Stephen Watson Fullom

# History of William Shakespeare, Player and Poet

With new facts and traditions. Second Edition

Stephen Watson Fullom

**History of William Shakespeare, Player and Poet**
*With new facts and traditions. Second Edition*

ISBN/EAN: 9783744748391

Printed in Europe, USA, Canada, Australia, Japan

Cover: Foto ©Raphael Reischuk / pixelio.de

More available books at **www.hansebooks.com**

# HISTORY

OF

# WILLIAM SHAKESPEARE,

## PLAYER AND POET:

## WITH NEW FACTS AND TRADITIONS.

BY S. W. FULLOM,

AUTHOR OF "THE GREAT HIGHWAY," "THE HUMAN MIND," "THE MARVELS OF SCIENCE," ETC.

"An honest man is able to speak for himself."—SHAKESPEARE.

"I would rather express that sentiment to you in the language of our great writer, Shakespeare, a man who seems to be imbued with a sort of inspiration from Heaven."—*Speech of* LORD OVERSTONE *at Nottingham, January* 23, 1861.

Second Edition.

LONDON:

SAUNDERS, OTLEY, AND CO.,

66, BROOK STREET.

1864.

*[The Right of Translation is Reserved.]*

# PREFACE.

THE justification of a new Life of Shakespeare should be furnished by its contents, not depend on a Preface. This work, therefore, must be left to speak for itself, and I trust that the light it throws on the subject will obtain indulgence for its deficiencies in other respects. I have here only to express my acknowledgments to those from whom I have received assistance. My best thanks are due to Mrs. Lucy, of Charlecote Park, for valuable information, which is a key to the whole history of Shakespeare; to Lord Willoughby de Broke for an obliging note on the Verney pedigree; to the Reverend G. Granville, Vicar of Stratford, the Reverend Donald Cameron, Vicar of Snitter-field, and the Reverend John Fagg, Vicar of Aston Cantlow, for access to the Parochial Registers;

and to W. O. Hunt, Esq., of Stratford, for permission to inspect the Corporative Records, and much personal kindness.

There is no probability that anything remains to be discovered respecting Shakespeare in his native county. I have followed every vestige of his steps, and explored every source which offered the remotest chance of a fact or tradition. The only quarters likely to repay a further search are the family archives of the Earl of Shrewsbury and the Earl of Pembroke; but I believe the Pembroke papers have already been investigated.

A public subscription has just secured to Stratford the possession of Shakespeare's Gardens; and it may not be out of place here to express a hope that the custody of them will be given to Mrs. Baker, the last representative of the Hathaways, and a most deserving person, now in poverty.

S. W. FULLOM.

TUDOR VILLA, SURBITON, S.W.
*December*, 1861.

# CONTENTS.

CONTENTS.

## CHAPTER X.



## CHAPTER XI.



## CHAPTER XII.



## CHAPTER XIII.



## CHAPTER XIV.



## CHAPTER XV.



## CHAPTER XVI.



## CHAPTER XVII.



## CHAPTER XVIII.



## CHAPTER XIX.



## CHAPTER XX.



## CHAPTER XXI.

## CHAPTER XXII.



## CHAPTER XXIII.



## CHAPTER XXIV.



## CHAPTER XXV.



## CHAPTER XXVI.



## CHAPTER XXVII.



## CHAPTER XXVIII.

# SHAKESPEARE.

## I.

### THE SHAKESPEARE FAMILY.

PHILOSOPHERS may see a moral in the fact that the greatest luminaries of modern times have risen from obscurity. Columbus was a cabin-boy; Luther, the son of a labouring miner; Copernicus was an unknown curate in the wilds of Lithuania; three mechanics of Strasburg invented the printing-press; the great Bishop Butler was the son of a grocer; Franklin was a printer's devil; Burns, a ploughman; and George Stephenson first saw the light—the divine light of science—in a coalpit.

Nothing could more clearly show us that greatness is independent of lineage. These men sprang, like Adam, from the ground. They were not, as we are accustomed to say, self-made; they were created; and the image of God stands freshly out upon them, a special impress. The source of their nobility is Nature; and this is a patent that needs neither blazoning from heralds, nor recognition from kings.

Of this master-type was WILLIAM SHAKESPEARE, the father of our drama, our literature, and almost of our language, but whose origin is so obscure, that an interval of barely three hundred years shrouds it in the mists of ages

Indeed, the same cloud envelopes his whole history; for the personal traces he has left behind are like the impressions of a leaf on a fossil rock; while his mighty works, which embalm this relic, are the rock itself. The very orthography of his name is a subject of dispute, as nearly everyone who bore it had his own variation; and it thus takes as many shapes as Ariel. Shakespeare is its most modern form, and being also the most familiar, claims our acceptance.

But the poet's admirers derive little satisfaction from settling only the spelling. The patronymic of Shakespeare has been thought to hold within it the germ of the family history, its foundation incident; and rare Ben Jonson has been made an exorcist to draw this forth:—

> "Look how his father's face
> Lives in his issue: even so the race
> Of Shakespeare's mind and manners brightly shines
> In his well-turned and true-fill'd lines,
> In each of which he seems to *shake a lance*,
> As brandished at the eyes of ignorance."

The suggestive name of the poet thus yawns before the eye, like an ancestral vault; and discloses a line of ghostly progenitors, who burst their cerements, and appear, like the Royal Dane, in "complete steel." Camden, Verotegan, and Bogan consider that it was originally given to a soldier; but we must remember that surnames had been in common use for a full century before it assumed the form of Shakespeare, and what we know of the family shows that the spade and the crook, rather than the spear, would best typify its pursuits.

The most diligent research has failed to trace the poet's ancestry to a higher source than his grandfather, Richard Shakespeare, of Snitterfield, although Shakespeares were settled in Warwickshire from a much earlier date, and, under the various forms of the name, were plenty as blackberries. The roll of the guild of Knowle marks their presence in the county as far back as 1470, and they hold their place among the brothers and sisters of the body till 1512, blazoning the list with all the variations of their patronymic.

This guild roll is, indeed, the roll of Battle Abbey to the Shakespeares, carrying us back to their first appearance; and, as regards the variations of their name, it is confirmed by the register of the Stratford Bailiff's Court—another muniment of the family, which, though not so genteel, throws much light on its history.

Rowe, who wrote in an age when mere birth was more esteemed than now, and felt a laudable desire to give his hero this advantage, describes the Shakespeare family as long settled at Stratford, where, " as appears by the register and public writings," they " were of good figure and fashion," and " are mentioned as gentlemen." But Rowe acquired his information third-hand from Betterton, the celebrated actor, who, though he visited Warwickshire expressly to collect the fading traditions of the poet, seems to have made but a cursory inspection of " public writings," merely pioneering the way for future explorers. The discoveries of modern times refute the assertion of Rowe, though it continues to find adherents. Illustrious ancestry is not to be despised, yet no one can suppose that it would give stature to Shakespeare—

> " Not propped by ancestry, whose grace
> Chalks successors their way ; nor called upon
> For high feats done to the crown ; neither allied
> To eminent assistants ; but, spider-like,
> Out of his self-drawing web—Oh, GIVE US NOTE !—
> The force of his own merit makes his way ;
> A gift that Heaven gives for him !"[1]

---

[1] ' Henry the Eighth,' act i. 1.

Like Napoleon, Shakespeare could exclaim—indeed, has here shown us—that he was his own ancestor, deriving all his nobility from himself, "a gift that Heaven gives for him!"

The Shakespeares are united in one stock by the baptismal names of Richard, Thomas, John, and William, common to all the branches from the remotest generation. Genealogical statements are so dry and bewildering, that the early traces of the race, after the attention they have received from antiquaries, might be dismissed with this allusion, if they did not present us with another thread of connection, hitherto left unnoted. Indeed, when the facts are placed in order, which has not yet been done, the affinity of the several branches is brought so near as to be all but established.

Towards the middle of the sixteenth century they are found seated principally at Wroxhall, Warwick, Rowington, and Snitterfield, the two latter villages being within a short distance of Stratford. Richard Shakspere of Wroxhall is mentioned as early as 1523, when he was declared to possess goods of the value of forty shillings, on which he was assessed for the subsidy to the king. At this time he was tenant, jointly with Richard Wodham, of three fields and a grove belonging to the priory of Wroxhall; and in 1534 he appears as bailiff to the good nuns and collector of their rents, at a salary of forty shillings a year. This post he doubtless owed to the prioress, Isabella Shakespeare, who was probably his sister, and who appears to have taken good care of her relations, as we find two more of the name, John Shackspere and William Shaxespere, tenants of the sisterhood at the same date. It has escaped notice that Isabella the prioress is remembered by Shakespeare in one of his most beautiful creations, Isabella the nun, in 'Measure for Measure;' and this fact, conjoined with the baptismal names of the other Wroxhall Shakespeares, is almost a proof of their consanguinity. The next generation at Wroxhall presents one John and three William Shakespeares, who may well be considered the sons of the previous John and William. One of the Williams had already given dignity to that name; for in 1545 he is declared to be worth 6*l.*, being just treble the value of the worldly goods of old Richard the bailiff. But this wealth was of little advantage to the family, if he were the same William Shaxspeare of Wroxhall, husbandman, who made a will on the 17th April, 1609, bequeathing only a groat to each of the children of his brothers and sisters, and his remaining store to one Joan Shrive, whose baptismal name, however, so connects her with the Shakespeares, that we may conclude the testator had very good reasons for making her his heir. As the will mentions brothers and sisters, we can identify this William as the brother of John Shaksper of Wroxhall, labourer, who died before him; for in his will, dated December 17, 1574, John mentions a brother William, to whom he leaves a horsecloth and his best shirt, and a sister Alice, who is bequeathed a lamb.

The Shakespeares first appear at Warwick about 1545, just when William of Wroxhall, the millionaire of the family, was found to be worth 6*l.* From equally small beginnings they advanced, through a line of mercers, shoemakers, and butchers, up to "Thomas Shackspeere, gentleman," who, in 1614, became bailiff of the town, and is thus described in the ancient municipal record, called the Black Book of Warwick. An earlier Thomas Shakespeare is found in the black books of Coventry; for he is mentioned in the accounts of the bailiffs of that city as having been indicted there for felony. He did not, however, wait the issue of the trial, but quietly decamped, leaving the authorities to appropriate his goods—a poor revenge, as they all sold for two shillings. It is possible that he took refuge in Warwick, and there became founder of the line of Thomas Shakespeares, who rose, in the person of Thomas the Bailiff, to such an honourable position.

The Shakespeares of Rowington commence with John Shakesper, in whom the family seems to have **first made way**, as in the subsidy roll of 1524, which rates Richard of **Wroxhall** at forty shillings, **he is stated to be worth six pounds, a degree of wealth which** the Wroxhall branch **attained only in the next generation.**[1] At the same time, John Shakesper, "junior," doubtless the son of the preceding, is estimated to be worth forty shillings, and he must be the same John Shakspere who dates his will from Rowington in 1574, leaving, among other bequests, twenty pounds to his son Thomas, and a bushel of corn to his aunt Ley, **the** midwife. These two names supply a link of great importance, which has been strangely overlooked; for we shall see that it connects the Rowington branch with that of Warwick. The will of Thomas Shakespeare of Warwick, made three years later, mentions his daughter Joan, married to Francis Ley; and Joan **Ley, the daughter of this Thomas of Warwick, must certainly be regarded as the aunt Ley of Thomas of Rowington.** At the same date, the Rowington branch possessed a Richard Shakyspere, described as a weaver, who, in his will of the 15th June, 1560, bequeaths his loom to his son William, a small sum to his son Richard, and six and eightpence to each of his daughters. This son Richard

---

[1] A subsidy was raised by an impost on **the people of the realm in respect** of their reputed estates. Landed property **was the chief subject of taxation,** and was assessed nominally at four shillings **in the pound. But the assessment** was made in such a way, **that** it not only **did not rise in proportion to** the rise in the value of the land, or **to the fall in the value of the precious** metals, but went on constantly sinking, **till** at length the rate was, **in the** reign **of** Charles I., less than twopence in the pound.—Abridged **from** Macaulay's 'England,' vol. iii.

may be the same Richard Shakespeare whom we shall presently find in the same year in the neighbouring village of Snitterfield, in whom three families, bearing the same baptismal names for generation on generation, would thus be united, while Shakespeare's tender remembrance of Isabella the prioress seems to connect them all with Richard Shakespeare of Wroxhall.

Thomas Shakespeare of Warwick, the father of " Aunt Ley," mentions in his will three sons : Thomas, who became a butcher in Warwick ; John, who seems to have settled at Stratford as a shoemaker ;[1] and William, who is thought to be referred to in an entry in the parish register of St. Nicholas, Warwick, recording that a William Saxspere was, in June, 1579, drowned in the Avon, which still proudly bears its swan, William of Stratford.

Richard Shakespeare, of Snitterfield, is the first known progenitor of the poet. He was found by Mr. Collier to be one of the tenants of Robert Arden, whose daughter became the wife of John Shakespeare of Stratford ; and this association led to the conjecture that he was John Shakespeare's father. The supposition was confirmed by the discovery that Snitterfield was also the place of abode of Henry Shakespeare, described in the registry of the Stratford Bailiff's Court as the brother of John, who, having become his surety

---

[1] John Shakespeare, the shoemaker, first appears at Stratford about 1584, when the register, under date of November 25, records his marriage with Margery Roberts. There seems to have been no issue from this marriage, and Margery died in 1587, her burial being registered on October 29, in that year. The disconsolate shoemaker appears to have immediately married again ; for, unless there was a fourth John Shakespeare in the town, he must have been the father of Ursula, "daughter to John Shakspere," baptized March 11, 1588-9 ; also of Humphrey, baptized May 24, 1590 ; and Philip, baptized September 21, 1591. He could hardly have exceeded his twenty-fifth year in 1587, as he was then a borrower under Oken'scharity, which was expressly restricted to " young men." He had previously been elected a burgess, and served the offices of ale-taster and constable, the highest corporate dignity he attained.

for the payment of a debt, exemplified the warning of the wise king, and was served with a process for its recovery. It is an ominous beginning of Shakespeare's life that the identity of his family is thus ascertained through the sheriff's officer.

Richard Shakespeare is always described as a substantial farmer, but he had really no pretension to such a rank. **In an indenture of the 21st** May, 1560,[1] the Snitterfield **property is leased by Agnes Arden, widow, to Alexander Webb, husbandman, for forty years, contingent on her life,** at the **yearly rent of forty shillings, equivalent to eight** pounds in the present day ; and it is specified as comprising two tenements and one cottage, with a yard and a half of arable land, or about thirty-two acres, the old Warwickshire yard measuring eighteen acres. The addition of " all lands, meadows, pastures, commons, profits, and commodities in **anywise thereunto** appertaining" is, of course, a mere legal flourish, signifying nothing. The premises are described as " lying and being in the town and fields of Snitterfield," and in the occupation of Richard Shakespeare, John Henley, and **John Hargreve, so that we may conclude each to have rented a** third part, or ten acres, and one of the three tenements. As Alexander Webb, who obtains a lease of the whole, is only **styled a husbandman, Richard Shakespeare** could have been **little more** than a labourer, tilling **his small** holding with his own hands ; and, indeed, we have ascertained that the cottage pointed out as his residence by tradition, and which was pulled down only four years ago, was such as a labourer **would** occupy. As the site has never been mentioned, we **may observe that it stood on the Green, over a muddy brook, which must often have swamped its clay floor.**[2] Around rose the Snitterfield slopes, then bounding the forest of

<hr>

[1] It is given in the Appendix.

[2] The cottage was described to me by the Rev. Donald Cameron, Rector of Snitterfield, who was present at its demolition.

Arden; and the " yard and a half" of arable soil tilled by Richard Shakespeare and his neighbours must have been a mere clearing in the wilderness. Indeed, much of the surrounding land was waste within memory, and is still poor ground, though the adjacent hill of Ingon looks down on rich pastures and wide teeming fields.

In the reign of Henry the Eighth, and for at least half a century later, a large part of England was forest or common, and wore the wild, rude dress of nature, being here smooth as the sward of a park, there an impassable fen, or overgrown with blooming heather. Cultivation appeared only in patches, surrounding miserable hovels of lath and mud, which gave shelter to the farmer and his hinds. Snitterfield was but a couple of miles from the great forest of Arden, which still studs the country with copse and thicket and clumps of trees, far beyond Henley :—

> " That mighty Arden, even in her height of pride,
> Her one hand touching Trent, the other, Severn's side."[1]

The commons afforded pasture to numerous flocks, the care of which formed the chief employment of the rural population ; and it is not unlikely that it occupied some of the time of Richard Shakespeare. In that case he may be the original of Corin, in ' As You Like It,'—the venerable old shepherd, who lived " *in the skirt of the forest*," the forest of Arden ! Here were an ancestor ennobled by his own words :—" Sir, I am a true labourer : get that I wear, owe no man hate, envy no man's happiness ; glad of other men's good, content with my harm ; and the greatest of my pride is, to see my ewes graze and my lambs suck."[2] The pastoral characters of Shakespeare are all conceived in this strain, and breathe the same spirit,—an appreciation natural in one who had sprung from a dynasty of husbandmen.

[1] Drayton's ' Polyolbion.'    [2] ' As You Like It,' act iii. 2

There was nothing remarkable in a peasant of Warwick-shire, a wool county, possessing two or three sheep, as we may see by the will of John Shakesper, the "labourer," who left his sister Alice a lamb. Sheep were then of a diminutive size, and were valued at two and eightpence, about ten shillings of our money, which was not above the means of Richard of Snitterfield. The few he contrived to purchase naturally fell under the care of one of his sons, while the others assisted him in the culture of his acreage; and we may conjecture that some such early occupation determined the calling of his son John.

There is no means of ascertaining the ages of Richard Shakespeare's children, as the earliest Snitterfield register is dated only from the 13th of January, 1561, when they had attained manhood; for John Shakespeare is found residing at Stratford in 1552.[1]

The family seems to have consisted of three sons, John, Henry, and Thomas;[2] and as the Greens of Stratford called the poet their cousin, it is probable that Richard Shake-speare had also a daughter, who relinquished her poetic name to become a Green.[3]

---

[1] Malone did not meet with the name before 1555, when it appears in the records of the Bailiff's Court, and Shakespeare's other biographers all adopt this date as the earliest mention of the name. But the late Mr. Hunter discovered that John Shakespeare was present at a court held at Stratford on the 29th April, 1552, though he was not assessed to the payment of the relief granted in 1549–50; consequently, he must have taken up his residence at Stratford about 1551.

[2] The baptism of a son of Thomas Shaxper is recorded in the parish register of Snitterfield under the date of the 10th March, 1581; and an entry on the 4th September, 1586, mentions Henry Shaxper as god-father to Henry Townsend. The registry notes the burial of Henry Saxpere on the 29th December, 1596, and of Margret Saxspere, his widow, on the 9th February, 1596–7.

[3] The cousinship of the Greens may have been derived from the step-sister of Shakespeare's mother, Mary Hill, whose eldest daughter, Eleanor, married William Green, of Alne.

The cottage of a Dorsetshire labourer of the present day, the extreme of what we know of English misery, would appear to advantage by the side of the lowly dwelling of these Shakespeares. In the cabins of the peasantry, there was then neither floor beneath the feet nor ceiling overhead: the thatch and bending rafters were blackened with smoke, which could only escape by the door; and a table and rude benches, with the commonest household service, composed all the furniture. At night the family took their repose on a pallet of straw or a coarse mat, and their pillow was a log of wood or a sack of chaff. The first light called them again to labour, so that the sons of Richard Shakespeare were trained to industry from childhood, and received no teaching but in the sweat of their brow.

At what age John Shakespeare left Snitterfield, no one has ventured to conjecture, and the same uncertainty prevails as to his first calling. By a singular coincidence, the founder of the English drama, and Chaucer, the founder of English poetry, stand in the same situation in this respect; for while we are left in doubt whether Chaucer was the son of a knight, a gentleman, or a vintner, it is not agreed whether the father of Shakespeare was a glover, a woolstapler, or a butcher. But it would seem, after all, that we have made a millstone of a very palpable fact.

The first actual memoir of Shakespeare was composed a hundred years after his death, by the poet Rowe; and consisted of about eight pages. The author wrote under the inspiration of Betterton the actor, who, from constantly realizing Shakespeare's creations on the stage, conceived for the great dramatist a veneration such as it was customary for a pupil of ancient Greece to feel for his master. In this spirit he went down to Warwickshire to collect the traditions of his life, as Xenophon collected the vestiges of Socrates. We yield a ready respect to the statements of such a disciple, but his Memorabilia, unlike Xenophon's, come to us from another pen, and Rowe gives them his own colouring. A desire to exalt Shakespeare according to the notions then prevalent, led him in some cases to suppress, and in others to expand facts, which were doubtless faithfully communicated by Betterton, but now conveyed an erroneous impression. Thus the latter had seen that John Shakespeare was called "magister," and Shakespeare himself styled "gentleman" in the public records of Stratford, which draws from Rowe the flourish that his family were of figure and fashion in that town. In the same way, John Shakespeare is described as "a considerable dealer in wool," a calling he certainly followed in later life, but Rowe refrains from shocking his generation with the disclosure that he had previously been a butcher.

Such considerations had no influence with Malone, who may justly be called the historian of Shakespeare. Coming to the work about eighty years later, he followed the footprints of the poet and his family with unwearied diligence, exploring every source of information, bringing to light facts which but for him had been lost, and which form the staple of all later biographers. He found an entry in the register of the Stratford Bailiff's Court of an action tried before John Burbage the bailiff, on the 17th June, 1555, to recover the sum of eight pounds from "Johannem Shakyspere, de Stretford, in county Warwick, glover," and concluded that he had here ascertained the trade of the poet's father. But this John Shakespeare must rather be the person who is mentioned in the municipal records as having prepared the accounts of the two chamberlains on the 15th of February, 1566.[1]  Like the Clerk of Chatham, he could "write and

---

[1] The entry mentions "the account of William Tylor and William Smythe, chamberlains, made by John Shakspeyr the 15th day of February, in the eighth year of the reign of our sovereign lady Elizabeth."

read and cast accompt." It is now clearly established that the John Shakespeare we are in quest of could not write his name, but had to himself a mark, "like an honest plain-dealing man," though Mr. Halliwell pronounces him and the accountant to be one and the same person, overlooking the impossibility of an account being drawn up by a man ignorant of writing. The circumstance that the veritable John Shakespeare was himself afterwards chamberlain does not reconcile us to such a contradiction; for, like William Tylor and William Smythe, he might have his accounts prepared by another hand—by his namesake. Nothing is more certain than that he could not be the person here mentioned. **There were thus two Dromios in Stratford; and if so, we have not only no ground for believing, but every reason to doubt, that the poet's father was a glover.**

The memoir by Rowe was preceded by some valuable memoranda furnished to Dugdale by **Aubrey, the antiquary,** who was in the habit of going through the land, like Burns's Grose, "takin' notes." His account is always considered as being some twenty years earlier than that of Rowe, because that was the time it was given to the world; but a little examination will show that the facts were really acquired half a century before, in 1642. Aubrey was then at Oxford, and his attention had been directed to Shakespeare both by **Joseph Howe, who was a fellow-parishioner of** the original **of Dogberry, and by the traditions of the Crown tavern, so that he would naturally be tempted to visit Stratford while** he was in its neighbourhood. This was only twenty-six years after the poet's death. Many of his "neighbours" still survived; and from them Aubrey learnt that John Shakespeare was a butcher.

**In** whatever way John Shakespeare came to settle at **Stratford,** he was not in good odour at the moment when he **first appears; for** the earliest mention of him—in 1552,

when he was living in Henley Street—records that he was
fined twelve pence for not keeping his gutters clean.[1]  The
lesson was not without effect, as he seems to have reformed
for a time ; but in 1558 he is fined fourpence for the same
offence, together with no less a person than the master-
bailiff, Francis Burbage.  Justice was evenhanded in Stratford, reaching to the bailiff himself,—a hard case, inasmuch
as one of his predecessors, **five years** before, was, by orders
**emanating from the Court of Aldermen, specially allowed the**
privilege of keeping a dunghill.  It is a curious coincidence,
that the first notices of the Shakespeares in Stratford, both
of John the butcher and John the glover, should be thus
associated with the name of Burbage, afterwards so linked
with that of the poet.  More curious still, that the association should begin in a gutter !  If the dust of Cæsar may
end in patching a wall, from what may it not rise !

The fine of fourpence did not press heavily on John
Shakespeare, who was now a thriving man, having in 1556
acquired from George Turner, a publican and burgess, the
copyhold of a tenement in Greenhill Street, with a garden, a
croft, or small field, and **other** appurtenances ; and from
**Edward West, a tenement and garden** in Henley Street.  But
**we must not be misled as to the nature of these acquisitions
and their** marketable value.  The two tenements could have
been nothing but miserable hovels, supporting a roof of
thatch on walls of mud ; and the copyhold may have been
purchased for a couple of pounds, about ten of our present
money, which, however, was no small sum for John Shakespeare to have laid by, and indicates a young man of sober
and thrifty habits.

There is other **evidence that he had** now established a
good character in the town ; for in the same year he was

---

[1] This is the entry discovered by Mr. Hunter, in a court roll of April 25,
1552, in the Carlton Ride Record Office.

elected a juror of the court-leet, a stepping-stone to the highest offices of the corporation. The jury was composed of twelve good men and true, who were not only empowered to dispense justice in certain causes, but were charged with the function of nominating more important officers than themselves, the ale-tasters and affeerors. In 1557 the office of ale-taster was imposed on John Shakespeare, and he was sworn to watch over the assize of bread, ale, and beer.

The regulations to be enforced are embodied in the orders of the Stratford Court of Aldermen, promulgated in 1553 ; and, for once, make us feel a passing regret for the good old days of Philip and Mary. It was John Shakespeare's business to see that the bakers made bread of three different kinds or sizes, which were to be sold respectively for a penny a loaf, and two and three loaves a penny ; any default entailing a fine of twenty shillings. The two a penny are evidently those of which Jack Cade promised "there shall be in England seven halfpenny loaves sold for a penny."[1] The same heavy penalty was imposed on the brewers, if they failed to sell new ale at twopence the gallon, the gallons being sold thirteen for twelve, which would thus seem to be a brewer's as well as a baker's dozen. Not more than a penny was to be charged for two gallons of small drink, "good and wholesome." But this liquor never acquired repute with our ancestors ; for Jack Cade declared "I will make it felony to drink small beer."[2] The brewers of Stratford were enjoined to sell their beer "in a pot" encircled by three hoops, which was also abjured by Jack, who solemnly promised that "the three-hooped pot shall have ten hoops."[3] Englishmen have always complained of the hard times.

As a part of his functions, John Shakespeare was to make himself acquainted, not only with the dimensions, but

[1] 'King Henry IV., Part II.,' act iv. 2.   [2] Ibid.   [3] Ibid.

the contents of the pot, which was often done by something more than tasting. But this young tradesman would seem to have been less partial to malt than Sir Toby Belch ; for he did not avail himself of his opportunities. An entry in the register of the Court of Record notifies that he was fined for non-attendance on the 2nd of June, 1557. He could no doubt have satisfactorily accounted for his absence ; for he was at this time under the influence of a more powerful attraction than cakes and ale, as we shall see in the following chapter.

## II.

### THE MOTHER OF SHAKESPEARE.

ABOUT four miles from Snitterfield, where John Shakespeare was born, and as many from Stratford, stands the hamlet of Wilmcote, a nook of the parish of Aston Cantlow. It lies in the forest of Arden, the remains of which still dot the surrounding country, crown Great Horn Hill, and look from the Ditchcote ridge over meadow and corn-field. So late as forty years ago, as we learnt from old inhabitants, great part of the land was waste; but it has now been reclaimed by the plough, and brought within the pale of canal and railway. Nothing of the olden times survives but cottages and oaks.

Wilmcote was the residence of Robert Arden, the landlord of old Richard Shakespeare, and connected with his descendants by a still nearer tie. His pedigree, though looked upon as established, is far from being so clearly made out as that of his tenant, as presented in this work; and both rest equally on conjecture. The Norman invasion found in Warwickshire an old Saxon family, the chief of which soon afterwards assumed the surname of Eardene, or Arden, which, according to Dugdale, had been given to that region on account of its woodiness: hence the forest of Arden. The supposed descent of Robert Arden from this magnate is only carried back to Walter Arden, who, from the identity of their coat-armour, is supposed to have been the father of John Arden, squire of the body to Henry the Seventh. John's will mentions his brothers, Thomas, Martin, and

Robert; and in the Arden pedigree the names of John, Robert, Thomas, and Martin are borne by the sons of Walter Arden, by his wife Eleanor, daughter of John Hampden in Buckinghamshire, though another account represents the maiden name of their mother as Bracebridge.[1] The arms of Arden, impaled in the herald's draft with the coat afterwards granted to John Shakespeare, bear the martlet, the distinctive mark of a fourth son; and Mr. Hunter conjectures that Robert was the fourth son of Walter Arden, because John Arden, in the will already mentioned, names him the last of his three younger brothers. This order, however, is not preserved in the pedigrees, in one of which Robert appears as the second, and in the other as the third son; and, what is more conclusive, the arms thus quoted were never really borne by Robert Arden of Wilmcote. Armorial bearings always conferred the rank of gentleman, a rank which the heralds certainly assign to Robert Arden, styling him "a gentleman of worship," but old Robert himself was content with the humbler title of "husbandman." Such he describes himself in the legal documents bearing his name, and these carry more authority than the whole College of Heralds.

There is nothing in what we know of Robert Arden, then, to show that he was even remotely connected with the old family of that name. When he first comes under notice he is just raised above the condition of a labourer, being assessed on only ten pounds in the subsidy roll of 1546. An interval of twenty years presents him as the possessor of considerable landed property, which is to be accounted for by his enclosing and reclaiming tracts of the surrounding

---

[1] A pedigree in Harl, 1110, f. 24, quoted by Mr. Hunter. The wife of Walter Arden is there said to have been the daughter of William Bracebridge of Kilsbury, in co. Warwick, esquire, and the names of their sons are given as John Martin, *Robert* and Henry.

waste, a practice then very general, and in which we shall hereafter find Shakespeare himself engaged. The value of his land at his death may be roughly estimated at about 200*l.*, equal to 800*l.* of our present money.

It has always been said that no trace remained of the old homestead of this substantial farmer. The conclusion was too hastily adopted; for diligent inquiry brought us to the spot where it still stands. The first light came to us from an old man, named John Mills, to whom it was pointed out on his first arrival in the village forty years ago. A little time was now spent in looking for the oldest inhabitant, who turned out to be one John Price, a man of fourscore and four, and the very witness required. John Price remembered the house in the possession of the WEBBS. To them it must have come from Robert Arden's widow, whose maiden name was Webb, and who was vested with it by his will. The Webbs known to Price were two brothers, residing at Sherborne, but who kept up the family predilection for enclosing waste lands at Wilmcote; and John Price was employed, in his capacity of mason, to chip their initials on a boundary stone, which partitioned their respective portions. Finally we met with John Simms, who also counted his fourscore and upwards, and whose old master had purchased the house some forty years since from the Webbs, when the tenant's name was John Lane.[1] We have thus a more satisfactory pedigree of the house than of its ancient owner.

The hospitality once maintained under its roof is now as little represented in its aspect as its name,—Starve Hall, which well indicates appearances. But a little examination shows that the dwelling was originally of mark. It consists of two floors, the upper lit by dormer windows abutting from the roof, except where it rises in a gable, and here there is a

---

[1] John would seem to be a favourite name at Wilmcote. We shall meet the name of Lane in connection with the Shakespeares.

casement. The house formerly comprised two gables, with a compartment between, and an extension on one side; but the connecting portion has been pulled down, isolating the **outer** gable, and this is now a shed for carts. The walls are of plaster, ribbed with oak, on which five centuries have made little impression, and the plaster itself seems almost as enduring. The interior is in still better preservation. Three rooms are **formed of the old hall,** but we can trace its **ancient proportions, and there still is the** same chimney-**corner which gave a warm seat to Robert** Arden. The oak floor above treads like a rock, and we creep through an aperture in the partition into a pretty chamber, looking out on green fields and wooded hills, which often met the waking glance of the mother of Shakespeare.

Robert Arden was the happy father of seven daughters. Their mother died before 1550, when he executed a **deed** which mentions his second wife, Agnes Hill, and who was a widow at the time of their marriage.[1] It has escaped remark that either Robert Arden must have died in the prime of life, or there must have been some disparity in the ages of the worthy **couple, as Agnes** survived her husband twenty-**five years. In either case, matrons** of the present day will **admire her courage in undertaking the** charge of **seven** young ladies, the oldest of whom could be little younger than herself; for in 1550 Robert Arden's eldest daughter, also an Agnes, had, like her stepmother, passed through the state of widowhood, and taken a second husband.[2] No one will impugn the docility of the sex, but it is expecting much from woman's nature to feel sure that the **sisters**

---

[1] She was always regarded as Shakespeare's grandmother, till the discovery of her first marriage by **Mr. Hunter.**

[2] In a deed of the 17th July, 1550, conveying the property occupied by Richard Shakespeare, in trust for three of Robert Arden's daughters, after his own and his wife's death, she is described as wife of Thomas Stringer and widow of John Hewins.

received their stepmother with open arms. One after another, however, they left the paternal roof as brides,[1] till, in 1550, only three remained unmarried.

The youngest daughter of **Robert Arden was** named Mary. As already said, she was, like **the damsel of Words**worth's ballad, one of seven ; and we **shall presently show** reason for concluding that in 1550, when her sister **Margaret** appears as Mrs. Webb, she was in her sixteenth year. As the youngest of the family she would naturally be the most tractable to her stepmother, and was certainly the favourite of her father. This is apparent from **the tenour of** his will, which also indicates her age, character, and occupations; for these may be inferred from the bequests he makes her. The inventory of his goods affords a glimpse also of the interior of her home.

The great feature of the hall was **a cupboard, which, for** reasons good, may have been kept **under lock and key ; for** nothing is said of the " fair garnish of pewter " used **to set** off open shelves, **and which Harrison mentions** as the ordinary contents of a farmer's cupboard in the next generation. A " table-board " occupied the middle of the apartment, and the family sat round on forms furnished with cushions, while the servants and farm-labourers put up with benches. Three chairs afforded seats of honour, or were brought into service on state occasions, **when the clay floor was strewn with rushes,** and the wall hung with painted cloths. The kitchen boasted four candlesticks, and was provided with four pans, and as

---

[1] Johanna Arden married Edward **Lambert ; Katherine became the wife** of Thomas Etkins of Wilmcote, and **Margaret married Alexander Webb,** apparently the same Alexander Webb who is described as **the brother of** her stepmother. The two first are mentioned in the deed of 17th July, 1550, printed in its original barbarous Latin by Mr. Halliwell. The Etkinses still abound in Wilmcote, where they have been settled for ages ; and the first entry which met my eye in the oldest baptismal register was **the baptism of a** Thomas Etkins.

many pots, which, together with two cauldrons, a frying-pan, and a gridiron, supplied the whole apparatus of the cook. There were painted cloths also for the principal bed chamber ; and this favoured apartment could show a feather-bed, and its appurtenances of pillows, bolster, two pairs of sheets, and a coverlet. Two mattresses remain for the young ladies, who may also be allotted two **coverlets and a couple of bolsters, while five pairs of sheets make due allowance for changing. Cleanliness, however, was a** point on which our **ancestors were not** fastidious, **and on** which Robert Arden did not go beyond his age ; for, as far as appears, the toilet of the whole establishment was performed with one basin and three towels.

In the early morning, when the dew was on the grass, Mary Arden tripped across the meadow, perhaps carolling a pleasant ballad, to a spot where the cows awaited her, and came back with a full supply for her churn. The rest of the day was occupied in a round of household duties, till evening took her forth to the same task. **No part of her** time was given to books. The schoolmaster was abroad, indeed, but he had not reached **the sequestered** homesteads of **Wilmcote, and the daughters of Robert** Arden could neither **write nor read. Indeed, these accomplishments were not** looked for in women at a much later date ; and, in the next generation, Mary's own daughters were as unlettered as herself. The ardent love of learning which animated the Princess Elizabeth and Lady Jane Grey was shared by few of **their own sex,** even in the highest circles, and was not yet general among men ; for Latimer, in his famous ' Sermon of the Plough,' laments that schools are **not provided** for the young gentlemen of **England and the wards of Court,** declaring that **the people would** not neglect " godly learning " if they saw it sought and appreciated by the nobility. He urges the young King to multiply schools as the safeguards of a pure faith; and we know how the wise boy acted on his counsel; for soon every petty town had its **grammar-school**, as every village its church.

Though never benefited by these seminaries, Mary Arden did not grow up in ignorance. **We may presume,** that the natural talents which won her the confidence of her father, though they received no culture, were improved by exercise, by a faculty of perception, and a habit of reflection, absorbing what she heard, saw, and thought. For a quick intellect, there was an education in the objects around her, and in the startling events of the time. Born in the reign of Henry the Eighth, after the secession of England from the Church of Rome, **she might remember the moment when the** light of the Gospel first **peered dimly out from the mazes of** fanatical controversy. **A** far brighter **gleam broke over her** girlhood. The throne was filled by the Boy-King, and every village **heard the** glad **tidings which** Latimer and Ridley went forth to preach. The parochial church became a school of itself; for the services **were now solemnized in** the English language, and the priest read and expounded the hitherto sealed pages of the Bible, as full of suggestion as admonition to a thoughtful mind. The ideas thus communicated were then new; and Mary Arden was at that impressionable age when they took the form of lessons, which, apart from their **religious influences,** permeated her **faculties, and opened them to physical, as well as** moral **impressions—to the teachings of the glorious woods, of the** recurring harvest, and of the sky of the summer morning, so that she learnt to appreciate the beautiful, while she was indued with a sense **of the divine.** The **prayer which came** down from heaven, raised her thoughts up to it, and brought **her to** know, by a straighter way than books, all the bright qualities which adorn her sex,—submission, compassion, charity, humility, and patience.

Happily the impression was made before the light was suppressed; and it was then deepened by the character of the period. England became the theatre of tragic events, which rumour bruited swiftly through the land, and they were often **talked of** round the quiet fireside of Robert Arden. Mary was here told of a living Cain, as well as of him of the **Bible—of a brother who sent his brother to the** scaffold, **and expiated the crime on the same block.** Then she caught a whisper that all was not well with the young King—that he was dying—and, while men's hearts were failing at the coming evil, that he was dead. She heard of the accession of Queen Jane, his nine days' successor, and heard in the same breath of her fall. Then came the reign of terror, gloomily ushered in by the headsman; and scaffolds streaming with blood—the blood of Northumberland, Wyatt, Dudley, and the unhappy Jane—made way for more terrible executions.

Mary Arden was removed from the immediate presence of **these** events, but not from their actual influence. The revolution which convulsed the realm extended to her native village, and entered her **father's house—for** it brought back the old religion and the old superstitions. Inquisitors searched everywhere for Bibles; Gospellers raved in the public ways; and **faithful** Protestants were dragged to prisons, and consumed at the stake. The atrocities of the times seemed to move the visible wrath of Heaven; for the midnight sky beamed with luminous exhalations, which were regarded by the excited people as the reflection of the **martyr fires;** while each succeeding year brought plague and famine.

Thus **Mary Arden was** not left untaught, though she attended no school. She was educated by her own experiences, in a time of peril, change, and social commotion. Her teachers were **Nature, Religion,** and History.

Like the population at large, Robert Arden conformed to the restored faith, and in December, 1556, expired in the bosom of the Church. The first person mentioned in his will, which is dated only two or three weeks before his death, is his daughter Mary, to whom he leaves a portion of the Wilmcote property called Ashbies, and he seems to intimate her acquaintance with farming by including in the gift " the crop upon the ground, sown and tilled as it is." He also bequeaths her six pounds thirteen and fourpence, ordering this legacy alone to be paid before any division is made of his property. His daughter Alice is left, " besides the goods she hath of her own at this time," a third part of his chattels, movable and immovable, but not till after the payment of his debts and the other legacies, thus placing her in an inferior position to Mary. A legacy of six pounds thirteen and fourpence is bequeathed to his widow, contingent on her permitting Alice " quietly to enjoy" half his copyhold in Wilmcote, but the sum is to be reduced to three pounds six and eightpence, if she will not comply with this condition. Such a clause, with the provision of a separate home for Mary, suggests the impression that there was no love lost between the daughters and their stepmother. Something is to be learnt also from the amount of the legacies—six pounds thirteen and fourpence, coinciding with the sum bequeathed by Richard Hathaway to his daughters, Agnes, Catherine, and Margaret, the sisters of Shakespeare's wife, whose portions thus exactly correspond with that of his mother, a sufficient proof that his maternal grandfather was in the same position of life.

Robert Arden divides his remaining property equally among his " other children," without naming them; and appoints Mary and Alice joint executrixes, another proof of his confidence in Mary, while it shows us, at the same time, that she must now have attained her majority, though, as her youngest son was not born till twenty-four years later, she could but have just completed her twenty-first year.

Robert Arden left fourpence to each of the poor residents of Wilmcote, and they doubtless assembled to pay a last tribute to so good a neighbour, by following his body to the grave. If we may reckon his tenants also among the mourners, the funeral was attended **by old** Richard Shakespeare, and possibly **by his son John. Certainly it is not** unreasonable to think **that John** Shakespeare, on this or **some other occasion, was a** witness of the grief of Mary **Arden, and did not withhold his** sympathy. Pity is akin to love, particularly when inspired by a pretty and gifted maiden, such as tradition describes Mary Arden; and it may well be thought that John Shakespeare soon revealed this feeling. To a young tradesman, the match was **a** desirable one, though not what it has been represented; for the little farm Mary inherited from her father, which has always been computed at sixty acres, is described in the pleading of John Lambert in the Court of Chancery, as consisting only of "one yard and four acres of land," which makes the whole number of acres but twenty-two. The name of **Ashbies is now unknown at Wilmcote, and there is not the faintest tradition of where it stood.**

John Shakespeare became the accepted lover of Mary Arden, and in due time they were betrothed. The church of Aston Cantlow preserves no record of their marriage, as the earliest register dates only from 1573; but it may have been solemnized on that very 2nd of June, 1557, when the **ale-taster** of Stratford **absented** himself without leave, and was fined eightpence for neglecting his duties.

Neither of the hovels which pertained to John Shakespeare in Henley Street and Greenhill Street, afforded a fit home for his bride, who, besides being very pretty, brought him a portion of six pounds thirteen in cash, and twenty-two broad acres.

It is, therefore, reasonable to assume that the happy pair came at once to the dwelling in which they passed nearly the whole of their married life, and which, though still humble, was no unsuitable residence for a burgess of the town, a dignity conferred on John Shakespeare soon after his marriage.

The house that received Mary Shakespeare as a bride can hardly be realized from its present aspect. Perhaps the bells were giving a merry peal as she alighted at its door; for the ale-taster's nuptials were not passed unnoted by the ringers; and certainly there were curious eyes scanning the arrival from the casements of the neighbouring houses. Even coming fresh from the wooded fields of Ashbies, Mary might be pleased with her new home. It stood in a garden which swept from the back round the two sides, while the front looked on the street, where she might see the remnant of a trim hedge and, further on, a rural lane, running to Greenhill Street, possibly the present Back Lane.[1] The prospect, indeed, comprised another feature, which it is to be hoped did not meet her eye; for the regulations of the town council mark the upper end of Greenhill Street, by Nicholas Lane's hedge in Henley Street, as the authorized site of a " donghyll."

Mary's attention might be all claimed by the house, and on such an occasion it doubtless looked its best. Something had been done with paint, and something with flowers; for this was a mode of decoration then very general. Stephen Perlin, a French physician, describing England in the reign of Philip and Mary, states that the shops of all trades were open like those of the barbers in France; and that nearly

---

[1] We gather these points from an entry in the records of the Court Leet, notifying that Nicholas Lane's hedge at Green Hill was despoiled by the wife of Ralph Hilton, who was fined for the trespass of his worse half, she being " a hedge breaker."

all the houses of every town, though occupied by tradesmen, were, both in the lower and upper storeys, furnished with glass windows, in which it was customary to display "a great many flowers." We may believe there were "glass windows" in the house of John Shakespeare, but whether they were precisely such as it now exhibits, it may be as well not to inquire.

It was not a time for much rejoicing. The bride commenced her married life with a deep sorrow fresh in her mind, and surrounded by dearth and peril, domestic privation and public calamity. The horrors of Smithfield were at their height; and reverses abroad completed the measure of national misfortune. But while all was gloom around—while the Queen was tossing in agony on her bed, and nobles and girded knights knew not where to step or what to expect, Mary Shakespeare might look hopefully forward. In due time, the promise that was broken to Mary the Queen, the Mary of humble life saw fulfilled; and on the 15th of September, 1558, John Shakespeare presented at the font of Stratford church his eldest child, who received, under the rites of the Roman Catholic faith, the Shakespearean name of Joan.

But the days of the old religion were numbered, and in two months more the land rose against it, hailing with acclamation the accession of Elizabeth. The many new arrangements imposed by the change in Stratford, were evidently carried out zealously by John Shakespeare; for he was not only confirmed in his office of constable for another year, but appointed an affeeror, or petty magistrate, his jurisdiction comprising those small offences not specified in the laws. The Reformation was equally acceptable to Mary, to whom it gave back the faith of her youth. Her second child, born in November, 1562, was baptized by a priest of the Protestant church, and received the name of

Margaret, indicating that she was carried to the font either by Mary's sister, Margaret Webb, or by her sister-in-law, Margaret Shakespeare, wife **of** her husband's brother Henry. The new Margaret made but a short stay, dying in April, 1563, but the April of the following year repaid the loss, bringing the bereaved parents their first-born son, WILLIAM SHAKESPEARE.

## III.

### HIS CHILDHOOD.

Accoriding to the parochial register, William Shakespeare was baptized on the 26th April, 1564 ; and a later vicar of Stratford made a pencil note that he was born on the 23rd. This has grown into a common belief ; and, though not traceable to any authority, receives confirmation from the custom of the time. Queen Elizabeth and Edward VI. were both christened three days after their birth.[1] The practice of the present age generally defers this rite to the fourth week, which would carry the birthday of the poet into unseemly proximity to the first of the month. Such an association could not be admitted ; and, indeed, we should prefer to make him, like Leonata's daughter, a "March chick." But, though he has not the tears of Troilus, everyone will agree that "he is, an 't were, a man born in April ;"[2] for, like young Master Fenton, "he writes verses, he speaks holiday, he smells of April and May."[3]

This is a point in which we shall not seem to make much ado about nothing. The satirist of the day has said that nobody cares to hear where a great man's grandmother was vaccinated. Yet an illustrious name attaches interest to "trifles light as air," if they carry any meaning ; and it is no maudlin feeling that links our national poet with our national saint, by fixing his birth on St. George's day.

---

[1] Strickland's 'Queens of England.'

[2] 'Troilus and Cressida,' act i. 2.

[3] 'Merry Wives of Windsor,' act iii. 2.

The coincidence may now seem a presage, but could hardly look so then, for **a** general gloom veiled every promise. The April that gave England her poet was all tears. Nature, indeed, put on her vernal robe **as** in the blithest spring, but death was in the air. The plague, which had long been ravaging London, was now everywhere, and fell like a blight on Stratford.

The frequency of the epidemics of that age will not appear strange when we recall the habits of our ancestors, for nothing can be imagined more baneful. The practice of strewing the floor with rushes was alone considered sufficient by Erasmus[1] to perpetuate the plague in England. From him we **learn that one layer was thrown over** another till they formed into a mass, which was **sometimes left undis-** turbed for twenty years, and meanwhile was made the cover for every kind of filth. Shakespeare often trod these unsavoury heaps, and remembers them on festive occasions, making Grumio ask Curtis, on the expected arrival of Petrucio and his bride, "if the house is trimmed, rushes strewed?"[2] Romeo also refers to the practice :—

> " Let wantons, light of heart,
> Tickle the senseless rushes with their heels."[3]

Stratford had other preserves besides rushes. The town was odorous with seven "dongylls," distributed impartially over it, and only the fear of penalties restrained the popu- lation from increasing the number. But here the local authorities stoutly entrenched themselves. They kept their eye especially on Chapel Lane and Dead Lane, where every- one was enjoined to wash down his gutter ; but why this concern was shown particularly for one quarter of the town does not appear.

[1] ' Letter to Dr. Francis.' [2] ' Taming of the Shrew,' act iv. 1.
[3] ' Romeo and Juliet,' act i. 4.

Such was the situation in which Shakespeare met in his nurse's arms the full blast of the plague as it swept through Stratford. It raged so fiercely that, in six months it carried off nearly a fifth of the population, reducing it from 1428 to 1190 souls. But there's a divinity hedges poets as well as kings. Walter Scott's nurse had stooped to cut his throat, **when a** tender inspiration, which might be an angel's voice, stayed her hand; **and, as we cannot** say it **was natural causes, let us not call it chance that** averted death from the cradle of Shakespeare. The gutter before the door, the slaughter-house at the side, the reeking dunghill within sight, offered conductors to the pestilence; but, though it walked by noonday, it came not to him. As in ancient Egypt there was not a house where there was not one dead, but the destroying angel happily passed over the **dwelling of** John Shakespeare.

An entry in the corporation archives records that, on the 30th of August, 1564, when the plague was at its height, the council met in the open air, which shows that, though indifferent to cleanliness, they were fully aware of the importance of ventilation. **Nor were they forgetful of the** public good; **for they twice raised money for the relief of the** poor, **and the name of John Shakespeare** appears each **time among** the contributors,—first, as the donor of a shilling, and on the second occasion, of sixpence. The smallness of the amount is not consistent with his supposed opulence, and hence an apology has been made for it on the ground that he was at the time only a burgess. But it should be remembered that he had for two years held the office of Chamberlain, an important trust; and as he appears in the accounts of the corporation as a creditor for one pound five and eightpence, there can be no doubt that he was now in as good circumstances as at any period of his life. On the 4th of July, 1565, he was chosen an alderman.

This rapid advancement testifies to his good repute, which could hardly be based on a penurious **disposition;** and, indeed, we shall find him becoming surety for his friend and doing other acts of kindness, quite inconsistent with such a character. We must, therefore, conclude that the sums he subscribed for the poor fairly represent his means. As it raised him above his calling, his promotion in the corporation was indeed a doubtful advantage, though at the time it might seem a proud day for both his wife and himself when he first donned his aldermanic robe, and the fond mother **held up their little son to contemplate** his bravery. Whether **this comprehended an alderman's thumb-ring, through which Falstaff might have crept in his youth,**[1] **and an agate as big** as Queen Mab for **his forefinger,**[2] **imagination must decide;** but whatever the costume, **the office conferred** dignity. This even extended to his spouse, and Mary Shakespeare was now elevated into the deputy's wife of the ward.[3]

It seems reasonable to believe that the obscurity which envelopes the childhood of great men **hides from** us nothing of moment. The " child Samuel " is the only one, apart from our Saviour himself, of whom a glimpse is preserved in the Bible; and little import attaches to the few incidents of childhood embalmed by history. That period of life can, indeed, no more indicate the character and genius which **circumstances are required to** bring **out, than the blossom disclose its superior beauty before it is opened by the** sun. **The prodigy of the fond parent is, to an impartial observer, but an ordinary infant, inscrutable as a** sealed book. **As the mind expands in youth,** a **flash may break** forth **at times, but it is like the** sparkle **of the** millstone—on **the surface, telling nothing** of the **core.** Futurity is veiled

---

[1] ' King Henry IV., Part I.,' act ii. 4.

[2] ' Romeo and Juliet,' act i. 4.

[3] ' King Henry IV., **Part I.,**' act iii. 3.

as closely in the soul of the child as in the destiny of the man.

Yet the conditions under which great men have been nurtured must influence the formation of their character, and sometimes give a direction to their genius. Nor can we doubt that the ruling passion, strong in death, shows itself almost at birth, almost with the first efforts of intellect. But these feeble ebullitions are **the traits** of childhood which **are often least noted : and, like a ripple on** the brook, they pass so quickly, that they are quickly forgotten.

The disposition begins to mould itself in the same way, with dawning perception. Our first lessons are the incidents around us, the unheeding gossip and thoughtless actions of our elders. The atmosphere in which we live casts down its impressions, as the air its ova, and both take eternal root in the soil. Thus Napoleon declared that a man's character was formed by his mother. And here he was only echoing the opinion of Shakespeare, who says, " He's all the mother's, from the top to toe."[1] The poet remembered the source of his own first knowledge, and in another place tells us how **it** was imparted—

> " Those who do teach young babes,
> Do it with gentle means and easy tasks."[2]

By the loving admonition, by the kindly reproving look, and by her own example, Mary Shakespeare moulded his qualities and unfolded his mind, as she taught him to speak and walk. From such lessons he derived that habitual urbanity which **brought the** friends **of** his later **life to** call him " gentle Will." They gave him also, with his first impressions, a sense of the moral nature of woman, the tenderness of her heart, the depth of her love, and the purity of her aspirations,—and, familiarizing his mind with the good and

---

[1] 'King Richard III.,' act iii. 1.          [2] 'Othello,' act iv. 2.

beautiful in a living type, thus prepared him for conceptions of undying beauty, grandeur, and sublimity.

While the little fellow **was** beginning to count his years, the domestic circle grew wider, bringing brothers and sisters to divide his **mother's care and share his own affection.** He appears to have been most attached to his sister Joan; for, so far as traces **remain,** she was the only ône of the family for whom he evinced a lasting interest. The prefer-ence was natural, as their relative ages brought them more together, and they grew up in this fellowship. One of the last acts of his life was to provide her a home, realizing the sentiment he has put into the mouth of Camillo:—"They were trained together in their childhood, and there rooted between them then such an affection as cannot choose but branch now."[1]

Joan was born when Shakespeare was five years old, and was the second of **John Shakespeare's** children who received that name—the first Joan, whose birth has **already been** mentioned, having died **in** infancy. **Between** Joan and William came Gilbert, born in 1566.[2]

John Shakespeare was at the height of his good fortune at the period of Joan's birth. On Michaelmas day of the preceding year he had been elected High Bailiff, which made him for his twelve months of power the chief man in Stratford. He supported the dignity of the office in a liberal manner, and, while he sought to please his own class, was not unmindful of the poor. The Chamberlain's accounts

---

[1] 'Winter's Tale,' act i. 1.

[2] The other children of **John and** Mary Shakespeare were:— 5. **Anne,** baptized September 28, 1571; 6. Richard, baptized March 11, 1573-4; 7. Edward, baptized May 3, 1580. Rowe says there were **ten children, but** he evidently makes up the number with the three children **of John Shake-**speare, the shoemaker, the eldest of whom was not born till 1588, when the mother of the poet would, **as** we have shown, be at least fifty-three years of age.

show that twelve-pence was paid to Peter Starkey for "undersetting Mother Gill's house," preventing it from tumbling about her ears, a catastrophe which, from the disrespectful mention of her name, we may fear might not have been lamented by her neighbours. But whether a "wise woman" or a witch, or simply a poor old dame, Mother Gill enjoyed the protection of the High Bailiff, and so took no harm. It is of more import to note a payment to the Queen's players, and another to the players of the Earl of Leicester; apprising us that theatrical performances were first introduced at Stratford under the auspices of the father of Shakespeare.

The future dramatist was in his sixth year when he was a spectator of these exhibitions. The impression they made upon him may be partly conceived from the spell which was thrown over our own childhood by the first visit to the theatre, since we know how from that moment we all became stage-struck, learnt dramatic speeches, engaged our companions in extempore performances, and found in no toy the enjoyment derived from a miniature playhouse. The spectacle witnessed by little Will Shakespeare was not, indeed, invested with the attractions of modern representations. There were no gorgeous dresses to give semblance to the characters; there was no changing scenery to heighten the effect; no artificial light to gently aid the illusion, and lend it the air of reality. Above all, the performance wanted the charm imparted by the participation of woman, —her grace, pathos, and beauty. But these properties, as we should now call them, are not what fascinate the young; as the colouring of the piece, they catch the eye for the moment, but it is the action that leaves the impression. This sank deep in the memory of the future poet, sitting as a child at the feet of Thespis, and, even at that age, must have given a turn to his thoughts.

He received his initiation in the drama and in letters about the same time, as if the alphabet of the one, the elementary old play, were as necessary to his education as that of the other. To qualify him for admission to the free school in his eighth year, he was required to be able to read; and this brought him under the ferule of one of the starched pedagogues, who then kept guard, like dragons, at the gate of learning. A representative of the class is preserved in Holofernes,[1] who, Moth tells us, is "lettered;" for "he teaches boys the horn-book,"[2]—the primer being fitted for the destructive fingers of boys by a cover of horn. Elsewhere Shakespeare mentions the more familiar title, at the same time recalling the lesson :—

> " That is question now,
> And then comes answer, like an A B C-book."[3]

And, in another place, he finds a simile in the despair of a boy who has lost his A B C.[4]

The poet's next step on the ladder of learning has left no vestige, but he was soon brought up by the catechism, which he seems to recollect as a tough lesson. Rosalind cries out upon it to Corin, " To say ay and no to these particulars is more than to answer in a catechism."[5]

Fortunately Holofernes was not the only tutor of Shakespeare's childhood. He received more genial, and for him not less useful instruction from his mother, though she was unable to teach him his letters. As he passed those fingerposts of knowledge, he was led on the road by her hand, in the charmed ballad lore which teaches all by the ear. It was as if the steepness of the way were beguiled by some

---

[1] Warburton thinks that Holofernes was drawn from John Florio, but we shall show hereafter good reason for differing from this eminent critic.

[2] ' Love's Labour's Lost,' act v. 1.

[3] ' King John,' act i. 1.

[4] ' Two Gentlemen of Verona,' act ii. 1.

[5] ' As You Like It,' act iii. 2.

pleasant companion, who sang now a romantic ditty, now an historic lay, when he might have been wearied. The country then teemed with such compositions, forming **a sort of** Homeric literature, which preserved the memory of great national events among the common people. Our early histories **are** little more than these fugitive lyrics **hammered** into an **Iliad. But** those which escaped **the fusion are the most precious ; for they have come down to us in their native dress, with all the charm of antique melody.** We owe their preservation **to** the deep **impression they made on the** peasantry, who treasured them in their homes, like family traditions ; and it was from the lowly cottages of the poor that these gems of poesy were recovered by the learned, when they awoke, almost too late, to a sense of their beauty. In them we have found what history left untold—all **that is** known of King Arthur and his Round Table, of the **bold** outlaw, Robin Hood, **and the hapless** beauty, **Fair Rosa-**mond. Such legends were **then** the first **lessons of the** child, **and** might **be** recited **to little** Will Shakespeare **in** the **glades of the forest of Arden, where the** red-deer still **lingered, and the spreading boughs above and the copse around gave a colouring to their incidents. Like Master Silence, he could sing the ditty of** " Robin Hood, Scarlet, and John ; "[1] and his works show acquaint-ance with many another lay, revealing the lore of his childhood.

The poetic faculty does not come with a breath : it is an instinct, growing unseen—a living and active power, which, like the coral insect, is at work before the work is visible, before the breast is conscious of its presence. An irresistible attraction draws the rising poet to Nature, and to the beautiful and great, while such fellowship produces no apparent effect. So Shakespeare imbibed in childhood the sweet

---

[1] ' King Henry IV., Part II.,' act v. 3.

poesy of the old ballads, which afterwards revealed their presence in his mind, just as the bee passes from flower to flower, and gleans many a fragrant garden and many a pleasant field before he yields his honey. Not a few of the old Prolusions which preceded the regular drama were founded on ballads, and several of these have been attributed to Shakespeare, particularly the two based on 'The Duke of Cornwall's Daughter' and 'King Edward the Third and the Fair Countess of Salisbury.' No one has yet remarked the traces of this ballad lore in his dioramic spectacle of 'The Wars of the Roses.' He may have heard from his mother's lips, as he stood at her knee, the pathetic strain of 'The Banishment of the Dukes of Hereford and Norfolk,' the incidents of which are, as far as they extend, the same as those of the play of 'King Richard II.' Or she may have recited the ballad as he walked by her side on the top of the neighbouring hills, within sight of the spires of Coventry—

> " The king did grant this just request,
> And did therewith agree,
> At Coventry, in August next,
> The combat fought should be."

An appointment not forgotten in the play—

> " Be ready, as your lives shall answer it,
> At Coventry, upon St. Lambert's day;
> There shall your swords and lances arbitrate
> The swelling difference of your settled hate."[1]

The ballad told how the banished Hereford took leave of his native land—

> " O *England!* here I kiss the *ground*
> Upon my bended knee!
> Whereby to show to all the world
> How dearly I love thee."

---

[1] ' King Richard II.'

And the farewell is remembered in the play—

> " Then, *England's ground*, farewell! sweet soil, adieu!
> My mother and my nurse, that bears me yet!
> Where'er I wander, boast of this I can,
> Though banish'd, yet a true-born Englishman." [1]

The tragic history was continued in another ballad,—'A Song of the Deposing of King Richard **II.**, and How, after many **Miseries**, he **was** Murdered in Pomfret Castle.' Here we catch the first faint whisper of "No man cried God save him:" [2]—

> " Not one for his misery grieved,
> That late was in place
> Of royalest grace,
> Where still the distressed he kindly relieved."

The fine strain of 'The Battle of Agincourt between the French and English' may have been committed to memory at the same period. It relates a colloquy between York and Henry, which is reproduced in the play of 'King Henry V.'

> " With that bespoke the Duke of York,
> 'O noble King,' quoth he,
> 'The leading of this battle brave,
> Vouchsafe to give to me.'

> " ' God a'mercy, cousin York,' quoth he,
> 'I grant thee thy request;
> Then *march thou on courageously*,
> And I will take the rest.' "

In the play York makes the same request :—

> " My lord, most humbly on my knee, I beg
> The leading of the vaward."

And the King answers—

> " Take it, brave York.   Now, soldiers, *march away*." [3]

---

[1] 'King Richard II.'          [2] Ibid., act v. 2.
[3] ' King Henry V.,' act iv. 3.

The old ditty of 'Cupid's Revenge,' composed in the fifteenth century, is supposed to describe the marriage of Henry VI. with Margaret of Anjou, which forms the leading theme of the 'First Part of King Henry VI.' The Second Part takes up the story of Eleanor of Gloucester, and this is all recited in the ballad of 'The Lamentable Fall of the Duchess of Gloucester, Wife to Good Duke Humphrey, With the Manner of her Doing Penance in London Streets, and of her Exile to the Isle of Man, where she Ended her Days.' There is a more than accidental resemblance between the speech of the good Duke in the play and the lament of the Duchess in the ballad. Thus Shakespeare speaks in the first :—

> "This is the hour that was appointed me
> To watch the coming of my punished duchess,
> Uneath may she endure the *flinty streets*,
> To tread them with *her tender-feeling feet*."

And thus the duchess in the ballad—

> " *My feet*, that lately trod the steps of pleasure,
> Now *flinty streets* so sharp were forced to measure."

All the elements of the play of 'King Richard III.' are found in three ballads, which were very popular in the midland counties in the sixteenth century. 'The Most Cruel Murder of Edward V. and his Brother the Duke of York in the Tower by their Uncle the Duke of Gloster,' is the significant title of one ; the second embraces 'The Life and Death of the Great Duke of Buckingham ;' and the third is 'A Song of the Life and Death of King Richard III., Who, after Many Murders by Him Committed upon the Princes and Nobles of this Land, was Slain at the Battle of Bosworth, in Leicestershire, by Henry VII., King of England.' The series concludes with a lay on 'The Union of the Red Rose and the White by a Marriage between Henry VII.

and a Daughter of Edward IV.,' glancing at the cruel nature
of the long struggle, and telling us how—

> " Fathers unkind their children killed,
> And sons their fathers slew ;"

incidents vividly recalled by Shakespeare—

> " Who's this ?   O God ! it is my father's face,
> Whom in this conflict I unawares have killed."
>
>  *   *   *   *   *
>
> " But let me see ! is this our foeman's face ?
> Ah, no, no, no ! it is mine only son ! "[1]

These faint footprints are not unimportant, since they
guide us to the poetic influences which surrounded Shakespeare's childhood, and link it with his noblest productions.
They show how his thoughts were coloured from the first,
just as Walter Scott, at the same age, was impregnated with
the old Border songs and his uncle's reminiscences of Preston
Pans and the Pretender.  We are left to conjecture whence
Shakespeare derived this intellectual sustenance, but we seem
to discern it rising with his nurture from the same living
fountain, his mother's love.  Though she lived to see its
effect in his riper years, this is the last association of mother
and son now traceable.  The time had come when he was to
enter the school-room, and she is left at the door.

[1] ' King Henry VI., Part III.,' act ii. 5.

# IV.

## HIS SCHOOL DAYS.

ALTHOUGH the Grammar School of Stratford is usually said to have been founded by Edward the Sixth, an establishment of the same character had existed in the town for half-a-century before, when Thomas Jolyffe granted to the guild of the Holy Cross, all his lands and tenements at Stratford and Dodwell, on condition that the masters, aldermen, and proctors, the executive of the body, should find a priest competent to teach grammar, which was to be imparted gratuitously to all boys in the town without distinction of rank.

The guild of the Holy Cross was a voluntary association of the townsfolk for purposes of local administration, and curiously illustrates the antiquity of self-government in England. Guilds existed under a royal licence, which authorized their holding lands and revenues for the objects in view, and gave them a legal position. Though not free from abuses, they appear to have generally exercised their functions discreetly and in an efficient manner. Of course, one of their traditions was an annual feast, which was not forgotten by the guild of the Holy Cross; but all the good cheer was not monopolized by its chiefs, and there was no grumbling at such a practice, when the door of the banquet-hall was thrown wide, admitting the humblest member.

In 1485, the date of William Jolyffe's bequest, the

guild was the governing power of Stratford : and from that time it appears to have notably kept up the victualling points of the charter ; for in the reign of Edward VI. it had accumulated a store of rich plate, such as garnishes the board when substantial burghers sit around. The reforming spirit of the age **was** opposed to this conviviality, **and** one of **the young** king's last acts was to dissolve the guild **and raise** Stratford into a corporation. The royal charter provides for the maintenance of the free grammar school, according to the original foundation, and vests the revenues held by the guild for that and other purposes in the new authorities, the high bailiff and burgesses of Stratford.

The school is on the skirt of the town, adjoining the alms-houses, and was formerly entered from the street by a gallery on the outside. But it is pretty certain that this was not the *Alma Mater* of Shakespeare ; for the corporation books record that on the 18th of February, 1594-5, it was decided by the authorities that the school should no longer be kept in the chapel, an intimation that the chapel had been so appropriated up to that time. In fact, it is precisely the edifice in which the schools of the fifteenth century were established ; and at Kingston-on-Thames, a free grammar school—founded, like that of Stratford, prior to the reign of Edward VI., but relicensed by that monarch, and afterwards revived by Elizabeth—is carried on in a similar building to the present day.

Memorable was the morning when young Will Shakespeare made his first bow in the grey old chapel—for it was even then grey and old ; and the light came streaming through all the dozen windows on one terrible figure, a man most villanously cross-gartered, "like a pedant that keeps a school in the church."[1] But we must not be deluded into supposing that he was allowed time to take observations.

[1] 'Twelfth Night,' act iii. 2.

The discipline of the school was too practical, and a large swinging birch at the pedant's right hand was all that the eye noted. Solomon's idolatry of the rod had deeply infected our ancestors. Roger Ascham tells us that their schools were conducted on a system of terrorism surpassing belief. In the preface to 'The Schoolmaster,' he records a curious discussion on the subject at the table of the officers of the queen's household; and nothing could more clearly illustrate the practice of the time. Fear of impending punishment had excited some Eton boys to run away from school; and Lord Burleigh, on mentioning the circumstance, lamented that schoolmasters did not exercise more judgment in correction, declaring that they often punished the weakness of nature rather than the fault of the scholar. An educational Brutus, bearing the stern name of Pater, dissented from this view, contending that the source of all knowledge was the rod; and his opinion found a supporter in the severe Mr. Haddon, who maintained that the best schoolmaster was the greatest beater, "naming the person." This assertion drew a protest from Mr. Wotton, "a man," we are informed, "mild of nature, with soft voice," who considered that more was to be done by moral suasion than by birch; and finally, Sir Richard Sackville told Roger apart, that he was often so punished when a boy by his schoolmaster, that the fear in which he lived prevented him from exercising his faculties, and the grandfather of the most brilliant man of his age grew up a dunce.

Shakespeare was evidently brought up by "great beaters," such as would have even won a character from Mr. Haddon, and we shall not be blamed for following his example in "naming the persons." The first was Thomas Hunt, curate of the adjacent hamlet of Luddington, and the second bore the unpoetic name of Jenkins. Their beating power is attested by Shakespeare's recollections of school, which are all of the gloomiest kind, his most cheerful allusion being—

> " —— the schoolboy,
> With his shining morning face, and satchel on back,
> Creeping, like snail, *unwillingly* to school."

This schoolboy is more dismal in the hands of Romeo, who says :—

> " Love goes towards love as schoolboys from their books ;
> But love from love, toward school *with heavy looks*."[1]

Grumio left the church where Petrucio married Katharina " as willingly as e'er I came from school ;"[2] and good Duke Humphrey speaks of—

> " —— an effeminate prince,
> Whom, like a schoolboy, you may overawe."[3]

Speed considers it a sign of love in Sir Valentine that he has learnt " to sigh like a schoolboy ;"[4] and in another place we are told of " schoolboy's tears."[5]

About forty years earlier, in the reign of Henry the Eighth, the schoolmaster's throne was filled by the clerk of Stratford, who might have been found, like the clerk of Chatham, " setting boys' copies," [6] had he been visited by any Jack Cade of the day. The yearly salary of ten pounds received no addition from that time, while money had diminished in value ; and, as mental acquirements commanded a price in the reign of Elizabeth, such a pittance could secure only inferior teachers. But they were still equal to " setting boys' copies," and on the satchel which the little scholar carried on his back he learnt to " cast accompt," [7] while the injunction that every boy should be taught " grammar " was no doubt strictly observed. Shake-

---

[1] ' Romeo and Juliet,' act ii. 2.
[2] ' Taming of the Shrew,' act ii. 2.
[3] ' King Henry VI., Part I.,' act i. 1.
[4] ' Two Gentlemen of Verona,' act ii. 1.
[5] ' Coriolanus,' act ii. 2.
[6] ' King Henry VI., Part II.,' act iv. 2.     [7] Ibid.

speare was the first of his family who could write his name, and he gives us convincing proof in his plays, excepting those laid on English ground, that he would not have passed a Civil Service Examination in geography, **though** he was not more backward on this point than Napoleon and Marlborough in spelling. The round of instruction at Stratford was confined to "small Latin and less Greek," which Ben Jonson pronounced the extent of Shakespeare's acquirements; and Laneham, in his celebrated letter from "Killingworth Castle," describes his education at the higher public school of St. Paul's as not exceeding this limit.[1]

**But Shakespeare has himself given an inkling of the standard of instruction at a provincial** grammar-school, **and** of the mode in which it was imparted. **As Walter Scott** presented his schoolmaster in one of **his novels, so the great** dramatist seems to us to bring his **early teacher on** the stage. It will, we know, be pronounced heretical to avow such an opinion; for as no author ever looked at human nature with the same sweeping eye, **Shakespeare is be-**lieved to have never coloured his creations with personal reminiscences. But it is time to dismiss this superstition; for Aubrey has introduced us to the original of Dogberry, and in a later chapter, we shall establish the hitherto dubious identity of Justice Shallow.

It is in the play which Shakespeare has tinged deepest with his own experiences, and where he brings forward all his old neighbours, that we make the acquaintance of the Welsh schoolmaster, Sir Hugh Evans, who is also in holy orders, and, like Thomas Hunt of Luddington, a curate. Hunt is suggestive of Hugh, and it is not improbable that

---

[1] " I went to school, forsooth, both at Paul's and also at St. Anthony's: In the fifth form, passed Æsop's ' Fables,' I wis.; and Terence, *vos istæc intro auferte*, and began with 'my Virgil, *Tityre tu patulæ*. I conned my rules, could construe and parse with the best of them."—*Burn's Reprint*, p. 91.

Thomas Hunt was a Welshman; for not only is the name common in Wales, but several natives of the principality were settled at Stratford, and two were actually of the tribe of Evans; for the parochial register records the burial of *Evans* Rice and *Evans* Meredith. A Welshman, named Lewis ap Williams, was an alderman at the same time as John Shakespeare. The poet, therefore, **in his younger days, often** heard him speak, **and** hence **that** familiarity **with the Welsh pronunciation so** humorously exhibited in Evans and **Fluellin. The very name** of Fluellin occurs in the parochial register of Stratford ;[1] and, indeed, many of Shakespeare's characters take their names from his fellow-townsmen.

Sir Hugh Evans brings under notice one of his pupils, who is put through his accidence ; and Shakespeare seems to have designed this incident expressly to indicate his schoolmaster; for not only is it foreign **to the** piece, which argues a special object, but the boy's name is WILLIAM. Sir Hugh is not exhibited in an odious light like Holofernes, but retains the traits of the type ; for he seeks to **create an** impression of his learning by precisely the same means, always aiming **at grand** words, which **he** mispronounces and misapplies. **As he confesses himself** "full of cholers," and, **little William, when called up for** examination, approaches **in the** Romeo **style,** " with heavy looks," it is clear that he was a good beater. Hence we feel no surprise at the complaint of Mistress Page :—" Sir Hugh, my husband says my son profits nothing in the world at his book."[2]

Dead languages offer no attraction to a boy of high sensibility and quick intellect ; and Walter Scott, like Shakespeare, acquired " small Latin and less Greek."[3]

---

[1] The register records the burial of William Fluellin **on the 9th of July,** 1595.

[2] 'Merry Wives of Windsor,' act iv. 1.

[3] Sir Walter Scott, in his autobiographical fragment, says that he could not repeat the Greek alphabet.

William is encouraged to face Sir Hugh by his mother—
" Hold up your head, answer your master, *be not afraid!* "
The examination brings out all his points : he knows the
Latin for *fair*, shocks Mrs. Quickly with the genitive case
plural, and, though Sir Hugh threatens to breech him for
stumbling at his pronouns, astonishes his mother with the
extent of his learning—" He is a better scholar than I
thought he was."

But Shakespeare's superiority as a boy is not to be
traced in his school hours. The time to see him excel is
" a playing day." A hint is given that the school was
under the domination of Charlcote, and " Master Slender is
let the boys leave to play."[1] In the ground behind the
school, and still more, in the green fields and pleasant woods,
the little fellow was at his ease, and both his mind and spirit
were braced by the freedom. Some have contended that he
was lame ; for it is not enough to depict him as a chartered
libertine, he must be made a cripple. The metaphors of
his sonnets become literal facts in such hands :—

> " Say that thou didst forsake me for some fault,
> And I will comment upon that offence :
> Speak of my lameness, and I straight will halt,
> Against thy reasons making no defence."[2]

Shakespeare had no need to affect a limp in order to
expose his lameness, as it would have been apparent, if it
had existed, in his natural step.[3] But to suppose that the
allusion describes a physical defect is to take away its whole
application. A capricious mistress might make the lameness of a suitor a pretext for rejecting him, but it would

---

[1] ' Merry Wives of Windsor,' act **iv.** 1.

[2] Sonnet 89. The same allusions occur in Sonnets 38 and 90.

[3] Malone has made an almost similar remark :—" If Shakespeare were
in truth lame, he had it not in his power to halt occasionally for this or any
other purpose."—*Malone's 'Life of Shakespeare.'*

afford no excuse for the desertion of a friend, and these particular sonnets are addressed to a man.

If Shakespeare had been lame his contemporaries would certainly not have failed to mention his infirmity; but they afford us, on the contrary, the strongest proof that he had no such defect. Aubrey learnt from his neighbours that he was "handsome and well-shaped;" and we shall see hereafter that he was selected to play the king on account of his personal appearance, which could derive no majesty from a game leg.

Could we imagine little William entering the schoolroom with a halting step, we should think that he indeed required all the encouragement of his mother when he caught the awful citation of Thomas Jenkins—"Come hither, William; hold up your head—come." [1] To the plain questions addressed to Saunder Simpcox—"What, art thou lame? how cam'st thou so?" he must reply that it was by "a fall off of a tree." But it is vain trying to fence with Jenkins, who extracts the damning confession that it was "a plum-tree, master." What was he doing in a plum-tree? The question may well strike him speechless, and he may think himself fortunate to be let off with the law offered to Simpcox:—"Fetch me a stool hither by-and-by. Now, sirrah! if you mean to save yourself a whipping, leap me over this stool." [2]

In truth, the fall from a plum-tree might very well have happened to little William. An entry in the chamberlain's accounts records a payment of twopence to one Viland for "digging of the plum-trees;" and another entry speaks of the "chapel orchard," the chapel, as we have seen, serving as a schoolroom, so that the plums were in a most tempting situation, under the very eyes of the scholars. It may have

[1] 'Merry Wives of Windsor,' act iv. 1.
[2] 'King Henry VI., Part II.,' act ii. 1.

been a remembrance of the chapel orchard that suggested to
Romeo to "leap this orchard wall."[1]  Shakespeare, at any
rate, was both a leaper and climber.  His allusions to active
sports, and his familiarity with their details, all breathe
reality.  He could "win a lady at leap-frog" with Henry
of Monmouth.  He might not, like Master Page, have "a
fine hawk for the bush," but he went "a-birding;" and we
suspect that he was himself "the schoolboy who, being over-
joyed at finding a bird's nest, shows it to his companion, and
he steals it."[2]  There is no rough gambol of youth for
which he does not find a nook in his works.  Nor does
he forget in-door pastimes, but preserves a fondness for
"hoodman blind,"[3] and a tender memory of "flap-dragon."[4]
The "book of riddles," which Slender lent to Alice Short-
cake, was, in his boyish days, the property of Shakespeare
himself.  But before everything he enjoyed the open fields,
the merry greenwood, and the excitement of vigorous exercise.  As we read his animated verse, we come to think that
the match between Orlando and Charles the wrestler had
been rehearsed with a schoolfellow.  He loves to follow the
flight of an arrow :—

> " In my schoolboy days, when I had lost one shaft,
> I shot his fellow of the self-same flight
> The self-same way, with more advised watch
> To find the other forth ; and by adventuring both
> I oft found both."[5]

And Mazeppa could not be more at home on the back of a
horse.

But there were times, in the midst of this buoyant ac-
tivity, this fullness of life and action, when he showed that
his power was not of the body but the mind, though to those

---

[1] ' Romeo and Juliet,' act ii. 1.
[2] ' Much Ado about Nothing,' act ii. 1.
[3] ' Hamlet,' act iii. 4.
[4] ' Love's Labour's Lost,' act v. 1.
[5] ' Merchant of Venice,' act i. 1.

around him its source was, like the strength of Samson, a mystery. Day comes not with a burst; there is a twilight, a dawn. The child of the Muses disclosed the germ of his gifts even at this early time, and what afterwards spoke with a trumpet's voice rose now as the soft, fragmentary utterances of the Æolian chord. It has been so with all great poets. Byron lay meditating on the tomb at Harrow; Walter Scott lured his schoolfellows from play with his wild stories; and Goëthe relates how he diverted his playmates with tales of elves and fairies, composed as he spoke. At the same age could Shakespeare be dumb? All his surroundings, and all our experience, give other testimony. The era was one to quicken the poetic disposition—a period of change, when everything was in motion, and when, as among the Persian Magi, light battled with darkness. Before the alert boy was a new epoch, at his feet were the ruins of the old, and around rose a mist of traditions and superstitions, gathering in strange heaps and weird shadows —all the lore of witchcraft, astrology, sorcery, monastic legends, familiars, ghosts, and fairies. Strange it were if his charmed mind did not rise to the spell which so powerfully influenced his genius.

About the same time, a boy of nearly the same age stole away from his playmates to investigate the cause of an echo, which he had heard repeating their words. And the boy Shakespeare, like the boy Bacon, heard an echo. He knew the voice—it was the voice of Nature: great, beautiful, glorious Nature, which spoke to him like his mother. But whence came the echo? He stole away from his playmates to inquire, and solved the mystery. The echo was in his own breast.

The flow of poesy is heard from the first, like the babbling brook, which, as it proceeds, swells into a river; and Shakespeare was already a river to his young companions, as they sat round him under the shady trees on the banks of their own Avon: it might be at the Weir Brake, where the tall trees interlace like a wall, throwing out their boughs in bosses, and where, in summer, the little mounds in the river are one mass of flowers—island parterres, while the bright turf-slopes are smooth as a lawn. See the spot at night, with the moon throwing up the church spire and streaming on the river, and it will be easy to believe the tradition that hence came the inspiration of 'Midsummer Night's Dream.' Quince seems to point expressly to the Weir Brake :—" When you have spoken your speech enter into that brake."[1]

Young Will was no doubt as powerful at a ghost story as Hermione's little son, and it began in the same way—" there was a man dwelt by a church-yard." [2] The churchyard of Stratford was very suggestive of such themes. It was so packed with dead that the grave-diggers, as in 'Hamlet,' were continually turning up human bones, and these were collected together and deposited in the charnel-house, which then adjoined the church. Hence arose fearful rumours, which were not always without foundation ; for on one occasion the body of a lady was found turned in her coffin, indicating that she had been buried alive. Some such tales had reached the ear of Shakespeare :—

> " —— Hide me nightly in a charnel-house
> O'er-covered quite with dead men's rattling bones,
> With reeky shanks and yellow chapless skulls.
> * * * * *
> Things that to hear them told, have made me tremble." [3]

His familiarity with the churchyard, " loose, unfirm, with digging up of graves," [4] is strongly brought out in both 'Romeo and Juliet' and 'Hamlet,' and shows that it was

---

[1] 'Midsummer Night's Dream,' act iii. 1.
[2] 'Winter's Tale,' act ii. 1.
[3] 'Romeo and Juliet,' act iv. 1.      [4] Ibid., act v. 2.

one of the favourite haunts of his boyhood. Here it was that he learnt the mysteries of ghostdom, which so impressed his imagination, and thence come embalmed to us. But for him we might not have known that ghosts only visit the earth between the glimpses of the moon—that light, though it be merely a small taper's, keeps them at a respectful distance; and that the fresh morning air is **unsavoury in their nostrils. It is from him we** learn that **they come neither from heaven nor hell, but from a neutral region, which hangs** between both, something in the fashion **of** Mahomet's coffin, and which has a climate so trying that it quite accounts for their uncomfortable habit of roving. Old Truepenny was a different being from the modern goblin, who signifies his presence by a rap on the wall, and answers polite inquiries with his knuckles. He took a questionable shape, spoke in a voice that froze the blood, and, instead of hankering after evening parties, haunted the loneliest spots, where **he was** shy of appearing to more than one person at a time. **Such** are the marks by which a true ghost may be known.

Shakespeare is **just** as great an authority about fairies. The belief **in fairies was a bequest of** the middle ages, embracing the relics of paganism. The popular **creed was not adopted** by Spencer, **who constructed** a system **of his** own; but Shakespeare reflects it as still current in remote districts of England. The little folk were divided into three classes—fairies, elves, and urchins; the first being inoffensive, unless provoked; while the two inferior orders **were very malevolent.** All were immortal, and the superior class, though diminutive **in stature, possessed unfading** beauty. They lived underground, or **in the clefts of rocks,** only appearing on **the earth's surface at night, when they** held merry meetings **in field and** forest, **tracing rings with their feet** on the green **sward.** These places **of resort were all known to Shakespeare—**

> " —— On hill, in dale, forest, or mead,
> By paved fountain or by rushy brook,
> Or on the beachy margent of the sea,
> To dance our ringlets to the whistling wind."[1]

The elfin rings were sprinkled with dew, as the poet faithfully records;[2] and this was never touched by damsels gathering May dew, as it was reputed to spoil beauty. Any trespass on their haunts, indeed, was highly resented by the fairies, particularly if it occurred during their nocturnal meetings. Falstaff trembled when he heard the alarm—

> " But, stay, I smell a man of middle earth ;"

and the punishment was sure and swift—

> " About him, fairies : sing a scornful chyme,
> And, as you trip, still pinch him to your time."

Shakespeare appears to have learnt this statute of fairy law from a lyric called the ' Fairies' Dance,' found in a collection of songs then current,[3] and which contains a similar passage :—

> " Pinch him black and pinch him blue,
> Oh, thus our nails shall handle you."

But fairies, while they shunned men and women, were often so charmed by pretty children that they stole them from their mothers, leaving in their place urchins of the same appearance, who sickened and died. These changelings, as they were called, are repeatedly noticed by Shakespeare, who makes Puck declare that Oberon was enraged with the fairy queen Titania :—

> " Because that she, as her attendant, hath
> A lovely boy stol'n from an Indian king,
> She never had so sweet a changeling." [4]

---

[1] ' Midsummer Night's Dream,' act ii. 2.

[2] Ibid., ii. 1.

[3] The collection is entitled, ' Hunting, Hawking, Dancing, Drinking, Enamouring.'

[4] ' Midsummer Night's Dream,' act ii. 1.

The poet also refers to the fairies' love of cleanliness—

> " I am sent with broom before,
> To sweep the dust behind the door." [1]

The " household maid " who attended to this duty obtained the favour of the little folk, and, some fine morning, found sixpence in her shoe. But, on the whole, fairies interfered in human affairs rather for evil than good, and the devout nightly offered up a prayer against their devices. Thus Imogen exclaims—

> " To your protection I commend me, Gods !
> From fairies and the tempters of the night,
> Guard me, beseech ye." [2]

A special service against fairies was introduced by the priests and monks, who regarded them as evil spirits, and threw over the faithful the shield of religion. But their prayers did not exorcise the superstition from the mind of the people, and the fairies took refuge under the mantle of Shakespeare, who secured to them their ancient heritage,—immortality and perpetual youth.

The realities as well as the superstitions of the age, had their picturesque points, appealing to the imagination, and contributing to mould the wizard boy. As yet, they passed him unheeded, like the tints which the changing sky throws over a landscape, and which do not arrest us at the time, seeming a thing of course. Afterwards they were recalled, or rather he found them treasured in his mind, as they are preserved in a work of art, and rise unbidden to the trained eye. But the impression he received from all that was novel was not only permanent, but immediate. It has been conjectured that his allusion in 'Midsummer Night's Dream' to Queen Elizabeth's visit to Kenilworth

[1] ' Midsummer Night's Dream,' act **v. 2.**
[2] ' Cymbeline,' act ii. 2.

was inspired by an experience of his **early life ; and all
doubt** on the point will be removed, **when we show hereafter**
that the family were acquainted with **the** Earl of Leicester,
and owed much to **his protection.** Shakespeare **was in his
twelfth year when he beheld this** pageant, the last blaze
**of** baronial splendour. **Another** play introduces **Kenil-**
worth itself, by its old provincial name of Killingworth
Castle, and here Henry the Sixth receives the submission of
the Cadites after their defeat by Buckingham.[1]

Lancham describes the castle in its proudest day, when
**it was the dwelling of Leicester. On** the great occasion
of **Elizabeth's visit, the hall was thronged with lords and
dames and choked with retainers—gentlemen in suits of**
velvet, each **with a gold chain round his neck—sword and**
buckler men, **domestics, and lacqueys. From the terraces**
of the castle **the eye looked down** on the **park, which was**
studded **with** trees, and **surrounded a spacious lake, in the**
midst of which a green islet sparkled **in the** sunlight like an
emerald. Herds of deer browsed **on the sward, and copse**
and thicket aided the undulating ground in diversifying the
prospect. Each day of the Queen's sojourn brought new
pageants and shows, often protracted far into the night, for
which the moon lent her brightest beams. The state, the
blazonry, and the gorgeous parade **of feudalism** exhausted
their power in this display. **It was chivalry going out like
a rocket, in a shower of light, teaching Shakespeare more
than he could learn from books—showing the young scholar**
the image of the **past ere it** faded for ever.

<hr>

[1] ' King Henry VI., Part II.,' act iv. 9.

## V.

### HIS EARLY IMPRESSIONS **OF RELIGION.**

It may seem strange to affirm that the genius of Shakespeare received an impulse from religion. We know that religion formed Dante and Tasso, and, at a later period, inspired Milton; but who would look for a divine influence in the drama? Yet this it was, in a corrupted form, that gave the drama existence. The Greek tragedies aspired to exhibit the action of the gods in human affairs, and the performance commenced with a religious service. Religion, indeed, did not disdain to use the drama as a means of instruction, under the Christian dispensation, and it may be said to have been kept in chrysalis in the 'Moralities and Mysteries' till the period of its revival. The Christian faith was itself regenerated at the same time, and this auspicious conjuncture gave birth to Shakespeare.

The great movement in progress affected every phase of the epoch. It was so pervading, that we cannot now estimate the extent of its influence, though we see it reflected in almost every event, and can trace it in every sphere. Openly or in secret, it was the mainspring of all hearts. Throughout the realm, from the capital to the remotest hamlet, and, abroad, over the whole continent, it was in operation; vibrating through society like sound through the atmosphere, and everywhere shaping thought, policy, and action.

Shakespeare was born just within the verge of Protestantism, in such proximity to the old religion as to remind

us of the relation of Berwick-upon-Tweed to England and
Scotland; for he might be claimed on either hand but for
special mention.   His parents were married according to the
rites of **the church of** Rome; his eldest sister was christened
in the same faith; and it is only from the establishment
of a parochial register at Stratford a few months before his
birth, that we know he received baptism in the Protestant
communion.   But he is a prize too great to be surrendered;
and, in spite of the evidence of the register, the Roman
Catholic church claims him as a son.[1]   This, indeed, is
**no ground for reproach.**   Seven cities disputed for the
honour of being the birthplace of Homer, and rival religions
may contend for the merit of having moulded Shakespeare.
Dante, Tasso, and **Milton belong to sects: Shakespeare is**
catholic, embodying in his precepts the meek **endurance, the**
sweet sympathy, the soft flow **of love** and pity; **the simple,**
confiding faith, which are the breathing spirit of **the Gospel,**
and which he **brought home to the dullest perception in**
human actions.   Thus he may be said to have converted the
intellect: and Rome may be excused for claiming the glory
**of** such a missionary.

   But the dispute about Shakespeare's religion was not
allowed to rest on the facts: some ardent Roman Catholic,
who wished to link him with Dante and Tasso, enlivened it
with fiction.   **In 1771, the roof of one of the** Shakespeare
dwellings in Henley Street **was out of repair, and a brick-**
**layer at work upon it, on removing some old tiles, found**
on the rafters a folded paper, having the appearance of **an**
ancient manuscript.   This, on examination, professed to be
an exposition of the creed of John Shakespeare, who **was**
**made to declare** himself " an unworthy member of the
holy Catholic Church," enumerating its doctrines as his
articles of belief.   The document was forwarded to Malone,

[1] Chalmer's ' Apology for the Believers.'

and as he was known to be editing the works of Shakespeare, and searching everywhere for information respecting his life, nothing could have happened more to the satisfaction of its fabricator. There were points about it that ought to have excited suspicion. The phraseology, though studiedly antiquated, was not that of the sixteenth century. It was highly improbable that a religious confession should be deposited in such a place, and, indeed, there could be no motive for making it, if it was to be concealed. But these inconsistencies did not strike Malone, and, after taking some years for reflection, he published the document in his edition of Shakespeare as a statement of the creed of the poet's father. At a later period he discovered his error, and declared that papers in his hands proved that it was not written by any of the family. In fact, he ascertained that John Shakespeare himself could not write.

We may leave controversalists to decide whether the poet's father was brought up in the tenets of the old church; but as he must have been born after the secession of England in the reign of Henry the Eighth, and grew up in that of Edward the Sixth, the probability is that he was reared in the doctrines of the Reformation. At any rate, he was a zealous adherent of the Protestant faith under Elizabeth. One of the first acts of the new reign required all municipal authorities to take the oath of supremacy, and this was done by John Shakespeare, as he was appointed successively to the offices of constable, chamberlain, alderman, and bailiff of Stratford. There is even proof that he was something of a fanatic, for, in 1564, the chamberlain's accounts record that he paid two shillings for the defacement of "an image in the chapel."

But, after all, it is not with the creed of John, but with that of William Shakespeare that we are concerned. Of him we know that he was born under a Protestant sovereign, baptized in a Protestant church, and educated in a Protestant school. It is true that he shows himself versed in the Roman Catholic divinity; and the fact of his making a Catholic discourse of penance and absolution, unction and purgatory, exactly as a Roman Catholic should, is alleged as a proof that these doctrines were his own. We might as well infer that he was a believer in Jove, because his pagan characters profess paganism. Evidence against him is found in his very charity, and it is thought conclusive that he was of the old faith, because he not only abstains from reviling Catholics on account of their religion, but even presents monks and priests in the garb of humanity, when it was the fashion of the day to regard them as monsters.

But, though free from religious bigotry, and untainted with sectarian bitterness, Shakespeare never leaves us in doubt as to his religious predilections. These are not to be gleaned from isolated sentiments, but from the whole development of the characters he presents—characters so complete that, like persons in real life, they pass before us again and again ere their points are apparent, as if they were endued with the power of keeping them out of sight. The monk's cowl is even worn so close that it hides his nature from himself as well as others, so that he is not conscious of the little traits that creep out. The delicate touch is spread through the action, as in real life, and scrutiny is required to see that what has captivated us by a general resemblance is natural in every lineament. Such is the character of Friar Laurence, who wins our respect by his benevolence, and our love by his gentleness, but who, on closer acquaintance, will be found wanting as a Christian priest. Not only is God not in all his thoughts; He is not in his thoughts at all. Thus he is angry with Romeo for his threat of suicide; but instead of pointing

out the wickedness of such a design, and reminding him
of the Christian duty of endurance, he speaks to him as
a man of the world, seeking to reconcile him to life by
the advantages it has given him, and by making light of
his misfortunes.  On another occasion he promises to give
him "armour"[1] to resist his trials, and we might suppose
him to have in view "the helmet of salvation, and the sword
of the Spirit, which is the Word of God"—"God's Word,"[2]
as Shakespeare has it.   But all he proffers is

> " Adversity's sweet milk, philosophy,
>     To comfort thee when thou art banished."[3]

Well may Romeo exclaim, "Hang up philosophy!"

While Shakespeare marks the Christian character so
faintly in his model friar, he presents no trace of it in his
Romish prelates, those wondrous creations which we may
call the hierarchy of the drama.  The sleek insolence of
Pandulph, the restless treason of Scroop, the "monstrous
life" of Beaufort, who "dies and makes no sign," all attest
his antagonism to the old church.  Even his favourite
Wolsey, a butcher's son like himself, does not remember
his holy calling till his fall, and then but to tell how he
had neglected it—

> " Oh, Cromwell! Cromwell!
> Had I but served my God with half the zeal
> I served my king, he would not in mine age
> Have left me naked to mine enemies."[4]

But he is careful to throw the halo of sanctity over Wolsey's
end—

> " —— To add greater honour to his age
> Than man could give him, he died fearing God."[5]

In contrast with these types of the old priesthood,

---

[1] ' Romeo and Juliet,' act iii. 2.
[2] ' King Henry VIII.,' act v.
[3] ' Romeo and Juliet,' act iii. 2.
[4] ' King Henry VIII.,' act iii. 2.
[5] Ibid., act iv. 2.

Cranmer, accused by the fierce Gardiner of filling the realm with "new opinions,"[1] is portrayed as a saint, and vested with the attributes of a prophet. No provocation exhausts his patience, and he preserves his meekness and humility under every affront. In the darkest peril he trusts for deliverance from his enemies to "truth and honesty," and, above all, to God.[2] As we mark his demeanour, as we hear his words, the inspiration is obvious, and testifies as much to Shakespeare's creed as his own.

But, in truth, Shakespeare needs no witness: he speaks for himself. On the great dogmas of the ancient church he has unmistakably pronounced. Absolution he utterly rejects, deriding those who—

> " Purchase corrupted pardon of a man
> Who, in that sale, sells pardon from himself."

He denies the supremacy of the pope, and contemns his spiritual powers.[3]   He ridicules the notion that there is miraculous virtue in the shrines of saints, and brings forward Saunder Simpcox to show what tricks were practised at those resorts to keep up their odour and repute. The varying emotions of King Henry in this scene[4] form, indeed, a sermon of themselves, breathing such exquisite piety, such confiding faith, such fervent adoration. Even in delivering rebukes Shakespeare does not lay aside his excellent gift of charity. The childlike credulity of the gentle king, which disposes him to believe the miracle before he hears the report of it, is wrapped in the beautiful mantle of devotion—

> " Good fellow, tell us here the circumstance,
> That we for thee may glorify the Lord."

And we are taught that holiness may exist in every creed

[1] ' King Henry VIII.,' act iv. 2.  [3] ' King John,' act iii. 1.
[2] Ibid., act v. 1.  [4] ' King Henry VI., Part II.,' act ii. 1.

by his burst of heartfelt worship, in which all sects may
join—

> " Now God be praised that, to believing souls,
>     Gives light in darkness, comfort in despair."

Nor will the poet allow the exposure of the trick to bring
any humiliation on the king, but, by a master-stroke of
art, makes it draw out his piety and turn to the glory of
Heaven—

> " O God ! see'st thou this, and bear'st so long ! "

The old church sealed up the Bible : Shakespeare is for
having it open, declaring that where it is read "God shall
be truly known." [1]   He thought no evidence so strong as
" proof of Holy Writ." [2]   His sentiments, his imagery,
his very language prove that he searched the Scriptures.
Cranmer's prophecy over Elizabeth is a paraphrase of the
prophetic vision of Balaam. [3]   The noble words of the sacred
historian [4] lose none of their effect in the version of Shakespeare—

> " In her days every man shall eat in safety
>     Under his own vine, what he plants." [5]

Nor is the sublime exclamation of Isaiah, "How art thou
fallen from heaven, O Lucifer, son of the morning," [6] un-
worthily rendered by Wolsey—

> " And when he falls, he falls like Lucifer,
>     Never to hope again." [7]

The Psalms lend the poet their noblest passage—"Who
maketh the clouds his chariot, and walketh upon the wings
of the wind," [8] which is put into the mouth of Romeo —

---

[1] 'King Henry VIII.,' act v. 4.
[2] 'Othello,' act iii. 3.
[3] Numbers, xxiv.
[4] Ibid., xiv. 12

[5] 'King Henry VIII.,' act. v. 4.
[6] Isaiah, xxxvi. 16.
[7] 'King Henry VIII.'   ,
[8] Psalms, civ. 4.

> " When he bestrides the lazy-pacing clouds,
> And sails upon the bosom of the air."[1]

But we will not multiply examples; the works of Shake-speare abound with such passages, and indeed no poet has borrowed from the Scriptures to the same extent, as none could borrow with the same effect.

It is true that the blemish common to our literary patriarchs attaches to him, in his too familiar mention of the Deity. The practice had become conventional with our poets from the time of Gower and Chaucer, and this associaton of the holiest of names with the grossest ribaldry not only failed to shock the ear, but was looked upon as a natural mode of speech. Its prevalence would not excuse Shakespeare if he had merely yielded to the fashion of the time. But he aimed to represent nature as it stood, in all its aspects, even, as he says, in its deformity, that, in the mirror which he held up, vice might be frightened by its own features. He attained his object, but the means, judged by modern ideas, are not sanctified by the end; and it is only when we recall the licence around him—the general corruption which he so loudly condemns—that his comparative purity can be appreciated.

The most thoughtless must be struck with Shakespeare's religious consistency—his true catholic views of Christian duty and practice, maintained through so many changes and so many temptations; for he had not only to rise superior to the sectarian spirit of the time, but to pass through lights and shades seductive to a poetic, and perilous to a speculative mind. In his boyhood, the monasteries and convents that had covered the land were but just broken up; as yet, their walls were memorials, not ruins, and the country round preserved the vestiges of their rule. The eye might still rest on old abbeys, where the finger of

_______
[1] ' Romeo and Juliet,' act ii. 2.

monkish art was traceable in delicate stone-work. Shakespeare heard of the shows and processions, the festivals and holidays, which had overgrown the ancient church like ivy, and what looked rank when close, he might think picturesque in the distance. His imagination recalled the trains of pilgrims who visited the famous shrines of Canterbury and St. Albans, and Chaucer helped him to throw **over** them **the hues of romance.** A period more recent, almost **within his own** life, inspired more serious and deeper feelings. **From** his mother's lips he heard her experiences of the reign of Mary, and in the speech of Glendower seems to allude to the luminous appearances in the sky, which the people had supposed to be a supernatural reflection of the martyr fires—

> " The front of heaven was full of fiery shapes,
> Of burning cressets." [1]

What a rebuke to the fanatics of all sects is the retort of Paulina to Leontes :—

> " It is an heretic that makes the fire,
> **Not** she which burns in 't." [2]

Even Shylock **is made to reprove** the intolerance of the age :—" Hath **not a Jew** eyes ? Hath **not** a Jew hands, organs, dimensions, senses, affections, passions ; fed with the same food, hurt with the same weapons, subject to the same diseases, healed by the same means, warmed and cooled by the same winter and summer as a Christian is ?" [3]

In Shakespeare's eyes, religion was too sacred a thing to be made an object of contention. **The strife** of creeds swept away, indeed, the noblest spirits of the **age on both** sides, making them forget that the **first** injunction **of** Christianity

---

[1] ' King Henry **IV.**, Part I.,' act iii. 1.

[2] ' A Winter's Tale,' act ii. 3.

[3] ' Merchant of Venice,' act iii. 1.

is for men to love one another; but while the English
people were kept in a ferment by a succession of religious
convulsions, such as the struggle between the Huguenots
and Roman Catholics in France, the massacre of St. Bartholomew, the heroic stand of the Reformers in Holland, the
persecution of the Protestants in Germany, the attempted
invasion of England, and, lastly, the Gunpowder Plot, the
poet, whose life was hedged in by these events, still preached
kindness to all men. Self-denial, forgiveness of injuries,
integrity, forbearance, purity of life, and practical piety, are
the doctrines he always inculcates :—

> " Love thyself last, cherish those hearts that hate thee;
> Corruption wins not more than honesty;
> Still in thy right hand carry gentle peace
> To silence envious tongues.  Be just, and fear not;
> Let all the ends thou aim'st at be
> Thy God's and truth's." [1]

The works of Shakespeare keep perpetually before us a
sense of God's presence—almost as much as the works of
nature, of which they are the reflection. The appeals for
His protection, the testimonies to His mercy, and the recog-
nitions of His providence, occur, indeed, so frequently, that
they must have been a leading thought in the poet's mind
in the musings of his study. It would seem as if he looked
out from this little chamber, as from an observatory, in the
silence of the night, on the world, the heavens, and the
universe, and learnt from them the littleness of man, the
greatness of God. These are the images he presents to
us, impresses upon us, and takes as the text of all his
pleadings. They are not used to excite terror, but to
humble, admonish, and melt us. He speaks to us as " little
children; " for, in the illumination of his mind, he retains
his child's heart, as natural, as genuine, and as innocent in

---

[1] ' King Henry VIII.,' act iii. 2.

his latter as his early life.   And the whole burden of his doctrine is to be charitable ; to be forgiving, and to meekly follow the steps of our Great Exemplar :—

" Alas, Alas !
Why all the souls that were, were forfeit once,
And He that might the 'vantage best have took,
Found out the remedy : how would you be
If He which is the top of judgment, should
But judge you as you are ?   Oh, think on that,
And mercy then will breathe within your lips,
Like man new made."[1]

---

[1] ' Measure for Measure,' **act ii. 2.**

## VI.

### INCIDENTS OF HIS YOUTH.

STRATFORD was the very spot for the cradle of a poet who, moulded by nature, was to be nursed by the Muse of History. The surrounding country is not more remarkable for its picturesque scenery than its historic associations, linking it with the greatest events of earlier and later times. Almost within view rose the spires of Coventry, from time immemorial a city of mark, and fruitful of legend and fable. Still nearer were the walls of Warwick, with its ancient castle, the eyry of the king-maker; and not far beyond were Guy's Cliff and Kenilworth,—the one a memorial of the past, the other uniting the past and present. In the adjoining shires of Gloucester and Leicester, the White Rose and the Red had fought their deadliest conflicts, and it was only a ride to Bosworth Field, where they finally intertwined in a nuptial wreath.

Shakespeare displays a familiar acquaintance with Coventry, and whenever the subject permits, seems delighted to carry his imagination to this scene of his boyhood, where he first trod enchanted ground. He saw the fair town in its glory, when its abbeys and monasteries, though converted to other purposes, still clustered round its triad of spires, like a flock round its shepherds; and the whole was encircled by an embattled wall, renowned from time of old. It is before these ramparts that he parades the host of Edward, when he challenges Warwick to the field :—

> " Go, trumpet, to the walls and sound a parle."[1]

---

[1] ' King Henry VI., Part III.,' act v. 1.

And, looking down from their summit, Warwick hurls taunts
at his old favourite :—

> " Confess who set thee up and pluck'd thee down,—
> Call Warwick patron, and be penitent ?—
> And thou shalt still remain the Duke of York."

"**A public** road near Coventry" is selected by the poet
for the introduction of Falstaff to his native county, where,
of course, he is joined by Prince Hal—"How now, mad
wag! what a devil dost thou in Warwickshire?"[1]   Here,
also, the knight tricks his sharp lieutenant, and makes his
first essay in campaigning :—"Bardolph, get thee before
to Coventry: fill me a bottle of sack ; our soldiers shall
march through." But touching the "soldiers," Jack has too
much regard for appearances to exhibit himself at their
head ; and having got rid of Bardolph, takes his famous
resolution,—"I'll not march through Coventry with them:
that's flat."

Shakespeare's recollections of Coventry dated earlier
than historic times.  He had heard of it in the ballad of
Lady Godiva, on whom her lord imposed a penance as the
price of the remission of the city tolls :—

> " If thou wilt but thy clothes strip off,
> And by me lay them down,
> And at noonday on horseback ride
> Stark naked through the town."

The incident was commemorated in the city pageants,
which Shakespeare saw as a child, when he was also a spectator of the old 'Mysteries,' for which Coventry was renowned.  These performances were got up by the artisans
of the city, and were thought worthy of being played before
kings.  The mystery of 'The Slaughter of the Innocents'
was represented by the tailors and shearers of Coventry
before Henry the Eighth in 1534, and the king may have

---

[1] 'King Henry IV., Part I.,' act iv. 2.

taken a lesson from the hero of the piece, in whom he might recognize a kindred spirit. Herod is even himself sensible of his infirmity :—

> " I stamp, I stare, I look all about."

And this is emphasized by the stage directions,—" Here Herod rages again," an intimation which is quite superfluous. Shakespeare was much impressed with Herod's habit of swearing, and mentions it as characteristic of a tyrant :—

> " This would make mercy *swear* and play the tyrant." [1]

Harry the Fifth remembers Herod's " bloody‑hunting slaughter‑men,[2] and Hamlet does not forget his ragings, rebuking the players who " out‑Herod Herod." [3]

This recovery of the impressions of Shakespeare's boyhood in his works throws a light on the development of his genius, as well as on his early life. They look like the little dints in the steep sides of Parnassus by which he climbed to its summit. The Coventry ' Moralities ' seem puerile to modern eyes, but were most ludicrous, when they attempted to be imposing, for their promoters saw nothing absurd in paying eightpence for a link to set the earth on fire, or, in the mystery of ' Doomsday,' making an old barrel do duty for the world. But Shakespeare drew his instruction from the antique dresses and the flaunting banners, the dialogue and the action. What turned men into children, helped to make this child a man—king of men. He caught from the exhibition its salient points—the picturesque and the dramatic ; and even a fund of drollery from its trips. The ' Nine Worthies,' performed in his boyhood at Coventry, he has himself kept alive, and his version illustrates the fillip it gave to his humour no less than the

---

[1] ' Measure for Measure,' act iii. 2.
[2] ' King Henry V.,' act iii. 3.    [3] ' Hamlet,' act iii. 2.

freshness of his memory. We understand all the arrangements of the old "Morality," when Holofernes says, "This swain, because of his great limb, or joint, shall pass Pompey the Great." Not that stature, any more than aptitude, regulated the distribution of parts, for it is no obstacle to the personation of Hercules by the page that he is, as Armado says, "not quantity enough for that worthy's thumb." The difficulty is got over by deciding that "he shall present Hercules in minority," and Holofernes undertakes to "have an apology for that purpose."[1]

Something was to be learnt by the observant boy in his native Stratford. The ancient festivals, the local usages, even the weekly market offered points to attract his eye and enlarge his experience. We know there was, as Luce says of Ephesus, "a pair of stocks in the town;"[2] and to this humble fountain we may trace some of the coarse humour of Launce and Speed, Grumio and the Dromios. Scolds and termagants were provided with a cucking-stool, where, however, they did not sit "like Patience on a monument;" for it often broke down under their struggles. The repairs are duly registered by the Stratford chamberlains, and we find the stool debited with sixpence " for things to mend it withal," with eightpence for "a cuck," and the large item of eleven shillings for trees. Ladies may think treats would have been more to the purpose. But our ancestors never tried gentle means for the Taming of a Shrew; and he who knew how to manage scolds of every degree, from injurious Hermia and waspish Katherine to Dame Quickly and Doll Tearsheet, had not yet spoken.

Once a year Stratford was the scene of a "great fair," as it is called in the chamberlain's accounts, which in the same entry record a payment of eleven shillings to four Stratford champions for excluding the "Coventry men,"

[1] 'Love's Labour's Lost,' act v. 1.    [2] 'Comedy of Errors,' act iii. 1.

who took advantage of the fair to make themselves disagreeable. It may be noted that the cost of keeping order at the fair, and keeping the fair themselves in order, was precisely the same—eleven shillings for the four champions, and eleven shillings for the cucking-stool.

Probably we derive from "the great fair" the germ of Caliban. Certainly it was there, amidst the prodigies of the showmen, and in his boyish days, that Shakespeare learnt how his countrymen "will not give a doit to relieve a lame beggar," when "they will lay out ten to see a dead Indian."[1] So admirably did he catch up our smallest traits, that those he ascribes to our ancestors still crop out in ourselves. It is only a few months since that London found an attractive exhibition in a "talking fish," such as might provoke the rhapsody which Caliban drew from Trinculo:—"A strange fish! Were I in England now, as I once was, and had but this fish painted, not a holiday fool there but would give a piece of silver: there would this monster make a man." The accounts of the Stratford chamberlains record that, in 1577, when Shakespeare was in his thirteenth year, the monster actually visited Stratford. The entry relates to four shillings "paid when the MONSTER WAS HERE for a gallon-and-a-half of sack." Shakespeare remembered this potation in the speech of Stephano:—"My man-monster hath drowned his tongue in sack."[2]

Another feature of the fair was the mountebank doctor, who, we learn from Decker's 'Villanies Discovered,' announced his arrival in bills, posted in different parts of the town. The practice gives a sarcasm to Beatrice, when she accuses Benedick of blowing his own trumpet:—"He set up his bills here in Messina."[3]

---

[1] 'The Tempest,' act ii. 2.  [2] Ibid., act iii. 2.
[3] 'Much Ado about Nothing.' act i. 1.

According to Decker, the sovereign remedy of the travelling quacks was "salve," so that there is nothing new in Holloway's ointment. The salve was composed of herbs, which were described by the fine term of "simples," and Dr. Caius was evidently thinking of some such preparation when the great Simple himself came in his way:—"Dere is some simples in my closet dat I will not for the world I shall leave behind."[1]

But Shakespeare's **boyhood** had other experiences, more suggestive and more impressive. He was not, as we have been told, reared in the abode of affluence, and amidst the smiles of fortune. This would have been no training for the laureate of nature. To understand the deep susceptibilities of humanity, to be able to portray its emotions and weaknesses, he must pass under their yoke. For a time he was indeed to know a happy home, but adversity cut off its promise, as a frost nips the blossoms of early spring. In this sad experience he grew up, familiar with the broken hope, the crushed spirit, the cruel pressure of misfortune, and all the thousand sorrows of poverty. Nature trained him in her counsels, made them his **nurture and aliment. Thus he came to** be so gentle **and patient,** deprecating resentment, exalting the twice-blest influence of mercy, and preaching the great truth that sympathy, the interchange of kindly feelings, associates all mankind—"One touch of nature makes the whole world kin."[2]

Our reverence for Shakespeare increases as we see how he acquired these lessons, and at how tender an age. In the ripening days of boyhood, just when the sensibilities are quickest and pride most active, adversity, **instead of** embittering, softens and elevates him—raises him out of the

---

[1] 'Merry Wives of Windsor,' act ii. 4.
[2] 'Troilus and Cressida,' act iii. 3.

narrow circle of self, and makes his heart beat for every living thing—even for "the poor beetle that we tread upon."[1] At a later time, he might take to himself the words of the sacred poet,—" It is good for me that I have been in trouble ; " for without this probation he could not have been what he became. Thus he is an example to all who follow him ; for, like Bunyan's Pilgrim on a higher errand, he waded through the slough of Despond, crossed the valley of Humiliation, climbed the hill Difficulty, encountered Apollyon the Reviler, and yet never wavered in acts of kindness to others or in his frank, honest cheerfulness.

To trace the future poet along this sacred way we must return to John Shakespeare, whom we have seen rise, from so obscure a beginning, to rank and importance, accumulating property, and passing from one corporate office to another, till, in 1568, we left him in the bailiff's chair. He was elected Chief Alderman three years later, just as his son entered the grammar-school, and little William thus appeared among his schoolfellows as one of the aristocracy of the town. So far as transpires, his father's means were then equal to his position, for about this time, there was a considerable expansion of his business, and he seems to have kept up a larger amount of stock, since he found it necessary to rent some land at Ingon, hitherto described as a farm, but which legal documents mention as fourteen acres of "meadow," such as a thriving butcher might require for pasture.[2] We may conclude that the speculation was successful, as John Shakespeare continued to prosper, for in 1575 he became the purchaser of the house he had so long

---

[1] 'Measure for Measure,' act iii. 1.

[2] The land is described as in the occupation of John Shakespeare in a deed executed in 1570. A deed, bearing date May 30, 1568, mentions it as in possession of another person.

occupied in Henley Street, and for which he paid forty pounds. The success, indeed, was such that it tempted him to deviate from the steady, prudent course he had previously followed, and engage in a new calling. Possibly, after filling the highest corporate dignities, he had begun to look down on his trade of butcher, or his increasing flock at Ingon meadows may have suggested to him a readier source of profit. **Certainly his situation underwent some change soon after the purchase of the** house in Henley Street, and **we may consider that** at this period he became a dealer in wool.

The worthy alderman's affairs now rapidly clouded. Not only did his new trade of woolstapler produce no wool, but it must have entailed a serious loss ; for, while in 1575 he was in a condition to lay out a considerable **sum in the** purchase of property, in 1577 he is evidently in straits for money, his embarrassments being matter of notoriety. This we gather from the indulgence he receives in the imposition of the local rates. An assessment for equipping three pikemen, two billmen, and one archer, made by the town council on the 29th of January, fixes six and eightpence as **the amount to be paid by the aldermen, but** makes an **exception in favour of Mr.** Plumley, whose liability is reduced to five shillings, and Mr. Shakespeare, who is to pay only three and fourpence, just half the amount exacted from the others. His circumstances had not improved in the following year ; for an order for a weekly poor-rate, which assesses every alderman at fourpence, excuses him altogether. It is useless to contend that the consideration thus shown to him was not on account of his inability to pay. There is other evidence of his poverty **of the same date ; for** in 1578 he **is** found **to** be raising money **on his** wife's inheritance at Ashbies,[1] which he mortgaged to Edmund

[1] **See Appendix.**

Lambert for 40*l*., the exact sum he had paid, only three years before, for the property in Henley Street.

These facts are no reproach to the father of the poet, for, on the one hand, the sympathy he awakened proves that he enjoyed the respect of his fellow-townsmen; and, on the other, it is shown that he exerted himself to meet his liabilities as far as his resources would permit. In short, he presents the spectacle of an honest man struggling with adversity,—a noble lesson for his son.

William Shakespeare had now completed his fourteenth year, an age at which he could appreciate such conduct, while he felt the change in his own position. Whatever his original prospects, he was not one to shrink from sacrifices when his father set the example; it became necessary that he should be placed in a way of earning his livelihood, and we may conclude that he raised no objection when, removing him from school, his father, whether influenced by a favourable opening or by old predilections, apprenticed him to a butcher.

# VII.

## SHAKESPEARE, THE APPRENTICE.

If it be incredible that Romulus, the type of Force, was suckled by a wolf, there would seem much more room to doubt that Shakespeare, the soul of kindness, was reared by a butcher. Who would suppose that poetry inspired by the deepest feelings of our nature, embodying the noblest conceptions, the highest aspirations, and the purest and tenderest sentiments, had its birth in the shambles! Mankind is as ready as ever to inquire if any good thing can come out of Nazareth. But the soil is not the parent of the tree, or the oak would never spring up in the cleft of a rock.

Shakespeare stands in literature in exactly the same aspect,—a towering, majestic oak, rooted in the unlikeliest spot. Nor is he singular in his position, though unapproachable in majesty; for tinker Bunyan, with his creative power, his sublime materialism, and his English undefiled, is as great a prodigy in his way as Shakespeare the butcher.

The nature of his calling is handed down to us by tradition, the authority of which is recognized by himself:—

> " But say, my lord, it were not registered;
> Methinks the truth should live from age to age,
> As 'twere retailed to all posterity,
> Even to the general all-ending day." [1]

And, in this case, tradition is confirmed by other testimony. The parish clerk told Dowdall, who visited Stratford in 1693, that Shakespeare was bound apprentice to a butcher.

[1] ' King Richard III.,' act iii. 1.

It has been objected to this witness, a patriarch of more than eighty winters, that he was only three years old when Shakespeare died, and, consequently, could not speak from personal knowledge. A similar point raised a doubt in Prospero:—

> "Canst thou remember
> A time before we came into this cell?
> I do not think thou canst; for then thou wast not
> Out *three years old!*"

And Miranda's answer is decisive,—"Certainly, I can."[1]

But the fact has been overlooked that the parish clerk was more than three years old in 1616, the date of Shakespeare's death, and might be even five or six; for Dowdall describes him in 1690 not as eighty, but as "*above*" that age.[2] Moreover, his statement is confirmed by Aubrey, who wrote his notice of Shakespeare six years earlier, when he had himself reached a green old age, and who declares that he acquired his information "*heretofore*"—that is, in 1642, when he was at Oxford—from Shakespeare's neighbours. "His father," says the old antiquary, "was a butcher, and I have been told heretofore by some of his neighbours that when he was a boy he exercised his father's trade." This does not necessarily imply that he was apprenticed to his father, though Rowe, who is the next authority, gives a colour to such a conclusion, mentioning the " want of his assistance at home " as one of the reasons which induced John Shakespeare to remove him from school. But it is most likely that " he exercised his father's trade " under his successor in the business—probably the " Henry Rogers, butcher," whom we shall hereafter find a joint-defendant with John Shakespeare in the Bailiff's Court.

The account of the parish clerk has never been fairly

---

[1] 'The Tempest,' act i. 2.

[2] The words are :—" The clerk that showed me this church is *above* eighty years old : he says that this Shakespeare was formerly in this town, bound apprentice to a butcher."

weighed.    In showing the monument to Dowdall, he represented the poet as "the best of his family," clearly intimating that the family was known to him ; and, in fact,
George Quiney, the brother of Shakespeare's son-in-law,
was curate of the parish till 1624, when the lowest estimate
would make the parish clerk twelve years of age.  Shakespeare's daughters were both living when he was in his
thirty-seventh year, and Judith did not die till 1661, when
he was nearly fifty, and probably officiated as clerk at her
funeral.   In any case, it is absurd to suppose that he could
grow old in so small a town as Stratford without knowing
all its inhabitants, particularly persons so prominent as the
daughters of Shakespeare ; and we must not forget that these
two representatives of the poet were still living when Aubrey
acquired the same information from his " neighbours."

It is thus indisputable that the great dramatist began the
world at fourteen as the son of a fallen man.  They who
have known a reverse of fortune at that age, and carry back
memory to the time, need not be told that he experienced a
thousand pangs in every relation of his position.  The cold
looks of friends, the taunts and gibes of old inferiors, the
mortified pride, the stifled resentment, recur to us as wounds
of yesterday.  So early did Shakespeare learn endurance !
The calling suddenly imposed upon him could not be to his
taste, but, with all his sensibility, he could hardly regard it
with loathing, as it had been always under his eye, and was
associated with his early home.  We know from Slender
that " upon familiarity will grow more contempt."[1]   Moreover, a boy soon adapts himself to things around, and these
must be gloomy indeed, if they do not afford some scope
for the spirit of youth.  Shakespeare's vivacity was inex-
haustible and irrepressible.  Old Aubrey calls it " a natural
wit "—as if it were not under his control, but burst forth

[1] 'Merry Wives of Windsor,' act i. 1.

spontaneously, so that it seems a logical thing for the same
authority to tell us that when the young apprentice killed a
calf, " he would do it in high style," prefacing the slaughter
with a speech !  Could we but recover one of those orations !
Crude it would be, no doubt, but we should see Mind
sparkling through it—the precious metal veining the quartz.
We may imagine there was a flavour of Touchstone and a
spice of Autolycus in the harangue, something of Jacques
in the forest and something of Hamlet in the churchyard,
winding up with the moral that the glutton, who to-morrow
feasted on the calf, should himself be a banquet for worms.
And the poor calf came in for a word of lament—

> "—— The butcher takes away the calf,
> And binds the wretch, and beats it when it strays,
> Bearing it to the bloody slaughter-house."[1]

The nature of Shakespeare's early avocations is not to be
ascertained from allusions in his works.  Such evidence
might be found to prove him acquainted equally with almost
every calling, from divinity, law, and physic, to haberdashery
and tailor-craft.  His thoughts were not the fruit of his own
experience, great as it was; but took the range of society,
sweeping both its surface and depths.  Yet, in connection
with the facts we have adduced, it may not be amiss to show,
for the first time, that he paid due honour to butchers, and
was master of all their mysteries.

As a beginning, we are carried with the drove on its way
to the shambles :—

> "—— And that's as easy
> As to set dogs on sheep." [2]

The butcher is represented sharpening his knife :—

> " No doubt the monstrous knife was dull and blunt
> Till it was whetted on thy stone-hard heart,
> To revel in the entrails of my lambs." [3]

---

[1] 'King Henry VI., Part II.,' act iii. 1.
[2] ' Coriolanus,' act ii. 1.        [3] ' King Richard III.,' act iv. 4.

The sheep is brought to slaughter :—

> " So first the harmless sheep doth yield his fleece,
> And next his throat unto the butcher's knife." [1]

The ox and the calf share the same fate :—" Then is sin struck down like an ox, and iniquity's throat cut like a calf." [2]  We hear the squeak of the pig in the like extremity :—

> " Weke, weke,—so cries a pig prepar'd to the spit." [3]

The poet shows us the interior of the slaughter-house :—

> " Lord Bassaim lies embrued here,
> All on a heap, like to a slaughtered lamb." [4]

Even its lesser operations are touched upon :—" And this way I take upon me to wash your liver as clean as a sound sheep's heart." [5]  Falstaff knows how the little Aceldama is cleaned out :—" Have I lived to be carried in a basket, like a barrow of butcher's offal." [6]  And we catch a glimpse of the shop itself, when the poet speaks of " butchers killing flies." [7]

Shakespeare's duties were not restricted to the slaughter-house and shop.  It was the custom of that day, as indeed of our own, to employ apprentices in the drudgery of the household ; and a citizen of 1657 relates that during his servitude he bore the water-tankard, cleaned shoes, and scraped trenchers. [8]  Shakespeare imposes similar tasks on Caliban, who, on rebelling, declares that he will no more " fetch in firing at requiring," nor engage in " scrape tren-

---

[1] ' King Henry VI.,' act v. 6.
[2] ' King Henry VI., Part II.,' act iv. 2.
[3] ' Titus Andronicus,' act iv. 2.
[4] Ibid., act ii. 4.
[5] ' As You Like It,' act iii. 2.
[6] ' Merry Wives of Windsor,' act iii. 1.
[7] ' Coriolanus,' act iv. 6.
[8] ' Life of a Satirical Puppy, called Nym.'

chering nor wash dish." [1] The poet has recurred here
to the days of his own apprenticeship. He may have
smiled over the reminiscence, without reflecting that it told
tales. But we think none the worse of King Alfred for
baking cakes.

The 'prentice lads of Stratford did not enjoy the dignity
or possess the liberty of the London apprentices. The
metropolis was just of the size to allow of such a body
making itself formidable—being of sufficient magnitude to
give numerical strength, and not too large for organization.
Rash were the man who ventured to attack the humblest of
the fraternity. At the cry of "clubs," apprentices of all
trades and ages, from the boy of fourteen to the athlete of
twenty, left task or bed to rush to the rescue.[2] Stowe says
that the apprentices went before their masters and mistresses
at night with a lantern, and "a great long club about their
necks." Though the Stratford authorities ordained that
apprentices should not carry weapons—"that is to say,
sword, dagger, or any weapon," [3] the form of the prohibition,
by its mention of sword and dagger, seems to imply that
clubs were not forbidden, nor could there be any danger of
the apprentices of a rural town being so animated by one
spirit as to muster their clubs in a fray. Shakespeare
makes the Porter's Man in Palace Yard "hit that woman
who cried out clubs," [4] but this cry would raise no alarm in
Stratford, where it did not, as in London, correspond with
the shout of "To your tents, O Israel!"

The authorities of Stratford may have permitted young
Will Shakespeare to go before his master at night with a
lantern, and certainly were not so ungallant as to forbid this

---

[1] 'Tempest,' act ii. 2.
[2] Stowe's 'Annals,' p. 1040.
[3] Orders of the Town Council, 1st October, 1 Mary.
[4] 'King Henry VIII.,' act v. 3.

attention to his mistress; but he was prohibited from taking a nocturnal stroll for his own pleasure. The orders of the town council were precise on this point, enjoining that no apprentice should leave his "master's house by the night after the hour of nine **by the clock**," and every breach of the regulation was punishable by a fine of twenty shillings, and a penance of three days in the stocks. **It is to be** feared **that** Will **Shakespeare was** often **guilty, but let us hope that he escaped the punishment.**

He was joined in his frolics by at least one companion. The name of this youth has not been recorded, and we only hear of his existence from Aubrey, who describes him as Shakespeare's "acquaintance and coetanian"—or one of the same age. He was also a butcher's son, and resembled the poet in other points, having a "natural wit," which we are told by Aubrey was not inferior to Shakespeare's, and, **though** this is incredible, we may believe that the **two boys** might then strike their companions, from whom Aubrey derived his information, **as** being equally gifted. One lived to exceed the promise of his **youth, the other** "died young."

Shakespeare **has left no reminiscence of the** "**coetanean,**" **unless he has remembered his wit in Dickon, the butcher. Dickon is a wag of the true shambles stamp, in** his playful moods overflowing **with** banter, but **ferocious at** the scent of blood. He makes a butt of Jack Cade on the march, but fights for him like a tiger at London Bridge, when he attempts to set the Thames on fire. The affray freshens his memory of the slaughter-house, and he even tells us what might be young Shakespeare's ordinary costume, declaring that honest men not only "go in their hose and doublets," but "**work in** their shirts, **too, as myself, for example,** that am a butcher."[1]

**But the** "coetanean" had nothing in common with Dick

---

[1] 'King Henry VI., Part II.,' act iv. 7.

of Ashford, but his wit, and, in a harmless degree, his love
of mischief—or he would not have been the companion of
gentle Will.    It is pleasant to think that the two friends
were kindred spirits.  They sang ballads together, and composed them, too—for Shakespeare could not be more backward than Dryden, who courted the Muses as a Westminster
scholar.    High festivals and holidays found them in the
same group of merry-makers, equally aiding the fun.  Whatever the sport, they were its life and pulse, full of jests, full
of pranks, but never betraying ill-nature.  May-day saw
them circling round the maypole, or they figured in the
morris, which Shakespeare thought so appropriate—"a
morris for May-day."[1]    The party was composed of Robin
Hood, Little John, and Friar Tuck, the fool, the piper, the
hobby-horse, the dragon, and Maid Marian, the Queen of
May.  The performers were all apprentices, and perhaps
Will Shakespeare's good looks procured him the part of
Maid Marian, which was always assigned to the handsomest
boy.  In his ungallant speech to Dame Quickly, Falstaff
recalls the awkward imitations of maidenly airs, which made
the principal fun in the morris-dance—"for womanhood,
Maid Marian may be the deputy's wife of the ward to you."[2]
The practice of dressing a boy in woman's attire rendered
the dance more odious to the Puritans, and it is denounced
as a breach of a "straight commandment" by the straight-
laced Fetherstone, who refers the incredulous to Deutero-
nomy xx. 5.  He also rebukes the "May Marrions" for
decking themselves with ribands, and is particularly shocked
at their wearing veils.[3]

We tremble for young Shakespeare and the "coetanean"
when we learn from another Puritan, the caustic Stubbs,

<hr>

[1] 'All's Well that Ends Well,' act ii. 2.
[2] 'King Henry IV., Part I.,' act iii. 3.
[3] 'Dialogue against Light, Lewd, and Lascivious Dancing.'

how the apprentices came by this finery, for, he says, it was "borrowed of their pretty Mopsies for bussing them in the dark."[1]   But Mopsa is represented by Shakespeare as receiving, instead of lending ribands.   "If I were not in love with Mopsa," says the Clown to Autolycus, "thou shouldst take no money of me; but being enthralled as I am, it will also be the bondage of certain ribands and gloves."[2]

The morris was not restricted to the early days of May. It was danced at most of the high festivals, and found particular favour at Whitsuntide.   This is brought out by Shakespeare in the Dauphin's speech :—

> "  —— Let us do it with no show of fear :
> No, with no more than if we heard that England
> Were busied with a Whitsun morris-dance."[3]

The Whitsun morris was danced at Stratford as late as 1717, when the chamberlain's accounts record a payment of five shillings to the morris-dancers, by order of the mayor.

It was not only customary for the dancers to be feed by the authorities, they were feasted by the townsfolk, and poor Stubbs goes mad as he enumerates the delicacies provided for their consumption, foremost amongst which stands good ale.[4]   He consoles himself, however, by reminding the various donors that by these gifts " they offer sacrifice to the devil and Sathanas "—thus dividing the Evil One into two persons, a power of sight which may account for his warranty of the " good ale."   Nor did the ale exercise a sobering influence on the morris-dancers, who became rather excited before

---

[1] ' Anatomy of Abuses.'

[2] ' Winter's Tale,' act iv. 3.

[3] ' King Henry V.,' act ii. 4.

[4] He declares that some contributed "good ale ; some, new cheese ; some, old cheese ; some, cracknels ; some, cakes ; some, flannes ; some, tarts ; some, cream ; some, meat ; some, one thing ; some, another."—*Anatomy of Abuses.*

they broke up, a circumstance not forgotten by Shakespeare—

> " I have seen him
> Caper upright, like a wild Morisco." [1]

What stirred the 'prentice world more than **morris and maypole** was the May pageant, Arthur's show, which inaugurated the shooting at the butts. This was quite distinct from the muster of the Duke of Shoreditch, which was held later in the year, and confined to London. Justice Shallow, indeed, declares that he figured as " Dagonet in Arthur's Show" [2] at Mile End, intimating that the same pageant was got up in the capital, but Falstaff warns us that all he says is not Gospel. There can be no doubt that the worthy **Justice** used the long bow in conversation, whatever might be his practice at the butts, though Sir Thomas Lucy was **not the man** to appear, like Shallow, as one of the butts himself,—for Dagonet was Arthur's fool.

Our ancestors rivalled the **Chinese** in **reverence** for the **bow-and-arrow**, which kept their place long after the introduction **of** fire-arms ; and John Shakespeare was assessed for the equipment of an archer in 1578, [3] the same year that his son William was bound apprentice. Some years later the Stratford chamberlain's accounts record a payment to Roger Welsh for carrying three loads of turf to make the **butts.** We have seen that Shakespeare could fly his shaft as a schoolboy, and neither he nor the " coetanean " would be absent, when the youth of Stratford were mustered at the **butts. The contest,** indeed, excited an **interest** among all classes, such as we see rising again in our own day, in every part of England ; and skill was stimulated by similar means. The prize was often a gun—a genuine brown Bess, repre-

---

[1] ' King Henry VI., Part II.,' act iii. 1.
[2] ' King Henry IV., Part II.,' act iii. 2.
[3] See p. 76, *ante.*

senting the Enfield or Westfield of modern times, though a contemporary tract records that the firing at a target on St. James's wall was for a gun, "made of gold," which was rightly "to be given to him that best deserved it." The competition created great excitement, and, according to Justice Shallow, betting ran high. "He shot a good shot: John **of Gaunt** loved **him, and** betted much money on his head."[1]

**Nothing was so attractive to** Shakespeare in his youth as **field** sports, the national recreation of Englishmen. This we know from tradition, but such testimony is not needed; for we have a living witness in his Muse. Only a sportsman could have written the beautiful description of coursing in " Venus and Adonis "—so animated, so life-like, so exact in the minutest details. If Shakespeare did not actually follow the hare in the chase, he followed him with his eye, knew all "poor Wat's" twists and turns—perhaps **crouched** down amongst his master's sheep in the field as he saw where they would lead—

> " **Sometimes he runs** among a flock of sheep,
> **To make the cunning** hounds mistake their smell."[2]

**He knew how to uncouple also**

> " —— **At the fox, which lives by subtilty,**
> **Or at the roe, which no encounter dare.**"[3]

And if ever a chance presented itself, he made a dash after the hounds; for he could ride a nag with any butcher's boy in Warwickshire. The doughtiest squire might have envied his seat, for we associate a natural grace with his lithe form. Leigh Hunt[4] applauds the way in which Byron **sat a** horse, when he praises him for nothing **else ; and the posture was** not less becoming to Shakespeare—

---

[1] 'King Henry IV., Part II.,' act iii. 2.
[2] 'Venus and Adonis.'
[3] **Ibid.**      [4] 'Lord Byron and some of his Contemporaries.'

> " Well could he ride, and often men would say
> That horse his mettle from his rider takes." [1]

His knowledge of horseflesh would make a fortune at
Tattersal's; and he gives a summary of the points of a
horse worthy of Rarey.

> " Round-hoof'd, short-jointed, fetlocks shag and long,
> Broad breast, full eye, small head, and nostril wide,
> High crest, short ears, straight legs and passing strong,
> Thin mane, thick tail, broad buttock, tender hide."

All this shows the intense nationality of Shakespeare—
the strong leaven of English feeling, habits, and tastes by
which he was animated, and which make him the impersonation of our national character. We shall see him manifest
the same spirit in every relation and at every stage of life.
But his fondness for animals, and his scrutiny of their pecu-
liarities, were quickened by his love of nature. He did not
observe them merely as a sportsman, but as a student.
They were to him as the flowers, as the trees, as the everlasting hills—words in the great volume ever open before
him, the Book of Life. They were lessons in a boundless,
unfathomable philosophy, such as schools could not teach.
Since he was master of small Latin and less Greek, men
ask where he acquired his wondrous knowledge, that knowledge which comprehends everything—which is more than
all the learning of the Egyptians. We need not inquire
when he so explicitly tells us—when he says that he found—

> " —— Tongues in trees, books in the running brooks,
> Sermons in stones, and good in everything." [2]

That was the burden of the sermons—of all that he observed and learnt : good in everything ! Not that he was
an optimist, beset with one idea, but that he looked upon

---

[1] 'A Lover's Complaint.'
[2] ' As You Like It,' act ii. 1.

everything in its relation to the whole. His far-seeing wisdom ranged beyond the immediate effect, and saw the comprehensive scheme to which it was tributary, and which had no flaw.

The wise King of Navarre looked at nature through his own crude notions, drawn from the inventions of Ptolemy, and **believed that** he could frame a better system, but **Shakespeare, with only the same light to guide him, searched deeper and further,** and recognized the handiwork **of Omniscience.** Thus it softened his heart, expanded his mind, elevated his soul. There was not an object—down, as he says, to the very stones, from which he did not gather instruction. His faculties were always in exercise. Nature was to him like a scroll in cipher, and he studied it till he found the key. Then he unlocked her deepest, darkest secrets. There **was** neither speech nor language, but her voice was **heard** in his breast. Linnæus could not speak **so** glibly **of our** English herbs and flowers, though the poet's Latin happily did not serve to give them unintelligible names. We like them better as—

> " Hot lavender, mint, savory, marjoram." [1]

And so through the list.

Shakespeare, **if** little in Latin, was less, we are told, in Greek, but he had the genius of the old Greek sages, grappling with the unknown like Socrates, and solving the problems of the material world like Pythagoras and Plato. He observed the falling apple before Newton.

> " —— **The strong base** and building of my love
> **Is as the very centre of the earth,**
> *Drawing all things to it."*

To him the minutest **effect shadowed a** mighty end, which **was** being worked **out by the ministry of an** over-ruling

---

[1] ' Winter's Tale,' act iv. 3.

Providence. The dust that crumbled into the stream, as he strayed along its banks, plumbed for him the depths of creation, disclosing the slow but certain process by which it shall be folded up as a vesture and be changed. Thus he was the prophet of geology before it found an expounder in Werner.

> " O, God ! that one might read the book of fate,
> And see the revolution of the times :
> Make mountains level, and the continent—
> Weary of solid firmness—melt itself
> Into the sea ; and, other times, to see
> The beachy girdle of the ocean
> Too wide for Neptune's **hips.**" [1]

This is the old Greek leaven ; the same intuition, the same grasp of universal knowledge. The one touch of nature makes Shakespeare and Aristotle kin ; and, as the Stagyrite was the first to **dissect the human body,** Shakespeare unfolded the mechanism of the soul, probed the **breast of** life, and showed its range of suffering, from the pang of the crushed insect, great as when a giant dies, to the agonies of Ophelia's heart and the paroxysms of Hamlet's brain.

Such were the lessons and the instinctive acquirements of Shakespeare's youth. It were idle to conjecture what he read or where he procured books. We only know that he did not, like Benedick, draw his wit from the ' Hundred Merry Tales.' [2] It **came rather from** " Nature's infinite book of secresy," [3] not only its pictured page, the great and beautiful and sublime, but, what might be thought small and mean, its most familiar lines. He did "reverence" to the " sun's uprising," [4] but he drew light also **from "the** fiery glowworm's eyes." [5] These taught humility as well as

[1] King Henry IV., Part II.,' act iii. 1.
[2] ' Much Ado about Nothing,' act ii. 1.
[3] ' Antony and Cleopatra,' act ii. 1.
[4] ' Titus and Andronicus,' act iii. 1.
[5] ' Midsummer Night's Dream,' act iii. 1.

wisdom; and he found that the widest human study and observation will, after all, leave worlds unnoted. "There are more things in heaven and earth, Horatio, than are dreamt of in your philosophy."[1]

More indeed! He might see an example in himself, growing up in the kennel, with a consciousness of superior powers, and with his sharp trial of humiliation and sorrow, not dreamt of in any one's philosophy. It was enough to teach him humility, to have a perception of all things, and find that he was nothing. "All is darkness," said Galileo in his dungeon, "yet it still goes round." The world did not stop on its course because its oracle was in chains. There was marriage and giving of marriage in Stratford, though Shakespeare was in eclipse.

John Shakespeare continued to be dogged by misfortune, and it drew him down deeper and deeper, for he was now visited with domestic affliction. In 1579 he lost his daughter Ann just as she attained her eighth year, an age which endeared her to her brother as much as her parents. We may still acknowledge a solemnity in the bereavement which first brought our poet and the King of Terrors face to face. This was a scene to awaken in him, even at the age of sixteen, some flashes of that perception with which he seems almost to light up death, as if he showed us the immortality of the soul through the grave-clothes, transfigured by its own thoughts. Imagination sees him join the sad group at the bedside of his little sister. The younger ones around, his pretty favourite Joan, the bent form of his father, and his mother with her pale face and streaming eyes—all receive a loving glance. Perhaps he turns an inquiring look on Falstaff's " wise woman,"[2] who officiated at his sister's birth, and now sadly watches her last moments,

---

[1] 'Hamlet,' act i. 5.          [2] 'King Henry IV.'

as a " wise woman" attended those of Queen Mary.[1]   She can give no hope, and he waits by the bed while the child passes softly away—

> " If thou and nature can so gently part,
> The stroke of Death is as a lover's pinch,
> Which hurts and is desired."[2]

Nor is he absent at the almost sadder moment when the lid of the narrow house is to close like a door between the dead and living, and all gather for a last look—

> " Death sits on her like an untimely frost
> Upon the sweetest flow'r of all the field."[3]

It is contended that John Shakespeare could not be in poverty at this time, because he incurred the expense of hiring a pall and having the bell toll at the funeral.  The parochial register shows, indeed, that on the 4th of April, the day of the interment, he paid eightpence for this last tribute to his child.  But there is far from being reason to suppose that he was now in funds, for on the 11th of the previous month he was returned as a defaulter for three and fourpence in an assessment for the local contribution of arms for national defence.   At the same time, we must remember that he was still an alderman, and therefore likely to make efforts to keep up an appearance.   His daughter could not be smuggled to the grave like a pauper, with Ophelia's maimed rites.  She must be borne thither in the sight of his neighbours, with all observance.  Some sacrifice would be made to accomplish such an object, and, though shaken in credit and much reduced in means, John Shakespeare yet commanded resources.  These, indeed, were now to undergo a severe strain, and the consequent arrangements opened new experiences to SHAKESPEARE THE APPRENTICE.

[1] Strickland's ' Queens of England.'
[2] ' Antony and Cleopatra,' act v. 2.
[3] ' Romeo and Juliet,' act iv. 5.

## VIII.

### STUDYING THE LAW.

It would be strange if Shakespeare, who observed everything, had taken no note of the uses of the law, the balance which regulates all the relations of life. And, in fact, no expectation that might be formed on this point could exceed the reality. Even jurists are astonished at the extent of his legal knowledge, and it has been thought to show that some period of his life was passed in a lawyer's office. This conjecture was originated by Malone; Mr. Collier came to the same conclusion; and it was more recently affirmed by an authority as high in law as in literature, no less a person than the late Lord Chancellor of England.[1]

From such a judgment there would seem to be no appeal. When the oracle recognized the wisdom of Socrates, it was acknowledged by all Greece. None will dispute Shakespeare's law, when it is endorsed by a Lord Chancellor! We accept it as from a Daniel come to judgment. What the woolsack pronounces unimpeachable, can be no "crowner's quest law,"[2] no Brummagem notions: it must be "the laws and statutes."[3] But, while joining issue on this point, we demur to the rule that this proficiency was acquired in a lawyer's office; and claim to show cause why it should not be made absolute.

Though there may seem to be no association between

---

[1] Lord Campbell's 'Letter to J. P. Collier, Esq.'
[2] 'Hamlet,' act v.  [3] 'Comedy of Errors,' act v. 1.

law and poetry—between hard matter-of-fact and the ideal, the atmosphere of the lawyer's office has not proved ungenial to the Muses. It was a spoilt lawyer's sonnets to his mistress that awoke Europe from the sleep of the dark ages, as Shakespeare describes the lark singing at heaven's gate at the first dawn; and Chaucer, the father of English poetry, received the same initiation in legal mysteries as Petrarch. The lawyer's office gave us also the two greatest poets of modern times—Goethe and Walter Scott. Poor Chatterton was a lawyer's clerk, and drew from the jargon of legal documents the fine old Saxon words, which enabled him to forge his antique ballads. There was nothing, then, in such a situation to repress Shakespeare's poetic instincts. His "natural wit" could not find a better soil; for a lawyer and wit are correlative terms, and there is no limit to the vivacity of lawyers' clerks. They are but the stone-breakers of the law, indeed; but, in paving the road for its decrees, they strike many a bright spark from the flints.

All this, however, does not bring home a legal novitiate to Shakespeare. The conjecture may satisfy believers, but it is not, like the compact of Fortinbras, "well ratified by law and heraldry."[1] Neither record nor tradition afford it the smallest warrant. "Mr. Beeston," who was acquainted with Shakespeare's early life, gave no hint of such a fact to Aubrey; the parish clerk never mentioned it to Dowdall; Betterton did not report it to Rowe. Nearly a hundred years intervened before it was put forward hesitatingly as a surmise by Malone. He was led to the impression by what he conceived to be the internal evidence in Shakespeare's works, and the only colour of testimony adduced from a contemporary source is an allusion by Nash, which has been quoted threadbare. It occurs in an epistle in Greene's 'Xenophon,' published in 1589, and is too obscure

_______________
[1] 'Hamlet,' act i. 1.

for the application to be understood in the present day.
The passage refers to a set of scapegraces—"a sort of shifting companions," who seem to have been in literature what
in the middle ages the free companions were in war, as they
are said to "run through every art and thrive by none."
They **even had** the presumption to make **a** raid on the
drama, which Nash and his friend Greene regarded as their
**private domain; and** we are **told that** they busied themselves "with **the endeavours of art,**" instead of pursuing
their own calling. This is sarcastically described as "the
trade of noverint," which, being a word usually found at
the beginning of old deeds, is supposed to mean a lawyer's
clerk. It is not surprising that such intrusion made Nash
and Co. gnash their teeth, particularly when we hear that
the "shifting companions could scarcely latinize **their**
neck-verse if they had need," which fortunately **they had**
not, as the audiences of the day cherished **a vulgar** preference for English. So far there is nothing to suggest
a reference to Shakespeare, unless we imagine a thrust
at his small Latin. But the application of the passage
**may be thought** to lie **in the close, as the sting in the**
**wasp's tail.** "Yet English Seneca, read by candlelight,
**yields many good sentences, as 'Blood is** a beggar,' and
so forth; and if you entreat him fair in a frosty morning, he will afford you whole *Hamlets*, I should say handfuls of tragical speeches." But this burst of sound and
fury signifies nothing in connection with Shakespeare. His
plays, indeed, are often read by candlelight, and sometimes even by firelight, if this be what is meant by
"the fair entreaty **of a** frosty morning"—for Walter
Scott relates that firelight helped him, when a **boy, to his**
first look at their pages.[1] But, with all their **abundance**
of "good sentences," they nowhere tell **us that** "Blood

[1] Sir Walter Scott's 'Autobiographical Fragment.'

is a beggar." Old Kent says, "I am a gentleman of blood"[1]—of "blood and breeding;" and such he approves himself. Nor do their tragical speeches come either in handfuls or mouthfuls, but "trippingly on the tongue."[2] The comparison with 'Hamlet,' then, must be regarded merely as a passing sneer at Shakespeare, not implying that he was a noverint, but that the noverints were Shakespeares.

The poet's knowledge of the law is, in truth, easily explained—more easily than most of his acquirements. Though not brought up in a lawyer's office, he was not without legal preceptors, and we can tell their very names. They were the firm of Snare and Fang, the familiars of Sir John Falstaff; and still represented in the profession by John Doe and Richard Roe. Their system of instruction was painful, but impressive, and what was learnt in the cold shade of the world's neglect, in privation, anxiety, and sorrow, stamped itself on Shakespeare's memory. He was in constant apprehension of seeing his father dragged to prison. The writ was out, exercising the subtlety of Snare and Fang; and, in fact, their scent was so keen that John Shakespeare could only avoid a gaol by shutting himself up at home. He was even afraid to venture once a month to appear in his place at church on Sunday, which was the test of orthodoxy prescribed by law ; and, in the returns made by the commissioners, he was more than once reported as absenting himself, pleading in excuse that he "came not to church for fear of process for debt."[3] How it can be contended, in the face of such evidence,

---

[1] 'King Lear,' act iii. 1.

[2] 'Hamlet,' act iii. 2.

[3] A Report containing the name of John Shakespeare was found by Mr. Collier in the State Paper Office. It is dated 1592, but it gives " the names of all such recusants as have been *heretofore* presented," so that it proves that the sword of the sheriff had been hanging over him for a long time.

that he had not fallen into poverty, we are unable to conjecture.

The unfortunate alderman made a stout struggle to maintain his credit. For some years he propped himself up by shifts, sacrificing portions of his property, or placing them in jeopardy, to obtain momentary aid, and these supplies, by meeting the most pressing demands, kept him afloat when he was really insolvent. He seems to have hoped that he might eventually right himself, by adroitly playing stake against stake, redeeming one security with another just before it became forfeit. Such a situation brings into view every possible source of relief, however remote, as every chance of succour is estimated by a beleagured garrison ; and John Shakespeare, besieged by Snare and Fang, could not forget that he would be put in possession of additional property by the death of his wife's stepmother, who was now very old, and in declining health. Mary Shakespeare was then to succeed to a share in the land at Snitterfield, held for life by Agnes Arden, and her husband's arrangements were evidently influenced by this expectation, which might be realized at any moment, but which continually broke down.

To derive advantage from this property in the bush without disposing of his interest in it, John Shakespeare had risked what was actually in his possession ; and in 1578 pledged his wife's farm at Ashbies to Edmund Lambert, his brother-in-law, for forty pounds, covenanting that it was to be forfeited at Michaelmas, 1580, if not previously redeemed. In the interim, his circumstances, instead of improving, became worse. We have seen him presented as a defaulter in 1579, apparently for the first time ; and his urgent need of money increased as the year advanced ; for on the 15th of October, he and his wife joined in an indenture, by which they sold to Robert Webb, apparently one of the brothers of the widow Arden, their share in two tenements and the appurtenances at Snitterfield, being perhaps the very premises once partly occupied by Richard Shakespeare. The sum thus raised was only four pounds, and could have done little to relieve their necessities; for the alderman was soon driven again to Edmund Lambert, who, perceiving that he was likely to retain Ashbies on the easy terms of the mortgage, and perhaps influenced by his wife, Mary Shakespeare's sister, lent him further assistance. This is established by a memorandum attached to the will of Roger Sadler, a baker of Stratford, which mentions, under date of 1580, that Edmund Lambert had joined Mr. Cornish as surety for the payment of five pounds—" the debt of Mr. John Shaksper."

Five pounds, measured by the money standard of the time, was a heavy bill for bread, even for an embarrassed alderman; and the credit of John Shakespeare must indeed have run low, if he had sunk so deep in his baker's books. But it is plain, from the statement of his debts, that Roger Sadler sometimes supplied his customers with money as well as bread, evidently considering that the one was as much the staff of life as the other; and this places the item in a clearer light. The Sadlers and the Shakespeares were hereditary friends. We shall trace the intimacy through three generations; and the transaction that affords our first glimpse of it deserves more than the bare mention yet accorded. It brings before us, in fact, a whole group of the family, dropping a whisper of its history. We find ground to believe that Roger Sadler had opened his purse to John Shakespeare at a time when he was in distress; and we discover the poor alderman, after his friend's death, involving himself further with his sharp brother-in-law that he may repay the money. The list of Roger Sadler's debtors records a claim also of six pounds eight and fourpence against Richard Hathaway, alias Gardiner, of Shottery, thus extending the connection to the poet's future father-in-law, and showing that he was largely trusted by Roger Sadler at the same time as his father. Nothing could more clearly attest the friendly relations of the three families at this period, and we learn from the precepts of the Stratford Bailiff's Court, that the same intimacy subsisted between John Shakespeare and Richard Hathaway fourteen years before, for in 1566 John Shakespeare forgot the warning of Solomon, and became surety for his friend. The payment of the alderman's debt to Sadler brings forward also the covetous Lambert, who, under pretence of assisting his brother-in-law, is, as we shall presently see, really taking advantage of his necessities, and drawing him into his own toils. In short, the whole transaction indicates that thereby hangs a tale.

Edmund Lambert might blind his brother-in-law, but he stamped a clear impression of his character on his nephew. Shakespeare learnt to know him as one who " might be in's time a great buyer of land, with his statutes, his recognizances, his fines, his double vouchers, his recoveries."[1] We must believe that the young poet watched these proceedings with deep attention. His father's credit, and good name, and some twenty-four broad acres, his own inheritance, were in danger. Well might he be versed in the law, for it came visibly into his home, into his own breast, with every surrounding of dramatic interest,—presenting the distressed father; the dejected mother; the avaricious, plotting uncle; himself the rightful heir, and in its action, the incidents which kept the fortunes of his family in suspense. This it was that made him learned in the wisdom of the lawyers. He knew every arrow in the attorney's quiver—" his quiddits

[1] 'Hamlet,' act v. 1.

new, his quillets, his cases, his tenures, and his tricks :"[1]
and, perhaps, there were times when he could almost have
accepted the proposition of Dick the butcher,—"The first
thing we do, let's kill all the lawyers."[2]

John Shakespeare was now in the situation of Antonio,
when his last argosy was wrecked in the Narrows ; and his
involved affairs led to many councils between himself and
his wife, which could not be concealed from their eldest son,
who, in his seventeenth year, must have given tokens of
his great capacity. It was plain that there was but one
thing to be done : they must raise the forty pounds required
to free Ashbies by Michaelmas, or Lambert would have his
bond. John Shakespeare must " make money," and unhappily this could only be done effectually on Roderigo's
plan :—

" I'll go sell all my land."[3]

The share in the cottages at Snitterfield was already disposed of ; Ashbies was mortgaged ; and now, to redeem
Ashbies, he parted with the reversionary interest which was
to devolve to his wife on the death of her stepmother. We
learn from the registry of a fine in the Chapter House that
the reversion was conveyed, in the Easter term of 1580, to
Robert Webb, the widow's kinsman, who had previously
bought the cottages ; and the purchase money is stated to
be forty pounds, the exact sum obtained on the Lambert
mortgage. There can, therefore, be no doubt that it was
specially raised for this purpose.

On or before Michaelmas day, John Shakespeare went
to Lambert's house, at Burton on the Heath, and there
tendered him the forty pounds. He may have gone on
the errand without a misgiving, in the confidence of a trust-

---

[1] ' Hamlet,' act v. 1.
[2] ' King Henry VI., Part II.,' act iv. 2.
[3] ' Othello,' act i. 3

ing kinsman, **and** even with a grateful recollection of the several little aids he had since received in **moments of** pressure. But these loans, which he had accepted as tokens of **kindness,** Lambert professed to regard as **additions** to the mortgage. He demanded the immediate payment of the whole debt, as the condition of surrendering the **property.** That, **he maintained, was** the **bond :** his **ducats, or the pound** of flesh **nearest** Antonio's heart—the **dower** of his wife, and the heritage of his children. Perhaps Shakespeare was present at this interview ; **and,** if so, it gave him as full a revelation of the law as he could desire. He learnt nine of its points in one word—possession ! On the table was the open deed, which signed away the last remnant of **his** heritage ; **and** there was the well-known **mark of his father** traced **on the parchment.** We may imagine **the reflection** it called up in his mind :—" **Is not this** a lamentable thing, that of the skin of an innocent lamb should be made parchment; and that parchment, being scribbled o'er, should undo a man ?"[1]

[1] ' King Henry VI., Part II.,' act iv. 2.

## IX.

### BAD COMPANY.

THERE is a remarkable similarity in the situation of Shakespeare at this period of his life and that of Burns at the same age. In his youth, Burns, like Shakespeare, saw his father constantly involved in difficulties, overtaken by one misfortune after another, yet still struggling—manfully working on to the last. In this atmosphere of gloom, a helpless spectator of the reverses of his family and the blight of his own prospects, he had ever before him his mother's troubled face, and often blended his tears with hers. So the two poets of nature rose under a similar discipline, in the daily experience of disappointment, and in the midst of privation and sorrow. God unlocked the pent-up sympathies in their breasts with the selfsame key.

It is related of Burns that the dark influences around him never destroyed his inherent cheerfulness. If the distress of others cast him down one moment, in the next his trouble was forgotten, and all around were inspirited by his ringing laugh and voice. So it was with Shakespeare. His disposition typified his natal month ; and if the sorrow of his home sometimes brimmed his eyes, the tears soon gave way to smiles, to his heart's innate sunshine. As he says of Troilus, " he was, an't were, a man born in April."[1] Tradition reports that his " natural wit " was always in motion, as if it flowed through his mind like the blood

---

[1] ' Troilus and Cressida,' act i. 2.

through his veins—slipped from him like his breath." So near akin were these two rare spirits, born wide apart and of different races, but inspired, though in an unequal degree, by the **one** divine Muse.

Shakespeare went down with his fortunes, as **men sometimes sink** in a wrecked ship, raising **no** outcry **and making no effort to keep afloat.** He **might have met a sudden fall in a different temper.** Then **pride and self-respect** would have **buoyed him above his position in** associations and **feelings; and** memory **would** have clung to the past, wherever he had **been** swept by calamity. But reverses came upon him by stealth, like a sleep—like a dream; and he passed through the strange transformations that occur in dreams without surprise or repugnance. We have just compared him with those who remain passive when **their** ship is foundering : he **was** rather like the wild **men who, in** this extremity, drink deep from the **spirit casks, mock the** raging **of** the **storm,** and meet the engulphing **waves with** defiance. He **became desperate and** reckless.

**Could we forget his character, we might look upon his submission to circumstances as natural at so thoughtless** an **age.** Poverty and he had become bedfellows; **they dwelt and messed together; and inured to the** companionship, finding himself bound and knit to it, he might accept it as destiny. We know that they are happiest in humble life who content themselves with their position ; for to rise from it is given to few. The attempt costs the one precious moment which life affords for enjoyment, and may fail. Let us remember that to each of us the sphere in which we are born, **or to which** we have **been reduced, opens** its own pleasures **and diversions, and that these are forfeited by an** ambitious struggle, often without being **recompensed by** those of a higher **grade.**

John Shakespeare may have relied for success on merit,

on exertion, on rising up early and lying down late, on will, energy, and perseverance, but his experience verified the admonition, **that** "the **race is not to** the swift, **nor** the battle to the strong." Hair prematurely grey, **a shrunken** cheek, a furrowed brow, eyes that would not sleep, and perhaps broken health, brought conviction to his mind, and these marks of his struggle may have taught his son that success is the prize, not of effort, but of accident, opportunity, or favour. Life is too short for such a contest ; and like Michael Scott's fiend, to whom one night sufficed to dam the Tweed, and another to cleave a mountain, Shakespeare **may have learnt that no industry will avail to weave ropes of sand.**

**The stature of his youth is not to be measured by the same rule of thumb that usually applies to** that period **of life ; and such considerations, if they did not wholly** govern him, **rose too obviously from his situation not to** influence his conduct. Without yet knowing what spirit he was of, he could not be unconscious of his mental superiority ; and when he "off-capped" to some magnate of the little Stratford world, in which he ranked as a serf, must have chafed under his servitude. Society seemed a community of animals to Æsop, galled by his chain ; and it now took some such form to Shakespeare.

**The " ambushed days of youth,"** while surrounding him **with discouragements, beset him with unusual temptations. If looked down upon by** the class in which he was born, **he was courted and caressed by that** into which he had fallen. His good temper and good nature, his humour and fun, were just the qualities to produce this effect, captivating minds that could neither discern nor appreciate his opening genius. They made him both a favourite with his elders, and an oracle to lads of his own age—the coetaneans ! But the vivacity and wit that gave such a charm to his fellowship, brought around him, too, all the loose, dissolute spirits of the town, and, carried to scenes of riot and dissipation, they fell among worse company than themselves. Unfortunately, he came to look upon these scamps as his natural companions, with whom he must cast in his lot—whose habits must be his habits, and whose tastes his tastes; so that he was ready to shout with the loudest, " Let us eat **and drink to-day, for to-morrow we die."**

**Some of the revels he** attended grew out of his calling, and were innocent in themselves, if not sullied by excess. Both his father's trade of woolstapler, and his own occupation as a butcher's apprentice, introduced him at the annual feasts of the sheep-shearers, and he may even have been employed as a shearer himself. Everyone will admit that his delineation of these rustic festivals is drawn from life, from personal observation and experience; for the scene attests its **own reality.** So completely, indeed, are we carried away **by its sweet** touches of nature, its living colouring, and its mingled pathos, vivacity, and humour, that the mind has no room for any other thought. Its very trips mark the ground which furnished the **picture. This is so well** understood, that we are not surprised to hear Pagans of ancient days talking of " Whitsun pastorals "—**to find that they name their** daughters Mopsa **and** Dorcas, or even that they are on convivial terms with a " Puritan "—for Mopsa and Dorcas were the names commonly borne by Warwickshire lasses in the time of Shakespeare's youth, and the shearers were then just beginning to be leavened with puritanism, which looked indulgently on the sheep-shearings, on account of their honourable mention in **the Old** Testament. Autolycus is classic only in name: his **roguery** is thoroughly English, and all his allusions have a national character. **Thus the** scene preserves **to us the rural** life of old England, in its merriest time; and the range of pastoral poetry can present no group to match the simple, hospitable old shepherd, the good-hearted clown his son, the snappish rivals, Mopsa and Dorcas, and " the mistress o' the feast," sweet Perdita.

**Here** Shakespeare's thoughts were diverted from family misfortunes, and the merry-making brought out his glee and the buoyant spirit of his years. He entered into it as Burns into the mysteries of Halloween. The raw material of the pies and confections is so accurately known to him, that we suspect he must have seen Mopsa or Dorcas before the feast, and received a private revelation,—" Three **pounds of sugar, five** pounds of currants, rice! I must **have saffron to colour the warden pies."** This hint **might have come from Menschikoff, when he was** selling pies in the streets **of St. Petersburg, and** proves that **Shakespeare was already behind the scenes.** " Mace, dates—none : that **is, not of any note ;** nutmegs, seven ; **a race** or two of ginger, but **that I may beg ; five** pound **of** prunes, and as many of raisins of the sun." [1] Stubbs, who was so enraged at the provision for the morris-dancers, would have been maddened by such a programme, particularly if he heard that the feast was to be attended by a Puritan, who would " sing Psalms to hornpipes." [2] Both in singing and dancing power the party was strong, " three-man song-men all, and **very** good **ones ;"** Shakespeare himself having " songs for **man or women of all sizes,"** with " the prettiest love songs **for maids."** [3] There is no mention of " good ale," which was **presented as such an** important feature **by** Stubbs, **but we fear** that **it was only** too largely supplied, and that the warden pies, rice, currants, prunes, raisins, nutmegs, and ginger hot i' the mouth, formed but the ha'porth of bread in comparison.

" Good ale " did not bring good company. We are told by Rowe, that Shakespeare had, " by a misfortune common

<hr>

[1] 'Winter's Tale,' act iv. 2.   [2] Ibid.   [3] Ibid.

enough to young fellows," picked up with bad associates.[1] The sea of troubles drove his spirit to revolt, to throw off its allegiance to society, and seize the license of the hour. Youth is often none the worse for a dash of wild oats, and Shakespeare is charged with nothing more ; but looking at his situation at the time, we shall see that he was not solely **actuated by the pursuit of pleasure. This** had, indeed, **attractions for him. Neither poverty nor servitude** could **repress the gaiety of** his nature, and it burst forth in the darkest moments. Opportunities for indulgence were never wanting ; for wherever there was appreciation for good songs or sparkling wit, there he was sure of welcome. But his character was self-denying, gentle, full of sensibility and sympathy ; and he would not have torn himself from his family at this crisis, and plunged his parents into new sorrow by his conduct, for a mere revel. The temptation may have done something ; but the real impulse was his desperation, a dogged indifference to anything that might happen, because he was helpless to resist it. This it was that made him familiar with all the idle haunts of Stratford, where his few leisure **hours were spent—**

> " —— 'mongst the taverns there ;
> For there, they say, **he daily doth frequent,**
> With unrestrained loose companions,
> Even such, they say, as stand in narrow lanes."[2]

Goethe, at the same age, ran a similar course ; for though he is too sentimental to own to potations pottle deep, he confesses his frequent visits to the "narrow-lanes" of Frankfort, and "the taverns there," with "unrestrained loose companions." **But he lived** under a more auspicious star than Shakespeare ; **and was carried** away rather by vanity than youthful **infatuation—by the homage which** his **low** associates paid **to** his talents, and **their not disin-**

<hr>

[1] Rowe's ' Life of Shakespeare.'　　[2] ' King Richard II.,' act v. 3.

terested admiration of his verses. His thirst was for applause—not " good ale !" and here it was gratified. We may believe that the youthful Muse of Shakespeare also won plaudits, but it was with a jovial song, rung out in chorus. It tended, indeed, to the same end. Both William Shakespeare and Wilhelm Meister were serving their Apprenticeship.

Our ancestors entertained the same admiration for a large consumer of beer that, in this sober age, we feel for a skilled cricketer or a crack shot ; and, aspiring to eclipse all rivals, the villages around Stratford established two fraternities, expressly to cultivate drinking power. One society was called the Sippers, and the other the Topers, in allusion to the mode of procedure followed respectively by each ; and their meetings were attended by delegates from Pedworth, Marston, Hilborough, Grafton, Exhall, Wixford, Broom, and Bidford, the last-named village being the favourite resort, as it contained not only the largest number of alehouses, but furnished the best liquor. Shakespeare never anticipated being pilloried by tradition for his participation in one of these orgies. But the story of such a lapse in his youth is, after three centuries, still fresh in the surrounding country, so true is it that " the evil that men do lives after them."[1] Hitherto, however, it has been very imperfectly given, the drollest points being omitted. The tradition now appears as it was related to us on the spot by Mr. Bagshawe, of Bidford, to whom it was told in his childhood by the old people of the village, which carries it back for at least a hundred years ; and it was confirmed to us by old people still living at Bidford.

It would seem that the Whitsun ales had rendered the Topers very pot-valiant, and they challenged All England to a drinking match. This stirred up the ardour of the

---

[1] ' Julius Cæsar,' act iii. 2.

Stratford apprentices, and they sent a party of seven, which included young Will Shakespeare, to engage the giants at Bidford. The seven champions set out on the Saturday half-holiday, Bidford being nearly eight miles distant, and requiring time for the walk. Meanwhile, the Topers had accepted a contest at Evesham fair ; and the tippling village could only meet the Stratfordians with the Sippers, whom they looked upon with contempt. But they had come out to do battle, and since they were too late to meet the Topers, and could not return without laurels, they were content to slay the Sippers.

Bidford still abounds with public-houses, but the inn selected for this great "contention" fell into bad circumstances about a hundred years ago, and came to the workhouse—or rather was converted into a workhouse itself, the only instance on record, perhaps, of a tavern incurring the usual fate of drunkards. Melancholy it is to look up at its venerable white face, with the high gable above, like a cocked-hat, betokening better days, and reflect that it may owe its present ill plight to bad hours. It now shows no sign, but tradition affirms that it was once decorated with a Falcon, though Swallow would have been more appropriate, remembering its connection with Topers and Sippers. The poor are still its tenants, though it is no longer a workhouse ; and an old woman leads us to the very room where the Sipping Giants, from all the surrounding villages, met the 'prentice lads of Stratford.

The ale was brought in, and the champions exulted over the slow progress of the Sippers, anticipating an easy victory We may imagine what raillery their cautious homœopathic drains elicited from Shakespeare, as his own Alexandrian measure—not the Alexandrian measure he received from his Muse—subsided under his draughts. The "natural wit" was no longer natural : it flashed and foamed like the ale, and was as heady and exciting. But the night wore on, and while the reeling brain of the young Bacchanal began to war those infinite jests which set the table in a roar, the Sippers were as sober as judges.

Such immobility awed the Seven Champions, and under the optical delusion incident to their condition, they magnified the Sippers into real giants—sons of Anak, while they seemed themselves as grasshoppers. Still they kept up till past midnight, but then their ranks began to break, and one by one they dropped off, leaving the Sippers masters of the field.

The poet did not feel the full effect of his potations till he came into the open air. Then, however, his steps gave him to understand that the great globe itself had no stability. It is doubtful whether his starting eyes, lately such magnifiers, were able to make out the old church, which directly faces the door, and might have reminded him that it was Sunday morning. His course lay another way, round the corner, and up the hill, which, from being the same height as the church tower, has received the name of Tower Hill. By some means or other he gained the summit. But, alas! his elevation was only a prelude to his fall, and we must record that Will Shakespeare, like many a worse man, lost his head on Tower Hill.

Even now he was befriended by the Muses, who lured their favourite to a secluded spot, where the green sward offered a couch, and a spreading crab-tree both sheltered him and screened. The tree was cut down within memory, but slips of it are growing in neighbouring gardens, and the rick-yard of the Tower farm still preserves its site. Here the king of 'prenticedom was laid low—alas, how low! "What's a drunken man like? Like a drown'd man, a fool, and a madman!"[1] His companions may shout for him

<hr>

[1] 'Twelfth Night,' act i. 5.

to come on, but he "won't budge an inch, boy."[1]   He has found a soft spot, and is asleep.   Yet

> "Were he not warmed with ale,
> This were a bed but cold to sleep so soundly."[2]

Shakespeare was aroused by the dawning day.  We may conceive his bewilderment on looking round and seeing the face of his mistress, sweet nature, peering up at the golden sky.  Assuredly he felt the reproach, as he collected his thoughts and recalled the night's debauch.  A soft mist might lie on the earth like a coverlet, but even as he looked it was rolled up, as by an invisible hand, and the fields showed their bright morning face, gemmed with dew.  The boughs which formed a bower above him were alive with birds, warbling their matins, and—

> " Hark, hark ! the lark at heaven's gate sings ! "

"Oh, that men should put an enemy in their mouths, to steal away their senses !   That we should, with joy, pleasance, revel, and applause, transform ourselves into beasts."[3]
Who can imagine the thoughts that, in that moment of reflection, poured into his mind, as the sunshine on the waking world?  He did not then dream that he should hereafter mould this text into a homily, which would endure for ever.  But he was awake—awake in his mind, as well as sight, and gazed down on the vale of Evesham, stretching away, through the Cleave and Marcliff hills, to the far Malvern, with the Avon winding through, like a stream of light, and wood and cornfield and rich green slope on every side. He could see the church *now*, standing among the graves at the foot of the hill, like a traveller who has accomplished his journey ; and it did flash across him that it was Sunday morning !

[1] 'Taming of the Shrew,' Ind.
[2] Ibid.              [3] 'Othello,' act ii. 3.

Sunday morning, and a man ploughing the field! Shakespeare could not believe his eyes. But beyond doubt there was the husbandman at his vocation; and under the influence of good resolutions, which aroused all his reverence for the day, he went up to him to remonstrate.

"Sunday!" cried the farmer, with a good laugh; "why it's Monday!"

Shakespeare was rather astonished, but a few words convinced him that he had actually slept through the Sunday and the Sunday night, and, in explanation, he owned that he had not gone to bed sober. In short, he told the story of the drinking match, which so diverted the farmer, that he would not be satisfied without knowing who were his antagonists. The villages represented by the Sippers can all be seen from the hill, and the poet replied to the inquiry by turning towards each, at the same time naming it in an impromptu epigram:—

> "Piping Pedworth, dancing Marston,
> Haunted Hilborough, and hungry Grafton,
> With dodging Exhall, papist Wixford,
> Beggarly Broom, and drunken Bidford."

While the farmer was still laughing, up came the other six champions, who had started at cockcrow from Stratford, intending to dare the Sippers to a new contest. They gave a shout as they saw the poet, and stating their purpose, claimed his company. But they had parted with Shakespeare drunk and found Shakespeare sober. He refused the challenge; and we may imagine with what a solemn look he spoke, as doubtless in a half-jeering, half-serious strain he rebuked their intemperance, adjuring them to amend. Then followed a conflict of wit, in which it is easy to conceive who had the mastery; and, indeed, tradition affirms that the Bacchanals were glad to move off, and leave the poet to his own devices.

Goethe relates that he once strolled forth alone, after an evening ramble with Lilli, and in the morning was surprised to find himself reposing under a tree, where he had passed the night. There was certainly room for surprise if not suspicion, and we could almost pair his situation with Shakespeare's, if we were not made to understand by the sentiment he has thrown over it, that he had drunk only the nectar of his own thoughts. At all events, the two adventures show a family likeness, and one may be looked upon as a romantic reflex of the other.

But if Shakespeare had committed a folly, we may hope that it was rather by surprise than intent, since he now turned back repentant to his father's house. While the prodigal was still far off, nature came out to meet him, and fell on his neck and kissed him; for on the top of the Bowden Hill, his eye must involuntarily sweep over the lovely scene which spread round for miles. Behind rose the blue ridge of Malvern, to which contrast and distance gave Alpine height; on his right the huge mass of the Breadon stood up alone, like a Titan in his strength; and to the left the country stretched away to the horizon, far beyond Snitterfield Bush. All between was forest and field, sloping green hills and spreading common, while before him lay the green hollow, in which his own Stratford, girded by the Avon, lay like a child in its mother's lap. There was his father's roof; the school; the grey old chapel of the guild; and there the older church, jutting up its spire through the trees, like a finger pointing to heaven.

The scene might make him sadder, but his excess had made him wiser; for he was coming home with that impression of the dangers of evil companionship, and the fascination it exercises over the young, which enabled him to impart an undying moral to the orgies of Eastcheap. In Prince Henry he gives us the most complete presentment of a scapegrace ever conceived. The creation is, indeed, no imperfect reflection of his own youth, though he goes out of himself in its colouring. Nor is the hoary old rip Falstaff drawn wholly from imagination. Oldyss affirms that the character was suggested by a Stratford man, who presented several points of resemblance, and was particularly noted as a cheat.[1] Certainly the ideal being heaves with the breath of the real; there is only one Falstaff, but he is the chief of a type; and as these seducers were not unknown in the haunts of olden Greece and Rome, as they were met with in the rookeries of medieval London, so they may still be found in our modern shades and taverns. There are few vicious resorts of the young that cannot show a grey-headed profligate, the oracle of the stye, versed in every wickedness, and making vice attractive by his good humour and wit. But Shakespeare at seventeen might already look on his boon companions with the eye of Prince Henry :—

> " I know you all, and will awhile uphold
> The unyoked humour of your idleness;
> Yet herein will I imitate the sun,
> Who doth permit the base contagious clouds
> To smother up his beauty from the world,
> That when he please again to be himself,
> Being wanted, he may be more wondered at." [2]

---

[1] MSS. notes to Langbain.
[2] ' King Henry IV., Part I.,' act i. 2.

## X.

### SHAKESPEARE IN LOVE.

Boccacio's Cymon, whom the spell of woman's beauty changed from a satyr to Hyperion, illustrates the transforming power of Love. But the tender passion does not produce the same effect on every nature, nor always show its might instantaneously. Over some breasts it sweeps as a zephyr over an Æolian harp, awaking a melodious strain, which only rises to expire. Some it pierces like lightning, and others it enters like light. In this way—softly and imperceptibly, like the dawn of a May morning—it stole upon Shakespeare.

A short walk from Stratford brings us to the little hamlet of Shottery, lying in the fields, between the roads to Evesham and Alcester; and here still stands the cottage of Richard Hathaway, whom we have seen on intimate terms with John Shakespeare as early as 1566, when the poet was only two years' old. There is, as already shown, reason to believe that this connection was never relaxed, and, indeed, the simultaneous recurrence of the same baptismal names in the two families points to a closer bond. When we find successive generations of Hathaways bearing the Shakespearean names of William, Richard, John, Edmund, Alice, Margaret, Anne, and Joan, and keep other facts in mind, it is difficult to escape the impression that they were not united to the Shakespeares by some tie of blood.

Whatever the ground of their connection, John Shakespeare gave Richard Hathaway the right hand of fellowship, and their children grew up together, and cherished the same feeling. Many a gambol had gentle Will Shakespeare with his young companions at Shottery, before he was drawn thither by a more powerful attraction. One of them, indeed, was a kindred spirit, whose society, as he was close upon his own age, must have had a special charm for him ; for we seem to meet with Richard Hathaway, the dramatist, in the following entry in the baptismal register of Stratford :—" Jan. 4, 1561–2, Richardus filius Richardi Hathaway, alias Gardner." Other sons there were, and daughters—Bartholomew, John, Thomas, William, Agnes, Catherine, and Margaret—as we learn from their father's will ;[1] but that document makes no mention of the bright, particular star of the galaxy, the first love of Shakespeare, ANNE.

Not mentioned by her father, unsung by her lover, and left in more than her native obscurity, Anne Hathaway has survived every neglect. Tradition guarded her home, preserved her footprints, and perpetuated her name, when Shakespeare was almost forgotten. For nearly three centuries this good odour has surrounded her: it is only our own age that has linked her with scandal.

Happily there is no ground for the imputations cast upon her. They rest on a perverted view of the facts, made in ignorance of the usages of the age. Anne Hathaway, enshrined in our imagination so long, maintains her place as the ideal of womanhood. We can feel that to her—to her character, temper, and qualities—we owe something of the illumination of Shakespeare. She and his mother were the two women who mirrored to his eye the attributes of their sex, and unfolded to him its destiny and mission. He saw in them the spirituality of woman. They were an inspiration to him, and a revelation. From them he learnt to conceive those beautiful, touching portraitures which exhibit

---

[1] The will of Richard Hathaway will be found in the Appendix. It was discovered by Mr. Halliwell, in the Prerogative Office, in 1848.

woman as little lower than the angels—pure, gentle, and
truthful, in thought spotless, in affection devoted, in faith
enduring, portraitures that, like those which the cunning
painter gives to the canvas, charm by their beauty, but are
most valued for their resemblance.   Innocent Perdita, faithful
Imogen, gentle, pleading Desdemona, romantic Juliet, admired Miranda, and sparkling Beatrice, are, with all their
diversity, alike in this, presenting the one common humanity
under every type of disposition.   The same exaltation of the
sex is perceptible, indeed, even in those characters which
embody its passions and frailties, or which show its fine delicate mechanism out of joint.   We trace it in wanton Cressida, as well as in chaste Isabella ; in Lady Macbeth, who is
deterred from murder by Duncan's likeness to her father ;
and in poor Ophelia, not less patient in her madness than in
her sorrow, when she mourns over **Hamlet "blasted with
ecstasy."** [1]

The deepest source of this appreciation of woman by
Shakespeare was the true woman's heart which was most
**open to him,** and constantly under his eye—the heart of
**Anne Hathaway.  This association we must** recognize.
**Then we gain a true perception of Anne Hathaway,** and can
**account for the tender impression** retained of her in her
**native** village, when documents seemed to prove that she
had never been connected with Shakespeare—that she was a
myth, and had never existed.   The memory of mere beauty
would have faded, like beauty itself : the memory of a gentle,
loving maiden became a monument, of which time preserved
the design, even when the inscription was effaced.

Nor has even the remembrance of her beauty passed
away.   Tradition depicts her as a counterpart of Perdita—

> " The prettiest low-born lass that ever
> Ran on the green sward." [2]

---

[1] ' Hamlet,' act iii. 1.     [2] ' Winter's Tale,' act iii. 5.

Indeed, she may have sat for that portrait, and the very sheep-shearing may have been held at Shottery, where, to this day, sheep dot the fields like flakes of snow. They formed the most available portion of Richard Hathaway's riches, for in his will he bequeaths a sheep to each of his nieces, and he makes special mention of his shepherd, Whittington. So perhaps it was, after all, Anne Hathaway, and not Mopsa, who betrayed the kitchen secrets to Shakespeare on the occasion of the shearers' feast.

We must expect that the love of Shakespeare would take a form different from that of ordinary men—that not beauty alone, not the mere bloom of a youthful cheek, swelled the poet's breast with the tender passion. And it was so. This passion of his rose under the genial influence of mind ; and as a plant always in the sun comes early to prime, it grew up in his boyhood and ripened in his youth. Anne Hathaway may have borne him in her arms when he was an infant, for she was then eight years old. Their ages were parted by such a gulf, that while he was still a child, she might have been a mother. The blooming girl of seventeen could without impropriety twine her arm round the boy of nine, push back his clustering auburn curls, and grace his forehead with a kiss. When he had attained the same age, she was a woman of five-and-twenty, in the full glory of her charms. It is said that the first love of every youth falls to a maiden older than himself. But though this be true, as we believe, the love thus given is ephemeral, a mere passing sentiment, and Shakespeare's was singular in being a passion. In tracing the course of love, he places, indeed, disparity of age second in its catalogue of obstacles :—

> " The course of true love never did run smooth,
> But either it was different in blood—
> Or else mis-graffed in respect of years." [1]

---

[1] ' Midsummer Night's Dream,' act i. 1.

But he speaks of this love as "*true*," that is, as earnest, constant, and abiding. If alluding to his own case, therefore, he asserts the genuineness of his love, and we learn from himself that his attachment to Anne was real and permanent.

Here, again, we meet a coincidence in the youthful experiences of Goethe. The German poet was also but a lad when he gave his heart to Gretchen, who was nearly as much his senior as Anne Hathaway was Shakespeare's. It was an attachment of the same kind—his first, his "*true*" love. The affairs with Frederika and Lilli were flirtations; he loved the Gretchen. All the tenderness he possessed while his nature was young and fresh, all his real sensibility and affection were given to her. The record of his meetings with her is a living romance. Nowhere does he rise in fiction to the same pathos and power, and tame indeed are his Charlottes, his Ottilies, and his Philinas, by the side of this "low-born lass," this Anne Hathaway of Frankfort. When she disappears he falls sick unto death, and the remembrance of her beauty, her natural grace, the pure spirit that animated her form, and which low associations could not sully, remains with him for ever.

Shakespeare tells us that "base men being in love, have then a nobility in their nature, more than is native to them."[1] How much more must the nobility which in him was native have shown itself under this influence! Time has not calendared the precise date when he became—

> "The lover,
> Sighing like furnace, with a woeful ballad
> Made to his mistress' eyebrow."[2]

But there are several reasons for concluding that he was a lover at seventeen. The fact may have been apparent to Anne before it was known to himself; and, perhaps, was mutually understood before it was avowed. And what

---

[1] 'Othello,' act ii. 1.          [2] 'As You Like It,' act ii. 7.

maiden, although she were twenty-five, could resist such a suitor—with the nobility aforesaid by her thoroughly known, even while it was under a cloud—with those deep eyes confronting **her and** appealing **to** her, lighting up that kingly forehead, still crowned with clustering auburn curls—this **suitor,** moreover, sighing like furnace! Would the few years' difference in age then seem indeed such a barrier! Anne could not but know her charms; and her glass did not remind her that beauty is but skin-deep. That moment of triumph, when she was listening to protestations more eloquent, more persuasive than maiden had ever heard **before,** was not likely to foreshadow the distant time when **her face would be wan and wrinkled, while his was** still **fresh; when she would be old, and he hardly in his prime.** She knew who **spoke, and** what was his innate quality, for he had grown and unfolded under her eye. If he pleaded, it was natural for her to yield; **and what he vowed, she** could *too* easily believe.

There was no need " to tell this youth what 't is **to love,**" for none knew better that—

> " It is to be all made of sighs and tears,
> It is to be all made of faith and service—
> It is to be made of fantasy,
> All made of passion, and all made of wishes,
> All adoration, duty, and observance,
> **All humbleness, all patience and impatience,**
> **All purity, all trial, all endurance.**" [1]

In this inflammable mood he strolls off to Shottery on his Saturday half-holiday. We can imagine his sunny face to reflect **the brightness of nature, which looks smilingly down** from the green Welcomb hills, lights up the sward of the common then surrounding Stratford, and gladdens his path

---

[1] In the last line of this quotation I have ventured to substitute the word "endurance" for " observance" as following most naturally after " trial ;" besides that Shakespeare would not repeat the word " observance " at an interval of only one line.

through the fields. Soon he catches sight of Shottery farm, standing then much as it does at present, with its old substantial house, its tiled barns, looking all roof, its ricks, and its orchard. Over the stile he is in the village road, and strides on to the brook, now bridged by a broad culvert, but which the passenger of those days crossed as he best could. It comes sweeping down beneath an arcade of trees, a sylvan **aqueduct, worthy of** being known to Jacques; for not in the **forest of** Arden could he have found a " babbling brook " **more** to his taste. Here Shakespeare could see the Hathaway cottage, basking in the sun under its thatched gable, and inhaling the balmy air at all its lattice windows. Perhaps he saw Anne, too, accidentally standing at the gate—of course, not thinking that he would appear. He quickens his pace; he is at her side; he—but we are not expected to tattle of what may not have occurred.

The aspect of the garden is changed since then, but persons living near remember what it was half a century ago, and they were told by old folks of that time that it had so existed **from** the **days** of Shakespeare. Thus are these **traditions cherished by the simple people of the village!**

A **walk shut** in by tall box led round the garden to an **arbour, also** formed of box, and screened from view by a high hedge. Here was a bench of oak, which fifty years ago was removed into the house, and is still preserved there. Tradition calls it the COURTING CHAIR.[1]

And on this bench they sat—so young, so beautiful, so

---

[1] This interesting relic, which has never been mentioned before, was shown to me by the present occupant of the cottage, Mrs. Baker, the great-grand-daughter of William Taylor, who married Susan Hathaway, the last known descendant of Richard Hathaway. She received the tradition **from** an old man who died in the cottage two years ago, and who was present when the bench was removed and the arbour cut down, on which occasion he was told their history **by** William Taylor.

full of life and hope and joy : those two lovers, whose graves we have just left in the church. All those joys, those hopes, that beauty, that radiant youth put out centuries ago! What a sermon is this Courting Chair! To think of the ardent vows and the whispered trust, the jests, the mirth, and, alas! the tears, of which it has been the witness! And all unknown—all passed, as if they had not been!

But not so the lovers! They are here still, despite the graves in the church. We open the register of visitors, and the last entry records the name of a resident of New York : a page back appears a Hindoo from Calcutta. The Brahmin has crossed the **dark water, the American has traversed the Atlantic, to tread this charmed ground! In the same way, the humble room in which Shakespeare was** born **exhibits tokens of pilgrims from all lands and of all** ranks. The register **contains the autographs of two** kings ;[1] the beam supporting the ceiling is inscribed with a tributary stanza by a Bonaparte ;[2] the mantelpiece bears the signature of Wellington ; the name of Walter Scott appears on the window ; and Byron's and Tennyson's on the wall. The mighty of the earth shrink before this worship of genius. In the little garden of Shottery, we ask what conqueror or autocrat, from Cheops to Napoleon, claims the veneration which is here shown for the butcher-boy of Stratford and his peasant mistress?

Shakespeare presented himself in the arbour as smart as Orlando when he paraded before Rosalind, and could have been **rallied by Anne** in Rosalind's words, seeing that **he** lacked all the outward marks of a true lover,—" a beard neglected, which you have not; but I pardon you for that, for simply your having in beard is a younger brother's revenue." The handsome pointed beard of later years was, in truth, not yet visible, and at seventeen there was

[1] George **IV. and** William IV.    [2] Prince Lucien Bonaparte.

only the faintest show of the delicate moustache.  **He was equally open to criticism** in his costume :—" Your hose should be ungartered, your bonnet unbanded, your sleeve unbuttoned, your shoe untied, and everything about you demonstrating a careless desolation.  But you are no such man : you are rather point-device in your accoutrements." [1]

**They walk round the** garden **to the cottage-door, past the moss-grown** well—his Helicon, where, while Anne stood by, he often drank inspiration and—water.  Perhaps it was here he produced his " woful ballad to his mistress' eyebrow."  But, in truth, he had to woo more seriously to remove Anne's scruples.  From the intimacy of the two families and his own winning manners, he always met a kindly reception at Shottery, but this did not extend to his suit.  An attachment so unequal in years suggested **to the** old husbandman and his wife little promise of **happiness for** their daughter, nor could they see an eligible son-in-law in a young lad whose father was insolvent, and who was **himself** sowing wild oats.  Anne knew what a nature was beneath this **cloud.  She discerned the generous** qualities, the **sterling worth, and the noble mind which her lover's lapses might obscure, but could not deface.  If his little trespasses made others shake** their heads, here she found assurance doubly sure.  Yet she had a misgiving, too.  There were moments when the little chasm of years between them looked wider, when she pondered over all that busy friends said of it, and trembled.  Well for her that she revealed her fears to him !  He could tell her that love depended not on the eye, but was enduring as the heart ; that her beauty was a prize indeed, animating **and inspiring him ; but** when her eye dimmed, when her **cheek** blanched, **when that sunny** brow was overcast by age, she would still be **the kindred**

[1] ' As You Like It,' act iii. 2.

spirit who had won his first love, endeared to him by associations more captivating **than** youth. Such are plainly the feelings which dictated his 116th Sonnet.—

> " Let me not **to** the marriage of true minds
> Admit impediments.   Love is not love
> *Which alters when it alteration finds,*
> Or bends with the remover to remove.
> Oh, no ! it is an ever fixed mark
> That looks on tempests, and is never shaken !"

Nothing could be **more** applicable to their courtship and the grave objections it had to **meet**. She would alter indeed, and he must see the alteration ; but that could not alter his love. This would remain firm, unbent, through every change, like the beacon which looks on the storm and is never shaken. For it was their MINDS that were to be married—their kindred, "true minds." And so he continues :—

> " **Love's not Time's fool,** *though rosy lips and cheeks*
> Within his bending sickle's compass come ;
> Love alters not with *his brief hours and weeks,*
> But bears it even to the edge of doom.
>      If this be error, and *upon me proved,*
>      I never writ and no man ever loved."

Time's " brief hours and weeks " are all the tenure he allows for Anne's "rosy lips and cheeks." Boy as he was, he did not contract this engagement without seeing its bearings.

The favourite time for declarations of love was St. Valentine's day. This probably arose from a Pagan custom connected with the Lupercali of ancient Rome, and was associated with St. Valentine by mere chance, for how he became the patron of lovers there is no legend to tell. The usage is mentioned by Shakespeare in the wild strain of Ophelia ;[1] and Theseus, in saluting his court in the wood,

---

[1] ' Hamlet,' act iii. 5.

alludes to an impression still current that birds choose their mates on Valentine's day—

> " St. Valentine is past ;
> Begin these wood-birds but to couple now ?" [1]

This sociable practice of the feathered creation appeared to the maids and bachelors of old a very rational proceeding, and as suitable to themselves as to woodlarks. Accordingly they were wont to meet on the eve of the festival to decide by lot who should be Valentines for the day. If not thus selected, the Valentine was usually the first person of the opposite sex seen in the morning. Maidens adopted the most subtle precautions to reserve this glance for the proper person ; and, indeed, there was generally an understanding as to the moment and spot for its delivery, so that the right swain might be in the right place. Thus, when Anne Hathaway stepped forth with closed eyes on St. Valentine's morning, she would not be greatly surprised to find Will Shakespeare at the door.

May morning was another festival for lovers ; for then young men and maidens went in the dark to the woods, to gather May dew at daybreak. Poor old Stubbs regards this custom as perfectly shocking, and the more so because, as he declares, it was followed by " both men, women, and children, old and young, even all indifferently." It was a sort of juvenile *fête* for the children, who were so wicked as to " spend all the night in pastimes," just as they do Twelfth Night in the present age ; and their elders deported themselves in such a manner as to prove they were only children of a larger growth. In the morning, they came home fresh enough for another night of it, " bringing with them birch,"— which Stubbs would like to have laid about them,—" boughs and branches of trees, to deck their assemblies withal." [2]

---

[1] 'Midsummer Night's Dream,' act iv. 1.
[2] ' Anatomy of Abuses.'

Such were the " May meetings " of Shakespeare's youth.
The notion that they **were** a pagan institution has been
adopted by himself, in ' Midsummer Night's Dream,' which,
though tripping **over the Christian St. Valentine, lays its
action** in pagan times. Nevertheless, he and Anne Hath-
**away held the custom in as much** reverence as Lysander and
Hermia—

> " No doubt they rose up early to observe
> The rite of May." [1]

We may believe that they could no longer meet without
difficulty. Anne's family did not look with more favour on
Shakespeare's suit, because he **persisted in it ;** and, **in that
case,** would afford **him few opportunities of** seeing her. **But**
love laughs at **locksmiths, and Shakespeare** would find a way
to secure **a meeting—**

> " If thou lov'st me, then,
> Steal forth thy father's house to-morrow night,
> And in the wood, a league without the town,
> Where I did meet thee once with Helena,
> To do observance to a morn of May ;
> There will I stay for thee." [2]

---

[1] ' Midsummer Night's Dream,' act iv. 1.
[2] Ibid., act i. 1.

# XI.

## SHAKESPEARE, THE WOODMAN.

It is remarked by Hume, that the character of our great Alfred has come down to us so free from blemish, and so untainted by the passions and frailties of human nature, that we are led to doubt that he ever existed. Some writers have whitewashed Shakespeare, as Malone did his bust in Stratford church, until his natural features, like Alfred's, are lost. The poet was not one to obtrude himself on the public gaze—" I love the people, but do not like to stage me to their eyes;"[1] and he might prefer his actions being forgotten; but since the world claims the story, we may hear him tell from the tomb in what spirit his life should be related—" nothing extenuate, nor set down aught in malice."[2]

However they may be disputed, the traditions of his youthful trespasses will never be plucked from the popular belief. In a biographical sense, they are as dear to us as his works; for they are almost our only impressions of his personal history, the remains of the man. Especially we cherish the old deer-stalking adventure, that turning-point of his life, and link between his life and works. But it would have little claim to this reverence, if it rested only on the loose statement of Davies,[3] or the idle fabrications of

[1] 'Measure for Measure,' act i. 1.

[2] 'Othello,' act v. 2.

[3] The Rev. Richard Davies was vicar of Sapperton, in Gloucestershire, and became possessed of some biographical memoranda by the Rev. W. Fulman, who died in 1688. One of these referred to Shakespeare, and simply mentioned his birth and death at Stratford, and that he was an actor and

Ireland. Rowe relates the occurrence in a different manner, and gives it the stamp of authority; for though he wrote a year later than Davies, he derived his information from Betterton. After an interval of a century and a half, during which it has been rejected by nearly all the biographers of Shakespeare, the tradition will now receive confirmation from the family archives of the Lucys, which enable us both to establish its truth and to present it for the first time complete.

The notorious Ireland affirmed that the adventure happened at Fulbrooke, and this awakens greater scepticism in Mr. Knight, who seems to have ascertained that Fulbrooke " did not come into the possession of the Lucy family till the grandson of Sir Thomas purchased it in the reign of James I."[1] But he cites no authority for the statement, and it has not been accepted as fact. Lately, however, a search in the old gatehouse at Charlecote, has brought to light the deed of sale, conveying Fulbrooke to the Lucys in January, 1615, and its discovery, as well as the precise date, is now first mentioned. Thus it is made clear that the deer was not taken from Fulbrooke, and Ireland is convicted of one more fabrication.

Nor must we receive implicitly the account given by Rowe. The offence becomes serious, if it was committed, as hitherto said,[2] when Shakespeare was a husband and a

---

dramatist. With this Davies incorporated a few lines of his own, relating the deer-stealing adventure, of which he had evidently heard the facts, though it is equally clear that they had become addled in his memory. He forgets the christian name of Sir Thomas Lucy, and is no better informed as to the name he received from Shakespeare, for he makes the poet satirize him, not by the familiar designation of Justice Shallow, but as Justice Clodpate !

[1] Knight's ' William Shakespeare : a Biography.'

[2] Rowe does not give any date, but he says that Shakespeare was married at the time ; and it has become orthodox to maintain that he left Stratford in 1586-7, when he was in his twenty-third year.

parent ; and, moreover, this is irreconcilable with the statements of Aubrey and Dowdall, who wrote nearest to his own time, and concur in affirming that he quitted Stratford during his minority. Their report of the time of departure bears out the tradition still current on the spot, while, on **the** other hand, the date always assumed is acknowledged to be conjectural, and **rests** on no evidence whatever.

**Rowe** intimates that Shakespeare engaged "more than once" in a raid on the deer, so far agreeing with Davies, who charges him also with stealing rabbits. It is certain that he was a cunning "woodman." He understood the whole mystery of "coney-catching;"[1] and knew both how to stuff a rabbit with parsley,[2] and how it turned on the spit.[3] Northumberland might excite the suspicions of a sharp gamekeeper, ignorant of **his rank, and** who heard him exclaim,—"So doth the coney struggle in the net ;"[4] and violent hands might be laid on Clifford, when he betrays such familiarity with the strife of "the woodcock with the gin."[5] But, suggestive as these experiences may be, tradition confines the poet's depredations to one raid and one occasion ; and we can admit no wider indictment on the present evidence.

The proof of the story is a note in a manuscript pedigree of the Lucys, made about ninety years ago by an old man named Ward, who derived his information from the family papers then in his hands. This version of the incident has been obligingly communicated to us by Mrs. Lucy, **of** Charlecote.

Shakespeare was but one **of a party in** the enterprise—

---

[1] 'Merry **Wives** of Windsor,' act i. 1.
[2] 'Taming of the Shrew,' act iv 4.
[3] 'Love's Labour's Lost,' act iii. 1.
[4] 'King Henry VI., Part II.,' act i. 4.        [5] Ibid.

whether the same who were worsted by the Bidford Sippers is uncertain, but we may believe that they were no better than they should be. They all lent a willing ear to Somebody's suggestion,—" Come, shall we go and kill us venison?"[1] and we are not left in doubt who was the spokesman; for a little bird has brought down a rumour of the day that the venison was coveted by Shakespeare for his approaching nuptials. Alas! why not content himself with the bride's warden pies, coloured with saffron! He might be sure that no " bribe buck "[2] would stop Richard Hathaway from asking awkward questions, when it came under his roof, and there would certainly be a suspicion that it was, as Justice Shallow says, "*ill* killed."[3] But suppose the marriage was to be, like the buck, a stolen one! Then, indeed, we may understand how young Wilful risked pains and penalties to " furnish forth the marriage tables."[4]

It was, doubtless, after the forbidden hour of nine,—the curfew of Stratford apprentices,—and on a dark night, that the marauders began to muster at the rendezvous, which Shakespeare, as a young butcher, might appoint at the 'Shoulder of Mutton,' on the other side of the bridge, waggishly intimating that the next course would be Haunch of Venison. The same old house is still there, and we could almost believe the same Shoulder; for it by no means looks fresh on the sign board. Here the party may have put " fourteen pence on the score for sheer ale,"[5] not without objections from mine host—though, perhaps, his growl is hushed by the appearance of some suspicious-looking dogs, not to mention a few cross-bows, arousing a distant scent of

---

[1] ' As You Like It,' act ii. 1.
[2] ' Merry Wives of Windsor,' act v. 5.
[3] Ibid., act i. 1.
[4] ' Hamlet,' act i. 2.
[5] ' Taming of the Shrew,' Ind. 2.

venison cutlets. For, truth to speak, the 'Shoulder of Mutton' must then have been very unlike what it appears at present, if it was a house where " bribe buck " would be met by awkward or any other questions.

It is growing late when the little band sally forth, much as Sir John Falstaff and " all his company " proceeded along Gad's Hill. The road lies straight from the door, and as they move along, they may hear the flow of the Avon through the osiers. On each side rise the hedges, hiding the broad fields, and making the lone road lonelier, till they reach Toddington, a mile further on. Its little sprinkle of dwellings has somewhat increased during the last twenty years, but allowing for this patch, it is still the Toddington of Shakespeare, and the same old wigwam cottages are still there, with their thatch of many winters. The party take care to pass very quietly, so as to provoke no notice, bearing in mind that there will be a hue-and-cry on the morrow, on the discovery of their depredation. It was not an hour when many were likely to be astir, though Toddington does not want a neighbour, being close to the little hamlet of Alveston, which they see rearing its gables through the darkness as they leave it on the left. For a time, elm and oak deepen the shadows, but presently the road pierces a clear space, spreading before them the sward of Charlecote park.

A moment is given to reconnoitring. All is quiet, and as everyone's blood is up, they are soon over the low fence. One leads the way, pointing out an eligible station—

> " Hereby, upon the edge of yonder coppice,
> A stand where you   ay make the fairest shoot." [1]

We look round the park for the spot. It must surely be here, where the turf slopes steeply down to a brook, and the

[1] ' Love's Labour's Lost,' act iv. 1.

closely packed trees are centuries old.    The poachers breathe
more freely beneath **their shade** :—

> " Under this thick-grown brake we'll shroud ourselves ;
> For through this haund anon the deer will come ;
> And in this covert will we make our stand,
> Culling the principal of all the deer." [1]

We are here in the very place where the deer might be
expected to come.    Here they can drink with the water just
covering their hoofs, while the Avon yonder, though not
**deep,** is broad, **and** runs close to the house.    The woodmen
**may have to wait ; but this were no great trial in the com-**
pany of Shakespeare.

> " And, for the time shall not seem tedious,
> I'll tell thee what befell me on a day
> In this self-same place." [2]

**Not the** adventure with the keeper's daughter !    Shakespeare **was** not, like Goethe, one to kiss and tell.    But **the**
recital, if one there were, would, whatever it might be, find
a willing audience, who did not give ear for the first time.
Not a breath stirred the bush in the front or the young wood
behind, and down the glade before them, paved with turf
and overarched by the boughs of spreading trees, they see
**only** darkness.    Yet something **may stop the tale, and** hush
the speaker.    Perhaps he hears a coming herd, or the
stealing step of keepers.    No ! a bird singing—" the nightingale's complaining notes," speaking to her poet, reproaching
him, awaking in his breast a thousand harmonies, which make
him forget his purpose.    But there is no time for the operation of the spell.    The deer are at hand : they come
stalking on, unsuspicious of danger, and reach the ambus-
cade.    The bows are raised ; the shafts loosed ; the dogs

---

[1] ' King Henry VI., Part III.,' act iii. 1.          [2] Ibid.

rush barking out; and in a moment the herd is in flight. A buck is seen to stagger, and the poachers start in pursuit.

Whether short or long, the chace was successful, **and the dogs fell on** the drooping stag, and pulled him down. **They were still by** the side of the brook—

> " **Under** an oak whose antique root peeps out
> *Upon the brook, that brawls along this wood,*
> **To** the which place a poor sequestered stag,
> That from the hunter's aim had ta'en a hurt,
> Did come to languish." [1]

With his butcher's knife in his hand, and even while fulfilling his vocation, Shakespeare was not unobservant of the scene, or indifferent to the sufferings of the "wretched animal." It had been wiser to have kept watch. The deer was cut **up;** the spoil apportioned; and **the party** jested and laughed as they pushed through **the** trees. But they had begun to whistle before they were **out of** the wood. Suddenly there was an alarm, but too late: the keepers **were** upon them. **It was** a fair stand-up fight. **If blood flowed, it was from** broken **heads;** for Shakespeare **never thought of using** his knife. **That was a resource unknown to our ancestors.** But, however **carried on, the** struggle **ended in** the rout of **the poachers,** and Shakespeare was left a prisoner.

It is not to be supposed that he received much comfort from his captors as they dragged him off. The discourse on such occasions is not reassuring; and prisoners who have killed deer and broken keepers' heads are made to understand that they will have to **pay for** their **sport.** It was with full information **on this** point that Shakespeare was left to ruminate on his situation in the **strong-room of** the gatehouse at Charlecote. **His captors, we may** believe, took

---

[1] 'As You Like It,' act ii. 1.

counsel on the facts before they separated, and resolved to lose no time in bringing him up for judgment. In this mood they may have burst into the room on the following morning. But vain are the purposes of men. The bird had flown, and the room was empty. "Knight, you have beaten my men, killed my deer, and broke open my lodge."[1]

[1] 'Merry Wives of Windsor,' act i. 1.

# XII.

## HIS WORSHIP THE JUSTICE AND HIS FRIENDS.

CHARLECOTE HOUSE stands on the south bank of the Avon, **rather** more than four miles from Stratford. In Shakespeare's day it was the residence of Sir Thomas Lucy, who was, indeed, its founder, though the surrounding estate had been held by his family from the time of the Conquest. It is still in possession of his descendants, and the mansion presents much the same aspect as of old, **showing its ruddy face** behind the arched gatehouse, **like a country lass's of** the time under her wimple. We can now remove all doubt **as** to the founder of this antique pile, being the Justice Shallow of Shakespeare. The fact is mentioned by Ward, in the **manuscript pedigree of the family;** and it is worthy of remark, that the only one of Shakespeare's plays of an old date, found at Charlecote, **is a copy of the octavo edition of** 'The **Merry** Wives of Windsor,' published in 1619, which was lately discovered by Mrs. Lucy, among the family records. A careful comparison will show that the Justice Shallow of this play is the one of 'King Henry IV.'—with a difference! In short, we must regard him here as presenting not only **the better man,** but the truer portrait. Both are satires; **but in 'King Henry IV.'** the poet is avenging himself; and in 'The **Merry Wives of Windsor,'** while blending with **a** remembrance of his own quarrel an impression **that it was** too fiercely pursued, he **is, as** we shall hereafter see, but the **champion** of his patron.

Ptolemy identified the courtier who hoaxed Apelles by the profile which the artist drew on **the wall; and Shake**speare has given such outlines to Justice Shallow as **insured** his recognition **at Stratford.** Of the direct reference to Sir Thomas Lucy in the word-play on his arms we shall speak in another chapter, when the point of the satire, which has never yet been shown, will be made more apparent.

Let us now merely remark how beautifully Shakespeare, throughout ‘The Merry Wives,’ seems to preserve the original mould of the character, while shading it imperceptibly off, **so that** Shallow becomes an unsophisticated, and indeed **lovable, country gentleman,—still a little vain, in**deed, keeping up all his old consequence, and with a sharp eye to his own interest, but disposed withal to join everybody in making things pleasant. **The portrait in ‘King** Henry IV.’ is drawn **in a different spirit, under the sting of resentment, and with his quarrel fresh in his mind.** Here the Knight appears with every marked feature prominent— a swaggerer and simpleton, **the** dupe of Davy and the butt of Falstaff: yet, even in his fury, gentle Will keeps bounds. There is a good-nature about this old country Justice after all, and, somehow or other, we get to like him. **Nor** is his simplicity without a leaven of shrewdness. He allows Falstaff to wheedle him out of a thousand pounds, but it had **the** look **of a very fair investment at the time, and** it was not **the act of a simpleton when the luck turned to strike in for halves, though he found it impossible to get butter out of Falstaff’s throat.** The **Justice would have had a good return, if** “sweet **Jack”** had **remained** powerful **at court.** He was to be “my Lord Shallow.” Falstaff would “make the king do him grace.” Is this said without meaning, or does it imply that Sir Thomas Lucy was aspiring to the peerage—to the extinct barony of De Lucy? The family archives have just disclosed a fact, which now first appears in

print, but which could easily have been known to Shakespeare,—namely, that Sir Thomas Lucy had sent a fat buck
as a present to Queen Elizabeth.  This both proves that he
was paying court to the queen, and removes all doubt as to
there being deer in the park, which, indeed, may be thought
to have **been already done by Mr. Collier.**  When the
**rumour** of the present reached Stratford, more than Shakespeare might imagine that Sir Thomas was aiming to be *my*
*Lord Lucy,* and, in truth, as the heir of the **Lords de Lucy,**
and inheritor of their name, **he might** feel warranted in
aspiring to this dignity.

Shallow's attempt to recover his money from Falstaff,
when the case was perfectly desperate, gives point to an
entry in the accounts of the Stratford chamberlain, which
shows that Sir Thomas Lucy entertained the same repugnance to surrendering bad debts.  He there " prayeth allowance for five shillings and fourpence for the rent of the tythe
of Little Wilmcote ; for that he could not receive it of
Mr. William Underhill."  Why he should expect to receive
it of Stratford is not stated, but it is evident that Sir Thomas
**was not particular as to who paid** it, so long as it was paid.
**The claim would seem to have** been too unreasonable
**to be entertained by the Stratford authorities, for** it obtains
**no** further mention, though they were most anxious to
keep him in good humour.  This is proved by their outlays
for providing him with refreshments, whenever duty or
pleasure carried him to the town—which was not often, the
visits of justices being in this respect more like angels' visits
in those days than they are understood by modern delin-
quents.

From the items **entered in the** chamberlain's accounts,
we learn that Sir Thomas had a special liking **for** sugar.  In
1578 he was regaled with " a pottle of wine and a quartern
**of sugar."**  The refection provided for him on the 12th of

January, 1583, consisted again of "a quart of sack, a pottle of claret wine, and a quartern of sugar." It is amusing to find the records which furnish this testimony, noting that "Sir Thomas Lucy sat in commission for tipplers," particularly as the same entry registers another payment for "wine and sugar," which he consumed on the occasion. It was not because he was virtuous that there was to be no more sack and claret, and sugar sweet i' the mouth. Sugar, indeed, was always provided, and always in the same proportion. It must have come in under a Morrill tariff, the price being eightpence a pound, equal to two and eightpence of our present money, but, whatever the cost, Sir Thomas expected his "quartern" every time he visited the town. An entry of eighteenpence, for "a quart of sack and a quartern of sugar *burnt* for Sir Thomas Lucy," shows, by this expression, that it was literally for his own smoking.

Such a consumption of sack and claret carries us back to the days when Justice Shallow was as wild as young Will Shakespeare; though, like the Irishman, we may believe what we please of his confessions, for they are scouted by Falstaff. The family records do not show that Sir Thomas Lucy was ever a member of Clement's Inn; but it is worthy of note that his son, the second Sir Thomas, did enter that society, which raises a suspicion that the family were not then connected with it for the first time. Even when no longer representing "mad Shallow," the worthy justice retains some of his old tastes, such as bear out the entries in the Stratford accounts, and the misadventure of his man, William, shows that he had not lost his relish for sack :— " Sir, do you mean to stop any of William's wages about the sack he lost the other day, at Hinckley fair ?" [1] The Justice seems to have an impression that it was himself who lost the sack, and that William had drunk it, for he curtly replies,

[1] 'King Henry IV., Part II.,' act iii. 2.

" He shall answer it."   The determination to make William " answer it," may point at WILLIAM himself.

Shallow is described as a justice of " the county of Gloucester," while Charlecote is in Warwickshire ; but from **the** windows of his mansion, Sir Thomas Lucy could see the **Cotswold** hills, **which** are mentioned by Shallow, when he speaks **of Will Squele,**[1] again turning up William—and squealing ! **Nor** does Slender forget this **feature of** Charlecote, **for** he **tells Page** how his greyhound **was outrun at " Cotsall,"**[2] the **local name** of the hills.   The places mentioned in the case on which Shallow is to **sit in** judgment, although in Gloucestershire, are also within a short distance from Charlecote.   " I beseech you, sir, to countenance William Visor, of Wincot, against Clement Parkes, of the Hill."[3]   A farm, two fields distant from Stratford church, on the other **side of the Avon,** is still known as **the Hill farm, and the present owner is** spoken of as Mrs. Newnham, "*of the Hill.*"   **A part of the old** house remains to this day, and when we lit upon it, **an** old labouring man described to us how it had stood in his youth, when it was always pointed out **as** the farm mentioned by **Shakespeare.   A** walk **of three miles and a half,** through **the villages of Clifford,** Atherstone, and Preston, and then **through a** dozen fields, brought us to Wincot, the residence of the " knave " Visor, and here **we met with visible traces** of Shakespeare's steps, of which we shall speak hereafter.

Shallow declares " Visor is a great knave, to my knowledge ;" but this is no rebuff to his man Davy, who admits the fact.   " I grant your worship that he is a knave, sir ; but yet, heaven forbid, sir, but **a knave** should **have some** countenance at his friend's request. . .   I have served your worship truly, **sir,** these **eight years ; and if I cannot once**

[1] ' King **Henry IV.,** Part II.,' act iii. 2.
[2] ' Merry Wives of Windsor,' act i. 1.
[3] ' King Henry IV., Part II.,' act iii. 2.

or twice in a quarter bear out **a knave against an honest man,** I have but a very little credit **with your worship."** Measured by **this gauge, Davy's credit seems to have been** little indeed ; for Shallow will **promise only that Visor** " shall have no wrong." We are thus left under the impression that Shallow was not a man to let justice go by favour, and we find that Shakespeare, even when he lampoons, is careful not to libel.

It has been conjectured that Shakespeare took the name of Davy from one Davy Jones, who was then living in Stratford. This may pass with landsmen, but, making a mortal **of Davy Jones, will never be credited by sailors.** Nor does **the mere name throw any light on the individual; for** **it is not pretended that Jones was connected with Sir** **Thomas Lucy.** But a list of the holders of corn and malt **residing in Stratford during the great dearth of 1598, gives** **us a clue** to Davy himself—the real **Davy ; for** it reports that **thirteen quarters of** corn are in the possession of " Robert **Pennell, Sir Thomas Lucy's** servant." Robert Pennell's store reminds us that Davy was entrusted with the superintendence of Shallow's crops—"and again, sir, shall we sow the head-land with wheat?"[1] And it also makes his principal farm-servant a resident in Stratford, where he might **play** such fantastic tricks before high bailiffs, as to draw down the lash of Shakespeare. **Nor is it improbable that he** may have lent his Christian name of Robert to his master, Robert Shallow, esq., and then—gone to Davy Jones himself.

The Lucy papers afford no aid in identifying Slender, but it cannot be that he was **not a real person,** one in authority at Charlecote, and known to Shakespeare from his schooldays—for does not Sir Hugh Evans tell us that " he gave the boys a playing-day."[2] It is possible that he may be alluded

---

[1] ' King Henry IV., Part II.,' act iii. 2.
[2] ' Merry Wives of Windsor,' **act i. 1.**

to in the following passage, in a letter written in 1597–8, by Abraham Sturley, a Stratford man, to a friend in London, and preserved in the Stratford records :—" Yesterday I spoke to Mr. Sheldon, *at Sir Thomas Lucy's,* for the stay of Mr. Burton's suit, and that the cause might be referred to Mr. Walker, of Ellington ; he answered me that Mr. Burton was now in London, and, with all his heart and good will, the suit should be stayed, and the matter so referred." The Sheldons are still in the neighbourhood, as well as the Lucys, and the landed proprietor near Charlecote, who now represents the name, may be descended from Master Slender, for the latter, though he kept " but three men and a boy " at Windsor, and was living " like a poor gentleman," intimates that he is to come into something handsome on the death of his mother.[1] Sheldon may be transposed into Slendoh, which is very close on Slender, and though we did not find the name in the Lucy pedigree, at Charlecote, it must be stated that the cousinships of those days are rarely traceable in pedigrees.

Silence is also introduced to us as the cousin of Shallow, or rather his cousin's husband, and his own brother-justice,—" My cousin Silence, in commission with me."[2] This description precisely answers for the magisterial colleague of Sir Thomas Lucy—Humphrey Peto, who married in the family of Verney of Compton, which gave a husband to Jane Lucy,[3] the sister of Sir Thomas's father, and, by the custom of the day, the Lucys and Verneys were hence regarded as cousins. " And how doth my cousin, your bedfellow."[4] It is clear that Peto was in the mind of Shakespeare at the time, for he gives his name to a character in

<hr>

[1] ' Merry Wives of Windsor,' act i. 1.
[2] ' King Henry IV., Part II.,' act iii. 2.
[3] Jane Lucy married George Verney, of Compton.
[4] ' King Henry IV., Part II.,' act iii. 2.

the same play, and has even thus used it in the 'First Part,' **where he** does not introduce Shallow ; **Peto, who is** latterly **an attendant on Prince** Henry, being there one **of** the hangers-on of Falstaff. But Ward does not connect the worthy magistrate with the prosecution **of** Shakespeare, and therefore we must **not** introduce him in our next chapter.

## XIII.

### SHAKESPEARE, THE PRISONER.

IT is not difficult **to imagine what must have been the feelings of** poor John Shakespeare and his wife, when they **heard of** the situation of their son, whose first impulse might naturally lead him to fly to them for refuge, and confide to his mother that he was pursued by the officers of justice. There was nothing to be gained by concealment, which might delay his punishment, but could not avert it; and we may believe that the unhappy youth was soon **again in** custody, and on his way to the magistrate. It has been customary to represent the offence of which he was accused as one of a light character, but nobody can pretend that a raid on a deer-park **would be** considered a mere frolic in the present **day; and** our ancestors, with their strong **feelings** about game, were as little disposed as ourselves to look upon it with indulgence. Indeed, deer-stealing was **for a** long time felony, and, up to a recent period, punishable with death. The statute 5th of Elizabeth reduced the penalty to whipping and imprisonment, but offenders could also be brought before the Star Chamber, which was a sort of lay Holy Inquisition, exercising a rigour unknown to the ordinary tribunals. Its judges made a long arm of the law to **reach beyond** it; and anyone brought within their jurisdiction, might consider himself given over to the tormentors. **He was not** only **made to** pay his last farthing in fines and **fees, but he** might be kept in **prison for any length of time, without** an opening for **appeal. Such a strain of** authority at length became unendurable; the whole nation rose against it, and the destruction of this judicial bastille was the first act of the English revolution.[1]

It is clear that Shakespeare felt both the peril and the ignominy of his situation, though they elicit a smile from his biographers. His arrest was not accomplished without a mournful scene; and the shame of his father, the anguish of his mother, and the loud, accusing voice of his own conscience, awoke every better feeling of that gentle breast. He saw that he had brought reproach on his family, as well as on himself, and that no one could be connected with him without sharing his disgrace. This carried his thoughts to one dearer even than his parents; and it now seemed a duty to forego his engagement with Anne Hathaway, which he had pursued so eagerly, and which embraced all his hopes of happiness. With what bitter emotion must he have penned this surrender :—

> " Let me confess that we two must be twain,
> Although our undivided loves are one :
> So shall those blots that do with me remain,
> Without thy help, by me be borne alone."[2]

He declares that their affection will endure, though the spite of fortune compels them to separate, and that love itself will remain to them, though despoiled of its sweet hours of communion. Then he tenderly confesses that he has forfeited his claim to her hand, and leaves her free :—

> " I may not evermore acknowledge thee,
> Lest my bewailed guilt should do thee shame ;
> Nor thou with public kindness honour me,
> Unless thou take that honour from thy name :
> But do not so : I love thee in such sort,
> As, thou being mine, mine is thy good report."

[1] Not long after Shakespeare's adventure at Charlecote, Lord Berkeley instituted proceedings in the Star Chamber against twenty persons for stealing his deer; and a letter from the Earl of Derby, in the Talbot collection, dated only a few years later, 1589–90, mentions the conviction by his lordship of a Staffordshire deer-stealer, whom the earl declares that he will call "into the Star Chamber in the next term."

[2] Sonnet xxxvi.

But whatever his remorse—whatever the emotions swelling in his heart, it was with no faltering step that he entered the hall of Charlecote, where family tradition reports that he stood arraigned. Time and modern taste have made little alteration in this noble apartment, which, omitting the pictures on the walls, presents much the same aspect as when it beheld **Shakespeare a** prisoner. Then, as now, the wide recess-**window** disclosed the garden without, extending to the gate-house, and radiant with flowers, of which he could tell all the names. His eye glanced up at the same stained glass and the same richly-carved ceiling, winding round to the curiously-wrought chimney-piece, from which fine marble busts of Sir Thomas Lucy and Queen Elizabeth now, as they look down upon us, recall the very age and body of the time. Here is the stone floor, and here a long oaken table, such as tradition affirms stood on the self-same spot **on that** eventful morning. In the bust we recognize Justice Shallow himself, his sharply-cut face and beard—" such bearded hermit staves as Master Shallow." [1]   Falstaff, sawed into quantities, would make four dozen of him. It is the face of a very thin, **almost emaciated man**—" a man made after supper of a cheese-paring." [2]   There is an impress of sober sadness on it, though, which makes **us think that Sir Thomas Lucy** had both sense in his head and the milk of human kindness in his heart.

Such was the man whom we must imagine ringing out his rustic oath of " cock and pye, sir!" as Shakespeare is brought up to the lower end of the table ; and, at the same time, threatening that " the council shall hear it: **it is a** riot." This speech may be **a** hit, indeed, **at a previous** occurrence, connected with the **right** of pasture on commons —for such a cause had **brought to** grief **thirty-five** inhabitants of Stratford, as **we learn from a paper** in the Rolls

[1] ' King Henry IV., Part II.,' act v. 1.     [2] Ibid., act iii. 2.

Office, giving " the names of them that made the riot upon
Master Thomas Lucy, esquire."[1] But, however the proceedings might be opened, there can be no doubt that Sir
Thomas Lucy was not in the sweetest temper. " You have
beaten my men, killed my deer, and broke open my lodge."
Shakespeare could not deny the indictment. The venison
was there in court : there, too, we may believe, were the
broken heads ; the very lodge could be seen from the window.
Of course, he had something to say for himself. It might be
that he did not actually knock down the keeper till he felt
his grasp on his throat ; and, as for the deer, his worship
was a woodman, and knew how naturally a bolt flew from a
cross-bow when a fat buck was in view. But Sir Thomas
refuses to hear the voice of the charmer, charm he never so
wisely. He meets Shakespeare's appealing looks with a
frown, and scoffs at his gentle speeches. " Tut, a pin ! this
shall be answered."[2] He is a Daniel come to judgment—a
Lord Angelo, who will follow the letter of the law, and not
dilute justice with mercy. Good words—or, as Parson
Evans has it, " good worts " weigh no more with him than
with Falstaff—" good worts, good cabbage ! "[3] He is determined to put down these practices with a high hand, and
Shakespeare is to be made an example. " Sir Hugh,
persuade me not: I will make a Star-Chamber matter
of it."[4]

Shakespeare was committed to prison—probably to the
county gaol at Warwick ; but on this point tradition is silent.
He was confined in a cell by himself, if we may trust the
sonnet :—

> ' I all alone beweep my outcast state."[5]

---

[1] Published by Mr. Halliwell.
[2] ' Merry Wives of Windsor,' act i. 1.
[3] Ibid.     [4] Ibid.        [5] Sonnet xxxix.

His unspeakable misery welled up in tears. This was not the emotion of a milksop, but the agony of a manly heart, and indicated that sensibility which is an unfailing characteristic of genius. His tears flowed from the same fount as those of Burns, when Walter Scott saw him weep over the picture **of a** wounded soldier, and as those which were observed stealing down the check of Byron as **he listened to a** plaintive piece of music. They were the tears of sorrow, indeed—of repentance ; but they were also **the** tears of sympathy. He was thinking of others—this poor, erring prodigal ; and of the shame and grief he had brought upon them. His eye—his mind's eye—turned from the dark, narrow cell to his once happy home, and to the cottage garden at Shottery, bringing up before him the bent form of his mother and the saddened face of his mistress. But sympathy, as he tells us, is like mercy : it is twice blessed, blessing as well those that give as those to whom it is given ; and it brought him comfort in the ties it recalled, and the images it conjured up. Anne Hathaway would not sever herself from him. In his misery and abasement, her faith in him **was unshaken** ; and she found **means** to apprise him of her constancy. These are the revelations we educe from the Sonnet, which evidently applies **to this** passage of his life :—

> " When in disgrace with fortune **and men's eyes,**
> I all alone beweep my outcast state ;
> And trouble deaf Heaven with my bootless cries,
> And look upon myself and curse my fate,
> Wishing me like to one more rich in hope,
> Featured like him, like him with friends possessed,
> Desiring this man's art, and that man's scope,
> **With what** I most enjoy, **contented least ;**
> Yet, in these thoughts **myself almost despising,**
> Haply **I** think on thee."

In his despondency he cries out, like **Job, against** his **own life.** He weeps over his disgrace and isolation ; he

arraigns Heaven; he curses his fate; he would be anyone
but himself: **and then comes a change:—**

> " Haply I think on thee; and then my state—
> Like to the lark, at break of day arising
> From sullen earth—sings hymns at heaven's gate;
> For thy sweet love remembered such wealth brings,
> That then I scorn to change my state with kings."

Heaven is no longer unjust; the vaulted roof of his cell
becomes the vaulted sky; he bursts forth in hymns of
thankfulness and praise; and thrones seem as nothing to the
place he occupies in his mistress's heart.

Nor was he forgotten in his captivity. The note by
Ward in the manuscript pedigree of the Lucys, informs us
that his friends interested in his behalf the most important
man in Warwickshire, no less a person than Robert, Earl of
Leicester; and this great magnate now interceded with Sir
Thomas Lucy, and prevailed on him to abandon the prosecution. We know not how this powerful friend was
secured. It could not be through the Ardens; for the
wealthy branch of that family must have been on bad terms
with the earl, as Dugdale asserts that Edward Arden, who
was executed in Smithfield for treason in 1583, was condemned to death at Leicester's suggestion. We are left to
suppose that John Shakespeare may have been brought in
communication with the earl in his municipal character,
probably when he was High Bailiff of Stratford;—for he is
then found patronizing his players; and the connection
which we shall show to have long existed with Leicester
may have sprung from that time. At any rate, the earl
stepped between Shakespeare and ruin. And strange it is
that an act so honourable to him should be now first mentioned, after his character has undergone three centuries of
criticism, no one ever suspecting that he was any way associated with our great poet, much less that he was his earliest

benefactor.   The service was afterwards to be requited. Here Leicester steps forward to rescue Shakespeare from Sir Thomas Lucy: by-and-by **we** shall see Shakespeare tilting at Sir Thomas Lucy in the quarrel of Leicester. But now the prison-door is open, the penitent scapegrace steps **forth free**; and as kindly faces and loving hands gather **round him, we** almost hear him exclaim,—"In **War-wickshire** I have true-hearted friends."[1]

[1] 'King Henry VI., Part III.,' act iv. 8.

## XIV.

### REVENGE AND FLIGHT.

SHAKESPEARE was once more in the streets of Stratford, but found that he was not in the same fair odour. In such a community his misadventure left a mark upon him, almost as deep as Cain's; and, indeed, those watching his course might well think that he was in no good way. Such expressions of opinion possibly reached his ear as he passed along; and he may have seen some avert their heads, and some shake them. Whatever his disposition, he could now have no companions but such as were under a cloud, like himself; for as it would be thought that all seen in his company were tarred with the same brush, everybody whose character was untarnished gave him a wide berth. There can be no doubt that he bitterly felt his position, which, in the Sonnet we have just quoted, he calls "my outcast state." We may fear that he was met by cold looks wherever he went. The fallen condition of his family, the increasing difficulties of his parents, and his own wild courses, had been enough to alienate friends before, but they were now kept aloof by his disgrace. Even the cottage-door at Shottery was shut against him; for we shall presently show that there was a breach between Anne Hathaway and her father, and this is explained by her persistence at this time in her attachment to Shakespeare.

Whatever happened, Shakespeare looked upon Sir Thomas Lucy as the author of all his misery. It was by

him that he had been committed to prison, by which he had
been brought into such odium; and the abandonment of
the prosecution did not, exasperated as he was, atone to
him for previous severity. In truth, he was enduring the
punishment still—feeling it in the look of every familiar
face, and the altered tone of every friendly voice. He
carried his prison about with him—in his own shame and
the public report, which made it as plain to the eye as a
convict's chain. But, as he felt the extent of his abasement,
his breast swelled against the oppressor, and the crushing
heel, which provokes the worm, stirred up the little venom
of gentle Will Shakespeare. Sir Thomas Lucy was to
learn that this worm could sting.

The poet determined on revenge, a revenge worthy of a
poet, had he not made his resentment his inspiration. But
he was now in the eddy of his passion, swept round and
round by it,—by his wounded love, his sullied honour, and
the thousand agonies of a humbled spirit. The landless
French troubadour made Henry Beauclere wince on his
throne under his satirical rhymes; and Shakespeare felt
that he possessed the same power over Sir Thomas Lucy.
Stripling though he was, he would go forth against this giant,
sheathed in the panoply of authority, and whose staff of the
law was like a weaver's beam, and strike him down with a
ballad. It was a brave resolve, and not more brave than
memorable; for but for the incidents that quickly followed,
Shakespeare might have remained a rustic, and the world
never have heard of its greatest poet. He was not led on
by Revenge as he thought, but by Destiny.

The note by Ward agrees with Rowe as to the course
he pursued. The ballad was nailed on the park-gates at
Charlecote,—on the very gatehouse in which he had been
confined, and from which he had broken forth. No one has
done justice to the spirit of this exploit—for not only was it

poetic in its conception, but it presents something heroic,—
for heroic it was in this poor country lad, a butcher's apprentice, daring to come to the manorial hall, and nail his
defiance on the very door, a door that had so lately closed
on him, a prisoner. The deed belongs as much to chivalry
as the ballad to literature ; and the past could give us no
welcomer relic than those boyish rhymes. We may rejoice
that they are not wholly lost. After a long interval, chance
recovered two stanzas, which have floated down to us like
a fragment of a wrecked ship—fortunately that part of the
vessel which shows whence it came. The verses are indeed
regarded with suspicion, as being unworthy of his genius,
but, though their literary merit is small, they reveal the
Shakesperian touch, such as those who have studied his
works cannot mistake. This touch he describes himself, when
he says :—

> " That almost every word doth tell my name." [1]

As the production of a lad of eighteen, they are not to
be measured by the standard of later compositions, although
they display sufficient familiarity with versification to dis-
prove the conjecture of Rowe that this was " probably the
first essay of his poetry "—a probability which few will
admit, since it would hardly have occurred to Shakespeare to
seek vengeance by such means without previous experience
of his strength.

From the fragment preserved, the ballad appears to
have been a defence of himself, as well as an attack on Sir
Thomas, reciting the case, and, perhaps, concluding with
the two surviving stanzas :—

> " Sir Thomas was too covetous,
>     To covet so much deer,
> When horns enough upon his head
>     Most plainly do appear.

---

[1] Sonnet lxxvi.

> Had not his worship one deer left?
>   What then?   He had a wife
> Took pains enough to find him horns,
>   Should last him during life."[1]

The imputation conveyed is alone a presumptive proof of the authenticity of this fragment; for Sir Thomas Lucy has inscribed on his wife's tomb so emphatic a testimony to her conjugal fidelity, that it could only be designed to refute a prevailing scandal.  The inscription takes the form of a solemn declaration, to which the witness appends his signature, converting the slab into a marble certificate. Beneath lies the effigy of the lady, preserving in her face the serene look of innocence, with the round lines of matronly beauty.  She rests in apparent peace under the inscription as if it absolved her before the world, and in perfect reliance that her worth will be acknowledged by all who read these loving words :—

"Here entombed lieth the Lady Joyce Lucy, wife of Sir Thomas Lucy, of Charlecote, in the county of Warwick, knight, daughter and heir of Thomas Acton, of Sutton, in the county of Worcester, esquire; who departed out of this wretched world to her heavenly kingdom the 10th day of February, in the year of our Lord 1595 ; and of her age 60 and 3; all the time of her life a true and faithful servant of her good God ; never detected of any crime or vice ; in religion most sound; in her love to her husband most faithful and true ; in friendship most constant; to what in trust was committed to her most secret; in wisdom excelling; in governing her house and bringing up of youth in the fear of God that did converse with

---

[1] The manner in which this fragment was recovered is not different from that to which we owe so many local ballads, known only to the common people.  About 1690, Joshua Barnes, the Greek professor at Cambridge, was at an inn at Stratford, when he heard an old woman singing these stanzas, and, discerning the association with Shakespeare, offered her ten guineas to repeat the whole ballad.  This, however, she was unable to do, having forgotten the remaining portion.  A version of the ballad was afterwards promulgated by a man named Jordan; but it is a manifest fabrication.  The stanza purporting to be taken from the MS. notes of Oldys is equally spurious.

her, most rare and singular; a great maintainer of hospitality; greatly
esteemed of her betters; misliked of none unless of the envious. When all
is spoken that can be said, a woman so furnished and garnished with virtue
as not to be bettered, and hardly to be equalled by any. **So she lived**
most virtuously, so she died most godly. Set down by him that best did
know what hath been written to be true,

" Thomas Lucy."[1]

Perhaps the inscription had been read by Shakespeare,
and he may have had before his eye that fair chiselled
figure when he pictured Lucretia—

" Where like a virtuous monument she lies."[2]

Who, indeed, would scrutinize the touching eulogy for the
secrets of the crumbled breast beneath, even were its subject
not a woman! There is a fervour in the words of the bereaved husband that claims our sympathy, while it commands
our faith. Such encomiums could not be wholly unmerited,
and they go as far to raise the character of Sir Thomas
Lucy himself as to clear that of his wife. And yet, if we
give them a moment's thought; if we take not only their
plain meaning, but their interpretation, we contract an
impression that they do protest too much. Of what need to
declare that she was " never detected of any crime or vice,"
if none were laid to her charge? Why insist so strongly
that she was " in her love to her husband most faithful and
true?" And wherefore those significant words —" misliked
of none, *unless of the envious.*"

The common rumour against her, if such existed, could
not have escaped Shakespeare; and in his exasperation he
may, with the thoughtless malice of youth, have too hastily
adopted it. Lady Lucy may even herself have provoked his

---

[1] Some years ago, the old church of Charlecote, having fallen into decay,
was pulled down, and a new and beautiful fabric erected on the same site
at the expense of Mrs. Lucy, who has preserved the ancient monuments
with religious care.

[2] ' The Rape of Lucrece.'

resentment. It is not improbable that she took part in the proceedings against him, for the strong language of the epitaph as to her " governing her house " raises a suspicion that her governing cares extended to her husband, particularly as he expresses an exalted opinion of her " wisdom." She certainly accompanied him occasionally in his magisterial visits to **Stratford**; for **though it is** not recorded that she sat with him **"in commission for** tipplers," we know **that** she **once sat with him** tippling, the chamberlain having recorded **the payment of four** shillings for sack and claret wine, " for **Sir** Thomas Lucy and **My Lady** and Mr. Sheriff, **at** the Swan." This was all in accordance with prevailing usages; but as there was no impropriety in appearing publicly with the justices at the Swan at Stratford, Lady Lucy might be at his worship's side when the Swan himself stood in her own hall at Charlecote. The reflection on Lady Lucy may have inspired Shallow's complaint against Falstaff:— " He hath wronged me, Master Page," a complaint **which is** bitterly reiterated :—" indeed he hath ; at a word, he hath : believe me, Robert Shallow, esquire, says he is wronged." And **some reparation is** evidently intended when Page replies,—" Sir, he doth *in some sort* confess it." [1] Lady Lucy, if she indeed busied herself in the deer-stealing affair, was **now forgiven**; and it is honourable **to Shakespeare that** he did **not** introduce her in the family group **on** the stage.

The ballad was discovered before it had been long exposed on the park-gate, and enraged Sir Thomas Lucy to such a degree, that he made its author feel very uncomfortable in Stratford. According **to** Capell, he directed **a** lawyer **at Warwick** to commence a prosecution against **him, but the Lucy note simply** mentions that Shakespeare judged it prudent to quit Stratford, **"at least for a time."** He had very likely **been** disposed **to** this step before by the bad

---

[1] 'Merry Wives of Windsor,' act i. 1.

odour in which he found himself, and did not affix the ballad
to the gate till he had fully decided on flight, for he must
have been aware that such an act would render it necessary.
Though strongly attached to Stratford, he could not be sorry
to absent himself temporarily from a place in which his
family were in eclipse and his own character was lost, while,
at the same time, his departure would release him from a
calling which he must now have begun to loathe.   Dowdall
was told by the parish-clerk that he " ran from his master to
London."   Prince Henry found that Francis, the apprentice
at the Boar's Head, was not unwilling to take a similar
liberty:—" But, Francis, darest thou be so valiant as to
play the coward with thy indenture, and show it a fair pair
of heels, and *run for it?*"   "Oh Lord, sir! I'll be sworn
upon all the books in England I could find in my heart." [1]

We must suppose that Shakespeare's intention was con-
fided to at least two persons—his mother and Anne Hathaway.   A wide-spread tradition reports that he went through
the ceremony of betrothal with Anne, and no fact of his life
is more worthy of credit.   The ceremony, it is true, was not
now a religious one, but it was deeply rooted as a popular
custom, and survived the changes effected by the Reformation.   Shakespeare was the very embodiment of those
old usages.   Whatever customs prevailed amongst the
people had for him the authority of a religion, and he became their chronicler and exponent.   His plays present us
with no less than four betrothals, each of a different
character, besides introducing nearly all his lovers as betrothed.   It is he alone who has informed us that a practice
existed amongst lovers of privately plighting their troth,
when circumstances enforced a temporary separation; and
the scene between Proteus and Julia [2] may embalm a re-

---

[1] ' King Henry IV., Part II.,' act ii. 4.
[2] ' Two Gentlemen of Verona,' act ii. 2.

membrance of his own betrothal. The venison taken from
Charlecote had, says tradition, been designed for the
marriage feast. The marriage was indefinitely postponed,
and he could only avoid utter ruin by flight. In such a
situation he naturally conformed to the popular usage, and,
before parting, exchanged his troth with Anne Hathaway.

**All** the tortures of Julia must have pierced Anne's breast
**at** the thought of their separation. She would surely reflect
**that** nothing could be so subversive of her ascendancy as absence, or more adverse to their attachment, since every day
must detract from her beauty, while it developed and augmented his; and the pang was sharper from coming at the
moment when they had proposed to be united for ever; when
she was prepared to share his evil report and hard portion,
and for his sake even to fly in his father's face and her own.
It was now that he was carried far beyond her influence, and
exposed, in the flower of his youth, to the blandishments of
other and younger maidens. Her faith in him was strong,
but the timid heart of woman leads her ever to doubt her
power, particularly in absence; and such misgivings must
**too often have risen in that gentle** bosom at Shottery.

**Tears were shed when she placed the ring on** Shakespeare's finger :—

> " Keep this remembrance for thy Julia's sake."

But they flowed more softly at his words :—

> " Why, then, we'll make exchange : here, take you this." [1]

They **" seal** the bargain with a holy kiss," and clasp hands
for "true constancy," when the simple ceremony is complete.

And now they must part—perhaps at the garden-gate—
perhaps at the "brawling **brook**," **with the** soft twinkling
stars beaming **down upon** them, **and shining as** brightly as if

[1] 'Two Gentlemen of Verona,' act ii. 2.

they never looked upon the sorrow and anguish and guilt of this unquiet world.

Let us imagine Shakespeare stopping at the corner of the village-road, ere he turned into the footway across the fields, to cast a glance back. The familiar gable-roofed cottage peered through the darkness, and he saw Anne, too, though she might not be substantially present, in all her beauty and all her truth, with his "mind's eye :"—

> " Here is her hand, the agent of her heart ;
> Here is her oath for love, her honour's pawn ;
> Oh, *that our fathers would applaud our loves*,
> To seal our happiness with their consents!"[1]

Whether he quitted Stratford by night or day, tradition does not report. Perhaps he stole from his loft, like Whittington, in the early morning, while it was still dark, and the whole town was locked in sleep. As he issues from his master's house, and softly closes the door, a hasty glance at the sky may show him that " Charles' wain is over the new chimney."[2] He has no time to lose, yet possibly he found a moment to take a farewell look at his father's house, and throw a pebble at his mother's window, ere, with heavy heart and quickened steps, he made his way through the broad market-place to Clopton's bridge. One look at the flowing river ; one fond glance behind, where the town lies in a shadowy but familiar mass, like his past life ; and he turns his face forward, where lies the unknown future. But, whatever his regrets, or whatever his misgivings, he must now go on. He has crossed the Avon!

[1] ' Two Gentlemen of Verona,' act i. 3.
[2] ' King Henry IV., Part II.,' act ii. 1.

# XV.

## ON THE TRAMP.

Those poor despised lads of bygone time—those *wight-errants*, who, without either lance or shield, gold or friends, set out on their adventures—our Dick Whittington and Will Shakespeare, claim from us an interest which we do not give to King Arthur and his Round Table. We tread that lumbering, crumbling old bridge over the Avon with a feeling of veneration, as we reflect that it was there Shakespeare took leave of his native town, and passed on into the wide world. He passed on,—with his gentle, open heart, his breast flowing with the milk of human kindness, his soul heaving with generous aspirations, — and "no man cried God save him."[1] In silence and darkness he went on his way, leaving home and kindred and friends behind.

Aubrey tells us that he was now eighteen; and his report is confirmed by Dowdall, who says he broke his indentures to run away. Tradition, as we have seen, asserts that the venison was taken when he was unmarried; and it is undeniable that he left Stratford within a few days of that adventure : consequently, before his nineteenth year. Thus the two oldest authorities agree with tradition in the date ; and against this joint testimony later writers adduce nothing but conjecture, with which they would fain persuade us that Shakespeare did not leave Stratford till he was twenty-three.

The raid on Charlecote Park was a mere lapse in the

---

[1] 'King Richard II.,' act v. 2.

lad of eighteen : in the man of three-and-twenty, a husband and parent, it would be a crime. It is beside the question to say that Shakespeare was in Stratford at a later date ; for the Lucy note intimates that he only absented himself "*for a time ;*" and Aubrey, though he makes him depart at eighteen, informs us that he always visited Stratford once a year, so that his subsequent presence there affords no argument. Rowe, who is followed by all later biographers, is not an authority on the point, as he came after Aubrey and Dowdall, and his information—some of which has been proved incorrect—was not obtained by personal inquiry.

The flight of the poet was certainly accomplished on foot. The ordinary mode of travelling was on horseback, in company with the carrier, whose horses were employed for the conveyance of passengers, as well as goods, just as mules are still used in Spain. We learn from the carrier, in the ' First Part of King Henry IV.,'[1] that marketings and packages were transported in panniers :—" I have a gammon of bacon and two cases of ginger to be delivered as far as Charing Cross." His mate apprises us that live stock were conveyed in the same manner. " Odsbody ! the turkeys in my pannier are quite starved."[2] The roads of those days were not made for carts ; and even the carriages of the gentry could only be dragged slowly along by six horses, which did not prevent them from sticking in the mud, or often altogether breaking down. Indeed, the roads were spoken of as mere horseways, as when Edgar declares that he knows the whole route to Dover,—" both stile and gate, *horseway* and footpath."[3]

Shakespeare shows a familiar acquaintance with the uses of carriers, as of every other mystery :—" I prithee, Tom, beat Cut's saddle : put a few flocks in the point ; the poor jade is wrung in the withers out of all rest."[4] But he did

---

[1] ' King Henry IV., Part III.,' act ii. 1.    [3] ' King Lear,' act iv. 1.
[2] Ibid.    [4] ' King Henry IV., Part I.,' act ii. 1.

not travel in their company on this occasion; for besides that the few pence in his pocket would not meet such a charge, there were special reasons why he should keep out of their way, inasmuch as they were noted as carriers of tales as well as of bacon and turkeys, and he had now a particular objection to giving a clue to his address. We may be fully **satisfied** that as he was so valiant as to play the **coward with** his indenture, he showed it " a fair pair of heels and run for it." He " *run from his master to London.*"

" Methinks I scent the morning air." It came sweet and fresh from the hedges and fields, as he trudged along the London road, now picking his way through a brook, now floundering in ruts deep as his knee. From the ridge of the Red Horse he could sweep his eye over the old loved valley behind—over the winding Avon, the tapering spire of Stratford, and far on to soaring Ingon and old Snitterfield bush. But it was too near home to linger, and during the early part of his journey he was not likely to let the grass grow under his feet. It is not to be imagined that his second day's stage fell short of **Oxford, which is a** bare forty miles from Stratford, **no great feat for a sturdy lad. But night must have fallen ere he entered the classic city, to him** so venerable, **and,** indeed as the seat of the Muses, almost **holy. What a** commentary on human institutions, that the king of poets first entered it as a vagrant, and, perhaps, found no bed but the step of a college gateway! Not that either man or beast would find any lack of accommodation in the roomy inns; for old Harrison avers that "every comer is sure to be in clean sheets, wherein no man hath lodged since they came from the laundress, or out of the water wherein they were last washed. If the traveller have a horse, his bed doth **cost** him nothing; but if **he go on foot, he is sure to pay a penny** for **the** same." [1] If he **was sure to pay no more,** inns have

<hr>

[1] ' Description of England.'

degenerated in their charges **as well as** their **sheets ;** and
Oxonians of the present day, with their Scriptural predilections, may sigh for the age which asked from the **traveller no**
more than the twopence paid by the Good Samaritan, whose
payment to the host was thus a fair remuneration at the **time**
of the translation of the Bible.

Possibly, Shakespeare now made his first acquaintance
with the " Crown tavern," to which he was afterwards wont
to come on horseback, an honoured guest ; but if he preferred to save his penny, a hale young fellow would find no
bad chamber in the porch of **St.** Mary's church, where our
Lady kept watch, from her niche above, over his slumbers.
**Shakespeare might " sit here on the church bench till two,"**[1]
and then resume his way, **fearing to wait for dawn. It may
have been on this occasion that he met with the constable** at
Grendon, **where he might arrive at the close of** the fourth
day. Aubrey, indeed, says :—" I think it was Midsummer
night that he happened to lie there," associating the immortal Dogberry with 'Midsummer Night's Dream,' instead of ' Much Ado about Nothing.' But we shall make
it appear that Shakespeare was on his way to London in
April, and this, in fact, quite agrees with the statement of
Aubrey himself, who says that he started when he was
" about eighteen," and he would then be just that age, his
**birthday occurring on the 23rd.**

**When Aubrey was at Oxford in 1642, Dogberry was still
living ; and it is mentioned that he was personally known to**
his friend **Joseph Howe, who came from** the same parish.
Shakespeare was more **likely** to have made his acquaintance
on this journey, when he was a fugitive, than at any other
time, for it was one of Dogberry's functions to " comprehend
all vagrom men,"[2] and, indeed, he makes it the whole duty
of the watch, a fact rather significant. Travellers in those

---

[1] ' Much Ado about Nothing,' act iii. 1.    [2] Ibid., act iii. 3.

days were obliged to give an account of themselves, and lodgers for the night were nowhere admitted without permission of the authorities, particularly of the constable.[1] In the present case appearances were suspicious: a jaded lad arrived at nightfall in a secluded village on his way to London, and to persons dreaming of runaway apprentices and "vagrom men," must have looked very like a whale. Dogberry naturally charged him in the prince's name, Stand! It does not follow that he took him to the gaol to "examination" him, as he did Borachio and Conrade. Shakespeare was a muscular fellow, having the air of one who could stand a battle with constables, as he had stood one with gamekeepers, and not come off the worst. Dogberry, on the other hand, was merciful :—" You have always been called a merciful man, partner," and, by his own account, he was prudent :—" How if a' will not stand ?" " Why, then take no note of him, but let him go."[2] He would appear to have acted on this principle with Shakespeare, though not before he was writ down ass.

Harrison computes the distance from Oxford to London at forty-eight miles, which is rather less than the present measurement; and, from entries in the accounts of the Stratford chamberlains, the journey from Stratford would seem to have occupied six days when performed on foot. One Thomas Vigers receives twelve shillings for "six days' journey to London, to make oath against Mr. Underhill and his man." This hard swearer, who was considered a match for both Mr. Underhill and his Friday, was quite as vigorous a pedestrian, for he must have covered his fifteen miles a day. We must believe that an active young fellow

---

[1] An order of the town council of Stratford decreed that "no inhabitant dwelling within this liberty from henceforth receive nor have any inmate, but only such persons as shall be appointed by the High Bailiff, CONSTABLE, and other officers, &c."

[2] 'Much Ado about Nothing,' act iii. 3.

like Shakespeare, with good reasons for haste, would not proceed less rapidly ; in which case the sixth morning after his departure from his native town found him on Hillingdon Heath,[1] looking forward to the end of his journey.

Here the poet may have thrown himself down on a patch of soft turf, and, as he stretched his tired limbs, cast his eye round on a prospect not wanting in interest. In the distance he saw the stately castle of Windsor, which was to receive a new halo from his muse, and which even now called up in his mind a host of associations. The level surface was everywhere relieved by wood ; and around him spread a sea of furze, its green expanse crested with gold. On his flank rose the verdant hill of Harrow, with its royal school and taper spire, thus confronting the birthplace of Henry of Windsor, whose sad story this poor wandering lad was to tell to all ages, with his noblest monument. We are pleased that Shakespeare's glance lingered on a spot which has been consecrated by Byron. In social and poetic rank, as in order of time, they were indeed widely sundered, but intellect makes them fellows ; and as we think of the plebeian youth of old toiling along the road in search of bread, and the modern lordly idler gazing musingly down from the haunted tomb in the churchyard, the gulf that divides them seems bridged, and all distinctions merge in the kindred nobility of genius.

But Hillingdon Heath, though unexceptionable in its associations, bore, as is sometimes the case amongst nobly-connected men, a very indifferent character, and Shakespeare may have heard sufficient of its ill fame to look up with curiosity if he suddenly caught the sound of horse's hoofs. followed by the appearance of a gallant-looking rider. Of course the "horseman" would sport a plumed steeple-hat

---

[1] The old road from Oxford, according to Harrison, came round through Uxbridge.

and a high ruff, and his sturdy legs would show the fashionable frilled boots, heeled with gilt spurs. There would be altogether a finish about him that might alarm a lad with a purse in his pocket, but not being burdened with that commodity Shakespeare could behold him unmoved, perhaps with **an** instinctive perception that he belonged to the **respectable class** which Gadshill designates as **Trojans:** —" **No** foot land-rakers, no long-staff sixpenny strikers, none **of** these mad, moustachio purple-hued malt-worms;"[1] but unmistakably one of "St. Nicholas's clerks." It was on such **a spot** that, only a few years later, the bold Ratsey overtook some strolling players, and relieved them of two pounds he had given as largess an hour or two before, when they amused him with their performance at an alehouse. But he consoled the chief of the strollers with a compliment which made ample amends, for he compared him with Shakespeare's friend Burbage, the Roscius of the age. **"Get thee to London,"** he is reported to have said, " for if one man were dead, they will have much need of such as **thou art.** There would **be none, in my opinion, fitter than** thyself **to** play his **parts. My conceit is such of thee, that I durst all the money in my purse to play Hamlet with him for a wager."**[2]

Ere the day closed Shakespeare reached the spot where **poor** Ratsey was to come to grief, a spot where many a crime was expiated, but where, in the name of justice, many more terrible were perpetrated. No one would have looked for such an Aceldama in a scene so peaceful. Trim hedges and green fields here stretched away to Primrose Hill and Highgate, and smiling lanes turned off from the high road, winding along **by copse** and wood, or disappearing in their shades. Just before him flowed **a pleasant brook, which,**

---

[1] 'King Henry IV., Part II.,' act ii. 1.

[2] ' Ratsey's Ghost; or, The Second Part of his Mad Pranks and Robberies,' quoted by Mr. Collier, in his ' English Dramatic Poetry.'

rising at Hampstead, poured its unrippled tide through the
fields into St. James's Park, and thence **into the** Thames at
**Chelsea. This was the too famous Tyburn, or Tie Bourne,**
and near it **stood the gallows or Tyburn-tree,** called the
Deadly Never-Green, rising from three **legs, in the form**
of a triangle. Gentle **Shakespeare must have** looked with
a shudder on the hideous object, for **his mention of it does**
not more vividly figure its construction than the impression
on himself.

> " Thou makest the *triumviry* the corner cap **of society,**
> The *shape* of Love's Tyburn that hangs up simplicity." [1]

**Tyburn-tree was indeed in those days the corner cap of
society, as often hanging up simplicity as villany, and well
points a rebuke from** the greatest **of Reformers.**

[1] **' Love's Labour** 's Lost,' act iv. 3.

## XVI.

### HIS FIRST VIEW OF LONDON.

IMAGINATION loves to colour a poet's life with hues akin to his art, but the reality is often common place. Its poetic aspect is in himself—in his feelings, aspirations, and sympathies, and these strike no eye but his own. The crushed affection, the poignant sorrow, the hope deferred or blighted, those workings of the human breast, have an outward and visible sign, which partakes of their nature—is often touching or majestic; but the impulse which gives them existence, comes in the shape of an ordinary event. Calamity is not foreshadowed by portents, nor do omens prefigure success; and we may remember that William of Normandy stumbled into a kingdom, while the sun of Austerlitz looked not more brightly on victory than on defeat. There is no royal groove for the lives of eminent men. Everything happens to them as to others, the former rain and the latter in their season, and we no longer expect that a comet will flash in the sky when they appear on the stage of their future greatness, or that an eagle will light on their shoulder. All that they have special is innate: the Genius of Socrates walked by his side, but was visible only to himself.

Yet no one will conceive that Shakespeare entered London under an inauspicious sky. We associate such an event with a summer evening, when the sun was sinking in glory behind our old abbey, and roseate clouds gave promise of a bright morrow. No doubt he peeped over the fence which then enclosed **Hyde Park, and** saw "a careless herd" couched on the turf, or breaking through **a thicket,** recalling the cause of his troubles. Deer had **been kept** there from the reign of Edward VI., when the French ambassadors hunted in Hyde Park with the king. But Shakepeare's eye would now be attracted by newer objects, and after resting a moment on the dark pile of the abbey, sweep over a hundred spires to the soaring tower of St. Paul's. He might hesitate a moment, whether to pursue his way down the green lane of Tyburn, now Park Lane, or follow **the broader Tyburn** Road, now forming Oxford Street; **but the latter was too direct not to be preferred. It brought him to the little, straggling village of St. Giles-in-the-Fields, where he cast a look at the church, and what remained of the old hospital, of which it had been part—now only remembered by its donation of a bowl of ale to** the condemned on their way to **execution.**

Hence the road was again flanked by fields as far **as** Holborn Bars, the boundary of the city liberty, and a spot associated with Shakespeare; for at the mansion which caught his eye at the side of the road, he was one day to be received by the graceful Southampton as his worthiest guest. He now entered the suburb of Holborn, or Old Bourne, where tall houses on either side, pretty closely packed, yet, here and there, showing a glimpse of garden, foreshadowed the adjacent city. He climbed the steep ascent of Holborn Hill, then called the "heavy hill," but so trod down by the feet of centuries, that it now presents but a gentle rise. From its summit he could overlook the city, catch a peep of the broad river, see the distant Tower and Castle Baynard, distinguish the noble mansions that bordered the Strand, and judge of their magnificence by **one** under his eye, the lordly residence of Sir Christopher

Hatton, surrounded by the large and stately garden which bore his name.

A block of streets shut off Smithfield, which, from being the scene of so many frays, then bore the slang name of Ruffian's Hall; but he paid it a visit at a later period, when he remembered **that** Bardolph went there to buy **Falstaff a horse.**[1] **The** road took a curve up Snow Hill to **St. Sepulchre's** church, then called St. Pulcher's, our ancestors having a Shakespearean reverence for brevity; and the vicinity **of the frowning** walls of Newgate may have reminded him **it was here that** criminals stopped on their way to execution at Tyburn, to hear a prayer and receive a nosegay. From this point he might look down Giltspur Street, at Pie Corner, celebrated for its cooks' stalls, and, during Bartholomew fair, for roasted pigs. Dame Quickly complains of Falstaff that "he comes continually to Pie Corner (saving your manhoods) to buy a saddle."[2]

Passing under the massive arch of Newgate, Shakespeare followed the throng of passengers to Cheapside, called **by** old Howes the " Beauty **of** London;" and though the shops were **now closed, and nothing was to be seen of the** dazzling **stores of Goldsmith's Row, or the rich silks of the mercers, and the ruffs and** frippery of the milliners, the equipages in **the street,** the carts heaped with merchandise, the horsemen, the fops, and the courtiers, " the city woman," with " the cost of princes on her shoulders,"[3]—all this every-day tide of life and traffic, was to him a splendid pageant. He may have stopped here to drink at the conduit, and sat down to rest on its step, watching the passers-by, till, with the deepening twilight, their numbers sensibly diminished.

His way was on, on—he knew not **whither, and we can only** follow him by the footmarks **which his works** give to

<hr>

[1] 'King Henry IV., Part II.,' act ii. 2.
[2] Ibid., act ii. 1.        [3] 'As You Like It,' act ii. 7.

our imagination. **Chance may have taken him to London Bridge,** past the scene of Jack Cade' s **butcheries, which he** has made a note **of:—" Up Fish Street, down St. Magnus** Corner, kill and knock down ! throw them into **Thames !"** [1] A party of roysterers may burst out of the King's Head tavern, a favourite resort of the rakes of the day, and grave citizens draw back as they brush noisily by ; but Shakespeare moves on at the same pace, and, passing through the gate-house, finds himself on the bridge, which might well be garnished with a human head or two, the last harvest of justice. Houses on either side formed a street across the **river,** but with gaps at intervals, affording a peep of the **river, which, however, was but dimly seen through the shadows of** night, rushing **furiously through the narrow, dwarfed, and shaky arches. Lanterns surmounted** the doors of the principal houses, **displaying the regulation candle,** which furnished **old Decker with the quaint title of his book,** ' London by Lanthorn and Candlelight.' But **the light** they afforded was not sufficient to prevent one running **occa**sionally against a sign-post, or stumbling in a hole, though from the drawbridge midway across, the line before and behind had a picturesque effect.

From this spot Shakespeare brings a messenger to Lord **Scales to** announce the success of Jack Cade :—" They have **won the bridge, killing all those that withstand** them." [2] **He might still bear the story in his mind as he entered Southwark. Though our ancestors knew nothing of the splendid lamps which adorn the modern gin-palace, there was a strong display of lanterns** at the White Hart inn, which Hatton **describes** as " the largest sign about London, except the Castle tavern in Fleet Street;" and, though the sign might be veiled by night, the loiterers at its entrance would reveal its name. It was at the White Hart

<hr>

[1] ' King Henry VI., Part II.,' act iv 8.   [2] Ibid., act iv. 5.

that Shakespeare wound up the struggle of the Cadites,
when there was an end of poor Jack:—" Hath my sword,
therefore, broke through London gates, that you should
leave me at the White Hart, in Southwark?"[1]   Hard
by was the Tabard, whence Chaucer took his departure
with the Canterbury pilgrims, and this ancient inn, indeed,
is standing at the present day in much the same condition
**as of yore.**   We first meet Shakespeare in London in the
Borough—some seven years later it is true, but that was
not his actual first appearance on that stage.   Was it at
**one of these famous** hostelries that the poor, travel-worn lad
**now** put up for the night?—at the White Hart?   It is
possible that he might have arrived in London without the
means of obtaining even this temporary shelter.   But if he
had slept on the church bench, or under a haystack, on his
way up to town, the want of a lodging would not seem **a**
great hardship.   He might wander on to St. George's
Fields, where he makes York appoint a rendezvous :—

> " Soldiers ! I thank you all : disperse yourselves,
> Meet me to-morrow in St. George's-field."[2]

Gerard, writing some ten years later, tells us that
he here gathered " water violets," but it was impossible
to proceed far without making the discovery that water
had rather the advantage, both of the violets and the
fields.   St. George's Fields were the Great Dismal Swamp
of merry old England.   One building loomed up at night
through the darkness, which might afford the wanderer a
resting-place : it was a windmill.   " Oh, Sir John, do you
remember when we lay all night in the windmill in St.
George's Fields?"[3]

[1] ' King Henry VI., Part II.,' act iv. 8.
[2] Ibid., act v. 1.        [3] ' King Henry IV., Part II.,' act iii. 2.

# XVII.

## SHAKESPEARE ON THE STREETS.

WHATEVER the expectations floating in his mind, Shakespeare did not find that his fortune was made by merely coming to **London.** Some of his biographers affirm, indeed, that there is no truth in the popular notion of his indigence on his first arrival in the capital, but they cannot ignore a tradition which carries such authority. Let them not think that he loses caste by the descent. It rather, in a moral sense, adds a cubit to his stature. We may even see that a severe ordeal was necessary for the development of his character and genius. Youth's bright hopes and the dreams of a glowing imagination it might, indeed, tame, but it inspired resolution, diligence, and alertness. Energy does not come from illusions. It is drawn out by what is immediately in view—rather the passing moment than the future, and is present most when thought is given only to the hour, from hand to mouth. We shall now see it excited in Shakespeare while he retains all his natural gaiety, the sparkle of youth. This will open to us our first glimpse of the master-quality of his mind and character—his aptitude. It was this that made him the greatest of men. He addressed himself to the circumstances of his position, whatever they might be; and grasped all their bearings. Thus he excelled in whatever he undertook. " When he killed a calf," says Aubrey, " he did it in high style." Here we have the moral of his life. If we reject it—if we repudiate the traditions of his early struggles, and attribute his success to fortune, opportunity, or position, to anything but his own exertions—we deprive ourselves of the noblest lesson **in the gift** of biography. But this we cannot do unless we shut out the facts ; for, **as already** said, they are their own witnesses, **and their tenour is unmistakable.**

**Through** all the vicissitudes of the past and all the poverty **of home,** Shakespeare **had at** least found bread, but it may be feared that he now felt the pinch of want. Certainly he saw it before him as what must be ; and looked it in the face, not shutting his eyes, and sitting helplessly down in the street, to await its approach. Curiously enough, the nephew of his friend Hamlet Sadler ran to the capital from Stratford a few years later in much the same way—probably following his example ; and, as we are told, "having no acquaintance in London to recommend or assist him, he went from street to street, and house to house, asking if they wanted an apprentice, and though he **met** with *many discouraging scorns and a thousand denials,* he went till **he light on Mr. Brookshank, a** grocer *in Bucklers-bury.*"[1]  **This is exactly the mode** of proceeding we should ascribe **to Shakespeare. He also** passed **from** street to **street, and house to** house, offering himself for any service **required ; and** was also met by discouraging scorns and **a** thousand denials, "the spurns that patient merit of the unworthy takes."[2]  Who need care for the proud man's contumely, when it did not spare Shakespeare !

The London of Elizabeth's reign was not the huge Babylon of our time, but, though diminutive in comparison, the poet is lost to **us** in its thronged streets. **We must** again, therefore, take his **plays for our guide-book, if we** would follow **his** steps, **and "satisfy our eyes with the**

[1] **'The** Holy Life **of Mrs.** Elizabeth Walker.'
[2] 'Hamlet,' act iii. 1.

memorials and the things of fame that do renown this city."[1]
Let us begin at Eastcheap, which, though only a vestige
of it remains, even now is haunted by his genius. The
famous "Boar's Head" is mentioned as a tavern as early
as 1537. It was destroyed by the Great Fire; but preserving the halo thrown over it by Shakespeare, the site was
appropriated to a tavern of the same name, which we remember being taken to see in our childhood, before Eastcheap was swallowed up by London Bridge, and then a
stone bas-relief did duty over the door as the identical sign
of the "Boar's Head" of Dame Quickly. Shakespearean
critics have omitted to note that Eastcheap was chiefly occupied by butchers. Stowe says,—"This Eastcheap is now a
flesh-market of butchers, there dwelling on both sides of the
street." Shakespeare's familiarity with the quarter suggests
the possibility of his having one time been engaged here
in his old calling; and it is far from improbable that he,
like his brother-adventurer Sadler, lit on some "Mr.
Brookshank," or Sheepshank, who gave him temporary
employment in Eastcheap on his first arrival in London.
Destitution reconciled him to any work, and an opening
was most easily secured by his actual calling, however
he might be determined to abandon it on the first opportunity.

But in imagination we see him pass on to the Tower,
whose four turrets he discerned from London Bridge, and
longed to survey more closely. It were a lesson to know
the train of thought awakened in his mind as he loitered on
the neighbouring hill, then uninvaded by houses, and appropriated to the scaffold, the frontispiece of that granite
history! The cruel murder of Henry the Sixth, the butchery
of the two princes, the execution of Hastings, all the dark
deeds he was to portray, were surely there, teaching and

[1] 'Twelfth Night,' act iii. 3.

developing, though without giving form. They were not yet conceptions, but impressions,—broken dreams and shadows.

Near Tower Hill stood Aldgate, which, if his course were in that direction, brought him within the city walls, and here he came upon the rich, open shops, displaying in their windows **every variety of** merchandize, and **each distinguished by a** gorgeous sign, a monster **or an angel, a gilded** Bible **or a shield.** Our ancestors were happily unacquainted with **bricks and** mortar, and the **tall** houses were composed of plaster, enframed in curiously-distorted beams, which supported three or four storeys abutting over each other, but indented **with** balustraded recesses, all capped by a tiled gable. Shakespeare did not pass down Lombard Street without looking for the house that once pertained to Goldsmith Shore, remembering that,—

> " Shore's wife hath a pretty foot,
> A cherry lip, a bonny eye, a passing pleasing tongue." [1]

A huge, ungainly sign assuredly stopped him also **at the door** of a great silk shop, the **windows of which parade** the richest fabrics of the **loom, and attract the fair wives of many a goldsmith. Would that on this day he had had the good fortune of Falstaff, who was " invited to dinner to the Lubber's Head, in Lumbert** Street, to Master Smooth's, the silkman." [2] **But** we may believe that his notions about dinner were now very humble, and that he looked round for an opportunity of earning the price of a sheep's head, instead of dining Smoothly at a lubber's. Thus he might come to the Stocks Market, another resort of butchers, now the site of the Mansion House, and stroll on till he found himself at Moorgate, looking so downcast that Prince Henry **would pronounce** him as " melancholy as **Moorditch." [3]** That gloomy

<hr>

[1] ' King Richard III.,' act i. 1.
[2] ' King Henry IV., Part II.,' act ii. 1.
[3] ' King Henry IV., Part I.'

outwork stretched along beside the city wall, receiving the drainage of Moor Fields, a region now absorbed by the borough of Finsbury, but which then brought the fresh open country to the citizen's door. The green turf was sprinkled with the labours of the city laundresses, who, however, were not so busy as to deny a glance to the adjacent parade of the train bands—the Volunteer Rifles of that day—making Shakespeare inquire, " Is this Moor-fields to muster in ?"[1] Within the wall, he is led round to Aldersgate Street, and soon involved in a labyrinth of narrow, crooked lanes, where the tumble-down houses accord very strikingly with the evil aspect of the population. He has indeed entered the lowest depth of the metropolis—Pistol's " manor of Pickthatch," as it is called by Falstaff,[2] and from which he presents terrrible gleanings in ' Measure for Measure' and ' Pericles.' Almost every door displays Boult's sign of " the sun,"[3] which Prince Henry links with the robe of " flame-coloured taffeta," as " the blessed sun himself."[4] Decker affirms that the entries stood " night and day wide open, with a pair of harlots in taffata gowns, like two painted posts, garnishing out those doors."[5] Along the street tramped the " swash-buckler," the " bully-rook," the " pick-purse," and the " costermonger," and none passed unnoticed by Shakespeare.

The rookery spread into Turnmill Street, called Turnbull by Falstaff, who, speaking of Shallow, says,—" This same starved Justice hath done nothing but prate to me of the wildness of his youth, and the feats he hath done about Turnbull Street."[6] A brook which, from having formerly turned several mills, gave name to the street, ran alongside,

<hr>

[1] ' King Henry VIII.,' act v. 3.
[2] ' Merry Wives of Windsor,' act ii. 2.
[3] ' Pericles,' act iv. 3.
[4] ' King Henry IV., Part I.,' act i. 2.
[5] ' Villanies Discovered ; or, The Belman's Night Walks.'
[6] ' King Henry IV., Part II.,' act iii. 2.

carrying down an unsavoury contribution to the Old Bourn, with which it poured into a swift little stream, called the Fleet. This was navigable for boats and barges, from the Thames at Blackfriars to Holborn, and formed the approach to the Fleet prison, which then had a water entrance, **like** Traitor's Gate at the Tower. It was to the Fleet that the **stern Chief** Justice committed Falstaff:—"Go, carry Sir **John Falstaff to** the Fleet: take all his company along with **him.**" [1]

Shakespeare has left no note of Fleet Street, nor even of the maypole in the Strand, but the latter region obtains honourable mention for its apprentices, whom the cry of clubs brought so promptly to the rescue of the haberdasher's wife :—"I might see from far some forty truncheons drawn to her succour, which were the hope of the Strand, where she was quartered." [2] From amidst the shops rose the unfinished range of Somerset House, the hospital of the Savoy, and the proud mansions of the nobility, including the residence of the great minister, Burleigh. By this chain of buildings, the village of Charing was now almost united with **London,** continuing the way to the house of the **great** cardinal, of which our poet has given the history in so few words—

> "Sir,
> You must no more call it York-place; that is past;
> For since the cardinal fell, that title's lost;
> 'Tis now the king's, and called Whitehall." [3]

The road passed under a gate-house through the midst of the palace, running out from a similar structure at the other end, near the present Cannon Row, where the **eye** caught sight of **the historic Abbey and** Hall, the Parliament

---

[1] 'King Henry IV., Part II.,' act v. 5.
[2] 'King Henry VIII,' act v. 3.
[3] Ibid., act iv. 1.

House, and Palace Yard, all of which are associated with Shakespeare. Palace **Yard was used as a place of punishment, and,** perhaps, he now saw one or **two framed heads** "in a pillory, looking through," in a plight more deplorable than Hortensio's, and receiving the sympathy of a jeering crowd in a shower of rotten eggs.

The favourite highway of Elizabethan London was the river, which, like the canals of Venice, was continually traversed by boats and barges, besides being crossed by ferries which opened up the whole capital. Only poetic **licence can fix when** Shakespeare was first pulled over the **broad, clear stream, but though** we cannot trace him on **its breast, we meet him on its banks, in the scenes he has represented at Castle Baynard and in the Temple Garden.** By the last, he has made **the Lycæum of the law one of** the sanctuaries of our **history, and the Thames as classic** as the Ilissus; for the great champions of **York and Lancaster here pluck their thorny flowers, the emblems of their** respective factions. The Temple Garden no longer bears roses, but, as we look around, we can imagine a time when it produced both white and red, worthy to be the device of rival princes. Then there was meaning in Plantagenet's challenge :—

> " Let him that is a true-born gentleman,
>     And stands upon the honour of his birth,
>     If he suppose that I have pleaded truth,
>     From off this brier pluck a white rose with me."

And Somerset could fairly answer :—

> " Let him that is no coward, nor no flatterer,
>     But dare maintain the party of the truth,
>     Pluck a red rose from off this thorn with me."[2]

In Shakespeare's day, the garden was appropriated to the

---

[1] 'Taming of the Shrew,' act ii. 1.
[2] 'King Henry VI., Part I.,' act ii. 4.

Temple students, who saw more attraction in its borderland,
the slums and dens of Whitefriars; and, indeed, were so
constantly met in that region, that they were ultimately
deprived of their laced gowns on account of the clue afforded
by this dress to their recognition and the consequent scandal.
Shakespeare **has** not unveiled the mysteries of Alsatia,
**though they were** daily exposed to his eye, as he threaded
**its dark ways to the** play-houses, all in its vicinity; but he
**leads us through** Whitefriars in company with history.  It
**is there** that he brings the funeral train of Henry the Sixth
by the peremptory order of Gloucester,—" To Whitefriars :
there attend my coming." [1]

On the verge of this sink stood Bridewell, at that time a
poor-house and prison, but originally a palace, and connected
by a gallery over the Fleet river with the monastery of
Blackfriars.  Shakespeare adheres strictly to history in representing it as the scene of the fall of Wolsey.  Its **diver-**
sion to the double uses of a refuge and gaol, by a grant
from Edward VI., changed the character of the locality,
and ought to **have transferred to it the** name of the neighbouring quarter; for, attracting to the spot the **crime and
poverty of the whole city, it made** Whitefriars **blacker than
black, while in comparison Blackfriars became** white.

Close by was another prison, hoary **old** Ludgate, which
gave admission by a narrow archway to the city; and as
the poor debtors called from above for alms, Shakespeare
may have looked up, and discovered that the law still held
by the principles of Cloten :—

" And on the gates of Lud's town set your heads." [2]

Ludgate Hill led **steeply up to Paul's Cross, which was**
connected with many historic **incidents and episodes,** and

[1] ' King Richard III.,' act i. 2.
[2] ' Cymbeline,' act iv. 2.

e-pecially interesting to Shakespeare, as the scene of Doctor Shaw's sermon,—

"Go, Lovel, with all speed to Doctor Shaw." [1]

The stone steps of the massive cross supported a pulpit, from which a sermon was delivered weekly in fine weather to a congregation standing in the open air; and often a court preacher improved the occasion for political objects. Thus even crook-backed Richard did homage to public opinion.

In his search for employment, Shakespeare may have been directed to St. Paul's cathedral, where it was customary for servants to wait in one of the aisles to be hired. It was here that Falstaff engaged Bardolph:—"I bought him in Paul's." [2] A seat round one of the pillars is called by Decker "the servants' log," and was their recognized station. The cathedral was, indeed, so perverted from its sacred uses, as to form, like the Temple of Jerusalem, a standing scandal. Not only was it a resort for money-changers, but as a public lounge, attracting the lowest dregs of society, it became literally a den of thieves. The company was like a fusion of the Exchange and Rotten Row of our day, with Houndsditch and Brixton. Men of fashion and men of substance, courtiers and gallants, with dames of quality and city madams, having the upper part of the face masked, and their fair chins bedded in delicate mufflers, rustled down the walk in velvet and silk, with pickpockets and nymphs, staid citizens and dandy apprentices, the "gents" of the era. Shakespeare ascribes to the ladies' masks the virtue of preserving the complexion; for when Julia "threw her sun-expelling mask away," the air "starved the roses in her cheeks." [3] But very different is the testimony of the ungallant

---

[1] 'King Richard III.,' act iii. 5.
[2] 'King Henry IV., Part II.,' act i. 2.
[3] 'Two Gentlemen of Verona,' act iv. 4.

Stubbs, who says :—"They have masks and visors made of velvet, wherewith they cover all their faces, having holes made in them against their eyes, whereout they look. So that if a man who knew not their guise before, should chance to meet one of them, he would think he met a monster or devil, for face he can see none, but two broad holes against their eyes, with glasses in them."[1]   It is charitable to suppose that Stubbs here used "devil" in the sense of fallen angel, and in "monster" he may have had in view the "fat woman of Brentford," whose muffler served to disguise Falstaff, when he was hard pressed by Master Ford,—"She's as big as he is ; and there's her thrummed hat and muffler, too."[2]   But though both mufflers and masks were met in the "Mediterranean isle," as Decker terms the central walk of the cathedral, pretty milliners in the shops at the side did not scruple to exhibit their faces, which were equally distasteful to poor Stubbs, who declares that the gallants, as they strolled along, ogled them between the pillars. The pillars served also another purpose, their massive blocks being hid by boards, inscribed with the epitaphs of the dead, as if the stones cried out at the profanation around.

Smoking was allowed, and brought a roaring trade to the New Tobacco Office in the central walk.   But the greatest throng was at the steps of the tower, which were ascended every day by the celebrated horse, Marocco, whose fortunate owner was such a lion, that Decker recommends all who would be thought finished, to make his acquaintance.[3]   It is not certain whether this perfection was reached by Shakespeare, but he was acquainted with Marocco, if not his master :—"How easy it is to put years to the word three, and study three years in two words, the dancing horse will

---

[1] 'Anatomie of Abuses.'
[2] 'Merry Wives of Windsor,' act **iv. 2.**
[3] 'Gull's Horn-Book.'

tell you."[1]   It was not always easy, however, to escape the penalty of such cleverness, which St. Peter's regarded with a different eye from St. Paul's ; and on exhibiting afterwards at **Rome, poor** Marocco and his master were convicted of magic, and both condemned to the stake.

At the end of the walk was "the great dial," which gave the dandy of the day an excuse for displaying his watch, as he could feign to set it by St. Paul's.  The two wooden figures, called Jacks, which struck the hours, furnished Shakespeare with a simile :—

> "  —— But my time
> Runs posting on in Bolingbroke's proud joy,
> **While I stand fooling here, his Jack o' the clock."**[2]

At two o'clock, which was the fashionable **dinner hour,** every one pretending to **gentility disappeared, leaving the** impression that he had gone to dine at **an** ordinary ; and those who had not the means of such indulgence, ashamed of being seen in the promenade, retired into the " left alley." This retreat was especially dedicated to " the dinnerless," who, in seeking its shades, were said to dine with Duke Humphrey, the monument of Humphrey Duke of Gloucester, Protector under Henry the Sixth, being the great feature of the aisle.

This old proverb seems to throw light on the space occupied by Duke **Humphrey on the poet's canvas.**  Was it **here, in his meditations among the tombs, that he conceived the outlines of that great portraiture ?  Did** he come to dine with the statue, instead of anticipating the hospitality of Don Giovanni, and inviting the statue to dine with him ? In short, could he at whose behest the tomb unclosed its ponderous jaws, sending forth the mighty dead to act his part again before the world, have stood here wanting bread ?

[1] ' Love's Labour 's Lost,' act i. 2.
[2] ' King Richard II.,' act v. 4.

It is a pregnant thought for struggling men, particularly struggling men of letters. We may take courage in remembering that there are few, indeed, who have endured greater extremities than Shakespeare.

One who visited the cathedral in search of employment could not overlook the *Si Quis* door—then, as the "best medium for advertising," daily covered with placards, in which aspirants for employment mingled their tenders with the puffs of fashionable quacks and perfumers, and it might be here that Shakespeare first saw a London playbill. What if it apprised him that a performance was to take place that very afternoon at the playhouse in Blackfriars—the piece to be represented by the servants of the EARL OF LEICESTER! That name, hitherto not suspected of any relation with him, we shall now meet, indeed, in every page of his life. He was not likely to suppose that any of the players would remember him since he was five years old, when they were entertained at Stratford by his father, the worshipful High Bailiff; but he might think to tell them that he was known to their great patron, the Earl. Whatever the attraction, and whether with or without credentials—there he stood at the playhouse door.

The theatre had been erected four or five years before by James Burbage, the father of Richard, the tragedian; and was a plain, rough building, standing on the spot now occupied by the publishing office of 'The Times.' Before it was an open space, which still bears the name of Playhouse-yard, and which was intended to afford turning-room for the visitors' carriages. But this purpose it very inadequately fulfilled, particularly as the male portion of the audience came on horseback, and carriages were thrown out by the irruption. The conflict of interests led to conflicts between coachmen and grooms, sometimes ending in loss of life, and blocks in the neighbouring streets, which the city authorities press on the Privy Council in a petition, as their principal complaint against the Blackfriars theatre, calling for **prompt redress.** On the other hand, it was made a grievance by the company's patrons, who could rarely find their **horses on** coming out of the theatre, and sometimes discovered that the boy in charge had got tired of waiting and decamped; of course in company with the horse.

Shakespeare had not been long in the yard before he was sensible of this vocation, and fortunately was seen by a dashing courtier, who threw him his bridle as he drew up. Perhaps the stranger was not more amused by the performance within than the observant horse-boy by the proceedings without, which indeed were, to speak in homely phrase, as good as a play. Comedy alternated with tragedy, or at least melodrama, on this not mimic stage ; for when sword-and-buckler men brought **up my lady's coach by a charge,** they were so stoutly opposed by varlets in tawny and by varlets out of tawny, **and out at** elbows too, that the collision led to more than one broken head, and counted fallen, though not slain. But this was a rare incident, as the majority evinced no love for blows, but warred chiefly with sarcasms, which flew about in all directions, like the fragments of an Armstrong shell, and everywhere let in daylight for that watching eye.

Seeing everything, and hearing and marking, Shakespeare still kept in view his present business. In the cottage occupied by Peter the Great at Zaardam, while he worked as a journeyman shipwright, a queen has written up her belief that TO A GREAT MAN NOTHING IS LITTLE ; and this is the precept we are taught by Shakespeare. He looked upon nothing as beneath him, as nothing was above; and threw his whole mind into whatever he took in hand, holding a horse, as he killed a calf, *in high style.* There he was at his post, bridle in hand, when the gorged house poured forth its audience; and the courtier no sooner appeared than he was presented with his horse. Such attention both surprised and pleased him, and attracted the notice of others, whose horses had disappeared in the jam, leaving them to walk home. All asked the name of the new equerry, and declared that no one should thenceforth hold their horses but Will Shakespeare.

Thus he stepped into a calling at once, and a few days **raised** the calling into a small position; for his reputation spread, and brought him such a troop of horses that he was obliged to engage assistants. There were plenty at hand, and collecting the best, he organized a horse-boy brigade! The varlets out of tawny and elbows now found their occupation gone. There was no more decamping, and no more horse-stealing; but the horsemen rode up, calling for Shakespeare, and being met by a cry of "I am Shakespeare's boy, sir! I am for Shakespeare," unhesitatingly resigned their steeds, knowing that, at the close of the performance, they would find them at the door. The boys held the horses, and Shakespeare took the charge. He did it in high style!

**The order he had established outside** the theatre was **soon observed from within, and naturally recommended** him **to** the players, who could not know him without discovering **his** merit. Whether on this account, or from learning who he was, and that he had been present when the company performed under his father's auspices at Stratford; or whether from being aware that the family were countenanced by the Earl of Leicester, Burbage felt an interest in his young countryman, and, according to Dowdall, took **him** into the theatre, "as a servitor." A manager's nod changed the horse-boy into a scene-shifter! and opened **the stage** to Shakespeare.

# XVIII.

## SHAKESPEARE, THE STROLLER.

THE boards of a theatre animate the inertest organization, and not only animate, but leaven. It would seem that the habit of appearing in different characters on the stage infects the character of the actor, just as familiarity with dramatic dialogue tinges his discourse, and he carries into real life the same disposition to play many parts. Such is the phase in which we are now to view Shakespeare. Hardly has he disappeared behind the scenes, when he comes forward in a new character, and tradition and his own words present him to us as a strolling player.

His early career was thus a continual training. He had run from his master the butcher, but he kept his indentures to nature and human life, and was still SHAKESPEARE THE APPRENTICE. Adapting himself to his situation, whatever it might be, he drew out all its points, and made it yield him wisdom as well as subsistence. His occupation, his fellow-workers, and what he could hear and see, became in this way his study and books; and every fresh experience opened to him some new lore. He was led to it, indeed, by no set purpose, but it gave vigour and scope to his faculties, and these were ever on the watch, and looked into everything. For, while he was attracted to the beautiful and great, his craving for knowledge was such, that he would not pass the little and mean, and all became gold in the crucible of his mind. It lay there unused for the present, and possibly unthought of, as if he was unconscious of its value, but, in truth, it was from ignorance of his powers, though these burst forth at times in glorious song, and the measure of others showed him his own stature. Not that this was necessary; for though Cromwell saw the phantom of his greatness while he was busy **with his** plough, it **is** Cromwell who **says that men never climb** so high as when they know not where they **are going.** No phantom came to Shakespeare; **and greatness, though** he achieved it, **was thrust upon him.** His sonnets prove that it was never an aspiration, and still less now, when all his thoughts were given to the moment—to his mistress, to the duties of a new vocation, and the attractions of a new companionship. The position suited the temper he was in; and the loose, wild habits which, once formed, could not easily be dropped. At this period he seems to come and go before us, as in a play, passing behind the scenes in one dress, and reappearing in another in a new scene, and with new aims. We can hardly be wrong **in** thinking that he was exhibiting the same variableness to those amongst whom he moved; now excelling in his part, whatever it might be; now meditating **alone in some solitary spot; now running riot with the most reckless of the company.**

The revival of the drama had spread a taste for theatrical **entertainments** through the community, except among the Puritans, who denounced them in the strongest terms, but could not convince the public. The players had thus a wide field, and it was occupied by a number of companies, most of which were continually on the move, and did not leave behind a good impression, either by the characters they sustained on the stage or their own. Hence arose many complaints, and it was determined to bring the whole body under the curb of authority, which was accomplished **by the Poor Act of 1572, when** the liabilities of " rogues and vagabonds " **attached to all " fencers, bearwards, common players in inter-**ludes, and minstrels, not belonging to any baron of this realm, or to any other honourable personage of greater degree." It now became customary for players to associate under the licence of a person of rank, and describe themselves as his servants, assuming his name or title, and they could then pass freely over the country, performing in the various towns in their way, as we have seen the players of Lords Leicester, Worcester, Warwick, and Derby successively visit Stratford. But unlicensed companies maintained their ground in spite of repressive enactments; and, surviving the hostility of the authorized players, and even the Puritan proscription, wandered over the land almost down to our own day, exercising their vocation in booths and barns, and always finding an audience. A tradition exists in Leicester, that Shakespeare was enrolled in a company that once visited that town, and performed in the Guildhall, perhaps under the patronage of the earl; and a similar tradition prevails at Worcester. There is every reason to believe that it happened at the period of his life we are treating of; for the theatre at Blackfriars, being a winter house, closed about the end of May, which deprived him of his employment there; and we shall show that he was now rambling about. The Blackfriars company, indeed, spent the recess in visiting the provinces, and he naturally went in their train; but, even if his services were not required, he would easily find a place in some troop of strollers. Time shrouds from us his companions as well as his position; but we may safely conclude that he began at the humblest point. As those around him must be struck by his " natural wit," before they discovered his other gifts, he might seem to have a special aptitude for the low comedy of the day, which made great demands on the humour of the actor. It startles us to think of Shakespeare playing the clown, though our fathers employed Burns to gauge beer; and, truly, Alexander has stopped a bunghole oftener than we suspect. But what matter to Shakespeare, who took everything as it came, and left it something different, but was never different himself. How he would jeer among the company over his own position at each step of advancement—from the horse-boy to the scene-shifter, and the scene-shifter to the clown, declaring he would now forswear low company, and only associate with fools! He never dreamt that it would one day be thrown in his teeth—that Greene would call him a "shake-scene" and "ANTIC." Nor, indeed, would any thought of the future now have been a check on his mad spirits.

This roving season has left **a** deep impression in his works, in the traces they present of personal acquaintance with almost every part of England and Wales. Only as a stroller could he have accomplished such wanderings, though they led him to scenes he yearned to visit—scenes hallowed by history or endeared by romance. Now he began to feel an irresistible impulse towards some mysterious aim, he knew not what; but he was stirred up to try to embody it in rhymes and metaphors. He was like a child learning to **speak—striving to** tell the unutterable things in its mind, **and mastering only a few broken** syllables. The idea was **there, but not the language—not the power of** expression. **This he was** to obtain by degrees, almost word by word, drawing it from the English undefiled of the people, stored up in the old stock-plays and many an old ballad. We can see his Muse thus stammering and straining in some of the earlier sonnets. But, if it was yet weak in utterance, it was strong in conception; and what he could not describe to others, glowed in his own imagination. Here every striking object left its impress, whether the scenes were "the Wilds of Gloucestershire"[1] or "the Coast of **Wales**."[2] It even grew under his eye,—changed, suggested to him something more beautiful, or something greater and grander. From

<hr>

[1] 'King Richard II.,' act ii. 3.       [2] Ibid., act iii. 2.

the smooth green turf and spreading oaks of an English park, threaded by a pleasant stream, sparkling in the sunshine, he could picture the garden of the Hesperides ;[1] and he made the hills of Wales a stepping-stone to " the frozen regions of the Alps."[2] In fact, his imagination as much transcends what he saw, as his knowledge what he learnt. We read the sea scenes in 'The Tempest'—see the storm raised by this literary Prospero, and retain no recollection that he never beheld the sea. Let us stand on the same spot—on Shakespeare's cliff, and think what the narrow Channel could tell him of the vastness of the Atlantic, or even the width of the Mediterranean. Yet his vivid perceptions occur to us in the midst of both, and we are not more struck by their grandeur than their fidelity. Comparing this " confined deep " to the span of the ocean, he was as blind as Gloucester in what he saw, but there was no bound to the deep of his imagination. From the path which now edges the cliff, " the very brim of it,"[3] and which breaks away from our foot as we " look fearfully " down, he could fancy the waters stretching off into immensity, having no limit and no bottom. Here he came to muse, indeed—fresh from his performance in the inn yard, or a glass with his merry comrades in the inn tap—running up to pass an hour with the waves ere the company moved off to another stage. He bears away with him every point in the picture—from the dread summit of the chalky bourn to its base, where it rises " perpendicularly " from unnumbered idle pebbles and murmuring surge, showing half-way down the daring plucker of samphire,—and the crows and choughs in mid air, all diminished in gradation with the fishermen on

<hr>

[1] 'Love's Labour 's Lost,' act iv. 3.

[2] 'King Richard II.,' act i. 1.

[3] 'King Lear,' act iv. 1. Shakespeare's Cliff has, I believe, been invaded by the railway, since I visited it ten years ago, and there may now be no vestige of the path.

the beach and the tall, anchoring bark and its boat.[1]  And,
perhaps, he had stolen up here at night, to mark the same
scene " beneath the moon,"[2] or when the moon only peered
out weirdly from black, lowering clouds, and the sky—

> "——— would pour down stinking pitch,
> But that the sea, mounting to the welkin's cheek,
> Dashes the fire out."[3]

**We may think** that he stood here in the fury of the gale,
**when it lashed the** waves to madness, and the whirl of both
caught the same tall anchoring bark, and dashed her among
the rocks.

> " Oh, I have suffer'd
> With them that I saw suffer ! a brave vessel,
> Who had, no doubt, some noble creature in her,
> Dashed all to pieces." [4]

But it was not only in her inanimate realm that nature
was now unfolding to him her deepest counsels : she **was**
enlarging also his knowledge of man and human life.  **His**
vocation introduced him to all classes, and familiarized him
with every **rank, carrying him as** often **into** the halls of the
**nobility as into the barn or the inn yard.  Rarely** did a
**strolling company fail to report themselves at the mansion
of a nobleman if** it **fell in their way.**

> " An't please your honour, players,
> That offer service to your lordship."[5]

And equally rare was the occasion when they were not
welcomed, and even retained for several days—for the
dull country life of the time could spare no recreation.
The practice continued in Germany as late as the end of
the last century, and the troop engaged **at** the Count's

---

[1] ' King **Lear,' act iv. 4.**

[2] Ibid.

[3] 'Tempest,' act i. 2.

[4] Ibid.          [5] **'Taming of the** Shrew :' Induction.

castle furnished the most effective scenes in ' Wilhelm
Meister.'   A strolling company is twice introduced in this
situation by Shakespeare, and more fortunate than the party
described by Goethe, they are hospitably treated on both
occasions.   The most liberal entertainment was provided
for the players engaged by the Lord, in the Induction to
' The Taming of the Shrew,' —

> " Go, sirrah, take them to the buttery,
>   And give them friendly welcome, everyone :
>   Let them want nothing that my house affords."

They receive the same consideration from Hamlet, who
spurns the proposition of Polonius to treat them according to their deserts, which might easily be under-rated,
and prescribes a golden rule,—" Use them after your
own honour and dignity." [1]   Perhaps our English William,
like Wilhelm Meister, was not without some experience of
cold receptions, and here had it in view.   Certainly he
speaks with a purpose when he warns the great ones of the
earth to avoid offending players,—" Do you hear, let them
be well used ; for they are the abstracts and brief chroni-
cles of the time : after your death you were better have a
bad epitaph than their ill report while you live." [2]   Shakespeare stood by his order.

[1] 'Hamlet,' act ii. 2.          [2] Ibid,

# XIX.

## WHERE HE WAS MARRIED.

SOME time between July and September, 1582, Shakespeare returned to Stratford. Doubtless his absence had permitted a friendly arrangement to be made with his master for the remission of his unexpired apprenticeship, freeing him from a calling he disliked, and it might be hoped that he would now have nothing to fear from the resentment of Sir Thomas Lucy. The family affairs evidently brightened about this time; for John Shakespeare presented himself twice at the meetings of the town council, which he had not attended for nearly four years, and, though hitherto passed over without comment, this sudden resumption of his public duties coincides so remarkably with the return of his son, and his temporary settlement at Stratford, that we cannot but connect it with some change of fortune, which opened to him new prospects. Certainly he could not be so near Stratford as Worcester without wishing to return; for he cherished an almost romantic attachment for his native town through the whole of his life, and an event had just happened which made it the centre of his thoughts. At the beginning of July he must have heard of the death of Richard Hathaway, which removed an obstacle to his early marriage with Anne, and even imposed it upon him as a point of honour, for it would appear that her determination not to reject his suit—possibly their avowed betrothal—had deeply incensed her father, as his will not only leaves her without a provision, but does not mention her name. She thus became dependent on her family, which placed her in a **situation as painful as** humiliating, and one from which a **lover would be** impatient to free her.

His wild ramble, and its hard, stern lessons, had made a salutary impression on Shakespeare. **Veiled from us as** they are, we **yet** see that they had done something to steady, if not to elevate him, to bring out his self-respect, and make him both ashamed of the past and hopeful of the future. In those days strolling-players were considered mere rogues and vagabonds, and, indeed, were literally so described in the statutes, **so that** his assumption of such a calling was **felt as a reproach by his** friends, particularly **as he** appeared in the character of Clown. He frankly acknowledges that he had given them ground for complaint :—

> " Alas, 't is true, I have gone here and there,
> And made myself a MOTLEY to the view."[1]

But, evidently **pleading with Anne Hathaway, he goes on** to affirm that his derelictions had had the effect of settling his character. Most true, he had wounded his self-esteem, abused his gifts, aggravated his old offences by yielding to seductions of a different kind—which implies that his association with strollers was thought as great a stigma as his previous connection with poachers ; and, to crown all, he had "looked on truth askance and strangely." But he solemnly avers that these excesses had brought about a beneficial, instead of an injurious result—" these blenches gave my heart another youth ;" while, as regarded Anne herself, his worst trespass had only proved that she was his " best of love." All was now over ; he would impose no further trial on her affection and patience ; but remain hers for ever :—

> " Then give me welcome, next my heaven the best,
> Even to thy pure, and most, most loving breast."

---

[1] Sonnet cx.

Fanciful though they are, and seldom to be taken in a literal sense, his sonnets testify that he was ever too ready to blame himself. They unfold to us, sometimes in myths, sometimes in the clearest manner, the secret depths of the kindest, noblest, and truest of hearts. In this instance he kneels at **the confessional**; and renouncing his **errors, and giving a solemn pledge of** amendment, claims **from his mistress absolution.** He urges, indeed, **a plea** which makes **this secure; for he can aver** that all his follies and transgressions have never shaken his love for herself.

The newspapers **lately told us of a Clown in a panto-**mime triumphantly playing **his** part, and, at the fall of the curtain, reeling behind the scenes to die. While he had kept the audience in a roar, he was writhing in his last agonies; their acclamations rang in his ear while the death-rattle was in his throat, and he laid down life like a bauble, with the paint on his face and the fool's frippery on his back. Just the contrary result was developed in Shakespeare. This shroud, as it was to him, covered the generation of new vitality—*gave* **his heart another youth.** He **came out of it, as the worm out of the chrysalis, a different being, and was now conscious of new instincts and a new life.**

We have said that his flight from Stratford occurred in the spring :—

" From you have I been absent in the spring." [1]

Let us now recapitulate the facts, and we shall see that they bring out a passage of his life. The Lucy note reports that the satiric ballad obliged him to quit Stratford—" at least, for a time," which **implies that he was absent but a** short period : Aubrey says that he left when he was " about

[1] Sonnet xcviii.

eighteen "—that is, when he was not quite that age, but close upon it, which would be the end of March; here the sonnet tells us that he was absent in the spring, and another sonnet will presently mention April; the Blackfriars playhouse closed at the end of May, when, as we have seen by a third sonnet, he goes "here and there" as a "motley," which explains what was meant by Green, when he called him an "antic" or clown; and we know positively that he was residing at Stratford in September.

Four of the sonnets[1] seem to apply so closely to his separation from Anne Hathaway that we may wonder they have not been so interpreted before. He dates his departure, as we have just said, from "proud-pied April," intimates that he remained away all the summer,[2] and returned about the middle of the "teeming autumn." Here we are brought to the very time when he was certainly in Stratford. The harvest in Warwickshire—"the rich increase"—is all gathered in by the commencement of September, and this is the epoch obviously marked in the 97th sonnet. In the 100th sonnet he calls upon his Muse to "return:" and, evidently recurring to what has been said about the disparity of their ages, warns his mistress that he will examine whether time has really impaired her beauty,—

> " Rise, restive Muse, my love's sweet face survey,
> If Time have any wrinkles graven there."

No light threat to a maiden of twenty-five, after a separation of four months, passed by her in anxiety and sorrow, but so expressed as rather to take the form of a graceful compliment.

Neither biography nor fiction gives us anything comparable to this honest, uncompromising attachment, so ideal

---

[1] Sonnets xcvii to c.

[2] " And yet this time removed was summer's time."—Sonnet xcvii.

yet so abiding, so romantic yet so real.  It exhibits the
English heartiness of Shakespeare in its whole breadth.  He
did not, like Petrarch, cherish a sentimental passion for
another man's wife ; nor, like Tasso, fall in love **with a
princess ; nor** did he shroud the object of his **vows in mystery like Ariosto.**  He loved openly, in his own station, and
**with no feelings that he** could **not express.**  This love was
**from the** beginning—his first impression, contracted in his
**childhood ; and,** perhaps, cradled in little Anne's arm when
**he was a** prattling infant.  Though " handsome and well-
**shaped,"** though endowed with every attraction of person
and mind, he did not look to marriage as a means of improving his fortune.  In love, as in everything else, he
thought little of himself; and returning, as it were, from
banishment, was proud to win a portionless maiden.

The marriage was not traced till 1833, when a bond
authorizing the ceremony was discovered by Sir Thomas
Philips in the archives of **the** diocese of Worcester.  **Previously** there was some **doubt as to Anne Hathaway, of
Shottery, having really been the wife of** Shakespeare ; for,
**though reported from the earliest time, the alleged union
was apparently refuted by an entry in the parochial** register
of Stratford, showing that nearly five years before the supposed date of his **nuptials—namely, on the** 17th January,
1579, Anne Hathaway, of Shottery, married William
Wilson, an alderman of Stratford.  But the marriage bond
from Worcester established the old fact.  We are now
aware, indeed, that as there were three John Shakespeares
living at one time in Stratford, so there were three contemporary **Anne** Hathaways, and these Warwickshire Graces
were all resident in Shottery.[1]

---

[1] **They were Anne Hathaway, who married William** Wilson ; Anne
**Hathaway, entered in the Stratford register as** "daughter to Thomas
**Hathaway ;" and the Anne of our history.**

Shakespeare's marriage presents features which, though no way peculiar in that day, are not reconcileable with the stricter propriety of our own, and hence has been made a subject of scandal. Mr. De Quincy cannot speak too severely of a woman of twenty-five, who allowed herself to be led astray by a youth of eighteen ; and, harping on this inequality of ages, sees an allusion to Anne in 'The Merry Wives of Windsor,' when Falstaff, escaping from Ford's house as the fat woman of Brentford, is described by Sir Hugh Evans as "a woman with a peard." The sarcasm is not very obvious ; and we must see far into a millstone to persuade ourselves that Shakespeare would thus publicly insult his wife, the love of his youth and the mother of his children. We should rather look for a reminiscence of Anne Hathaway in that character of the play to whom he has given her name—ANNE Page, "*sweet Anne Page !*" Fenton, indeed, tells Anne that one of her father's objections to their marriage is what we may believe was urged by Richard Hathaway as an objection to Shakespeare—

" My riots past, my wild societies." [1]

But he declares, as we have shown that Shakespeare declares to Anne herself, that his true, honest love, has wholly changed his nature.[2] Finally, he justifies their stolen marriage by affirming that they were " long since contracted ;" and, considering the deep local colouring of this play, there were friends in Stratford who might see a nearer application in the words—" The offence is holy that she hath committed." [3]

If the betrothal took place, as we have conceived, before

---

[1] ' Merry Wives of Windsor,' act iii. 6.

[2] Sonnet cx.

[3] ' Merry Wives of Windsor,' act v. 5.

Shakespeare's departure in the spring, they were, when he returned in September, "long since contracted." The death of Richard Hathaway was too recent to admit of their being immediately married, without disrespect to his memory ; and for this there was no inducement, as, by the usages of the day, Shakespeare was already her husband.[1] His position was recognized by Anne, and both Mr. De Quincy and Mr. Hunter evince a forgetfulness of prevailing customs in making her submission a reproach. When the question has been so warmly discussed, it is strange that no one has cared to ascertain in what light it was viewed by Shakespeare himself, particularly as he has expressed his opinion very emphatically—the speaker, in his assumed character of friar, giving it a religious weight, while he connects it with one of his purest conceptions of the sex, Isabella the nun, whom we may suppose to represent Isabella Shakespeare, the prioress of Wroxhall. It is with Isabella's full assent that the Duke urges Mariana to keep the assignation with Angelo :—

> " Nor, gentle daughter, fear you not at all :
> *He is your husband on a pre-contract :*
> To bring you thus together 'tis no sin." [2]

The marriage bond is dated the 28th of November, 1582.[3] It licenses the marriage of " William Shagspere " and " Anne Hathaway, of Stratford," maiden, " with once asking of the banns of matrimony ; " and Fulks Sandells and John Richardson, described as husbandmen, bind themselves in forty pounds as securities to the Bishop against

---

[1] " Every man lykewyse must esteme the parson to whom he is hand-fasted, none otherwyse than for his owne spouse, though as yet it be not done in the church nor in the street."—*Christian State of Matrimony, London,* 1543.

[2] ' Measure for Measure,' act iv. 1.

[3] The bond will be found in the Appendix.

any legal consequences. Mr. Halliwell thinks that "the bride's father was most likely present when Sandells and Richardson executed the bond; for one of the seals has the initials **R.H. upon it;**"[1] but he forgets that the will of Richard Hathaway, which was brought to light by himself, proves that he had now been at least five months in his grave, probate having been granted on the 9th of July, 1582. Mr. Hunter has spoken of the bond with the same want of caution:—"Two more unseemly persons to attend at a poet's bridal can hardly be conceived than Sandells and Richardson, two husbandmen, who were unable to write their names."[2] And he asks indignantly where were the friends of the family? This question is answered by Richard Hathaway himself, who mentions Fulk Sandells in his will as his *trusty friend and neighbour*, desiring him to be one of its "supervisors," and John Richardson affixes his mark to the will as one of the witnesses. Surely the bride could not have two fitter friends on such an occasion. It is true, they were both husbandmen, but her father was nothing more; and the reproach of being unable to write does not apply more to the poet's two bondsmen than to his own father.

Churches have been rummaged and registers explored for the record of the marriage, but the search has proved fruitless. Malone seems to have thought that it was solemnized at Luddington, where, after finding that Anne Hathaway, of Shottery, had married William Wilson, not William Shakespeare, he supposed the bride to have lived; and it is not unlikely that she took refuge in that village, when the death of her father deprived her of a home. We have room to fear that she was reduced to this strait; for Shakespeare must have had some deep ground of offence against the Hathaways, as they never come again in con-

<hr>

[1] 'Life of Shakespeare,' p. 117.
[2] 'New Illustrations.'

nection with him, and none of them are mentioned among the friends remembered in his will. If they still opposed the match, and made Anne suffer for her constancy, his alienation is explained.

It had been well if Malone had extended his researches to Luddington, when he was inquiring about the marriage; for there the missing record would have been found. But the little chapel of Luddington had just before been burnt to the ground, and he was not aware that the fire had spared the registers, which contained the memorable entry. Strange that it should have perished within memory without being brought to light, or even attracting to the spot any attention, while explorers were searching for it in every neighbouring church!

A hope of recovering some faint tradition of the event carried us to the village, and we were soon standing in its ancient burial-ground, now a garden, where we still find the old parsonage. The house is occupied by a family named Dyke, respected for miles round, and here the report of the marriage can be traced back directly for a hundred and fifty years. Mrs. Dyke received it from Martha Casebrooke, who died at the age of ninety, after residing her whole life in the village, and not only declared that she was told in her childhood that the marriage was solemnized at Luddington, but had seen the ancient tome in which it was registered. This, indeed, we found, on visiting the neighbouring cottages, was remembered by persons still living, when it was in the possession of a Mrs. Pickering, who had been housekeeper to Mr. Coles, the last curate; and one cold day burnt the register to boil her kettle!

There were good reasons why Shakespeare should go to Luddington to be married. Then, as now, it was a most secluded spot, reached by a road through fields, where its dozen thatched cottages, the same which have stood there for centuries, form a world of themselves, and it was desirable that the marriage should be private, on account of the still recent death of the bride's father, if not her own **position**.   Moreover, the nuptial knot could here be **tied by a** friend, no other than his old schoolmaster, Thomas Hunt, who **was curate of** Luddington, and, under the sanction **of** the licence, would doubtless **be willing** to render this service, though the young couple were not his parishioners. **He had** even, like Sir Hugh Evans, a compliment for Mistress Anne—that mysterious Anne, who ever flies from our approach, or only stands revealed in the inscription on her tomb, as if she spoke to us from the grave.

## XX.

### SHAKESPEARE, THE MARRIED MAN.

WE could wish imagination to carry us back to the first
lowly home of Shakespeare and his bride. Scant was the furniture, and of the plainest description, yet we cannot believe
that this penury had not something bright—something that
marked *his* presence. It might be but the cast of the light,
a little taste in arrangement, or even a few flowers ; for a
mind generative of beauty imparts it by a touch. One way
or another, the humble dwelling wore a cheerful look ; for
Shakespeare loved to image that the light of the body is the
eye. There was no blank in **his perceptions. In his pro-
foundest reverie, in the sublimest flight of his Muse he kept
in view the real and practical. He did not require to be
dragged by force to his dinner, like** Archimedes,—though,
**more successful** than the Syracusan, he found a stand-point
from which to move the world. And now his gaiety was
in its zenith, and could not be obscured by his worst necessities: rather, like the glow-worm's light, the darker the
hour the clearer it appears.

It is proverbial to say that Poverty at the door drives
Love out of the window, but, after all, this is shallow
doctrine, and must **have** come from one who knew **not the**
constancy of the human **heart. It is the notion of a sordid
mind, hardened by prosperity and contact with the** world,
**and which can tell nothing of what it** has not experienced—
**the** softening **influence** which, in the midst of its trials,

poverty exercises on the affections. The effect was understood by Shakespeare; for it was his own aspiration—"let me but bear your love, I'll bear your cares."[1]  If this were not an impulse of nature—if fellowship in suffering did not beget communion of feeling, from how many breasts must love be excluded! What the adage makes the death of sympathy is, in truth, its life; drawing us out of ourselves, and making us a part of others, alive to their misery, and strengthened by their participation of ours. The sorrow or privation shared with another is lightened in the same degree as a material burden, and inspires the same mutual reliance. There are moments when the temper yields to the burden equally with the back, but the affections are unbent, and derive new vigour from the trial.

Such is the testimony of Shakespeare; and it is by this that we must judge his married life; for it clearly expresses what he felt. It proves that his wife retained the love which he gave to Anne Hathaway, and that what he was to her she was to him, under all vicissitudes and adversities abidingly and unchangeably faithful—

> " Kind is my love to-day, to-morrow kind;
> Still constant in a wondrous excellence."[2]

Three centuries, indeed, were content to regard this marriage as a true love-match, when modern criticism suddenly discovered that it was out of joint. Mr. De Quincy describes the married life of Shakespeare in different terms from those used by himself.[3]  He represents it as passed in incessant bickerings, till the maddened poet flies for relief to London, leaving wife and children at home—like the truant ladybird in the nursery rhyme. We are perplexed to

---

[1] ' King Henry IV., Part II.,' act v. 2.

[2] Sonnet cv.

[3] ' Encyclopædia Britannica.'

conceive what can have led to such a theory; for, beyond the muttered conjectures of other commentators, it has not a shadow of ground. All the facts point to an opposite conclusion. Within three years of her marriage Anne Shakespeare presented her husband with three children— Susannah, baptized at Stratford on the **26th of** May, 1583, **and a twin son and** daughter, baptized **as Hamlet**[1] and Judith, on the 2nd of February, 1584–5. At the very time when he is said to have been worn out by their "**conjugal discord**," she is attaching herself to him by new ties, the dearest in nature's gift; and it is at the same moment that he addresses to her one of the most beautiful of his sonnets,[2] which, read by the light of its obvious meaning, affords, indeed, a noble revelation of his feelings. The wife of thirty, and mother of three children, might now recall the disparity of their ages, as she looked on her husband of three-and-twenty, and saw him adding to his attractions, while her own were on the wane. But **how** must she be reassured, when her fears call **forth such** tender words **as these :—**

> "**To me, fair friend,** you never **can be old,**
> **For as you were,** when first your eye **I eyed,**
> **Such seems your** beauty still!"

**He** reviews the three years **they** have spent together, commencing with winter, which, **as they** were married in November, pointedly marks his wife :—

> "Three winters' cold
> Have from the forests shook three summers' pride,
> Three beauteous springs to yellow autumn turned,
> In process of the seasons have I seen;
> Three Aprils' perfumes in three hot Junes burned,
> Since first I saw you fresh, which yet are green."

---

[1] This name was sometimes given as Hamlet, and sometimes as Hamnet; Shakespeare, in his will, spells it with l.

[2] Sonnet civ.

The change made in her appearance by maternity is imaged with surpassing delicacy —

> " Ah ! yet doth beauty, like a dial-hand,
> *Steal from the figure, and no pace perceived :*
> So your sweet hue, which methinks still doth stand,
> Hath motion, and mine eye may be deceived."

It may be an illusion, but he sees the same maiden bloom on her cheek, and the same grace in her form, so that her charms, though they may be declining, seem to his watching eye, unchanged and stationary.

His love for her not only survived their marriage and lit up their home, but was still the inspiration of his Muse. Thus it seems to open the door of his little dwelling, where we see his poetic instincts rising, as if they were a fountain, and hither he comes with his wife, in their pain and weariness, to drink and rest. One of his biographers has said that a good poet may be a bad man, and unhappily it would not be difficult to prove the fact; but we deny that it could be true of Shakespeare. The poet who is the interpreter of the noblest susceptibilities of the human heart must himself feel and respond to them. To believe he could be their oracle to all ages without this participation, were, indeed, to reduce them to leather and prunella. Virtue alone can image virtue. Libertines may give us a Parisina, but it requires a pure and refined mind, as well as the highest genius, to conceive a Miranda, and a Perdita, an Imogen, a Desdemona, and an Ophelia.

So these sonnets of Shakespeare's now remove the cloud both from his married life and his good name. Instead of appearing as a thrall or a reprobate, he stands forward in his natural character, as the tenderest of husbands and the fondest of parents. Poetry is nurtured in his breast by affection, unites with it, and takes its hue and likeness, so that they seem two lovely berries moulded on one stem.

Now he entwines them in the tresses of his wife ; now they form the plume for his little son :[1]—

> " What's in the brain that ink may character,
>   Which hath not figured to thee my true spirit ?
>   What's new to speak, what new to register,
>   That may express my love, or thy dear merit ?
>   Nothing, *sweet* boy !  But yet, like prayers divine,
>   I must each day say o'er the very **same**,
>   Counting **no thing** old, *thou mine*, *I thine*,
>   Even as when **first** I *hallowed thy fair name* ;
>   So that eternal love, in love's fresh case,
>   **Weighs** not the **dust** and injury **of age**,
>   Nor gives to necessary wrinkles **place**,
>   But makes antiquity for aye its **page** :
> >   **Finding** the first conceit of **love there bred**,
> >   **Where time and outward form** would show it dead."

That it is indeed his son he thus addresses as "sweet boy," the whole tenour of the sonnet declares.  In whom else could he find " the first conceit of love there bred ;" that is, its first hope and fruit embodied ?  Who else could be a reproduction of his own childhood, when the lapse of time and his matured **form witnessed** that it had fled **for ever?** The love pledged eternally to his wife was here re-cast " in love's fresh case," in which there was no sign of the defacing wear of years,—the " dearth and injury of age," or "necessary wrinkles," perceptible in himself.  Thus love ever makes antiquity "its page," **shows a** man his youth renewed in his children, presents him again **as a young** boy.  The poet saw "figured" in his prattling **infant** his own inmost nature —"his **true** spirit," even to the last thought in his brain ; and he could find nothing to say or write that would newly express either his own affection or the child's " dear **merit.**"  Yet he continually remembered them, dwelt **upon them, and** went through the **unvarying** reflections **they** suggested, as **he repeated daily the same prayers,**—

> " **Like prayers divine,**
>   I must each day say o'er the very same."

---

Here the father appears himself a child, in the beautiful revelation of his faith.

Is there any fact to lend even **a colour to the theory of** his defamers? Look on this picture, and on this! **Four** years of domestic strife, following an enforced marriage! This would class Shakespeare with Dante, as the man who had been in hell. But how different is our impression of the stricken Florentine,—our awe of his ghostly genius, from the notions we have formed of the warm, living sympathies of Shakespeare!

It was in a different way that these first years were **a** time of trial, for such they doubtless were, though the humble position of the poet screens him from view, and veils even his occupation. It is always assumed that he is described by Rowe as following at this time the trade of his father; but Rowe merely says that "he seems to have given entirely into that way of living, which his father proposed to him," which may equally mean that he was a butcher, a woolstapler, or anything else. We receive a fuller revelation from Aubrey, who learnt from "Mr. Beeston" that "he had been in his younger years a schoolmaster in the country." This account, indeed, is confirmed by tradition, which cannot be refused belief, when we receive a like tradition of Homer from nearly a thousand years before the Christian era. As Chios exhibited the hollow tree which formed the rostrum of Homer, so Stratford preserves a lumbering old schooldesk, reputed, on equally doubtful evidence, to have belonged to Shakespeare. It has been surmised that he was employed as assistant in the Free School, where he had once been a pupil; but the corporation records show that in 1585 this post was held by Sir William Gilbert, and we may conclude that he had filled it for at least four years before, for in witnessing the will of Richard Hathaway, in 1581, he signs himself curate of Stratford, so that he was then on the spot, and in the very position to secure it. Any way, such a situation was not likely to be conferred on one who, whatever his present conduct, had very recently been an indifferent character, and, besides, was justly obnoxious to the powerful family at Charlecote, which, as Master Slender **was able to** grant the boys "a playing-day," we know exercised **a** control over the school. In fact, Aubrey implies that he set up a seminary of his own, for which there might **well** be an opening, as boys were not admitted to the Free **School** before **they** had learnt to read, and it was in his " younger years " that he was thus engaged.

It must have been at this time that **he** lived near the church, close to his loved Avon, to the Weir Brake, the scene of 'Midsummer Night's Dream,' and the charnel-house and churchyard.[1] Wherever it stood, the school was not conducted on the terrorist principles of the day. The pupils of Homer, in that time of patriarchal sternness, might be ruled by awe, and the teacher's rod seems **not** unsuited to Milton, but Shakespeare can only be connected with "gentle means **and easy tasks.**"[2] **The** discipline imposed **on himself was of a sterner** kind, and never pressed, **heavier than now; for** while every **day brought** new **burdens, he could** obtain but the barest subsistence. **But** this simply made him more considerate for others, and less thoughtful for himself. We can see that the rubs of life never ruffled his temper or bruised his spirit. On the contrary, they softened and chastened him, so that he came to look upon them as wholesome discipline :—

> " Sweet are the uses of adversity,
> Which, like the toad, ugly and venomous,
> Wears yet a precious jewel in its head."[3]

---

[1] I have been told that **he writ the scene of the Ghost in** Hamlet at his house, which bordered on **the charnel-house and churchyard.**"—*Gildon's Langbaine.*

[2] 'Othello,' act iv. 2.  [3] 'As You Like It,' act ii. 1.

These touching words give us a history,—the history of
the darkest, but who shall say the unhappiest, portion of
his life ?  For do they not tell us of privation, borne with
courage and patience ;  of anxiety, soothed by counsel ;
of care, lightened by sympathy ;  and of toil, cheered
by love ?

The decline in the fortunes of his family and the increasing pressure on himself, must, as he grew older, have
frequently led him to reflect on the smallness of the field
open to his exertions in Stratford, and once more directed
him to London.  True, he had derived little advantage
from his first visit to the capital, but it had taught him
that he might at least rely on a subsistence, and this was
encouragement to venture again.  It is always contended
that he was in Stratford in 1585, because his twin children
were baptized there in that year, but the fact does not sustain
the conclusion.  Aubrey says that he made a journey to
his native town every year, and, as he probably first settled
in the capital alone, his children may have been born in
his absence, or during one of his annual visits.  Certainly
he had established himself in London shortly after the birth
of his first child, when he was in his twentieth year.

## XXI.

### ON THE STAGE.

MANY will be astonished by the announcement that Shakespeare began his career as an author before he was twenty years of age, and, indeed, we might shrink from making it, in face of the criticism it will provoke. But the fact is established by his connection with the Earl of Leicester, now first adduced, and, instead of confusing his history, it will be found to explain much that has hitherto appeared contradictory.

Before twenty he was an author—on his road to Fame ! But we must not think that the way did not present obstructions, because they are no longer traceable ; for this is the surest proof that he was toiling in obscurity. "There was a man dwelt by a churchyard"[1]—this is all we know, except that it was here he wrote 'Hamlet.' His ramble with the players had given him a perception of dramatic composition, and in the hours unoccupied by his school, it turned his thoughts in that direction, and inspired a wish to give them form. The name afterwards given to his son at the font was derived, perhaps, rather from his first play than from his friend Hamlet Sadler. But we must not think that it was the finished play : it could be only the outline, and rather a prophecy than a performance. He set out for London with this skeleton in his wallet—or it might be but a skull, but the skull was Yorick's. One day it would be turned up, and be recognized by princes.

[1] 'Winter's Tale,' act ii. 1.

He commenced the terrible struggle for bread by authorship at the greatest disadvantage; for he knew but the rudiments of learning, and was poor, friendless, and unknown. But he was prepared to suffer, and able to endure, and we shall see him who had once been made reckless by misfortune now draw from his trials constancy and courage.

There is a story of the scion of a beggared house leaving his alienated heritage with a vow that it should one day again be his; and in the course of years returning from the subjugation of India to be Lord of Daylesford. Perhaps a kindred resolve swelled the breast of Shakespeare when he started on his present expedition; for he steadily pursued a similar object, and, like Warren Hastings, eventually came back to restore the dignity of his family in his native place.

But the task to him was more arduous, while the success was more splendid. No friend secured him an opening; no accidents of fortune favoured his advancement; he owed nothing to interest, opportunity, or collusion. Warren Hastings riveted the chains of millions of slaves, but it was a greater work to humanize millions of freemen; and this is what was accomplished by Shakespeare. This was his mission, and it was worked out, like every mission, in weariness and pain, after many a strong effort and many a silent failure. The story he has left untold will not rise to our imagination; for it goes further back than we see, and all the action is behind. It is like the Ephesian's picture: we cannot remove the curtain, for nothing but the curtain is there.

These blanks too frequently interrupt our history. Shakespeare is like a periodic star, which vanishes for a time, and then reappears in its old position. So we now find him again at the playhouse in Blackfriars, the spot where he was last seen. He sprang on Parnassus from

the stage, and though there is little to mark the way, it is
thence that we must trace his steps.

A notion prevails that he was deficient in histrionic
talent, and never excelled as an actor : but we may **judge**
what was his **quality** by Hamlet's instructions to the players.
One who could **so well "suit the** action to the word and the
**word to** the action," and who **so** fathomed " the purpose
of playing," could **be** no ordinary performer.  Rowe says
**that** " the top of his performance was the Ghost in his own
Hamlet," but this, if true, is no reflection on his powers ;
**for** the Ghost is always assigned **to the** second tragedian in
**the** company, and as we know that Hamlet was played by
Burbage, the part of the Ghost might well devolve on
Shakespeare.  It is certain that he was accounted a good
actor by his contemporaries ; for his performances obtained
for him both rank in his profession and popularity with the
public.  Aubrey reports that he did " act exceedingly well,"
though he denies this merit to his friend Ben,—" now, Ben
Jonson was never a good actor, but **an** excellent instructor."
Chettle, **who must have often** witnessed his performance,
describes him as " excellent in the quality he professes,"
and what that was we learn from Dowdall, who calls **him**
" **our** English Tragedian."  Dugdale also speaks of him as
" William Shakespeare, the late famous Tragedian," and we
know that he habitually played the King, which, in his own
dramas, is always the part of a leading actor.  His graceful
personation of Royalty is attested by his friend Davies, in a
poetical address to himself as our English Terence, Mr.
William Shakespeare :—

> " Some say, good Will, which I in sport do sing,
>> Had'st thou not **played some kingly parts in sport,**
> Thou had'st been a companion for a king,
> And been a king among the meaner sort." [1]

---

[1] ' Scourge of Folly.'

Capell avers that a tradition was current at Stratford of a
very old man there having told some of his neighbours that
he remembered seeing Shakespeare brought on the stage on
another man's back; and this was interpreted as proving
that he had played Adam in 'As You Like It.' The very
old man is transformed by Oldyss into "one of Shakespeare's
younger brothers, who lived to a good old age, even some
years as I compute after the restoration of Charles II." It
is strange that such a statement should be constantly repeated, as it has been ever since, when it is open to the
easiest refutation, for the youngest of Shakespeare's brothers
was Edmund, who was himself a player, and died in 1607,[1]
five years before the poet. His brother Richard also preceded him to the grave, and their elder brother, Gilbert, is
supposed by Malone to have died before 1611–12, but at
any rate he cannot be thought to have been living "some
years after the restoration of King Charles II.," when, as he
was born in 1566, he would be upwards of a century old.

Even if better attested, this story would not assist us to
fix the position of Shakespeare as an actor; for as we know
that he began at the bottom of the ladder, and in his way
upwards fell into whatever place he was temporarily assigned, he may have played Adam in 'As You Like It,'
just as he sustained other inferior characters. The superior
parts came to him as promotion, as he displayed his superior
merit; and he took rank by the election of his fellows and
the preference of the public. Our great dramatist was
never above his business, were it ever so humble—never
above the relations of the position in which he happened to
be thrown. Whatever his consciousness of innate capability,
he did not claim to be recognized as a Heaven-born Roscius; and he would, indeed, have smiled at the conflict-
ing pretensions of the modern green-room, the terror of the

[1] Collier's ' Memoir.'

dramatic author of our day. The characters of a play appeared to him only in one aspect, as the embodiment of the performance, and they were to be cast in such a manner as would present this to the greatest advantage. The actors were to be selected for the parts, not the parts for the actors; and he looked rather to fuse all in a harmonious whole than to parade each as a brilliant. No one better knew that there would be as little profit in a company composed entirely of Burbages as in a drama presenting nothing but thunder; and to his eye the clown who did his inimitable fooling after the pattern of nature was not less a " well-graced actor " than the successful personator of Hamlet. The player, in fact, is told that his part is distinct from himself—" What's Hecuba to him, or he to Hecuba," [1] and the ambitious are admonished not to imitate Bottom, who makes us more alive to his ass's head when he attempts to play Pyramus.

His association with inferior parts exalts instead of dwarfing Shakespeare; for it is a proof both of the native greatness of his character and the versatility of his gifts. It brings out, also, his practical worth and modesty as well as his aptitude, so that the comic and the tragic Muse, as they alike inspire his pen, seem to have equally prompted his action. To him was given the rare power of excelling both as Pyramus and Bottom.

He was now in a situation to draw out, too, his taste for composition, and raise it into a pursuit. His wallet may not yet have thrown up the skull of Yorick, nor its other relics, for it had shut also on Venus and Adonis, and his sonnets. But he was revealing his abilities, and his productions must come to light when he drew light on himself. He found an opening in the old stock-plays of the theatre, which it was his daily task to con and study; and which, he saw, called for wider range in the scene, and scope in the characters.

<hr>

[1] ' Hamlet,' act ii. 2.

Perhaps his power was first displayed by a few adroit touches thrown into his own part, or that of Burbage, or by the restoration of some antique copy, defaced by time or wear. However it came about, he was soon engaged in writing up the dialogue of old plays, and remodelling or amplifying their plots—chiselling them into shape, and making them exercises for his " prentice han." We know not where to look for the sparkling thoughts which were then sown broadcast, often we may fear on the command of some illiterate manager, or to meet a low public taste ; setting many a precious jewel in a swine's snout. But this same public taste was by this means refined. Thus his thoughts, though they were unclaimed, were not lost. They accomplished the object in view, and still leavening those old Prolusions, have come down fresh to us. We know not how long he was engaged in such jour-neywork, but as the advantage of his emendations was seen, the demand upon him increased, until pieces in which he had introduced a speech of " some dozen or sixteen lines,"[1] in the manner of Hamlet, were placed in his hands to be re-cast. Tradition credits him with seven plays never included among his works. They possibly owe much to his pen, though not to his conception. The 'Merrie Devill of Edmonton' exhibits such masterly touches that the German critics claim it as wholly his. Charles Lamb all but avowed the same opinion, and though it is one we cannot admit, some of the incidents do, it must be owned, bring the great poet forcibly to mind. All the action in the forest, the manœuvres of the poachers, and the proceedings of the keepers, so indicate a skilled " woodman," that we can hardly acquit him of a hand in the deer-stalking expedition. Perhaps the 'Merrie Devill' was a stock-play which he was engaged to dress up, and the task was executed at a time when these impressions were fresh in his memory.

---

[1] ' Hamlet,' act ii. 2.

Even in the present day stage carpentry is badly remunerated, and pieces are adapted from the French at the minor theatres for a pound an act. The same rate of payment, measured by the money standard of those days, would only give Shakespeare a pound for adapting a five act play. Oldyss affirms, indeed, that he received no more than five **pounds for** ' Hamlet,' the price which was paid to Milton for ' Paradise Lost,' so that the same sum purchased our noblest epic and noblest tragedy. Though incessantly at work, it is clear that he made no appreciable addition to his income; for he could do nothing to relieve the pecuniary embarrassments of his father, and he was himself living in the deepest obscurity. No research will open to us that corner of the great city in which he had taken refuge. He was toiling out of sight, like Stephenson in the mine; down in the deeps of society, the deeps from which he was to come up, like Schiller's diver, to tell fearful secrets. But his retreat, wherever it might be, was a home. There was no blight on that humble hearth. **We** see its kindly light gleaming in his thoughts, in his creations, and in his own cheerful spirit. Thus **" an honest man is able to speak for himself, when a knave is not."** [1] Shakespeare is not to **be** judged by the **weak** inventions of antiquaries, but by his life, and by facts —by his own testimony. After three centuries, he is still " able to speak for himself;" for though he was now burrowing underground, we hear his voice, as Hamlet heard the Ghost's, and he is still "Old Truepenny." We know that he is not alone. His wife is with him in this dreary hour of toil, cheering him as he works, chained to the oar. His " sweet boy " is in her arms, while little Judith and Susan nestle at his feet. It is difficult **for a " poor player " to fill** so many mouths, even with **the help of** an occasional sovereign for **embellishing old plays.** But his tender wife shares his

[1] ' King Henry IV., Part II.,' act v. 1.

burden, and if she thinks doubtingly of the morrow, as likely to bring new anxieties and new cares ; if unbidden tears brim her eye, he can chase away both doubts and tears—

> " What! we have many goodly days to see,
>   The liquid drops of tears that you have shed,
>   Shall come again, transformed to orient pearl,
>   Advantaging their loan with interest,
>   Oftentimes double gain of happiness !" [1]

[1] 'King Richard III.,' act iv. 4.

## XXII.

### CLIMBING THE STEEPS.

**Few** will believe in a period of Shakespeare's life when he was unknown to the Muse. He was a poet by birth; and rhythm came to him intuitively, as soon as he began to think. If Voltaire made rhymes in his cradle, how much more Shakespeare! No doubt there was an epoch when he was seized with a new impulse—when this rudiment of poesy struck out and unfolded itself. He had possessed the faculty from the beginning, but now it became a power; and with the first conviction of its existence he recognized his vocation. It was to deliver the whole story of existence, in every sphere and relation, in every phase and aspect. He must give expression to the thoughts and form to the images that thronged through his mind, and were ever reflected there, as in a wizard mirror. The tender aspirations of love, and its passionate emotions, with the sullen broodings of hate, and its fierce impulses—all the motives of man, all the susceptibilities of woman, and the common frailty of both: these were to be the themes of his Muse. And he must carry the tale through the infinite diversity of Nature, portraying in the recital her phenomena and features in all their grace, beauty, and sublimity.

It is related of Albertus Magnus that he once amazed the Count of Holland, who had come to visit him, by transforming a little court-yard into a garden, threaded by a meandering stream, and girt with woods, which resounded with the song of birds. The imagination of Shakespeare was no less potent ; for it changed the alley of the crowded city into a beauteous landscape, and conjured up at will green hills and smiling valleys, wild moor, and shady forest. The poet's eye, in a fine frenzy rolling, saw, as in a dream, meads dotted with sheep, fields yellow with harvest, and hedges hung with the wild rose, or laden with blossom. And he could bring up the birds too, and raise a concert from "the nightingale's complaining note,"[1] the "love-song" of the robin redbreast,[2] the "lark that tirra-lirra chants,"[3] the finch,[4] the "thrush and the jay."[5] There was no feature of nature hid from that eye, no point overlooked, nor tint forgotten. As he sat by the midnight lamp, or lay awake on his pillow, when the great city was hushed, and nothing broke the universal stillness, he was busy with this magic, and the scenes that he created, unlike the illusions of Albertus Magnus, are around us still.

He called poetry "sweet," and well called it ; for it gave him a retreat from the world, beyond its influence—a world of his own. Here he sat, as in a hermitage, and mused on the vanity of this mortal coil, its pleasures and sorrows, its trials and triumphs—such stuff as dreams are made of. He must act his part and bear his burden ; but that done, he could withdraw into himself. Thus neither his own poverty, nor the reverses of his parents, neither privation nor suffering, could break his spirit, or subvert his fortitude :—

> " Though fortune's malice overthrow my state,
> My mind exceeds the compass of her wheel."[6]

MIND was his world ; and here he could defy the malice of fortune, which, though able to mar his best-laid projects

---

[1] ' Two Gentlemen of Verona,' act v. 4.

[2] Ibid., act ii. 1.

[3] ' Winter's Tale,' act iv. 2.

[4] ' Midsummer Night's Dream,' act iii. 1.

[5] ' Winter's Tale,' act iv. 2.

[6] ' King Henry VI., Part III.,' act iv. 3.

in life, was powerless against the airy nothings to which he gave a local habitation and a name.

He could have been but a short time on the stage before he became known to Sir Philip Sidney, and it was apparently about the same time that he made the acquaintance of Spenser. Both these illustrious men were play-goers, and both were 'in England in 1584, Spenser having been driven here by the Irish rebellion, while Sidney had not yet proceeded to the Netherlands. Walter Scott tells us that Sidney was such an admirer of Shakespeare, that he slept with his sonnets under his pillow, just as Alexander, a more renowned but not greater hero, made a pillow of the 'Iliad', and though he does not mention his authority, he doubtless had ground for the statement. The facts we now adduce—that Shakespeare came to London before the death of Sidney, and enjoyed the protection of his uncle, the Earl of Leicester—lend it confirmation. The point is of great importance in his history; for it affirms the existence of the bulk of his sonnets before he was twenty years of age; and, indeed, induces a belief that they were his letter of introduction to Sidney. At that time, literary productions, and particularly poems, were rarely given immediately to the printer, but were circulated by the author in manuscript, among his patrons and friends; and Sidney's own ' Arcadia ' was passed about in this way, and only reached the press four years after his death. It was by sending him a portion of his ' Fairy Queen ' that Spenser attracted his notice; and Shakespeare may have fallen in with the custom of the day, in the hope that his compositions might be brought before the great Earl, who would recognize his name, and perhaps consider that the lad he had saved from prison was not so black as he was painted.

However this may be, he would soon become known to Sidney by his adaptations of old plays, amongst the first of which we must place the two **Parts of** 'King Henry IV.,' which, as well as the drama of 'King **Henry V.,' were founded** on a wretched stock-play, called 'The Famous Victories of Henry V.' Shakespeare took up the names of the old characters, and many of the incidents, working them in with new, and rejecting the dialogue and colouring. No one has hitherto placed the two Parts of 'King Henry IV.' at an earlier date than 1590, but we shall presently show that they must have been produced before 1586, and they are so tinged with the impressions now in Shakespeare's mind, that **we may** safely assign them to 1584. The First Part transforms the low buffoon of the old piece into the witty knight, **who** is said by Oldyss **to be a** reminiscence of a Stratford **man;** Prince Henry is changed from a rascal **into a mere** amiable sort of scapegrace, sowing wild oats, **but animated** by noble intentions—as if Shakespeare designed to lead **his** friends to the same impression of himself; **and finally, both** knight and prince are carried off to Warwickshire, to the spot first in his thoughts, the neighbourhood of his native town.[1] This reflection of home deepens in the Second Part, a proof that it followed quickly on the First, while the feeling was still fresh. Here he takes his revenge on Sir Thomas Lucy, and carries his scapegrace through another stage, finally bringing him to turn over a new leaf, as **he** has done himself. The drift of the two pieces must have **been understood by those who knew his history, and he would accomplish a great object, if it tended to remove any prejudice created against him by his past misconduct. Whether this was achieved or not, the play could hardly** fail to bring back the story to the memory of his old protector, the Earl of Leicester, and he was not deterred by his antecedents from securing such an ally. Bishop Warburton penetrated the allegory in 'Midsummer Night's Dream,' and maintained

[1] 'King Henry IV., Part I.,' act iv. 2., " A Public Road *near* Coventry."

that " Cupid all armed" designated Leicester—without having this key ; but as there seemed no reason why Shakespeare should so distinguish the Earl, when he had no acquaintance with him, and was supposed to be dead **at the** time the play was written, his interpretation has always been rejected.   **But** the question takes another shape when we find **the Earl** alive, and Shakespeare in his ante-chamber.   We **now** understand that,—

> " —— a mermaid on a dolphin's back,
> Uttering such dulcet and harmonious breath,
> That the rude sea grew civil at her song,"

is, as Warburton assumes, Mary **Queen** of Scots ; and when the poet adds :

> " And certain stars shoot madly from their skies,"

we recognize an allusion to a recent event, the conspiracies of the Duke of Norfolk, the Earl of Northumberland, and Throckmorton.   Capell is thought unworthy of credit in affirming that the play was printed as early as **1595 ; but** here it is found to be in existence in 1585.   Malone thinks it was produced in **1594, just** nine years later, but he is evidently guessing on Capell.   We must think that he had done more wisely to follow the leading of his own judgment, which never appeared to greater advantage than in the criticism **on** this play, since he pronounced it the work of Shakespeare's genius "*in its* **minority!**"   He might have said, indeed, that the poet himself was **in** his minority ; for he was scarcely twenty-one when it appeared.

'Midsummer Night's Dream' is as much leavened as ' King Henry IV.,' with reminiscences of Shakespeare's home. Tradition, as we have heretofore shown, lays its scene at the Weir Brake, on the banks of the **Avon, and Shakespeare** brings in all the fairy lore **of his childhood.**   The description of **the** splendid **pageants at Kenilworth** recalls, too, a scene of his boyhood, and, at the same time, enables him to pay a compliment, and, as we shall presently see, render a service to the Earl of Leicester. That Kenilworth was in his mind is evident from another allusion which has been overlooked by the commentators, though it is a reminiscence of "the mermaid on the dolphin's back," and a proof that Shakespeare was present on the occasion. The dolphin in the Kenilworth pageant was employed to bear Arion, not "a mermaid," and the representative of the minstrel prepared himself for the task by potations from the earl's cellar, which so washed his speech out of memory, that being unable to repeat it, he pulled off his mask and exclaimed that "he was none of Arion, not he, but honest Harry Goldingham."[1] This incident is recalled by Bottom :— " Write me a prologue, and let the prologue seem to say, we will do no harm with our swords, and that Pyramus is not killed indeed ; and, for the more better assurance, tell them that I, Pyramus, am not Pyramus, but Bottom the weaver."[2]

Thus the Two Parts of 'King Henry IV.' and 'Midsummer Night's Dream' form a series, tinged with the hues of the author's own character and experience. The first piece exhibiting a shadowing of himself, weakly yielding to every seduction ; the second presenting the prodigal reclaimed, and castigating his old adversary, Sir Thomas Lucy ; and the third paying a tribute to the nobleman who had come to his rescue and saved him from prison.

The allusions in 'Midsummer Night's Dream' to passing events leads, indeed, to the impression that Shakespeare received from Leicester some hints on this point, as the earl was making them a means of recovering his influence with Elizabeth. It was now that he formed his association for her protection from "Popish conspirators," and the Roman Catholic nobility were so terrified by his proceedings, and

---

[1] Laneham's 'Kenilworth.'
[2] 'Midsummer Night's Dream,' act iii. 1.

by the tone of the public mind—for which they had given some cause, that Lord Paget and Charles Arundel fled to France, and were being followed by the Earl of Arundel, when he was intercepted. The affection felt for Elizabeth by her subjects was deepened by these occurrences, and naturally **drew** a tribute from Shakespeare, who, though he refrains from ministering to the public excitement, or prejudicing any party or sect, frames it in such a manner as to revive her favour for Leicester. The compliment is not scrawled at night on the wall of her palace, like that of Virgil to Augustus, but is delivered in open day, before her court and subjects. Never did homage take a more winning shape ; for, by sinking the present in the past, it was at once flattering and true, and the faded Queen saw herself once more a beauty, surrounded by a scene of unsurpassed splendour, and with a lover at her feet :—

> " Thou remember'st
> Since once I sat upon a promontory,
> And heard a mermaid, on a dolphin's back,
> Uttering such dulcet and harmonious breath,
> That the rude sea grew civil **at her song:**
> **And certain stars shot madly from their spheres,**
> **To hear the sea maid's music.**
> **That very time I saw (but thou could'st not)**
> Flying between the cold moon and the earth,
> Cupid all arm'd : a certain aim he took
> At a fair vestal, throned by the west,
> And loos'd his love-shaft smartly from his bow
> As it should pierce a hundred thousand hearts :
> But I might see young Cupid's fiery shaft
> Quench'd in the chaste beams of the watery moon,
> And the imperial votaress passed on,
> In maiden meditation fancy-free." [1]

The three plays must have produced but **a small sum,** as they leave Shakespeare still in **obscurity, and it does** not appear that he received any **substantial mark of patron-** age from Leicester ; for he was unable to arrange **the affairs of**

[1] ' Midsummer Night's Dream,' act ii. 2.

his father, though he probably afforded him assistance. The better fortune which had apparently **visited the family at** the time of his marriage was a mere gleam, vanishing as it **came**; and he saw his parents daily overtaken by reverses, which grew more desperate as they advanced in years. **In** 1585 John Shakespeare comes forward in his old character, as an embarrassed man, being cited in the Court of Record on the 27th of October for a debt to John Browne. The family name, indeed, was now altogether in bad odour; for **about** this **time** proceedings were taken against "Thomas Shaxper," his first appearance on this stage; and respecting whom nothing further is known. **Browne's action** extended **to several hearings, which** carried **it over to the 19th of January,** 1586, when the claim **was established, and the poor alderman was served with an execution.**

The return made to the court is a painful revelation:— "*Johannes Shackspere nihil habet unde distr. potest*—" John Shakespeare had no goods to satisfy the distress! **On the** 16th February Browne obtained a *capias* against him, and on the 2nd March an *alias capias*; but we learn from a marginal note to the last entry that he took nothing by his motion—"*non sold., per Browne.*" This may indeed have resulted from his own forbearance, as he might shrink from stripping a fallen man, once the **chief** magistrate, and still **one of the aldermen of** the **town; but the words** suggest a less favourable construction. **At the same time, it is clear that John Shakespeare was** treated with **great lenity in his distress. His brother** aldermen reduced his rates and **assessments; and, as he was in** constant fear of arrest, connived at his absence from their meetings, though it was against their rules—for there is no record of his having been fined for non-attendance. But this indulgence could not be extended to him in perpetuity. As long waiting wore out the patience of creditors, long absence weakened the sympathies of aldermen ; and at last there were murmurers in the assembly. Some friendly warning reached John Shakespeare, for, regardless of duns and bailiffs, he took the bold step of attending the council on the 21st of August, 1586, within five months of the issue of the "*alias capias*." After an absence of four years, his appearance at the table must have been as startling to his colleagues as that of Banquo at the board of Macbeth, but he came too late to save his dignity. At the next monthly meeting, on the 6th of September, he was formally deposed :—

"At this hall William Smythe and Richard Courte are chosen to be aldermen in the place of John Wheler and John Shaxspere ; for that Mr. Wheler doth desire to be put out of the company, and Mr. Shaxspere doth not come to the hall when he be warned, nor hath not done of long time."

The statement that John Shakespeare had absented himself for a considerable period has led to a conjecture that the mention of his name as present on the 21st of August, is a mistake ; but the words—" nor hath not done of long time," refer to a practice, not a single occasion, and no way impeach the previous record. We may, in fact, believe that his connection with the council, now that he was a hopeless insolvent, was thought a public scandal, and that this was the real cause of his deposition, though non-attendance was made the pretext.

While these events were passing in Stratford, Shakespeare was engaged in a hard struggle in London. He had now lost what countenance he received from Sidney and Leicester, as the expedition of 1585 carried them both to Holland, and there would seem to have been, about the same time, some change in the public taste, which discouraged him from composing another play—for this must be the period pointed at in Spenser's ' Tears of the Muses,' written about 1585, though not printed till five years later. He so withdrew himself from **authorship that Spenser mourns him as dead, while he already pronounces him the oracle of the Muses**—

> " And he, the man whom Nature's self hath made
>    To mock herself, and Truth to imitate
>    With kindly counter under mimic shade,
>    Our pleasant Willy, ah ! is dead of late ! "

Spenser presently explains that he is not really dead, but that the public could only be attracted by " scoffing scurrility," " scornful folly," and " shameless ribaldry," **themes** not **to the taste** of Shakespeare, and this kept him silent :—

> " But that same gentle spirit, from whose pen
>    Large streams of honey and sweet nectar flow,
>    Scorning the boldness of such base-born men
>    Which dare their follies forth so rashly throw,
>    Doth rather choose to sit in idle cell
>    Than so himself to mockery to sell."

**We are told in the present day that Shakespeare looked** to his Muse only as a means of making money, yet here one of his contemporaries records that he threw down his pen— lived in idleness, in a time of scarcity and at a moment of great family distress, rather than pander to a corrupt public taste. This corresponds with his own assertion ; for he **declares** that he **loved poetry, just as if poetry** were his **mistress.** His love for it was like his love for Anne—like the passion Anne cherished for music :—

> " If music and sweet poetry agree,
>    As they must needs, the sister and the brother,
>    Then must the love be great 'twixt thee and me,
>    Because thou lov'st the one and I the other."

What money he acquired **came, in** fact, by gift, and could never have been in his thoughts when he wrote. His inspi- ration was from Nature, not Mammon ; it came in the **glance** that he threw from **heaven to earth,** from earth to heaven, from the forms of things unknown! He did not woo the Muse, as Fenton first wooed Anne Page—for her gold. He was drawn to her by a fascination before he could dream that **poetry** was a **treasure, which would buy** him honour, station, and troops of friends. **Fame he dis-dained to pick** up, **when it** lay **at his feet. It would seem as though, in** respect to himself, he was **ever looking beyond this** little life rounded **with a sleep, and the** great globe itself. Coronation **in the capitol, by the vote** of the people, compensated Tasso **for a blasted** existence; Shakespeare neglected even to give **his works to the** printer. He knew, indeed, they were to live **for ever :—**

> "So long as men can breathe, or eyes can see,
>   So long lives this, and this gives life to thee."

But they were not to owe their preservation to himself, or to any interference on his part ; it was to be the effect of their own merit.

There is nothing so great in Shakespeare **as this con-**tempt for fame, unless it be his **acceptance at** all **times of his position.** Never **does** he breathe **a word of complaint, but always utters the** same **sentiments, expressive of brave en-durance, coupled with** incessant **exertion.** He speaks of **adversity in terms** almost **of affection, as of a** counsellor and **friend.** Instead of brooding **over reverses and** railing at fate, he sets himself to overcome all obstacles, **be** they ever so great, but gives up the contest when, as in the period of his life we are now reviewing, his way is barred by principle. He will not hire his talents to what Spenser calls " scoffing scurrility, scornful folly, and shameless ribaldry." " Our pleasant Willy " prefers the sharpest pinch of poverty **to such** baseness.

**His patron was about the same time encountering** diffi-**culties** on a greater stage, and **here he lost his** friend Sir Philip Sidney, who was killed at the battle of Zutphen, on the 22nd of September, 1586. His death was followed by a succession of reverses, culminating in the fall of Sluys; and this was such a disaster, that it destroyed all confidence in Leicester, who was angrily called home. On his arrival the council assembled in glee to witness his disgrace, as he had sunk so low with the Queen, that she grew furious at the mention of his name. But though now fifty-four, he was still her "sweet Robin," and came, saw, and conquered. The council were expecting him to appear on his knees, when he took his seat at the table, and Lord Buckhurst received a reprimand from the Queen for having counselled his recall. He was again master of the situation.

It requires some faith to accept the stories of his crimes, when we find him retaining this ascendency over Elizabeth through his whole life. Bearing in mind that it raised endless cabals against him at court, and combined with his haughty manners to render him odious to the people, while the Roman Catholics regarded him with intense hatred, it is easy to conceive that he was a constant mark for detraction. The scandals about him could have received no credit from the Queen, or her attachment for him must have declined; and he could hardly have lived on the friendliest terms with his step-son Essex, if he was believed to have poisoned his father. This, indeed, is not the place to vindicate his character, but we may be pardoned a word of digression in favour of the patron of Spenser and Shakespeare.

Leicester never displayed more arrogance than now. He took up his abode at a splendid mansion, near Temple Bar, long since superseded by Essex Street and Devereux Court, and changed its name of Paget Place to Leicester House. It obtains a grateful remembrance from Spenser:—

> " A stately place,
> Where oft I gained gifts and goodly grace
> Of that great lord." [1]

---

[1] Spenser's ' Prothalamion.'

The note in the Lucy pedigree affirms that he required Sir Thomas Lucy to adopt his badge of the bear and ragged staff, which he wished to see worn by the servants of all the gentry of Warwickshire, and the Charlecote Knight refused to comply, at the same time calling him an upstart. But it is dangerous to hurl opprobrious names at the friend of a poet. Leicester remembered Justice Shallow, and according to the Lucy note, he now applied to Shakespeare to take up his quarrel, by bringing Sir Thomas Lucy again on the stage. We could hardly obtain a stronger proof that the poet was not connected with the ancient Ardens, for Edward Arden, the representative of that family, who was executed in 1583 for his share in the Throckmorton conspiracy, declared that he was brought to the scaffold by Leicester because he had refused to wear his badge ; and it is incredible that Shakespeare could be persuaded to gibbet Sir Thomas Lucy on such a ground, by the man who had thus hanged his kinsman. The state assumed by Leicester in 1587, points to that year as the time at which he undertook this task, nor could we well assign an earlier date to 'The Merry Wives of Windsor.' No commentator has yet ranged it before 1595, but it is generally placed after 1596, as it was not till then that Dover established the Cotswold games, referred to by Slender in Scene I. But these were merely a revival, and Shakespeare is speaking of the original games, which existed in the reign of Henry IV. We have now established that the play was produced at least seven years earlier than any one has surmised, since Leicester, at whose behest it was written, died in 1588, and the reasons we have adduced point indeed to the previous year as the date of its production. What Mr. Collier justly considers a surreptitious copy, found its way to the press in 1602, and another surreptitious edition was printed in 1619. We have already remarked that a copy of the latter edition was lately discovered in the Lucy

archives at Charlecote, showing how it had been sought at
the time by the family ; and as it is extremely rare,[1] we sub-
join a transcription of the title-page :—

A Most Pleasant and excellent Comedy of Sir John Falstaffe
and the merry Wives of Windsor,
With the Swaggering Voice of Ancient Pistol and Corporal
Nym.
Written by W. Shakespeare.
Printed for Arthur Johnson,
1619.

It has always been said that ' The Merry Wives' was
written to please Elizabeth, who had expressed a wish to see
Falstaff in love.  This is a tradition[2] we cannot relinquish,
and it is quite consistent with the statement in the Lucy note,
which must otherwise have set it aside.  It accounts, too, for
the scene being laid at Windsor, an unlikely resort for a
Gloucestershire Justice, unless the design were to compliment Royalty.  The Benediction of Windsor Castle, and the
Notice of the Forest and of the Order of the Garter, confirm
this impression, and were assuredly meant for the Queen's ear.

> " Search Windsor Castle, elves, within and out :
>     Strew good luck, ouphes, on every sacred room ;
>     That it may stand till the perpetual doom,
>     In state as wholesome, as in state 'tis fit ;
>     Worthy the owner, and the owner it.
>     The several chairs of order look you scour
>     With juice of balm, and every precious flower :

---

[1] A reprint of the edition of 1602 has been produced by the Shakespeare
Society.  The edition of 1619 was known to Theobold and Steevens.

[2] The tradition first appeared in print in 1702, when we learn from
Denwes, the critic, in an epistle prefixed to a transversion of ' The Merry
Wives,' that " this play was written at he command of Queen Elizabeth."
Seven years later it is repeated by Rowe, who adds that the Queen, having
seen the Two Parts of ' King Henry IV.' desired to see Falstaff in another
play, which should represent him in love.

> Each fair instalment, coat, and several crest,
> With loyal blazon, evermore be blessed !
> And nightly, meadow-fairies, look, you sing
> Like to the Garter's compass in a ring :
> The expressure that it bears, green let it be,
> More fertile-fresh than all the field to see ;
> And, Honi soit qui mal y pense, write
> In emerald tufts, flowers purple, blue, and white :
> Like sapphire, pearl, and rich embroidery,
> Buckled below fair knighthood's bending knee :
> Fairies, use flowers for their charactery." [1]

The commentators are so puzzled at the set made in the play at Shallow's arms, that many question the application to Sir Thomas Lucy, while others admit it cautiously, as having some appearance of probability. The truth is, that it catches up, in a few words, the armorial history of the family, in a manner not to be misunderstood by his neighbours ; and this was naturally made the point of retaliation by Leicester, as a sneer at his own arms was the ground of offence. The attack is first brought to bear on the family pedigree. Slender declares that Shallow writes himself *armigero*, " in any bill, warrant, quittance, or obligation, *armigero*," which Shallow confirms—" ay, that I do, and have done any time these three hundred years." Slender grows warmer—" all his successors gone before him have done 't, and all his ancestors that come after him may ; they may give the dozen white luces in their coat." Here the shafts take direct aim, but the mark is unseen by the commentators, who are not aware that the family anciently bore the name of Charlecote, which was changed, in the twelfth century, for that of Lucy. This was assumed by Sir William de Charlecote in right of his mother, Cecilia Lucy ; and the same right gave him the Lucy arms. Thus the successive heads of the family had in 1587, written themselves " *armigero* any time these three hundred years." As the real name of the family was not

<hr>

[1] ' Merry Wives of Windsor,' act v. 5.

Lucy, but Charlecote, Sir Thomas's successors went before him, for they had a better right to the name, from bearing it later, than he had ; and his ancestors came after him, as his descendants would all be Lucys, and from the Lucys he claimed to have sprung. " They may give the dozen white luces in their coat." Ferne's ' Blazon of Gentry ' describes the arms of Geoffrey Lord Lucy, as " three luces hariant argent,"—the same three luces which we may see carved in stone on the gateway at Charlecote, placed there by Sir Thomas Lucy. But the " dozen white luces " have here a double signification, referring not only to the arms, but to their original owners—the dozen Lords de Lucy, the *white* or pure Lucys. " It is an old coat," says Shallow, " but the luce is a fresh fish,"—by which we are to understand that the contemporary Lucys were a fresh family who had taken an old coat of arms—the arms of the Lords de Lucy. It was these, the orriginal stock, who were the salt fish ; and " this salt fish is an old coat." There was salt in the satire, and we see what Shakespeare could make of a small subject ; but, after all, it admitted the family antiquity, and Sir Thomas Lucy might have joined in the laugh it excited.

This play has been pronounced Shakespeare's highest achievement in comedy ; and viewed as a whole, in the diversity of the characters, the flow and variety of the incidents, the range taken by the action within such narrow limits as a small country town, and the harmony of its parts, it cannot be surpassed in any language. As a picture of rural life in the days of our ancestors its value is inestimable ; and, though there are Elizabethan tints in the colouring, we may consider it to reflect the epoch of the Henrys, as tradition had reported it to Shakespeare.

The Queen was highly diverted with the new view of ' Falstaff.' To us his story would seem incomplete without his adventures at Windsor ; but they came to her like a little fresh scandal. The effect was heightened, if Leicester gave her any inkling of the concealed satire; of course, saying nothing of the bear and ragged staff, but throwing it all on the deer stalking. But Leicester himself was not aware how much **the play owed to** the local recollections of Shakespeare. We have **shown that** Sir Hugh Evans was drawn from his **schoolmaster, and has** left his name in the Stratford **Register: three of** the characters bear the name of Page, which occurs **in the will of** his step-grandmother, Agnes Arden.[1]  Anne Page presents reminiscences of his wife, and the Stratford Register notes the death of Samuel Brook—think of that, Master Brook! The whole play betrays where Shakespeare's mind was turned at the time he was writing.

At the commencement of 1587, his thoughts might well indeed be thus pre-occupied, for there was a dark cloud on his father's house. In the midst of his own embarrassments, John Shakespeare entangled his affairs with those of **his** brother Henry; and this led to his being cited in the **Court** of Record, on the 18th of January, 1587, **at the suit of** Nicholas Lane. `The transaction was **not** a recent one, and **had evidently caused disquiet to the family for some time; for one brother had come to the assistance of the other, so that Ni**cholas Lane*may have threatened proceedings—been playing the lion—a year or two before he commenced the action. Anachronisms are no strain to Shakespeare, but his fellow-townsmen would see a meaning in the interlude in 'Midsummer Night's Dream, which associates classic times with Nick Bottom the weaver.[2]  Nicholas Lane lived at the *end* of Greenhill Street, and his garden hedge extended to the *end* of Henley Street;[3] so that he might well be called

---

[1] "Item, I give and bequeath to **John Page and his wife, the longer liver of** them, six and eightpence."

[2] 'Midsummer Night's Dream,' **act iii.** 1.

[3] **See page 27, ante.**

Nick *Bottom*, and his attitude towards the Shakespeares is indicated by Quince, when he addresses him as " BULLY."

John Shakespeare entertained such misgivings of the issue of the action, that he avoided being present when it was tried, and we learn from the register that he was represented by Richard Hill, probably a son of John Hill, his wife's step-brother. There was real ground for his fears; for in spite of his precautions, he fell into the clutches of Snare and Fang, and the proceedings in the suit on the 29th of March refer to his producing a writ of habeas corpus, showing that he was at last in gaol.

It is singular that none of the biographers of the poet have remarked, at this point, a very significant fact, that while his father, his uncle, and the unknown " Thomas Shakxper"—in short, all who bore his name, are found plunged in difficulties, Shakespeare himself makes no appearance in the Court of Record, a clear proof that at the age of twenty-three, the very period when he is represented as leading a disorderly life, and consorting with evil companions, he was the only one of his family who was honourably paying his way, though weighted with a wife and three children. We have here, even without the evidence of the Lucy note, ample corroboration of the statements of Aubrey and Dowdall, as to the age at which he quitted Stratford, and tradition is vindicated in assigning his mad days to his early youth.

# XXIII.

## SUCCESS.

As we have adduced ground for concluding that the 'Merry Wives of Windsor' was produced in 1587, and Shakespeare then received a recompense from Leicester, it is easy to believe that he at once procured the liberation of his father, for nothing more is heard of the suit of Lane. The arrangement necessarily involved a visit to Stratford, and we seem to attend the poet as he releases him from prison, and restores him to home, and then taking a tender leave of his mother, again turns his back on Stratford, burning to redeem the tarnished honour of his family and his own.

The effect of his determination is immediately apparent in the fruits of his pen. He is said to have written 'The Merry Wives' in a fortnight, no doubt under the spur of the family distress, and the year had not closed when he produced 'King John,' which bears marks of having been written on the first rumour of the Spanish Armada. Patriotism never dictated a nobler strain than the concluding words of the play, which, after representing the dreadful spectacle of a foreign invasion aided by intestine feuds, here admonishes factions to forget their differences, and unite against the common enemy :—

> " This England never did, nor never shall,
> Lie at the proud foot of a conqueror,
> But when it first did help to wound itself.
>  *  *  *  *  *
> Come the three corners of the world in arms,
> And we shall shock them. Nought shall make us rue,
> If England to itself do rest but true."

'King John' was quickly followed by 'Love's Labour's Lost,' which bears the same impress of the time ; and indeed Armado, the Spaniard, is indebted to the Armada for his name. The critics have omitted to note that Shakespeare repaid the obligation, for this quiz on Spanish chivalry fore-shadowed Don Quixote.

It is true the resemblances of the two creations may be accidental, merely a coincidence of thought in men of kin-dred genius ; but, as a rap at Spain and the Armada, the play was likely to be translated in the Netherlands, and in the sixteen years that elapsed before the production of 'Don Quixote,' the translation might reach Cervantes.' The Knight of the Woful Countenance would certainly be thought to have suggested Armado, as presented in the King's de-scription, if he, instead of Armado, could have claimed the precedence :—

> " A man in all the world's new fashion planted,
>     That hath a mint of phrases in his brain :
> One who the music of his own vain tongue
>     Doth ravish like enchanting harmony ;
> A man of compliments, *whom right and wrong*
>     *Have chose as umpire of their mutiny :*
> This child of fancy, that Armado hight,
>     For interim to our studies shall relate,
> In high-born words, the worth of many a knight
>     From tawny Spain, lost in the world's debate.
> How you delight, my lords, I know not, I ;
> But I protest, I love to hear him lie,
> And I will use him for my minstrelsy.
>         Armado is a most illustrious wight,
> A man of fire-new words, fashion's own knight."[2]

The two characters vary in their development and even their conception, but they preserve such a resemblance as to mark them of the same stem. Don Quixote is as fond of " fire-new " words as Armado ; they equally see everything through a perverted medium ; and the Knight of La Mancha

---

[1] ' Don Quixote ' was published in 1604.

[2] ' Love's Labour 's Lost,' act i. 1.

elevates a peasant girl into a lady love, as Armado sees a divinity in Jacquenetta. The intuitive perception of Shakespeare caught up the characteristics of the Spaniards, whom he only knew by report, with the same felicity as their great countryman.

The **French** physician recommended his languishing **patient to go and see** the famous comedian, whose drollery **could not** fail to make him laugh. "Alas!" replied the **sufferer**, "I am the man." Shakespeare was diverting the whole nation, and writing comedies for latest ages, under a **load of** anxiety and care. But there are now symptoms of an improvement in his affairs, reflected in those of his father, which it is surprising that no one has noted; for in 1588 John Shakespeare appears in the Bailiff's Court at Stratford in a new position—as a plaintiff.[1] His liberation from prison and this change in his circumstances follow so close on the production of 'The Merry Wives of Windsor,' as to amount to a proof that he was then succoured by his son, **and the** impression is confirmed when we find him plaintiff in **another** suit in the following year.[2] Yet **putting aside the subsidy of** Leicester, it is plain that the poet's productions made little **addition to his means; for though the allusion in Greene's** '**Xenophon**'[3] **proves that 'Hamlet' was** a familiar play in **1589,** and, consequently, had been a long time on the stage, and though his comedies received high praise from Spenser some years before, he is still out of sight—still climbing the hill Difficulty. Inferentially, indeed, we may, for the first time, obtain a glimpse of his residence at this period, or rather show reason to conclude that it was in the same place as in 1596, when, we learn from a document found by Malone

---

[1] Jun. 20. 30 Eliz. Johannes Shaxpere queritur **versus Johaunem** Tomson, in placito debiti.

[2] April 23. 31 Eliz. **Johannes Shaxpere queritur versus Willielmum** Grene de **placito** debiti.

[3] Quoted at p. 96, ante.

amongst the papers of the celebrated actor **Edward Alleyn,** that he lived near Palace Garden. His name is included in a list of residents who complained **against the Garden as a** public nuisance, and which was discovered by Mr. Collier at Dulwich College. What leads us to believe that he dwelt here in 1588 is the allusion of Slender to the bear Sackerson —"I have seen Sackerson loose twenty times, and have taken him by the chain: but, I warrant you, the women have so cried and shrieked at it, that it passed."[1] The incessant uproar in the Garden must have been a great annoyance to Shakespeare, whose avocations, both as an author and actor, demanded quiet: " You'll leave your noise anon, ye rascals: do you take the court for Paris Garden?[2] He was, however, actuated in his opposition by a higher motive—abhorrence of the revolting exhibitions; for we see it was long before he petitioned for their suppression that he held up their patrons in 'Slender' to public derision. A place so disreputable created a bad neighbourhood, **and the list in** Dulwich College mentions one of Shakespeare's neighbours by the designation given to the accomplice of Boult and Pander, in 'Pericles.' Such disadvantages imply a low rent, and it is a fair inference that there was little increase in his actual income while he remained in this quarter.

The Garden derived its name from Robert de Paris, who resided here in the reign of Richard the Second, and a corruption of the name survived, after the Garden was swept away, in the adjacent Ferry, which was called Parish Garden Stairs. Here Shakespeare often took boat to Blackfriars, on his way to the theatre; and the buildings on the opposite shore were so many beacons to his Muse. They suggested to him the scenes for his great dramatic epic of 'King Henry VI.,' which begins in Westminster Abbey,[3] and ends

---

[1] ' Merry Wives of Windsor,' act i. 1.

[2] 'King Henry VIII.,' act v. 3.

[3] Part I., act i. 1., " Westminster Abbey."

in the Tower.[1]  Between came the Temple Gardens, where he makes the factious Barons pluck the fatal roses ; Baynard's Castle, which he also associates with the struggle, and where we shall presently see him an honoured guest ; and White-friars, where the unhappy Henry was entombed.  We can trace these poetic associations wherever he is met, as if he sought to surround himself with a world of his own, yet ever merged that of his fancy with the one in which he lived.

Mr. Collier found a paper in the Ellesmere archives, which represents Shakespeare as a " sharer " in the Black-friars theatre in 1589.  It purports to be a certificate of the good behaviour of the company, addressed to the Privy Council, and the same designation is applied to sixteen persons, amongst whom the poet stands fifth.  The document has been pronounced spurious,[2] but perhaps this opinion will be relinquished when it is seen that he was now the author of numerous plays, and not, as hitherto supposed, a mere novice.  The term does not imply that he was one of the owners of the theatre, but that he had a certain share of the profits ; and it was by no means uncommon for companies to be formed on such an arrangement.

Three years elapse before we again meet his name.  But his occultation was not a period of idleness, passed with the wits at the taverns, or a rumour of him would have come forth.  It was consumed in hard toil by the midnight lamp, which threw its light out on the world ; so we need not wonder that our next report of him is abuse.  The tirade comes in a pamphlet, entitled " A Groatsworth of Wit, Bought with a Million of Repentance," the last effusion of Robert Greene.  It was written when the unhappy author was at the point of death, in the last refuge left to his poverty, the house of a poor shoemaker, and was inscribed to

---

[1] Part III., act v. 7., " A Room in the Palace at the Tower."
[2] It is given in the Appendix.

three brother dramatists, Marlowe, **Lodge,** and Peele.[1] Forgotten by these old boon companions, and by the magnates
who had courted him in the hour of his popularity, **he**
addresses them in the bitterest spirit of reproach, holding
up to each his own image, mirrored by a mind blurred by
disappointment, and overshadowed by the remembrance of
opportunities lost and time misspent. We may fear that the
presentment of his three friends is, nevertheless, too truthful.
But our concern is not with this, for he pushes them aside to
show us Shakespeare, and we receive a forced recognition of
him in the middle of his career. He must be standing well,
indeed, when a brother author views him with such feelings,
and, from the bed of death, pronounces him a **despoiler and
impostor, and a** man out of the literary pale. **Because he**
has given life and soul to **plots which came to him dummies,**
he is described **as** one who pretends to improve the **work of**
others and merges it in his own. **He takes in his hand a**
rod, and throws it down a serpent, and the magicians of the
day only throw down their rods to see his swallow them up.
This is a trick in the eyes of Greene. He tells his brother
dramatists that the sweet swan is a crow, garnished with
their feathers ; a burr, cleaving to their keels ; an upstart,
antic, and ape. But we know what is at the bottom when
authors and critics call names—a bitter sense of inferiority,
or a deep personal **hate ; and this it was that made that**
galled spirit wince.

Greene does not mention any of his great rival's productions, but as he pictures him as having "a tiger's heart
wrapt in a player's hide," parodying **York's denunciation of**
Margaret, " O tiger's heart wrapt in a woman's hide,"[2] we
know that he had now produced the Second **and** Third Parts

---

[1] It is directed " To those Gentlemen, his Quondum Acquaintances, that
Spend their Wits in Making Plays."

[2] 'King Henry VI., Part III.,' act ii. 4.

of 'King Henry VI.' In 1592 they had been repeatedly performed—for a reference by parody would only be made to a familiar play. But the one shadow of the murdered King at Greene's bedside might have passed unnoted, if it had not been **preceded** by others, and if he did **not discern behind "many more," as clearly as** Macbeth. Here was **Shakespeare's crime.** To Greene he was already what he **was afterwards to Ben** Jonson—the "Soul of the Age," and **we** feel that it is to the reviler's eye, not his own, that he appears as "the only *Shake*-scene in a country." But the literary world will always have Greenes, and we may know how to appraise their abuse, when we see how they vilified Shakespeare! Burr, Crow, Antic, Upstart, and Ape—it is a miracle that he was not writ down Ass.[1]

The attack was contemned by himself, but it was taken up by others, and such an outcry raised as proves, in the clearest manner, that he was now a popular favourite. Greene was in his grave, but the pamphlet was **not received as the testimony of one who came from the dead.** It was declared to **emanate from a living pen—from either** Nashe or Chettle; but the latter, avowedly its editor, was **held responsible for its publication.** The feeling against him was so strongly pronounced that **it could not be left un**noticed, and he embraced the opportunity shortly afterwards

---

[1] The language used by Greene is so extravagant, that it may be necessary to give the passage, though it has often been printed:—" Base-minded men, all three of you, if by my misery ye be not warned; for unto none of you (like me) sought those burrs to cleave: those puppets (I mean) that speak from our mouths, those antics garnished in our colours. Is it **not** strange that I, to whom they all have been beholden, is it not like that you, to whom they all have been beholden, shall (were ye in that **case that I am** now) be both of them at once forsaken? **Yes,** trust them not; **for there is an upstart crow beautified with our feathers, that, with his ' tiger's heart wrapt in a player's hide,' supposes he is as well able to bombast out a blank verse as** the best of you; and being an absolute Johannes Fac-totum, is, in his own conceit, the only *Shake*-scene in a country."

afforded by 'Kind Heart's Dream,' to declare in the preface that the pamphlet had not been written either by himself or Nashe, but was really composed by Greene, at the same time he expressed his regret at the attack on Shakespeare, and, while retracting nothing in reference to Marlowe, Lodge, and Peele, made him full amends. It is impossible to overrate this tribute to his professional merit and personal character; for, though yielded to pressure, it comprises those points on which we most desire to be informed. To screen himself, Chettle might ascribe the slanders of his scurrilous pen to a dead man, who could tell no tales; but here he speaks of what is known to every one, and what would expose him to derision if he exceeded the truth. Such a consideration gives volume to his words, though they are but few; for they bring Shakespeare before us at twenty-eight as he appeared to his contemporaries—a portrait, though a miniature. They tell us that he is an excellent actor, a courteous and upright man, and an accomplished author, possessing the esteem of persons of rank, and an honourable reputation. His conduct in life, in its various relations, and the qualities of his heart and disposition, must indeed have stood spotless to wrest such testimony from a hostile witness.[1]

Shakespeare could no more be accused of plagiarism on the ground alleged by Greene than the same charge can be made against Canova, because a mason's hand shaped the

---

[1] Chettle's testimony claims to be given in his own words:—" With neither of them that take offence was I acquainted, and with one of them I care not if I never be: *the other whom at that time I did not so much spare as since I wish I had,* for that, as I have moderated the heat of living writers, and might have used my own discretion, especially in such a case, the author being dead, that I did not, I am as sorry as if the original fault had been my fault, *because myself have seen his demeanour no less civil than he excellent in the quality he professes;* besides, divers of worship have reported *his uprightness of dealing, which argues his honesty,* and his facetious grace in writing that approves his art."

marble which he fashioned into the Graces. Admitting that the block was already rough-hewn, it was Shakespeare who gave it the delicate form of art. The plays were still his, for it was to him they owed their shape, speech, action, and the breath of life. But, in this case, there is no vestige of the **alleged earlier** pieces which they are said to have **absorbed, and** Greene's insinuation must be directed at the **Two Parts of** 'King Henry IV.,' not the Three Parts of 'King Henry VI.' The supposed outlines of the great trifold **drama were** doubtless Shakespeare's own, before he had acquired his full power; and were improved and expanded as it matured—for he carried on this elaboration, as we find by the later versions, to the last. His Muse was naturally attracted by the story of the civil war, recorded in the loved ballads, and fought out in the haunts of his youth; and it must not be forgotten that we owe the first works of Scott to similar recollections.

The subject possessed no greater interest for **himself** than for his wife, for it could hardly be that he had not talked of it when **a lover, as** they strolled together over Bowden **Hill, or stood** in the streets of Coventry or **Warwick. Could imagination** call up their home **at this** time of promise, **the poet would be** found working **out** his plot mindful of those memories; and we should see the still **bright** eye of Anne grow brighter as the familiar incident expanded into a scene, the scene into an act, the act into a play. Here were an inspiration worthy of this great drama, the 'Iliad' of feudalism.

But Shakespeare's life derives from 'King Henry VI.' a light which needs no help from imagination. Chettle refers **to** the respect entertained for him by "divers of worship," and we find **that** the Third **Part was** originally played by the company **of the** Earl **of** Pembroke. This **is the** first trace of Shakspeare's **connection** with the Pembrokes, and we understand how it was formed, now we are aware that he was known to Sidney and Leicester; for the Countess of Pembroke was the sister of Sidney, and Leicester's niece. 'At Leicester House, indeed, we meet the whole circle of his titled friends; for the Earl was the step-father of Essex, who was the bosom friend of Southampton, and was allied to the Talbots, a fact which, conjoined with the prominence given to the two Talbots in the First Part of 'King Henry VI.,' raises a presumption that Shakepeare was now on friendly terms with that family. We may see a softer feeling than patriotism threading his portraiture of Talbot, Earl of Shrewsbury, whom he presents as the Bayard of the drama. Knighthood is made to dazzle us in this last of the Knights, for the poet invests him in defeat with all the panoply of chivalry. His frantic resentment of insult when, though a guarded prisoner, he tears up the stones from the streets to fling at the French rabble—his indomitable courage in battle, and his heroism in death, are beautifully contrasted with his grief for Salisbury, his friendship for Congreve, and his generous conduct to the Countess of Auvergne. All the gentler qualities of humanity thus blend in his breast with a passion for glory resting on loyalty to the King, and devotion to his country. To show, moreover, that his heroism is innate—that it springs from his soul, and is not the result of physical strength, the great warrior whose name the mothers of France held as a terror over their children, is described as small of stature and insignificant in appearance. At the same time we are brought to understand that the inherent tenderness of a gentle nature will survive even a life of warfare, and Talbot, surrounded and cut off, contends with his son which shall die for the other. They fall together, as neither will yield, and the incident sheds new lustre on the old historic name and title, which are still preserved on the roll of our nobility, and borne by the lineal representative of the race, the present Earl of Shrewsbury and Talbot. The link that, as we shall see, connects them with Shakespeare, gives them also a nobility in literature.

As the churchyard of Stratford attracted his childhood, the poet now loved **to haunt the** cemetery of History, and muse on its adamantine tombs. Nor was he unobservant **of the** history in progress, actually passing around him— panics, conspiracies, intrigues, and tumults, which almost caught him in their vortex. We may note the influence it exercised on his genius, by the vivid reflection presented in his works; let us see if we can trace also the emotions it awoke in his breast.

# XXIV.

## SHAKESPEARE AND HIS PATRON.

LEICESTER HOUSE was bequeathed by the Earl, at his death, to his step-son, the Earl of Essex, and took the name of its new master. We shall make it apparent that he continued the friend of Shakespeare, and it was doubtless under his roof that the poet met his noblest patron. Henry Wriothesley, Earl of Southampton, was the other self of Essex, and the roll of nobility contains no name so dear to literature. Happily we may reverence the man as well as the patron; for he is as honourably enshrined in History. He was indeed eminently adapted to figure in both. Nature and fortune had bestowed upon him all their gifts—rare capacity, a handsome person, high birth, hereditary honours, wealth, and repute. These ensured the homage of his contemporaries, but he owes the respect of posterity to himself; and it would be claimed by his fidelity to Essex, even if it were not due to his friendship for Shakespeare.

This connection was certainly formed before 1592, when Chettle speaks of the poet as highly considered by "divers of worship," but it could not yet have brought substantial advantages; for he was in no position to render effectual aid to his father, who is returned in that year by the commissioners as absenting himself from church "for fear of process for debt."[1] This fact sufficiently refutes the notion that he derived a large income from his plays, and we may safely estimate their proceeds by the price which Oldyss says

[1] See note to page 97, *ante.*

he received for 'Hamlet'—five pounds. But he was now coming on better days. In 1593 he published his poem of 'Venus and Adonis,' which he calls " the first heir of his invention ; " and, consequently, it must have been written ten years before it was printed. This, however, as we have seen in the case of the 'Arcadia,' was no uncommon occurrence, and it might have been read by his friends in manuscript long before; for we shall presently hear of his sonnets circulating in this way, though they were not given to the printer till nine years afterwards. Indeed, there were no need to describe the poem as a first production, if it were manifestly such, and not preceded by compositions which, though written later, were earlier known to the public.

It was then customary for authors to give their works to the world under the auspices of some illustrious person, who, in the dedication, was acknowledged as a patron, and thus shared the honour of the production. This association with literature is the coronet of the Elizabethan nobility. It fell, indeed, into abuse, and dedications were made a commodity, retailing flattery and adulation for a price. But the institution was a good one ; and it is an honour to Elizabeth that she considered herself honoured by the dedication of the 'Fairy Queen.' Her example influenced the Court, and there were few there of the temper of Cardinal d'Este, who repaid Ariosto with a sneer for his dedication of 'Bombastes Furioso,' while the brigands of the mountains, " albeit unused to the melting mood,"[1] returned the money they had stripped him of on hearing his name. The nobles of Elizabeth were munificent patrons. Sidney ordered fifty guineas to be presented to Spenser on merely reading a stanza of the 'Fairy Queen,' which had been left in manuscript at his door, and doubled the gratuity the next moment, when he had read a second, raising it to two hundred guineas on reading a third,

---

[1] 'Othello,' act v. 1.

when he ordered his steward to hasten away, lest he should give all he possessed.[1] We have seen that Spenser refers to the " gifts and goodly grace" that he received from Leicester, and that it was beyond doubt the subsidy of Leicester that enabled Shakespeare to aid his father and place him for **a** time at ease. Essex was of a **more** generous nature, but not possessed of the same means ; and, moreover, was surrounded by a host of dependents, who suffered none of his bounty to pass themselves. They could have no fear of molestation from Shakespeare. He did not appear amongst them in the character of a parasite, but as an adherent of the house and its master's friend. We may presume that he was a more frequent visitor at the mansion of Southampton, **at Holborn Bars ; and it was to this nobleman that in 1593 he dedicated ' Venus and Adonis.'**

**The dedication is a model of that species of composition.** It rather seeks to apologise for the **author than to praise the** patron, and does this **in** such a manner that we **see it is no** affectation. It differs from the dedications of the day, too, in its brevity, which is never more the soul of wit than in such cases :—

" To the Right Honourable HENRY WRIOTHESLEY, Earl of Southampton and Baron of Titchfield.

" Right Honourable,

 " I know not how I shall offend in dedicating my unpolished lines to your Lordship, nor how the world will censure me for choosing so strong a prop to support so weak a burthen : only if your Honour seem but pleased, I account myself highly praised, **and vow to take advantage of all idle** hours till I **have** honoured you **with** some graver **labour.** But if the first heir of my invention prove deformed, I shall be sorry it had so noble a godfather, and never after ear so

---

[1] Hughes's ' Memoir of Spenser.'

barren a land, for fear it yield me still so bad a harvest.   I leave it to your honourable survey, and your honour to your heart's content; which I wish may always answer your own wish, and the world's hopeful expectation.

> " Your Honour's in all duty,
>
> " WILLIAM SHAKESPEARE."

**The prevailing** taste ran on gods and goddesses, and the **beings of classic** fable.  Divinities and monsters, nymphs and **satyrs, furnished the** characters of all the pageants and all the court masques ; and the first composition of Shakespeare naturally partook of the regulation pattern.  A set form was prescribed for poetry as for sculpture, and he submitted to the one as in later days Canova bowed to the other. But the submission was only in appearance and in name ; for the Venus of the boy poet, like the Orpheus of the boy sculptor, was in all else human.  Canova broke into what he called " the sculpture of the heart," and Shakespeare into the poetry **of the heart.  He could represent** nothing **but nature,** what he had **seen and knew, and** this brought his **goddess down to a woman, the** point **to which we all** bring **our goddesses.  The** poem **of 'Venus** and Adonis**' is** a **delineation of** human passions and feelings, presented visibly **to the eye** in a narrative play.  All the details are beautiful reflections of life.  " The myrtle grove," " the bushes in the way," " the brake" " the flying hare," and " the flap-mouthed hound," give us the very image of the scene and action. Meanwhile the ear is charmed by the soft flow of the metre and the harmony of the rhyme, while a delicate touch veils those points which would otherwise be too prominent, and impart a too voluptuous tint to the poem.

**The** publication **was a great success, and the** " unpolished lines" were pronounced " honey-flowing verse."[1]   It

---

[1] Barnsfield's ' Poems, in Divers Humour.'

became an immediate favourite, and passed through several editions. But the proceeds of the poem, even if the copyright was not sold for a trifle, were the least of Shakespeare's recompense; for Lord Southampton was so gratified by the dedication that he soon afterwards presented him with a thousand pounds. Rowe speaks of the occurrence with some hesitation, but it is affirmed positively by Oldyss,[1] and comes to us as an immemorial tradition. Some later biographers believe in the present, but discredit the amount. " This amount," says Mr. Halliwell, "must be exaggerated; for, considering the value of money in those days, such a gift is altogether incredible."[2] How incredible? when we find that in 1596, only three years later, an estate worth eighteen hundred pounds was presented to Bacon by Essex. Indeed, the gift to Bacon was probably suggested by that made to Shakespeare, as Essex was one who would not be outshone, even by Southampton, and though encumbered with debt, he involved himself further to eclipse his friend.

The next year gave to the world the " graver labour" of " all idle hours," for which the poet stood pledged in the dedication of ' Venus and Adonis.' This was the poem of the ' Rape of Lucrece,' also dedicated to Lord Southampton, in accordance with the same promise; and the tradition of his gift here receives corroborative testimony from Shakespeare himself:—

---

[1] Rowe was a believer, as he could not resist the evidence :—" There is one instance so singular in the magnificence of this patron of Shakespeare's, that if I had not been assured that the story was handed down by Sir William D'Avenant, who was probably very well acquainted with his affairs, I should not have ventured to have inserted—that my Lord Southampton at one time gave him a thousand pounds to enable him to go through with a purchase which he heard he had a mind to." Oldyss merely states the fact :— " Wriothesley, E. of Southampton, gave him 1000l. to complete a purchase."

[2] ' Life of Shakespeare,' by J. O. Halliwell.

" To the Right Honourable HENRY WRIOTHESLEY, Earl
of Southampton, and Baron of Titchfield.

" The love I dedicate to your Lordship is
without end, whereof this pamphlet, without beginning, is
but a **superfluous** moiety. The warrant I have of your
honourable disposition, not the words of **my** untutored lines,
**makes it** assured **of acceptance.** What I have done is yours;
**what I have to do is** yours; being part in all I have devoted
**yours.** Were **my** worth greater, my duty would show
greater; meantime, **as** it is, **it** is bound to your Lordship;
to whom I wish long life, still lengthened with all happiness.

" Your Lordship's in all duty,

" WILLIAM SHAKESPEARE."

There is no reference to pecuniary obligations in the
dedication of 'Venus and Adonis;' but it is difficult to mis-
understand what we are told here—" all I have, devoted
yours." *All I have!* In truth, the thousand pounds given **by**
Southampton formed **nearly** the whole **property** he ever
**possessed; and if he obtained** high prices **for his** plays, even
**as much, we are informed, as** a thousand **a year,** we are
**reduced to ask** what became of the money—for no vestige of
**it can** be traced.

" The love I dedicate **to** your Lordship is without end."
**Mr.** Collier conjectures **that** Southampton's gift was in
acknowledgment **of the dedication of 'Venus and** Adonis,'
and every one who weighs the evidence must share his
opinion. We will take the Dedication's word for a thousand
pounds, though it is attested only by tradition. Mr. Collier,
indeed, thought that he **had** discovered confirmation **of it in**
other facts; for he found in the State Paper **Office** a document purporting to be **a petition to the** Privy Council from
**the " Owners and Players"** of the Blackfriars theatre in

1596, soliciting permission to render the **house more commodious**; and here the thousand pounds **appeared to have** found an investment, as Shakespeare, before only **a " sharer,"** stands on the roll as one of the owners, all of whom have " put down sums of money according to their shares in the said theatre." Malone thinks that it was about 1596 that the Blackfriars Company erected the Globe at Bankside, and it is adverted to in the petition as a portion of their property—" in the summer season your petitioners are able to play at their new-built house on the Bankside."[1]   But no inference is admissible from this document, as it has been pronounced spurious.[2]

The 'Rape of Lucrece' is a more perfect work **of art** than ' Venus and Adonis,' because it adheres still closer to **Nature.**   It throws off the trammels off the critics, which **the first** poem had infringed, **and takes a range equal to the** subject.   The dramatic power rises to the sublime, **imparting** a living force to the illusion. **We are reconciled to** the absence of the charming scenery of ' Venus and Adonis' by graphic pictures of old Roman life, exhibiting its patriarchal simplicity, its virtue and heroism, while we are interested alike by the rapid succession of the incidents, the exciting tenour of the narrative, and the grandeur of the characters. The art of representation by words is carried to perfection, and the truthful colouring of the poem stamps it an English " Æneid."

[1] The petition will be found in the Appendix.

[2] It may be desirable to give the report upon it :—" We, the undersigned, at the desire of the Master of the Rolls, have carefully examined the document hereunto annexed, purporting to be a petition to the Lords of Her Majesty's Privy Council, from Thomas Page, Richard Burbage, John Hemings, Augustine Philips, William Shakespeare, &c., in answer to a petition from the inhabitants of the Liberty of Blackfriars, and we are of opinion that the document in question is spurious." The report is signed by Sir Francis Palgrave, Sir Frederick Madden, J. S. Brewer, T. D. Hardy, and N. E. S. A. Hamilton.

There is nothing to guide us to the date of the two minor poems of Shakespeare, 'The Lover's Complaint,' and 'The Passionate Pilgrim,' but they are obviously early productions, and but for his own declaration, we should place them before 'Venus and Adonis.' They are of far inferior merit, being trifles in comparison, but they are happy and sprightly, and, as the effusions of an idle hour, no reproach to his genius.

His Muse threw off 'Venus and Adonis,' and the 'Rape of Lucrece,' as the printing-press throws off the sheets—with a resistless effort, which at once achieves the object. Their publication created a demand for his dramatic productions which excited the cupidity of piratical booksellers, and the 'Rape of Lucrece' was soon followed by what we must consider a surreptitious edition of the Second Part of 'King Henry VI.' This was published as the First Part, and in a very crude form, for which poor compensation was made in the fullness of the title—" The First Part of the Contention betwixt the Famous Houses of York and Lancaster, with the Death of the Good Duke Humphrey and the Banishment and Death of the Duke of Suffolk, and the Tragical End of the proud Cardinal of Winchester, with the notable Rebellion of Jack Cade, and the Duke of York's first Claim unto the Crown." It was the fashion of the day to make a title speak volumes. Shakespeare knew that such a result was best attained by brevity, and this principle is carried out in the first collected edition of his works, where the same play appears as the 'Second Part of King Henry the Sixth.' The surreptitious edition was so favourably received, that it encouraged the publication in 1595 of 'The True Tragedy of Richard, Duke of York, and the Death of good King Henry the Sixth, with the whole Contention between the Two Houses of Lancaster and York, as it was several times acted by the Right Honourable the Earl of Pembroke's servants.' Here we meet the Third Part of ' King **Henry VI.**,' but in a form so different from what **we have received** it from Shakespeare in the collected plays, that a disposition prevails to consider it as a mere rudiment by some **other** hand, on which his play was built, but looking at it as **his** first conception, the differences are not greater than might be expected in that age in **a** copy printed from notes taken while the play was being performed.

## XXV.

### THE USES OF THIS WORLD.

The tide of Shakespeare's prosperity was immediately felt by his father. We have seen that he employed his first good fortune for his benefit, and there is proof that this was a mere windfall, such as a gift from Leicester, in the relapse of John Shakespeare in 1592, when he appears in the black list of the Warwickshire Commissioners. But his affairs were again soon arranged, leaving him to go peacefully to church, for his name is not included in the next list of recusants, though he figures in a squabble in the Bailiff's Court just before the publication of ' Venus and Adonis.' We hear nothing more of him for a couple of years, and as we now understand his case as one in which no news is good news, it is a safe conclusion that he was held up by the hand of his son. It is difficult, however, to throw off old habits, and he gravitated towards the Bailiff's Court, as to a natural centre, so that we are not surprised to meet him there again in 1595. But in this instance he is apparently involved by others, being a joint defendant with Philip Green, chandler, and Henry Rogers, butcher. The action was brought by Adrian Quiney, for the recovery of five pounds ; and his liability, whatever it might be, was promptly met ; for the subsequent notices of the action omit his name, confining it to Green and Rogers. It is his last appearance in the Bailiff's Court, and we have already pointed to it as showing him to be connected with a butcher, who was probably his successor in that business, and the old master of Shake-speare.

He was now able to sit down quietly under his fig-tree, but, as Charles the First said of Bacon, he was not disposed to go out like a snuff; and, released from pecuniary difficulty, and seeing himself restored to his former consequence in Stratford, he was revisited by ambitious aspirations. Whatever these embraced, they might be thought to be transcended in the position attained by his son. Yet it was not so. He imagined that his son, honoured by princes, courted by nobles, and acclaimed by brother poets, daily increasing in fame and substance, and, withal, possessing an heir to his name, still wanted one element of greatness. He had no coat of arms!

The antecedents of the family were of a character to come out lamely in heraldry, which has more to do with dragons and griffins than the " familiar beasts" known to the Shakespeares. Such materials could hardly be fashioned into a " coat" by the most inventive heraldic tailor; for, as Mrs. Quickly would say, " what's a joint of mutton or two" ¹ for the fabrication of joints of harness? But coats of arms were then in demand, as the hand of commerce was daily hoisting up persons of low birth, ready to pay for a diploma of gentility; and the occasion produced the required man. John Dethick, Garter King at Arms, could not be excelled in his vocation—which is saying much. He was to heraldry in that day what Professor Owen is to geology in our own; and as the professor needs but the tip of a tail to make a labyrinthodon or a pterodactyl, so Dethick asked but a name or a fact for the fabrication of monsters quite as prodigious, and which should typify a family lineage as fabulous as themselves. A rumour of his powers reached John Shakespeare, and in 1596 he applied to him for a grant of arms,

<hr>

¹ ' King Henry IV., Part II.,' act iii. 4.

stating his case. This Dethick at once turned inside out, finding the applicant, who could adduce no heroic Shakespeares, a new ancestry in the family of his wife, and while treating these Ardens as descended from the favourite squire of the body to Henry the Seventh, he equipped the ex-alderman with a spear out of his own name, to give colour to the transmutation. [1] The process terminated in the issue of a grant of arms, "gold, on a bend sable and a spear of the first, the point steeled, proper, and the crest or cognizance a falcon; his wings displayed, argent, standing on a wreath of his colours, supporting a spear gold, steel, as aforesaid, set upon a helmet with mantles and tassels." The grant was confirmed in 1599, when authority was also given to impale the coat with the arms of Arden.

So impudent a fabrication was considered to overstep even the licence allowed to the College of Heralds, which was then more observed than now ; and in conjunction with other cases, raised such a clatter, that Dethick and his coadjutor, Camden, were obliged to stand on their defence, coming forward with "The Answer of Garter and Clarencieux Kings at Arms, to a libellous scrawl against certain Arms supposed to be wrongfully given." But the defence is of the same temper as the arms, springing equally from Dethick's forge ; for in reference to John Shakespeare it alleges that the person to whom the coat was granted " had borne magistracy and was justice of peace at Stratford-upon-Avon ; he married the daughter and heir of Arderne, and was able to maintain that estate," though it need hardly be said that John Shakespeare, if magistrate during his year of bailiffship, was never a justice of the peace, and that his wife was

---

[1] The draft of 1597 describes John Shakespeare as " of Stratford-upon-Avon, in the county of Warwick, *whose parents and late antecessors* were for their valiant and faithful service advanced and rewarded by the most prudent prince King Henry the Seventh, of famous memory, since which time they have continued at those parts in good reputation and credit," &c

not *the* daughter and heir, but one of the seven daughters and co-heiresses, of Robert Arden, not "*Arderne*." She is, indeed, more accurately described in the grant of 1597 as "Mary, daughter and *one of the heirs* of Robert Arden of Wellingcote," but it did not suit Dethick to state her paternity with such precision in this instance. Indeed, he threw the responsibility of the first grant on a predecessor, who was dead, attaching a memorandum to the draft of the first grant, which affirmed that "this John hath a pattern of the arms under Clarence Cook's hand *in paper* twenty years past."[1]

The proceeding would be unworthy of so much notice if it were not commonly assumed that John Shakespeare applied for the arms at the suggestion of his son William; but it cannot be pretended that William exercised this influence over him as a boy, twenty years before, when he received the "pattern" from Cork, and became, in the language of the grant, " John Shakespeare, Gent.' Shakespeare had no wish to make his father a gent. After his severe quiz of the arms of the ancient family of Lucy, he could not wish to lay his own family open to juster derision, and barb his name with its own spear, as he jeered at theirs by the "luces in their coat." We may imagine his mirth when he first saw Dethick's trumpery, and hear him pronounce the "steel proper," very proper, as it imaged the steel which in old butcher days, both his father and himself had kept in constant use : the "falcon" commemorated the Falcon at Bidford, the scene of his memorable conflict with the Sippers; and the "helmet with mantles and tassels" figured his " accoutrements" on the stage. Slender's question of "I may quarter, coz?" which draws from Shallow the intimation

<hr>

[1] The memorandum gives a description of John Shakespeare similar to the recital in the defence :—" A justice of peace, and was bailiff, officer, and chief of the town of Stratford-upon-Avon, fifteen or sixteen years past. That he hath lands and tenements of good wealth and substance, 500*l.* That he married a daughter and heir of Arden, a Gent. of Worship."

" you may by marrying,"[1] would exactly apply to John Shakespeare's impalement of the arms of Arden, and draw from Sir Hugh the remark that it was " marring indeed"— marring the greatest name in existence with a silly pretence.

**It is certain that the arms** were never used by Shakespeare, **for** they do **not appear** on any of the deeds relating **to** his property, and his will bears no seal. An antique seal-**ring** of gold, believed to be his, was picked up near Stratford **church, and** it is merely inscribed with his initials—W. S., more honourable than a hundred quarterings. He remembered that his forefathers were trained to the spade, not the spear; they were, as we have seen, husbandmen. **"There** is no ancient gentleman", says the Clown in ' Hamlet,' " but *gardeners, ditchers,* and grave-diggers : they hold up Adam's profession. He was the first that ever bore arms. The Scripture says, *Adam digged.* Could he dig without arms ? "[2] The grave-digger gave a jibe to Lord Chesterfield, who ticketed the **portrait** of one of his ancestors **as Adam** de Stanhope, and inscribed Eve de Stanhope under another.

**At the time of the first application for arms in 1596,** Shakespeare was, in truth, thinking rather of the grave-digger than Dethick. He became sensible of a change in the appearance of his son, perhaps unmarked by others, but known by himself as the shadow of death. The mournful discovery is made the theme of a sonnet, as if he found relief in pouring forth his feelings in verse, though the composition, which is of a different structure from all the other sonnets, at first seems more expressive of distraction than anguish, and it is not till we look in its depths that we understand **the bitter-**ness **of his affliction.** Admonishing his " lovely boy,"[3] that

---

[1] ' Merry Wives of Windsor,' act i. 1.
[2] ' Hamlet,' act v. 1.
[3] Sonnet cxxiv.

he now holds in his power the **fickle glass of Time,**—that hour of life which, passing so swiftly, **may be called Time's** sickle,—he tells him that he is waning as he grows, **a proof** that decay is surely sapping also the beauty of his lovers, the maidens who fondle and caress him ; and if Nature, " sovereign mistress over wrack," continues to impair his strength as he advances in years, it is in order that her power of sustaining and protracting life may impose on Time the disgrace of killing him by minutes. The child learns that he **is but** the minion or creature of her pleasure, whom she **may detain** but cannot keep ; for her account, even if temporarily delayed, must be **rendered,** and the debt she is to pay is his life.

Enough is stated here to indicate the disease which was consuming little Hamlet, and was soon to strike him down ; and we discern the fond father at his bedside, noting its progress and **foreseeing the end.** Under this heavy burden he still toiled and composed—seeking comfort as of yore, in his MIND, while he both supplied the theatre with plays, and strutted his brief hour on the stage. His son appears to have been taken to Stratford, in the hope that he might benefit by his native air, a remedy often prescribed for consumption. It is not certain whether Shakespeare was present at the last sad moment, when, in his eleventh year, the little fellow's eyes were closed by death, making his father, who is said to be now suing for armorial bearings, reflect how weary, stale, flat, and unprofitable are all the uses of this world. He was buried in Stratford churchyard, and we find that the sexton has made the usual prief in his note-book:—" 1596, August 11, Hamnet, filius William Shakspere." We seem to catch the anguish of the bereaved parent in that despairing exclamation, " It is mine only son."[1]

---

[1] 'King Henry VI., Part III.,' act ii. 5.

It was doubtless before this sad event that Shakespeare resolved to make an effort to recover the inheritance of his mother, at Ashbies, though the cause did not come before the Court of Chancery till the following term. We may believe that he was its **promoter, or at least furnished the means of carrying it on,** though the proceedings were necessarily taken **in the** name of his parents. Nineteen years had passed since **the property was** pledged for forty pounds to his uncle, Edmund Lambert, now long dead: and the land had been eleven years in the possession of John Lambert, his first cousin, **and** apparently a true chip of the old block. John Shakespeare's declaration of the case in 1597, recurs to the tender he made in 1580 of the redemption money, according to the covenants of the mortgage, and its refusal by Edmund Lambert, on the plea that it had been swelled by other loans, which were also secured on the land. But John Lambert meets this statement with a flat contradiction. In an answer to " the bill of complaint," he avers that " the said complainant did *not* tender or pay the said sum of forty pounds unto the said Edmund Lambert," and **consequently that the latter had become the lawful possessor of the property, which had devolved to himself as** his next heir. As a proof **of** his right he affirms that he had hitherto enjoyed the land undisturbed, and that his title was only disputed now with the design of extorting some " further recompense," the land having greatly increased in **value, and** the approaching expiration of the old lease enabling him to let it on better terms. His whole pleading was indignantly denied by John Shakespeare, who, in his replication, maintained that " the answer of the said defendant is untrue and insufficient **in law** to be replied unto," and repeated his former **version of the transaction.**[1] The suit dragged along for nearly two years, when the parties seem to have discovered that they were

---

[1] The documents will be found in the Appendix.

both " o' the windy side of the law,"[1] which was blowing them to an equal distance from the land.  At any rate, they are presumed to have come to an arrangement, restoring the property to the poet's father, but he more probably received a " further recompense," as Ashbies was not in the possession of Shakespeare at his death.

The Chancery suit was not the only measure taken at this time by Shakespeare to restore his family to its former position in his native county.  The fixed purpose with which he quitted Stratford is proved by his now returning there to make his first purchase of property, particularly as the acquisition was a house and grounds, intended for his own residence.  This property was called New Place, and was bought, in 1597,[2] of William Underhill, whom we have seen withholding tithes from Sir Thomas Lucy, and afterwards involved in a suit with the town.  The purchase-money was sixty pounds, about two hundred of the present currency— for the difference in value, which was fourfold in the reign of Henry the Eighth, had greatly diminished by the end of the reign of Elizabeth, and this sum indicates a house that we may say, from valuations we made on the spot, would now[3] let in Stratford for twenty-five pounds a year.  It is described as comprising a messuage, two gardens, and two barns ; and as a list of the holders of corn in Stratford in the following year reports " William Shackespere " as holding ten quarters, we learn that the barns, though it was a time of dearth, were well filled.

---

[1] ' Twelfth Night,' act iii. 5.

[2] The date of the purchase of New Place was first stated to be 1597 by Mr. Collier.  It has since been established by the discovery in the Chapter House, Westminster, of a notice of the fine levied on the occasion

[3] New Place originally belonged to the Cloptons, and is said to have been then called the Great House, but this must rather have been the designation of another residence of the Cloptons, almost facing it, and which was of much larger dimensions.  Part of it is still standing, and is in the occupation of W. O. Hunt, Esq.

By the acquirement of a substantial residence, and the extrication of his father from poverty and debt, Shakespeare was presented as a prosperous man to his old neighbours, and began to receive attention where he had long been treated with neglect. Fortune drew around him troops **of friends in the little** country-town, as well as the capital, **and none pressed** forward more eagerly than the Quineys, **one of whom** we have so lately seen citing John Shakespeare to the Bailiff's Court. The relations they sought now to **establish are brought out in** a series of four letters, which have been interpreted to the disadvantage of Shakespeare, though they require only to be placed in their proper sequence to convey a different impression. In fact, they tell their own story, and so clearly, that it is hardly open to misconstruction.

It is necessary to premise that the Quineys were connected with the Corporation, which, indeed, they had made a sort of family appanage, the office of High Bailiff having been secured three times by Adrian Quiney,[1] and once by Richard,[2] **who** was apparently **his son. Some** office in the **Corporation was now held by Richard's son,** Richard the **Second,[3] for in** October, **1598, he is found** in London, engaged in a suit for the town. Unfortunately he run out of funds, and came to a dead lock at the Bell, in Carter Lane, and he then bethought him of a certain Will Shakespeare, who was accounted a very good fellow, and had credit, if not money, to help him out. Accordingly, he at once favoured him with the following letter :—

---

[1] Adrian Quiney was High Bailiff in 1559, 1571, and 1582.

[2] Richard Quiney was a second time High Bailiff, **in** 1601-2.

[3] The second Richard Quiney married Eleanor Sadler, **the sister of the John Sadler who followed Shakespeare to London ; and** joined him in busi**ness as a grocer in Bucklersbury, at the sign of the Red** Lion, probably the very house where Sadler had been received as an apprentice by Mr. Brookshank.

" Loving Countryman,

" I am bold of you, as of a friend, craving your help with £30, upon Mr. Bushell's and my security, or Mr. Mylton's with me. Mr. Rosswell is not come to London as yet, and I have special cause. You shall friend me much in helping me out of all the debts I owe in London, I thank God, and much quiet my mind, which would not be indebted. I am now towards the Court, in hope of answer for the despatch of my business. You shall neither lose credit or money by me, the Lord willing; and now but persuade yourself so, as I hope, and you shall not need to fear, but with all hearty thankfulness I will hold my time, and content your friend, and if we bargain farther you shall be the paymaster yourself. My time bids me hasten to an end, and so I commit this to your care and hope of your help. I fear I shall not be back this night from the Court. Haste. The Lord be with you, and with us all, Amen!

" From the Bell, in Carter Lane, the 25th October, 1598.

" Yours, in all kindness,

" Ric. Quiney.

" To my loving friend and countryman, Mr. William Shakespeare, deliver these."

Mr. Halliwell makes a strange remark on this letter :— " I am scarcely willing to hazard the conjecture, that after Shakespeare had obtained a capital in ready money, he increased it by supplying loans at interest; but there really seems to be fair grounds for such an opinion."[1]  Where are the grounds, and on what do they rest?  Quiney is bold of Shakespeare " *as of a friend,*" knowing him as a kind, generous, open-hearted man, his " loving countryman," not as a usurer, and he comes to him " *craving* his help," not inviting him to an investment. The thirty pounds, equal to

[1] ' Life of Shakespeare,' by J. O. Halliwell, Esq., F.R.S.

a hundred of our present currency, are to be lent on a joint personal security, one of the sureties being the man who requires it to pay off his debts, and Shakespeare, if not in sufficient funds himself, is to back up this arrangement with his own credit. " You shall neither lose money *nor* **credit** by me." **Is** this the language that would be addressed to a **money-lender** ?

The letter could **hardly have reached** Shakespeare when he hastened to Quiney's relief, and engaged also to obtain money for the town ; for Quiney wrote home to this effect on the same day. The facts are revealed in the reply made from Stratford, on the 4th of November, by Abraham Sturley, who had apparently married among the Quineys, and, of course, married the Corporation too. After a salutation in the highest evangelic style, Sturley, whose love of the current coin of the realm deserves the name of Sterling, comes at once to the point, to what is uppermost in his thoughts, money :—

" Your letter **of the 25th of October came to my hands the last of the same [that is, the 31st of October] at night per Greenway, which** imported a stay of suits by Sir Ed. Gr. **[Edward Greville's]** advice until, &c. . . . **and** that our **countryman, Mr.** Wm. Shak., would procure us money, which I will like of, as I shall hear when, and where, and how ; and I pray let not go that occasion, if it may sort to any indifferent conditions. Also, that if money might be had, for £30 or £40 a lease &c., might be procured."

We are here plainly told that Shakespeare was to " procure " the money, not lend it himself, and, in fact, **we see** that he was merely taking a kind interest in **the weal of his** native town. He was **not aware that the money was** to be expended in **bribing everyone, small and great,** who could forward the object in view, and that the parties really to be **benefited were the magnates of** the Corporation, the Quineys and Sturleys. All this comes out in the letter, but has been passed unnoticed, though it satisfies us that Shakespeare was now among sharks, and that our Puritan forefathers were acquainted with the Man in the Moon.[1]

Shakespeare desired to invest his own means in land, either in the town itself, or its neighbourhood, where it is evident that he was already making preparations to retire. He communicated his wish to Richard Quiney, apparently over a friendly glass at the Bell, and might as well have told the bellman ; for Quiney imparted it to his father, and his father to Sturley, who talked the matter over with the Corporation to see if they could bring to market some bargain of their own. The result was a prompt despatch to Richard, which, after prayers, went at once to business.

"This is one special remembrance from your father's motion. It seemeth by him that our countryman Mr. Shakespeare is willing to disburse some money upon some odd yard land or other at Shottery, or near about us. He thinketh it a very fit pattern to move him to deal in the matter of our tithes. By the instructions you can give him thereof, and by the friends he can make therefore, we think it a fair mark for him to shoot at, and not unpossible to hit. It obtained, would advance him indeed, and would do us much good."

This was evidently intended to be read by Shakespeare, but Sturley remembered his weak point, and followed it up with a hint in Latin, the drift of which has escaped notice, as no one recognized it as a quotation from Terence, bringing

---

[1] Nothing was to be left undone to secure **Sir Edward Greville,** who was to be admitted to halves if he would aid in an act of spoliation. " If it be the rest of the tithes and College houses and lands in our town you speak of, the one half were abundantly rich for us ; and the other half to increase Sir Edward's royalties, would both bear the charge, and *set him sure on.*" But Sturley was dreadfully afraid Sir Edward would swallow the whole !

before us a scene in which a slave conspires with his master
to impose on a third party. It is difficult to give the exact
sense in English, but it may be put thus :—" You must set
this going, and work it with all your might. Don't neglect
it ; for this will be of the utmost importance both to yourself and us. This toil, this labour, will cover you with
unusual honour and credit." [1]  Yet Shakespeare is represented as a sharp practitioner, **making** usury out of these
Pharisees, who, while they begin and end their letters with
prayers, are continually saying grace over schemes for
bribing and cheating. Unfortunately they persuaded him to
buy the tithes, which almost immediately involved him in a
lawsuit.

It is a sure sign of an improvement in his circumstances
that he is found at this time to be no longer residing near
Paris Garden. An assessment roll of the parish of St.
Helen's notes him as an inhabitant of Bishopsgate in 1598,
and as it refers to the first of three subsidies granted to
Queen Elizabeth in the previous year, we may conclude
that he lived in the same place in 1597. Saccherson, that
rugged Russian bear, drove him for quiet into the heart of
the city. But he turned from the mercenary crowd in its
streets, and peopled them with a past generation—still, as of
old, surrounding himself with his own thoughts, so that every
structure met his eye with poetic and heroic associations.
Thus the date of his migration is marked by ' King Richard
III.,' printed in 1597, and which rises from the neighbourhood of his residence as on a stage at the removal of the
curtain. In Bishopsgate stands Crosby Hall, King Richard's
palace, where Sir John Spencer, called " the rich Spencer,"

[1] Sturley's Latin is rather " small," though he **depends** on its baffling
Shakespeare. We give it **as** it is written :—" Hoc movere **et** quantum in te
est permovere ne necligas [negligas] hoc enim et **sibi** [tibi] et nobis maxi-
mi **erit** momenti. Hic labor, hic [hoc] opus, **esse** teximiæ, et gloriæ, et
**landis sibi [tibi]."

had just kept his mayoralty, and which consequently brought the poet into the presence of the " Lord Mayor, Aldermen, and Citizens," who so prominently figure in the play. His daily walk to the Blackfriars playhouse carried him by Lombard Street, which gave a residence to Jane Shore; further on he passed St. Paul's Cross, consecrated by the famous sermon; and often he turned to visit his friend the Countess of Pembroke, at Baynard's Castle, where, in a scene of unequalled grandeur, he brings Buckingham to offer Richard the Crown.

There is even a footprint to tell us where he went to church on Sunday. It was the church of St. Helen's; for as we enter the sacred edifice we catch a glimpse of one we could little expect to meet in such a place, no other than Falstaff. While Sir Oliver Martext was delivering his sermon, the poet's eye, and, we may fear, his thoughts, wandered to a monument, which Strype avers was erected here to Sir Hugh Fastolfe, and from behind which the great cozener seems to leer upon us, as he did on King Hal. We may thus understand that he was not only witty in himself, but the cause of wit in his dead progenitor, deriving from him a name which is wit's symbol. The name in the original play of the ' Famous Victories ' was Sir John Oldcastle, and this was taken up by Shakespeare like an old dress amongst the properties of the theatre, but in his hands, it is the dress on Liston or Matthews: the name becomes an impersonation. But Shakespeare was still harassed by the Greenes and Nashes whenever he left room for a stab; and they raised a cry that the character, which he had found existing in the old play, was intended as a lampoon on Sir John Oldcastle, the pious chief of the Lollards. The epilogue to the Second Part of ' King Henry IV.' contemptuously denied the charge—" Oldcastle died a martyr, and this is not the man." At the same time he changed the name to Falstaff, which removed the ground of objection, though it rather leads to heterodoxy, being a clear case of the transmigration of a soul; for Falstaff, like Pythagoras, remembers that he was once another person, and answers to the Prince's call of " my *old* lad of the *castle*." [1]

Shakespeare's facility in composition has never been equalled, unless by Lopez de Vega, who is said to have produced a short piece at a sitting. But Lopez worked for the hour; Shakespeare for all ages. The dramas of the one are forgotten, while those of the other—the most popular of his own day—were never so appreciated as at present. The vastness of his powers and his untiring industry are better understood when we remember how few were the hours he could devote to composition, as he was occupied nearly all day at the theatre, by his profession of actor, which exacted also a part of the night for preparation and study. But we can never properly estimate the difficulties he had to provide for, and the points and considerations he had to keep in view, in adapting such imposing subjects for dramatic representation—difficulties which his contemporaries declared insurmountable, [2] but which he triumphantly overcame. The rude means available for realizing his conceptions must have been ever in his mind; and with what art he measured the work to the means, the immediate popularity of his plays demonstrates. Yet he has presented us with every variety of character and scene, in their very semblance and image. Did he have no misgivings in entrusting to the rough handling of men and boys those delicate and fragile creations?—the sparkling Rosalind, a part in which Mrs. Siddons broke down; the shrinking Perdita, the loving Desdemona, and the too tender Ophelia! He seems, indeed, to point at the

---

[1] 'King Henry IV., Part I.,' act ii. 2.

[2] Ben Jonson's Prologue to 'Every Man in His Humour,' Henslowe's MS.

difficulty in 'Hamlet,' where the boy's advance towards manhood is marring his qualifications for representing woman—"What! my young lady and mistress! By'r Lady, your ladyship is nearer heaven than when I saw you last by the altitude of a chopine."[1] The voice became as unsuitable as the stature, and Hamlet bids the young actor pray that his "voice, like a piece of uncurrent gold, be not cracked in the ring." Perhaps Shakespeare foresaw a time when those ideal beings would be represented by beautiful women, able to portray both the deepest passion and the lightest coquetry—when even the witches in Macbeth would be personated by accomplished actresses, who, in appearance, voice, and gesture might be called witches indeed.

Some advance was made during his own lifetime. The celebrated Sir Henry Wotton, writing to his nephew in 1613, notices that a new play, called 'All is True,' had just been produced by the King's players at the Globe with a splendour almost regal. Matting, then found in Kings' anterooms, was laid over the stage; Knights of the Garter appeared in the insignia of the order; and guards in embroidered coats. The display terminated in a catastrophe. In one scene there was a discharge of artillery, when the wad of the cannon lodged in the thatch, and, after smouldering for a few moments, set the roof in flames. Less than an hour served to consume the whole building, but Sir Henry assures us that nothing perished but a few old cloaks, though the fire might have broiled one man, whom it seized by the breeches, if, with rare presence of mind, he had not drenched them with ale.

Much has been said as to the number of the plays he had written up to the year 1598. All the theories are based on a rather loose statement made in that year by Francis Meres, a clergyman of Lincolnshire, in a comparative discourse of

[1] 'Hamlet,' act ii. 2.

our English poets, given in a work called 'Palladis Tamia,
or Wit's Treasury.' Meres declares that, as Plautus and
Seneca excel respectively in tragedy and comedy among
the Latins, so Shakespeare combines the merit of those
authors among the English, being in tragedy and comedy
equally excellent. "For comedy," he adds, "witness his
'Gentlemen of Verona,' his 'Errors,' his 'Love's Labour's
Lost,' his 'Love's Labour's Won,' his 'Midsummer Night's
Dream,' and his 'Merchant of Venice;' for tragedy, his
'Richard the Second,' 'Richard the Third,' 'Henry the
Fourth,' 'King John,' 'Titus Andronicus,' and his
'Romeo and Juliet.' A little consideration shows that
Meres simply mentions in this enumeration some of Shake-
speare's productions as examples, and does not profess to
give them all. Indeed, we at once discern important omis-
sions, for nothing is said of the three parts of 'King Henry
VI.,' which we know to have been printed in 1594-5; of
'Hamlet,' adverted to by Nashe in 1589; or of 'The Merry
Wives of Windsor,' which we have proved to be written
before 1588. Hence the list, valuable as it is, must be pronounced imperfect.

While giving the names of plays, which are now household words, Meres mentions a comedy we do not possess—
at least under the same title—'LOVE'S LABOUR'S WON.'
What has become of this treasure? We are unwilling to
allow that any of Shakespeare's dramas have perished, for how
can things immortal die! A providence seems to guard them
through all the vicissitudes of nations and ages, so that man's
thought outlives his grandest monuments. The critics have
agreed that all we have lost of 'Love's Labour's Won' is its
title. Like Oldcastle, the play has changed its name, and
we have only to make out its identity. This, however, leads
us into as great a maze among these plays as a quest for the
Lost Tribes in ethnology. Shakespearean authorities have

all but unanimously pronounced for ' All's Well that Ends
Well;' but it must be admitted that the case is not a strong
one, as the same incident which obtains the preference in this
play occurs in ' Measure for Measure,' which therefore has
equal claims; for Isabella aids Mariana to circumvent Angelo,
exactly as Diana assists Helena to win Bertram. The name
of Mariana is borne by a character in both dramas, and their
development brings out coincidences which further assimilate
their pretensions. No such objection applies to ' The Taming
of the Shrew,' which has never been mentioned as the play,
but with every deference for the weight of authority on the
side of ' All's Well that Ends Well,' we venture to submit
that it has a superior claim. It does not appear in the list
of Meres, but we know that it was acted at Henslowe's
Theatre in 1593, and as the stage was already in possession
of a drama called ' The Taming of *a* Shrew,' on which it was
founded, there was a reason for giving it another title. Certainly the incidents of the piece—the series of mortifications
by which Petrucio conquers the temper and wins the love
of Katherina, may more properly be called "labours" than
the stratagem adopted in common by Helena and Mariana;
and, in fact, the task is placed in that light by Gremio,—

> " Yea, leave that LABOUR to great Hercules,
> And let it be more than Alcides' twelve."[1]

The triumphs that exalted Shakespeare before the world
did not raise his estimation of himself, still less infect him
with the proud man's contumely. They rather brought him
to see the emptiness of worldly distinctions, which no man
ever more contemned, and to look down kindly from his
eminence on all below. Those noble thoughts, which open
to us every virtue—those melting sentiments which bring
home the tender pleadings of nature to the hardest breast—

---

[1] 'Taming of the Shrew,' act i. 2.

those exhortations to pious trust in Heaven, and gentle dealing with our fellow-man, are linked in our minds with himself, and make us regard him as a counsellor and friend. Here is the secret of his world-wide influence; **reaching** every age, **and** not more recognized by the scholar in **his closet than by the** unwashed artisan **in the playhouse gallery. We see that he is in** earnest, and the **heartiness of his sentiments embodies them to the** eye, and attests his own participation. **An instance has come down** to us, indeed, of the **manner in which he carried them, like** the creations **of his genius, into real life, and** made them a part of his being. One morning he joined the actors at the theatre just as they were dismissing a literary aspirant whose play had been rejected, and saw him turn away with a despairing look. All his kind feelings were instantly aroused. He requested to see the manuscript, and we may imagine with what anxiety the author watched his countenance as he placed it in his hands, knowing that he alone was interested in his exclusion. But such **petty instincts never swayed** Shakespeare. **A moment satisfied him that the play deserved attention; and perusal having confirmed the impression, he not only procured its acceptance at the theatre, but undertook the principal part. This is the** only **instance** on **record of one** literary man befriending another without some previous acquaintance; but the Unknown **was** Ben Jonson, and the benefactor Shakespeare.

While rendering deeds of kindness to strangers, he discharged the highest filial duty in smoothing the declining years of his father. In 1601 John Shakespeare shuffled off this mortal coil. As he was a householder in Stratford in 1552, we may accept Malone's conclusion **that he was born** before 1530, which gives him **a life of three score** and ten, **and something to spare. His burial is noted in** the Stratford register—" 1601, September 8, Mr. Johanes Shakspeare"—

and his son has been censured for not placing a stone over his grave. Who is to say that he is open to this imputation? The oldest stone now in the churchyard bears the date of 1675, so that all before that time have been removed ; and, indeed, it has been customary to take away the obliterated stones from an early period. There is thus no proof that the grave was left without a memorial ; and we refuse to believe that Shakespeare, who was so thoughtful for the living, forgot what was due to the dead.[1]

[1] The Rev. G. Granville, the present excellent Vicar of Stratford, has sent me the following note on this subject :—" Several stones were removed many years ago of families that had long been gone, and were used to extend a walk on each side of the church after the soil had been taken away. None have been removed in my time, except such as had lost the inscription from age."

# XXVI

## SHAKESPEARE AT COURT.

NONE of the traditions about Shakespeare have so strangely survived as those which connect him with Queen Elizabeth. That she was an admirer of his productions we know indeed from one of his contemporaries, and no one can question what is sung by Ben Jonson :—

> "Sweet swan of Avon, what a sight it were
> To see thee in our waters yet appear,
> And make those flights, upon the banks of Thames,
> That so did take Eliza and our James."

But the instances of her manifestation of this interest come to us we know not whence, far as they may be traced back, and though the lapse of three centuries leaves them fresh, History forgot her office, and dropped a brilliant thread, in omitting them from her record. Such an association, indeed, adds majesty to the character of Elizabeth and lustre to her reign, even though we cannot picture her as sitting, in the manner of Augustus, with Shakespeare on one side of her board, and Spenser on the other.

We have seen that it was by the Bridge of Sighs that Shakespeare, inverting the Venetian tradition, passed from the prison of his father to the palace. He probably first became known to the Queen by his compliment in ' Love's Labour's Lost,' which was no doubt delivered by himself, as he always played the King, and the speech falls to Oberon. But it is not till we hear of ' The Merry Wives of Windsor,'

that their connection is mentioned. That comedy confirmed
him in her good opinion, as well by the art it exhibited in
carrying out her wishes, in a manner so flattering to her
pride, as by its merit as a composition. It is remarkable
that both 'The Merry Wives' and 'Midsummer Night's
Dream' introduce the fairies, as if Shakespeare wished
to show the Queen that they were not better known to
Spenser than himself. They maintained a friendly contest
for her favour, while they praised and loved each other. It
does not appear that she ever bestowed any gift on Shakespeare, but Spenser was more fortunate, as she once presented him with an order for a hundred pounds. This seemed
such a piece of extravagance to Burleigh, that he refused
payment. The great minister, gorged with three hundred
manors, looked upon authors in the same light as Pitt,
who replied to an application for some assistance to Burns,
that literature would take care of itself. Spenser received
for his order only a wise shake of the head; and on an
appeal to the Queen, Burleigh declared it was madness
to give "all this for a song." "Then give," said the
Queen, "what is reason." Burleigh still evaded payment,
which drew from Spenser an epigrammatic remonstrance
to Elizabeth—

> " I was promised, on a time,
> To have reason for my rhyme ;
> From that time unto this season
> I received nor rhyme nor reason."

This epigram exhibits the familiar relations to which the
poet was admitted by Elizabeth, and renders it probable that
the sonnets in which Spenser is referred to by Shakespeare,[1]
are also addressed to her. It is difficult to imagine who
else received the praise of every pen, taught "the dumb on
high to sing," and gave "grace a double MAJESTY." True,

---

[1] Sonnets lxxviii. to lxxxvi.

one of these sonnets salutes its object as "sweet love,' which creates a difficulty—

> "I grant, sweet love, thy lovely argument
> Deserves the travail of a worthier pen;"

but the **Queen allowed great latitude** on this point, and in the next **stanza** Shakespeare acknowledges that his Muse is a **"saucy bark."** Another sonnet may allude to Elizabeth's **acceptance of** the dedication of the 'Fairy Queen':—

> "I grant thou wert not married to my Muse,
> And therefore may'st without attaint o'erlook
> The dedicated words which writers use
> Of their fair subject, blessing every book."

But the succeeding lines could not apply to Spenser, as they censure the gross flattery of dedications, and that of the 'Fairy Queen' was not open to this reproach.

Elizabeth admired Shakespeare also as an actor, although "the top of his performance," as we have seen, is rather slighted by Rowe; and one so impressed as the Queen by personal attractions **was** naturally pleased by **his noble** appearance and gentle, **engaging manners. There is a story that** on one occasion, **when he was performing the part of majesty, she wished to see whether he would** maintain **his assumed** character, **if brought** to address herself; and **for this purpose dropped** her handkerchief on the stage, just **as** she caught his eye. Another time, **it** would have been a scramble for the Court, but now all kept their places by the royal command, appearing not to note the incident. It seemed to be really unnoted by Shakespeare. The scene progressed, the moment for his exit was approaching, and he still made no sign. But the "saucy" Muse knew what was expected and, at the last moment, he wound up **his** speech with this impromptu :—

> "Yet, ere we take to **horse, forbear a space,**
> Till **we restore our sister's handkerchief;"**

and the purpose was carried out in true kingly style.

Shakespeare never lent the influence of his Muse to the service of faction, at that time so busy, and engaging all his friends. Even in 'Midsummer Night's Dream,' where he alludes to Throckmorton's conspiracy and the captive Queen of Scots, he maintains his neutrality, and does homage to Leicester without abusing his adversaries. But a time had come when he must plunge into this whirlpool to drag out a drowning friend. The play of 'King Henry VIII.' is an appeal to Elizabeth for the life of Essex. The action is brought as near as possible to her own reign, introducing her parents and even herself, and exhibits all the unscrupulous means adopted by courtiers to ruin an enemy, particularly when in favour with the Sovereign. The presence of her mother reminds her how nearly she was touched by such intrigues, and she could not but see a bearing on passing events in the fall of the great favourite Wolsey. The absence of Essex in Ireland had afforded his enemies an opportunity of weakening his influence with Elizabeth, and this is pointedly adverted to by Surrey, who declares he was nominated to the same position, in order that Buckingham might be destroyed in his absence :—

> " Plague of your policy !
> You sent me deputy for Ireland :
> Far from his succour, from the king, from all,
> That might have mercy on the fault thou gav'st him." [1]

But an unmistakeable reference is made to Essex by the KING, by which Cranmer is to appeal to Henry, when the hostile cabal leaves him no other resource :—

> " If entreaties
> Will render you no remedy, this ring
> Deliver them, and your appeal to us
> Then make before them." [2]

The ring was intercepted in its way to Elizabeth, but she heard of it from Shakespeare, so deeply interested in this

---

[1] 'King Henry VIII.,' act iii. 2.  [2] Ibid., act v. 1.

transaction, not only on account of Essex but Southampton.
He tells her, at the same time, his opinion of the unhappy Earl :

> " He's honest, on mine honour.  God's blest mother !
> I swear he's true-hearted ; and a soul
> None better in my kingdom." [1]

Some of the commentators maintain that this play is the
one mentioned by Sir Henry Wotton as a new production in
1613, under the title of ' All Is True,' because the latter is
described as " representing some principal pieces of Henry
the Eighth."  The compliment to James the First, in the
speech of Cranmer, may seem to support their argument ; but,
in fact, it counts for little, as the passage is evidently wedged
in, cutting the tribute to Elizabeth in two.  The internal
evidence is more in favour of the view we have taken.

His feelings towards the Queen were entirely changed by
the execution of Essex, and he has left a record of the impression it produced upon him, which, though hitherto overlooked, admits of no misconception :—

> " Great princes' favourites their fair leaves spread
> But as the marigold at the sun's eye ;
> And in themselves their pride lies buried,
> *For at a frown they in their glory die.*
> *The painful warrior famousèd for fight,*
> *After a thousand victories once foiled,*
> Is from the book of honour razed quite,
> And all the rest forgot for which he toiled." [2]

He made no lament for the Queen at her death, though
it gave a theme to every poetaster in the kingdom ; and his
marked silence elicits a reproach from a contemporary :—

> " Nor doth the silver-tongued Melicert
> Drop from his honied muse one sable tear
> To mourn her death, that graced his desert,
> And to his lays opened her royal ear :
> Shepherd ! remember our Elizabeth,
> And sing her Rape, done by that Tarquin, Death." [3]

---

[1] ' King Henry VIII.,' act v. 1.
[2] Sonnet xxv.
[3] Chettle's ' England's Mourning Garment.'

He could hardly be expected to deplore an event which terminated the captivity of his friend the Earl of Southampton. As the news spread, such a throng went to visit the Earl, that the approaches to the Tower were blocked up with carriages, and, when even Bacon wrote to ask permission to present himself, Shakespeare must have been the foremost there. His patron was free, and this disposed him to feel kindly towards the new monarch even if he had possessed no other claims. But, as learned as Elizabeth, and, like her, an author, James was an admirer of literary merit, and a wor-shipper of the Muses. It does not appear that he conferred any substantial benefits on authors, but he treated them with great consideration, and Shakespeare was won by kindness when he could not be bought with gold. He was the more open to favourable impressions of the King, from the partiality he evidently entertained for the Scotch, and which he had manifested long before in his presentment of Captain Macmorris in 'King Henry V.' It is by no means improbable, indeed, that he was known to the King before his accession to the English throne; for he is supposed to have been one of a company which visited Scotland in 1601, and which is mentioned in that year by the designation of the "King's serwandes," in the register of the Town Council of Aberdeen. This record informs us that the players had visited that town, where the freedom of the guild was conferred on their chief, Laurence Fletcher. Shakespeare was undoubtedly a member of Fletcher's troop shortly afterwards; for James issued letters patent from Westminster on the 19th May, 1603, mentioning the "King's servants" by name, and "William Shakespeare" appears second on the list, next to "Laurence Fletcher." The patent licenses the players at the 'Globe,' and is headed "Pro Laurentio Fletcher et Willielmo Shakespeare et aliis."[1]

[1] See Appendix.

But the drama had little attraction for the Londoners at this time. For some months the city had been ravaged by the Plague, and now presented a dismal scene. The Court made but a short stay; the streets were no longer thronged with traffic; Paul's Walk was a solitude; there were no dinners at the ordinaries; the gay shops were deserted; and a royal ordinance closed the theatres, as a precaution against infection. The licence to Fletcher and Shakespeare authorized the opening of the 'Globe,' "when the infection of the plague shall decrease;" but, meanwhile, the players were deprived of their means of subsistence, and suffered great distress. They appear to have sought relief by performing in the country, for on the 20th of October, 1603, when the sickness had much abated, Mrs. Alleyn writes to her husband that "all the companies be come home, and well, for aught we know." Alleyn had taken advantage of the idle time to obtain a little country air, and, while his wife remained to watch events at home, was enjoying the old English diversion of hawking.

It is not clear where we are to look for Shakespeare at this crisis. Mr. Collier thinks that he has wrested the secret from the all but obliterated postscript of Mrs. Alleyn's letter, still preserved in the archives of Dulwich College, and which he considers to state that "Mr. Shakespeare of the Globe" had called upon the writer, in reference to a youth who had told her that he was known to him, but the poet stated that "he knew him not—only he heard of him that he was a rogue." This reading is not universally accepted, but it contains nothing improbable, for, as Mrs. Alleyn mentions that all the theatrical companies had returned, Shakespeare was very likely to be in London at the time. Towards the close of the year, he made his first appearance before King James on English ground. The monarch was holding his court at Wilton, the seat of Shakespeare's friend, the Earl of Pembroke, when, on the 2nd of December, his company of players was summoned to perform in the royal presence. We may conclude that they were previously acting to empty houses at Mortlake, beyond the city jurisdiction; for the Treasurer of the Chamber records a payment of 30*l*. to John Hemings, for "the pains and expenses of himself and the rest of his company in coming from Mortlake, in the county of Surrey, unto the Court aforesaid, and there presenting before His Majesty one play." Lord Pembroke may have availed himself of the opportunity to present Shakespeare to James, though the monarch was more likely, in his usual homely way, to renew their acquaintance himself, if he had seen the poet in Scotland. That he was well pleased with the performance, we may judge from the amount of his donation, equivalent to a hundred pounds of our money; and from the fact of his being so interested about the players that he soon afterwards ordered a liberal payment to be made to Richard Burbage, as a free gift to the company, in consideration of the losses they had sustained from the closing of the theatre, and their subsequent distress.

The suspension of his income from this source could now cause no inconvenience to Shakespeare, and, indeed, he is believed to have retired from the stage in 1603, as his name last appears as a player in that year, in a list of characters printed in Ben Jonson's 'Sejanus.' Otherwise it might lend colour to a statement in a letter found by Mr. Collier in the Ellesmere archives, from Daniel to Sir Thomas Egerton, to the effect that the dramatist had been an applicant for the post of Master of the Queen's Revels, which the Lord Chamberlain bestowed upon Daniel. The appointment was made at the commencement of 1604, when the distress in the theatrical profession was greatest. But the authenticity of the letter is disputed, and certainly its tenour does not claim a ready acceptance, for Daniel would hardly be preferred to Shakespeare. Nor is it credible that he was now looking for an appointment at Court. He was rather, as we shall presently see, pining for rest, and completing his arrangements to secure it. These had occupied his attention, for some years, especially since the death of his father, and indicate where his thoughts were turned, all his investments being made in Stratford. In 1602 he had bought of William Combe, of Warwick, and John Combe, of Old Stratford, a hundred and seven acres of arable land for 320*l.*; of Walter Getley, a cottage in Dead Lane; and of Hercules Underhill, a house, with horses, gardens, and orchards, for 60*l.* This property was now augmented by the purchase in 1605 of the unexpired tithes of Stratford, Old Stratford, Bishopton, and Welcomb, for which he gave 440*l.*, doubtless to the full satisfaction of his friends Quiney and Sturley.

Far from having a feud with the Court, we may believe that the kindness of the King to his fellows, and the consideration evinced for himself, led him to the subject of one of his noblest dramas. No prince ever received such a graceful compliment as he paid James in the play of ' Macbeth,' which did homage both to his national partialities and his ancient lineage, while it associates them with what may almost claim to be his greatest work. Nor can we escape the impression that its author had some personal knowledge of the scene of action. The weird heaths, the lonely old castles, the midnight silence, broken only by the screeching owl, the mountain cavern, and the dreary forest, seem indeed plainly to tell us that they are from the graven mould of memory. This sense of reality was so present to Mrs. Siddons, as she sat alone at night studying the character of Lady Macbeth, that she dropped the book from her hand, and flew from the room, not daring to breathe till she had joined her husband, and trembling at the rustle of her own dress, in her dread of some pursuing spectre.[1]

Yet the terrible and the awful are not the sole aim of the tragedy. As Alpine glaciers and precipitous rocks open dells of exquisite beauty, with the soft turf sloping to a clear though headlong stream, so we here catch glimpses of the noblest emotions,—compunction, filial tenderness, heroism, and devotedness.

Perhaps the revelations of witchcraft were the most attractive feature to the royal author of 'Demonology.' Those fearful scenes might persuade us that Shakespeare himself was tainted with the delusion of the time. When we find a man of the character and intellect of Sir Matthew Hale condemning an old woman to be burnt as a witch half a century later, it is indeed hard to believe that he was free from it, imbued as he was with all the traditions of the rustic population. But to him it came in a spiritual form, in the sense of surrounding mysteries which is habitual to men of imagination, and impresses them with things unknown. This it was that enabled him so to realize the supernatural, in its awfulness and sublimity. His witches are neither the crones of a secluded village, nor the wild revellers of 'Faust.' In the form of women, but lean, withered, and bearded, and made shadowy by fog and vapour, they "look not like the inhabitants o' the earth."[2] Possibly they are thus elevated from motives of humanity as well as art. Such weird attributes raised a doubt if every old woman was a witch, even when she was her own accuser; and the friendly interest they are represented as displaying in his ancestors might soften the King, who was now pursuing the suspected with more than Saul's animosity.

The obscurity which envelopes Shakespeare's connection

with the Court attests the extraordinary dignity of his character.  Almost any one in his position would have been continually boasting of the royal courtesies, and made them as
familiar in men's mouths as household words.  He received
them with sealed lips, though others report they were such as
might flatter the highest subject.  Lintot declares that James
wrote him a friendly letter in his own hand ;[1] and it appears,
from a note made by Oldyss in his copy of ' Fuller's Worthies,'
that this information came from the Duke of Buckingham,
to whom the letter had been shown by Sir William D'Avenant.
The favour he enjoyed draws a high compliment from his
friend Davies, in some verses addressed " to Mr. Will.
Shakespeare, our English Terence."

> " Some say, good Will, which I in sport do sing,
>     Had'st thou not played some kingly parts in sport,
>   Thou had'st been a companion for a King,
>     And been a King among the meaner sort."

The statement that Shakespeare had played "some
kingly parts in sport," has led to the conjecture that he
mimicked James on the stage, and Davies is supposed to
hint that this had given offence and prevented closer intimacy.  It has even been surmised that he personated the
King in the tragedy of ' The Gowry Conspiracy,' which was
acted by the Royal Company in 1604 ; and was, it must be
owned, not the most grateful return for the monarch's recent
donation.  But there is the strongest reason to conclude
that he retired from the stage in the previous year ; and
could we admit that he had incurred the royal displeasure, a
little reflection will convince us that such a fact would never
be selected as the theme of a complimentary sonnet.  At
the same time, we must consider it unlikely that he would
do anything unbecoming his relations with the King and his
own character.  "Kingly parts in sport" may be judged

---

[1] Advertisement to ' Shakespeare's Poems,' 1710.

to mean the part of **King** in **any** dramatic performance, such as he habitually sustained; and we **may understand** Davies to intimate that such was **the estimation in which Shakespeare was** held by James, that in all **probability he** would have made him his companion, if his profession had not raised a bar. Indeed, it was after the presumed rupture that Shakespeare was in most friendly communication with the King, for Malone and Chalmer agree in naming 1606 **as the earliest** date for ' Macbeth,' and **there** is no mention **of its having** been performed before 1610, when it was witnessed by Forman. It is considered to **have been suggested** by an incident **of the** King's reception at **Oxford** in 1605, when he was welcomed by **three** Collegians **of St. John's** personating the witches who met Macbeth and Banquo ; but we may rather think that the play suggested the incident. If produced at the beginning of 1605, it would be just in the height of its popularity at the time, and very likely to have this effect. In fact, everything attests that there was no interruption of the good understanding between Shakespeare and the King. Eighty years after he had been committed to the grave, Otway embalms this tradition :—

> " Our Shakespeare, too, wrote in an age so blest
> The happiest part of his time and best,
> A gracious prince's favour cheered his Muse,
> *A constant favour he ne'er feared to* **lose.**"

The " amicable letter," written by James, was addressed to him at Stratford, in his retirement; and we know that his plays were in high favour at Court at the very time of his supposed occultation. Mr. Cunningham's ' Revels at Court' contains notices of their frequent performance, as recorded in the accounts at the Audit Office.[1] Charles the First entertained the same veneration for Shakespeare, as we learn from Milton, who was not one of his eulogists; and, indeed,

---

[1] See Appendix.

he has left a memento of it himself, in his copy of the first complete edition of the poet's works, preserved in the library at Windsor Castle. This volume reveals traces of frequent and careful perusal, and perhaps was the companion of his solitary hours, in the gloomy chamber of Carisbrooke. It may **have prepared** him, by the story of the deposed Richard, to act his part as became a King, and throw over his end a majesty that redeemed his life. It is worthy of remark that Henrietta Maria took up her abode at New Place when she marched into Stratford at the head of the King's troops; and **it is** more reasonable to conclude that she was determined in this choice by other considerations than the size of the house. The daughter of Henry the Fourth felt the attraction of the daughter of Shakespeare.

## XXVII.

### HIS HAUNTS AND FRIENDS.

LITTLE is known of Shakespeare's intercourse with his friends, so little as to indicate that he went seldom into society during his residence in London. If he had been a man about town, we should hear something of his favourite places of resort, and they might even have found a niche in his works. But on this point we are met by the same obscurity that envelopes his social relations, and he cannot be tracked to a single haunt. It is said that he frequented the Mitre tavern in Bread Street, but the only ground for the assertion is, what seems rather illogical, that the Mitre was patronized by Ben Jonson. Rare Ben Jonson was notoriously partial to taverns, and the evidence on which he is convicted would not be wanting against Shakespeare had he been equally guilty. But no hint from his contemporaries, and no tradition of his life in town ascribe to him such a habit, or name any tavern as his retreat. It has been contended, indeed, that he resorted to a house with the sign of the Tabor, kept by Tarleton the Clown, and that it is alluded to in 'Twelfth Night,' "Dost thou live by the Tabor;"[1] but Tarleton's sign was the Saba, and the allusion is plainly to the tabor carried by the Clown. Nor can anything be urged in favour of the Falcon at Bankside, which he is said to have made a house of call. This tavern took its name from the Falcon Theatre, with which he was never connected; and it

---

[1] 'Twelfth Night,' act iii. 1.

did not lie in his way to the Globe, which stood near Maid Lane, within the space now occupied by Barclay's brewery.

Gifford affirms that Shakespeare was a member of a club which met at the Mermaid, under the presidency of Sir Walter Raleigh, and he professes to take the fact from Fuller; but Fuller does not give the least colour to such a statement. Indeed, it is very unlikely that Shakespeare would have made a boon companion of Raleigh, who was the political opponent of his patrons, and who, moreover, by his gasconading schemes provoked his own satire. Raleigh's pamphlet on "The discovery of the large, rich, and beautiful Empire of Guiana, with a relation of the great and golden city of Manva (which the Spaniards call El Dorado), &c., performed by Sir Walter Raleigh, Knight," had, by the wonders it set forth, produced a very mischievous effect on the public mind, exciting a universal disposition to speculate in the wildest enterprises, if they held out the bait of a large profit, and many were even tempted to embark personally in expeditions which, fitted out at their joint expense, were vaunted as promising a return of five for one, but ended in disappointment and failure. Shakespeare considered such a publication a fair object for ridicule; and 'The Tempest' assures us that there was at least one of Raleigh's contemporaries who did not believe —

> "That there were such men
> Whose heads stood in their breasts! which now we find
> Each putter out of five for one will bring us
> Good warrant of." [1]

---

[1] 'Tempest,' act iii. 3. The passage in Raleigh was as follows:—"Next unto Arai there are two rivers, Atoica and Cavra, and on that branch which is called Cavra are a nation of people whose heads appear not above their shoulders, which, though it may be thought a mere fable, yet, for my own part, I am resolved it is true, because every child in the province of Arronaccia and Cavari affirm the same; they are called Ewaipanoma; they are reported to have their eyes in their shoulders, and their mouths in the middle of their breasts."

It is quite possible that the "wit-combats" mentioned by Fuller as very frequent between Shakespeare and Ben Jonson came off at the 'Mermaid,' though not under the auspices of Raleigh. The 'Mermaid' is supposed to have been in Friday Street, and here we are close upon one of Shakespeare's footprints—London Stone,[1] which is niched in the wall of St. Swithin's church, in Cannon Street. Beaumont describes the 'Mermaid' as a perfect hotbed of wit, where the words flew about like subtle flame, so that each of the company seemed to condense his whole intellect in a single jest, as though—so hot was the contention—he would be satisfied to remain a fool for the rest of his life if he could excel for that moment.[2] This, it must be owned, was a fitting spot for an encounter between the two foremost wits of the time. Hot and fierce was the collision, in spite of all we have heard of a different tenour ; and we can almost imagine Ben floundering into the room as he is described by Fuller,[3]—"a Spanish galloon, built high in learning." Of course, he instantly gives his friend a full charge of Latin, and then parades his Greek fire, while Shakespeare, "the English man-of-war," as Fuller calls him, "lesser in bulk, but lighter in sailing," opens a broadside of good English hail, "turns with all tides, tacks about, and takes advantage of all winds," and "by the quickness of his wit and invention," makes the galloon either strike her flag or roll off, a log on the waves.

Shakespeare's small Latin was a constant target for Ben Jonson at this period. But the real grievance was his great English, and Ben would have given all his own Latin, and thrown in the Greek, for the same mastery of his native tongue. "Why, here's our fellow Shakespeare puts them

---

[1] 'King Henry VI., Part II.,' act iv. 6.
[2] Francis Beaumont's ' Poetical Epistle to Ben Jonson.'
[3] Fuller's ' Worthies.'

all down, ay, and Ben Jonson, too. Oh, that Ben Jonson is a pestilent fellow; he brought up Horace, giving the poets a pill, but our fellow, Shakespeare, hath given him a purge that made him bewray his credit."[1]

Almost the only anecdote that has come down to us of Shakespeare's intercourse with Ben Jonson refers to the small Latin, showing how good-humouredly he met the taunt, and how playfully he retorted. As the story goes, he was god-father to one of Ben Jonson's children; and, after the christening, fell into a brown study, as it appeared to his host, who inquired if he was suffering from low spirits. "No, faith, Ben," was the answer, "not I; but I have been considering a great while what should be the fittest gift for me to bestow upon my godchild, and I have resolved at last." Such an announcement made Ben prick his ears. "I prithee, what?" he asked. "I' faith, Ben, I'll e'en give him a dozen good Latin spoons, and thou shall translate them." The uninitiated may require to be told that latten is tinned iron, now employed chiefly for canisters, but then forming the material of much of the household ware in daily use.

There is no great point in this story, but it has a Shake-spearean touch, the reproof being at once plain and masked. Ben may either see it or not, but such a thrust can hardly excite resentment. The Ashmolean MSS. at Oxford contain another well-known anecdote, which bears the same character. The two friends were at a tavern, in a merry mood, when Ben was seized with an inspiration for his epitaph, which he began in this wise :—

> " Here lies Ben Jonson,
>     That was once one, — "

And then handed it for completion to Shakespeare, no doubt

---

[1] ' Return from Parnassus,' 1606.

expecting some high-flown compliment. But "pleasant Willy" gave the rhyme an unexpected turn:—

> " Who while he lived was a slow thing,
>   **And now, being dead, is nothing.**"

This recalls the sarcasm of Voltaire on Rousseau's address to Posterity—"Here is a letter which will never reach its destination." The drift is the same, but the words afford a different construction, in which it is kerneled. Ben was slow and heavy in his gait—"a slow thing;" and being dead, would be but dust—"nothing." He must smile at the literal meaning while gored by the point. By his own report he was to be remembered as "once *one*"—that is, Somebody, a person of eminence; by Shakespeare's, he was to appear "slow" by what he had done in life, and in death be forgotten. We cannot accept such an epitaph for one who redeemed his faults by his rare gifts, yet it contains a leaven of truth, notwithstanding; for his works are now little known, except in the study of the scholar, and the only one which keeps possession of the stage is, 'Every Man in His Humour,' which owed its acceptance to Shakespeare.

It is not to Ben's credit that the prologue of this very play made a direct attack on his friend :—

> " Though need make many poets, and some, such
>   As art and nature have not bettered much,
>   Yet ours for want hath not so loved the stage,
>   As he dare serve the ill customs of the age,
>   Or purchase your delight at such a rate;
>   As, for it, he himself must justly hate :
>   To make a child, now swaddled to proceed
>   Man, and then shoot up, in one beard and weed,
>   Past three score years; or, with three rusty swords,
>   And help of some few foot-and-half foot words,
>   Fight over York and Lancaster's long jars,
>   And in the trying house bring wounds to scars."

Such sneers could do little towards decrying productions

already enshrined by the people, and are the less graceful in Ben from preceding a flourish over his own performance :—

> " He rather prays you will be pleased to see
> *One such to-day, as other plays should be ;*
> Where neither chorus wafts you o'er the seas,
> Nor creaking throne comes down the boys to please :
> **Nor nimble squib is seen to make afeard**
> The gentlewomen : nor rolled bullet heard
> To say, it thunders : nor tempestuous drum
> Rumbles, to tell you when the storm doth come.
> But deeds and language, such as men do use,
> And persons such as Comedy would choose
> When **she would** show an image of the times,
> And sport with human follies, not with crimes."

Ben Jonson also satirized Shakespeare in ' Bartholomew Fair,' and, indeed, hardly ever spoke of him without some disparaging remark. His tribute to him after death is cited as evidence of the good understanding in which they lived. But the grave-clothes cover as many sins as charity, and he could afford to render him homage when he was no longer a rival. Yet, even then he was full of **wise** saws, rather looking **for some pitiful blemish** than dwelling **on his genius and virtues. "I loved the** man, **and do** honour **his memory, on this side of idolatry, as** much **as** any." In **those days, as in our own, there** were some who regarded Shakespeare as something more than an ordinary man—"*a man imbued with a sort of inspiration from Heaven*"—and this **was** idolatry in the eyes of his eulogist. He was weary of hearing the players **sing his praises.** " I remember that the players have often mentioned it as an honour to Shakespeare, that in writing, whatsoever he penned, he never blotted out a line. My answer hath been, Would he had blotted a thou-**sand !"** A thousand lines blotted out **of Shakespeare. Posterity,** to whom Ben addresses **this stage** confidence, will think **with the** players **that it was "a** malevolent speech." " His wit was in his own power : would the rule of it had been so too!" His wit could not be in his power if he had not the rule of it—if it were not under his control. But Ben Jonson sees the mote in the wit of Shakespeare, while he overlooks the beam in his own. He cites an instance of his trips, which is far from happy. "Many times he fell into those things, could not escape laughter, as when he said in the person of Cæsar, one speaking to him—'Cæsar, thou dost me wrong.' He replied, 'Cæsar did never wrong but with just cause,' and such like, which were ridiculous." There is no contradiction in the passage. It intimates that Cæsar never committed an act which might be wrong in itself, but for an object which rendered it just. It might be an arbitrary exercise of power—which was a wrong—to banish the brother of Metellus, but the measure was adopted "with just cause." Moreover, Ben Jonson quotes the passage from memory, as he had heard it delivered on the stage; for the earliest printed copy gives a different version :—

> " Know, Cæsar doth not wrong; nor without cause
>   Will he be satisfied." [1]

Critics are more unreasonable than Cæsar; for they are not to be satisfied, even with this reading. But if they only keep in view the context, and the Shakespearean mode of expression, the passage will not only present no obscurity, but remarkably illustrate the compactness of his style :—

> " Thy brother by decree is banished :
>   If thou dost bend, and pray, and fawn for him,
>   I spurn thee, like a cur, out of my way.
>   Know, Cæsar doth not wrong, nor without cause
>   Will he be satisfied."

This plainly means your brother is rightfully banished : bending and praying and fawning for him does not show that he ought to be recalled, but merely exhibits your own meanness.

[1] 'Julius Cæsar,' act iii. 1.

Know, Cæsar is not one to act illegally, nor will he be satisfied to rescind what he has done, without good reason.

The popular impression of rare Ben pictures a jovial, burly fellow, fond of his glass, and ever ready with a jest or epigram. But there can be no doubt that he had his cholers, as well **as Sir Hugh** Evans, and was a little testy and snap**pish.** Like his namesake of later times, he was something **of a** bear. The great Doctor could not always be civil even **to** Boswell. "Sir, you have but two topics, yourself and me, and I am tired **of** both." So Ben's waspish nature grew irritable under Shakespeare's gentleness. He tells us that pleasant Willy "was indeed honest, and of an open and free nature; had an excellent fancy, brave notions, and gentle expressions, wherein he flowed with that facility that sometimes it was necessary he should be stopped." Ben was obliged to put on the drag. "*Sufflaminandus erat*, as Augustus said to Haterius." But the imperial Roman would not have complained of Haterius if his facility had flowed in such "gentle expressions" as these :—

> "How weary do I journey on the way,
> When what I seek—my weary travel's end—
> Doth teach that ease and that repose to say,
> 'Thus far the miles are measured from thy friend.'"[1]

Such **is at least** the conclusion of Ben Jonson himself :— "There was ever more in him to be praised than to be pardoned."

His eulogistic verses to "the memory of my beloved the author, **Mr.** William Shakespeare," render, indeed, full justice to his friend; and there is not a word of rebuke to the "honey-tongued" Shakespeare of Weaver, and "silver-tongued Melicert" of Chettle, for his gentle **expressions.** Nor could we have clearer testimony than he affords, to the personal appearance of **his** friend, which he declares to be

[1] Sonnet 50.

faithfully presented in the portrait given in the first folio edition of his works :—

> " This figure, that thou here see'st put,
> It was for gentle Shakespeare cut ;
> Wherein the graver had a strife
> With Nature, to outdo the life.
> Oh, could he but have drawn his wit
> As well in brass as he hath hit
> His face, the print would then surpass
> All that was ever writ in brass :
> But since he cannot, reader, look,
> Not on his picture, but his book."

Nothing is preserved of Shakespeare's intercourse with Marlowe, yet he found a more congenial nature in that frank, reckless, and unhappy man. To him **alone,** of all his contemporaries, has he reared a tablet in the temple of his works—

> " Dead shepherd !  now I find thy saw of might ;
> ' Whoever loved, that loved not at first sight ? ' " [1]

Literature hardly yields such a touching *In Memoriam* as this. We almost see the tear fall, and are conscious of the shadow of a dark fate, though no allusion betrays it.

Shakespeare pays a tribute to Spenser, but it is one of a different kind. He mentions him by name, as the poet of the day, and his own favourite author :—

> " Dowland to thee is dear, whose heavenly touch
> Upon the lute doth ravish human sense ;
> Spenser to me, whose deep conceit is such,
> As, passing all conceit, needs no defence." [2]

They frequently met at Leicester House, in the saloons of their common patron ; and they were brought together by a similarity of disposition, by kindred tastes and habits, as well as by their situation. Spenser mixed as little as Shakespeare in general society, or he would not have passed away

---

[1] ' As You Like It,' act iii. 5. The line quoted from Marlowe is from ' Hero and Leander.'

[2] ' The Passionate Pilgrim,' vi.

without leaving a wrack behind; but they recognized in each other a spiritual affinity, which drew them into companionship. Never, indeed, did two poets exhibit this feeling in a higher degree. The sonnets in which Shakespeare refers to Spenser without directly naming him, beautifully express this feeling. He speaks of him as "a better spirit," as "of tall building, and of goodly pride," declares himself "inferior far,"[1] and then calls him "that able spirit," writing "with golden quill" and "well-refined pen," in "precious phrase by all the Muses filled,"[2] finally dwelling on "the proud full sail of his great verse."[3] Drayton and Daniel have been put forward as equally entitled with Spenser to the honour of these encomiums, but there was only one poet of that day to whom they could apply; and, moreover, the 86th sonnet contains such plain allusions to the 'Fairy Queen,' as removes all doubt:—

> " Was it the proud full sail of his great verse,
> Bound for the prize of all too-precious you,
> That my ripe thoughts in my brain inhearse,
> Making their tomb the womb wherein they grew?
> Was it his spirit, *by spirits taught to write*
> Above a *mortal* pitch, that struck me dead?"

No contemporary poet but the author of the 'Fairy Queen' could be said to be taught to write by "spirits," another term for fairies; the word mortal, which immediately follows, being always used by the little folk to designate mankind. The application grows clearer as the stanza proceeds:—

> " No, neither he, *nor his compeers by night,*
> Giving him aid, my verse astonished."

Night was the season for the fairies: it was then that they left their retreats, in the depths of the earth, and either kept high festival in sequestered spots, or stole into the dwellings of mortals. This was the time when they came to

---

[1] Sonnet lxxx.        [2] Ibid. lxxxv.        [3] Ibid. lxxxvi.

Spenser as compeers, " giving him aid,"—that is, revealing
to him their traditions and mysteries. Yet so far is this
meaning from striking the commentators, that Steevens sees
an allusion to Dr. Dee in the two following lines :—

> " He, nor that affable, familiar ghost
> That nightly gulls him with intelligence."

What possible influence could Dr. Dee and his familiar
spirit exercise on the inspiration of a poet, or how could such
a far-fetched notion be understood by the person to whom
the sonnet is addressed, and who, as we have heretofore
shown, was probably Queen Elizabeth? But the allusion is
transparent, when applied, with the context, to Spenser's great
epic. The "affable"—that is, gracious—"familiar ghost,"
which comes to him nightly, then stands forth as the Fairy
Queen herself, of whom he has the same glorious vision as
Prince Arthur. But her apparently unreserved revelations
are fabulous; she "gulls him with intelligence," just as
fairies gulled simple rustics with fairy money, and mothers
with changeling children; and all the splendid fabrics which
she presents to his eye are gorgeous illusions.

Spenser warmly responded to these friendly praises. It
cannot be doubted that he refers to Shakespeare in this well-
known passage :—

> " And there, though last not least, is Ætion ;
> A *gentler* shepherd may nowhere be found ;
> Whose Muse, full of high thoughts' invention,
> Doth, *like himself, heroically sound.*" [1]

We have already referred to the tributary verses in the
'Tears of the Muses,' which were declared by Dryden to
refer to Shakespeare, and, indeed, will not bear any other
construction. Malone quotes an elegy to show that the name
of Willy was sometimes applied to Sir Philip Sidney, who
is also said to have composed some masques ; but such pro-

[1] Colin Clout's ' Come Home Again.'

ductions, though flattery might assign them a higher rank than their own, could never be described as—

> " —— the sweet delights of learning's treasure,
> That wont with comic sock to beautify
> The painted theatres, and fill with pleasure
> The listeners' eyes, and ears with melody." [1]

**Nor could Sidney be** described **on such grounds** as—

> " —— **the** man whom Nature's self hath made
> To mock herself and truth to imitate."

Masques, **indeed, were unlike anything** in nature, and the last object of **their** composer **was to imitate** Truth. The difficulty **in** the application **to** Shakespeare is the date, as the verses **are** believed to have been written about 1585, two years before his supposed arrival in London ; but **this is removed** now we have shown that he was settled in the capital in 1583.

Another of Shakespeare's friends was John Florio, whom Warburton and Farmer consider the original of **Holofernes**. Whatever deference we **may feel for these eminent** critics, **it** must **be admitted that they rather jump to this conclusion, which all we know of Shakespeare and Florio, and their mutual relations, forbids us** to entertain. **It rests on no ground, indeed, but a** passage in one of Florio's **dedications,** prefixed to his English and Italian dictionary, which is supposed to intimate that he had been ridiculed on the stage—" Let Aristophanes and his comedians make plays, and scour their mouths on Socrates ; those very mouths they make to vilify, shall be the means to amplify his virtues." But this allusion must be viewed in its relation to what has gone before, which is an onslaught on literary, not dramatic, assailants, with a concentration of abuse on one H. **S. ; one** Deformed. Florio yielded to the **temptation** of comparing himself to Socrates, without **considering** that the parallel

---

[1] ' Tears of the Muses.'

broke down in Aristophanes, and, after all, his illustration is happier than his English. Wood tells us that he was born in England, and places his birth in the **reign of** Henry the Eighth, but as he was only 57 in 1611,[1] it must be brought into that of Mary, when the religious persecution in England obliged his father, a Protestant refugee from Florence, to fly to the Continent. Whether born in England or not, Florio is admitted to have spent his youth abroad; his parents were foreigners; and, though he subsequently matriculated at Oxford, he must have retained a foreign accent. Although the play is laid in Navarre, this peculiarity would be marked in Holofernes, as, in 'The Merry Wives of Windsor,' it is in Dr. Caius, if it was intended to hit Florio—and, in fact, we are told of the foreign derivation of Armado—"a Spaniard who keeps here in court;"[2] but Holofernes is throughout presented as a native of the place. Indeed, he has not a single point of resemblance to Florio. His language is wholly unlike, swelling with an affectation of learning, while that of Florio is merely the superlative phraseology of the time, touched with Italian varnish. Holofernes is the lowest type of pedagogue—"he teaches boys the horn-book."[3] Florio was a scholar, a linguist, and an author. As such he was countenanced by the very noblemen who were the liberal patrons of Shakespeare, for he may be said to have grown up under the protection of the Herberts; his maiden production, *First Fruits*, was brought out under the auspices of the Earl of Leicester, and in the dedication of his Italian Dictionary, he declares himself to be living in the " pay and patronage " of the Earl of Southampton. Sir William Cornwallis describes him in his Essays, as "a good fellow," and " wise man," and such a character would rather attract

---

[1] This is stated in the inscription to his portrait, in the second edition of his Dictionary.

[2] 'Love's Labour's Lost,' act iv. 1.      [3] Ibid., act v. 1.

Shakespeare, who was frequently thrown into his company at the mansion of Southampton, if not at Leicester House and Baynard's Castle. We seem, indeed, to have a memento of their friendship in the only book traced to his possession, which is Florio's translation of Montaigne, preserved in the British Museum, and in which he has written his name with his own hand.

But Shakespeare's friendships in town were formed chiefly among the players, who called themselves his "fellows;" and we find proof of the amiability of his nature in their espousal of his cause whenever he was assailed, though his great success, raising him into a superior sphere, might well have excited their envy. His chosen friends seem to have been Heminges and Condell, who became his literary executors, and Richard Burbage. It is curious that his intimacy with such a man as Burbage should have left no impression in contemporary gossip. A story, indeed, has come down, which associates their names, but it is such a palpable invention, that it refutes itself. We are told that a fair city dame was present at the theatre when Burbage played Richard the Third, and was so charmed with his performance that she invited him to come that night to her door, where an intimation that he was Richard the Third would secure him admittance. The tender message was overheard by Shakespeare, who determined to forestal his friend, and, accordingly, was first in the field. He had reconciled the lady to the change, when a knock at the door announced Burbage, who was challenged from within, and gave the concerted password—" 'Tis I, Richard the Third," on which Shakespeare replied, "But William the Conqueror came before Richard the Third," and so gave him his dismissal.

The association of the story with Richard the Third, a character so unlikely to be bidden to my lady's chamber, is unfortunate, leading us to exclaim "was ever woman

in this humour wooed, was ever woman in this humour
won ?"[1]    But it was the only **one of Burbage's parts that**
fitted his name, and, at the same time, represented a later
King than William the Conqueror, so that the difficulty was
unavoidable.    Mr. Collier found the story in a manuscript
diary of the time,[2] written by a Temple student, who is
assumed to have borne the name of Manningham ; and his
authority is supposed to be given in the conclusion—"Shakespeare's name Willm.—Mr. Tooley."    Mr. Collier states that
**Tooley** was the name of Burbage's apprentice, but both
Tooley and Manningham are very mythical persons, and
such a charge requires to be supported by "sufficient honest
witnesses."[3]    We can trace it to a much higher source—
namely, Margaret of Angoulême, who relates substantially
the same adventure in the 'Heptameron,'[4] which had then
**just made its appearance in an English dress, and thus
allowed of the sins of Bonnevet being transferred to Shake-**
speare.

The poet's alleged intrigue with the mother of Sir
William Davenant rests on equally credible report.    According to Aubrey, Mrs. Davenant was the wife of "a grave,
discreet man," who kept the Crown inn, at Oxford, where
Shakespeare was in the habit of putting up, as he journeyed
**to and from Stratford.    She was a woman of** great beauty,
and her personal attractions were heightened by her agree-
**able manners and sparkling wit.    Her moral character** did
**not stand so high,** and Aubrey reports her "a trader."
However this may be, Shakespeare was godfather to her
son, afterwards **Sir William, and Aubrey "heard Parson
Robert say,"** that he had seen him give the **boy a hundred**
kisses.    It is plain that neither Parson Robert nor Aubrey

[1] 'King Richard III.,' act i. 2.
[2] MS. Harl., 5353.
[3] 'Taming of the Shrew,' act ii. 1.
[4] Novel, xiv.

had a clear notion of what is expected from a godfather. A hundred kisses, even taking Parson Robert's round numbers as accurate, though he probably meant but a dozen, are within the canon, and would not secure an affiliation order. But it may be said that a whisper is dropped of more direct evidence. Solomon declares that he is a wise son who knoweth his own father, and, according to Aubrey, this proof of sagacity often broke from Sir William Davenant when he was drunk. He would then inform his boon companions " that it seemed to him that he writ with the very spirit that Shakespeare [did], and was contented enough to be thought his son: he would tell them the story as above." The story of the hundred kisses, with " Well, well, we know,"[1] and so on! But we cannot blacken Shakespeare on the insinuation of a reprobate in his cups, who makes no scruple of taking away the character of his mother, and fixing the vilest stigma of bastardy on himself, to look big as a poet.[2]

The age of Elizabeth was not a moral millenium, but it was purity itself compared with the era of the second Charles, and though Davenant saw no odium in a licentious life or a shameful origin, Shakespeare was of a different mould. We know that he possessed the esteem of the noblest characters of the day—of Sir Philip Sidney, the Countess of Pembroke, and the Earl of Southampton; and none of his contemporaries urge a word against him. Lady Pembroke allowed him to form a friendship with her son, while he was yet a youth, and we learn how this connection was prized by the family from the dedication by Hemings and Condell, of the posthumous edition of his plays to the two brothers, the Earls

---

[1] 'Hamlet,' act i. 5.

[2] The great value of Aubrey's ' Memorabilia' is attested by the appearance of this story in the MS. notes of Oldys, who received it from Pope, to whom it came from Betterton; but this only carries it back to the same source— Sir William Davenant, as Betterton must have been often present when, as Aubrey says, " he would tell them the story as above."

of Pembroke and Montgomery. The Earl of Pembroke is believed also to be the " Mr. W. H.," to whom he dedicated his sonnets. But this is a point that must ever remain unsettled, though perhaps the strongest fact in its favour is the initials, which, even with the prefix of Mr., present no link of connection with any other person. Even if we reject Sir Walter Scott's assertion, that the sonnets were in possession of Sir Philip Sidney, we know that they had been some time circulating in manuscript in 1598, when Meres calls them " sugared sonnets," which Shakespeare passed round among his friends. At that time Lord Herbert was only eighteen years of age, and, consequently the sixteen opening stanzas could have no application, if addressed to him ; but the case was different in 1609, the date of their publication. He had then become Earl of Pembroke, and was on the verge of his thirtieth year, so that Shakespeare might say—

> "  —— wasteful time debateth with decay,
> To change your day of youth to sullied night." [1]

The solemn exhortations to marriage are intelligible when addressed to a nobleman who is imprudently extending the days of bachelorhood towards middle life, when he ought to be training the heir to his title and estate. There is no advocacy of any particular match; on the contrary, the Earl is reminded that he may select from many maidens ; [2] yet, when his bride proves to be one of the three co-heiresses of Gilbert Talbot, seventh Earl of Shrewsbury, we are inclined to think that a particular object was in view. At any rate, she supplies the link that connects him with the illustrious house of Talbot, and though hitherto passed over in silence this is really an important point in his history ; for uniting the possible bearing of the sonnets on the marriage with the prominence given to the two Talbots in the ' First Part of

[1] Sonnet xv.          [2] Sonnets v. and xvi.

King Henry VI.,' it induces the belief that Earl Gilbert was one of his first patrons. He had probably been introduced to him by Sir Philip Sidney, who, in his vindication of the nobility of the Dudleys, lays great stress on this relationship to the Talbots, and Shakespeare may be thought to have favoured a union which cemented it by a new tie.

It would seem impossible that a man, known as the friend of so many powerful nobles, the foremost dramatist and poet of the time, and, as such, publicly honoured by two successive sovereigns, should need to be mentioned to the Lord Keeper in such terms as are used in a document found in the Ellesmere archives, and which, from being signed with the initials " H. S.," is pronounced a contemporary copy of a letter from the Earl of Southampton. The writer appeals to the Lord Keeper to protect Shakespeare and Burbage from the city authorities, who waged a crusade against the players, continually threatening them with legal proceedings in order to drive them from Blackfriars. But besides presenting internal **evidence of** fabrication, **the** paper is only tendered as **a copy, and,** as no one ever saw the original, this alone throws it out of court. Mr. Collier acted with his usual candour in bringing it forward, but even the weight of his name cannot supply what is necessary to its authentication—the Earl of Southampton's own signature.[1]

[1] The Letter will be found in the Appendix.

## XXVIII.

### LAST SCENE OF ALL.

HALLAM has remarked that the latter productions of Shakespeare are imbued with a feeling of gloom, as if his mind had undergone a change, and saw life from a darker point of view. He had reached an age when we all grow staider and think more soberly, and both his experiences of the few previous years and his own situation were calculated to produce such a result. In the height of his success he was reminded of the instability of earthly fortune by the death of his only son; the grave was next opened for his father; and he already saw it yawning for himself. It is impossible to misinterpret the allusions in his sonnets:—

> " No longer mourn for me when I am dead,
> Than you shall hear the surly sullen bell
> Give warning to the world that I am fled."[1]

And he evidently looks to an early dissolution:—

> " In me thou see'st the glowing of such fire,
> That on the ashes of his youth doth lie,
> As the death-bed whereon it must expire,
> Consumed with that which it was nourished by."[2]

Coleridge considers this passage to intimate that he was in a decline; but such a view is not reconcilable with his appearance in the bust in Stratford church, which Chantrey pronounced to be taken from a cast after death. There the face is full and plump, indicating a man inclined to corpulency—with fat capon lined. Nor does the verse apply to

---

[1] Sonnet lxxi.　　[2] Sonnet lxxvii.

the nourishment derived from food. It points to his blood, which should nourish, but consumed him, whence we may believe that he was subject **to** internal hæmorrhage, and, indeed, the **word** "consumed" **suggests** consumption rather than decline.

**Here we see** him, then, in broken **health, and familiar with sorrow,** while he still toiled **with his pen, and** it is no **wonder that a reflection of this** feeling **is** apparent in what **he writes.** The death **of** his son left him without induce- ment to continue his exertions when he had acquired **a com-** petence ; and he instantly began his preparations to retire, purchasing New Place in the following year. Other pur- chases followed, as we have seen ; and in 1605 a mighty effort completed the task he had set himself. It is all but certain that he then produced three of his noblest plays— 'Macbeth,' 'King Lear,' and 'Cymbeline.' We venture to look upon 'Cymbeline' as his latest production ; and, indeed, the dirge over Imogen seems to announce his retirement in a manner that **would be understood** by his **friends :—**

> " **Fear no more the** heat **o'** the sun,
> **Nor** the furious winter's rages ;
> Thou thy worldly task hast done,
> *Home art gone and ta'en thy wages.*" [1]

**The last** lines of the dirge apply to himself, far more than to Imogen :—

> " Quiet consummation have ;
> *And renowned be thy grave !* " [2]

No renown could attach to the grave of a nameless fugi- tive, whose very sex was unknown ; but how striking are the words in connection with Shakespeare ! [1]

The " wages" that he took home were little more than the thousand pounds **he received from** Southampton. The **whole of the purchases of property he is** known to have made

---

[1] 'Cymbeline,' act iv. 2.        [2] Ibid.

scarcely exceeds that amount,[1] so that he **could** never have obtained high prices for his **plays ; and the report of Vicar Ward** that he wrote two plays a year after his retirement to Stratford and sold them for 500*l.* each, is a pure fable. None of his plays can be proved to be written later than 1605. As for his means, his largest investment was the lease of the Stratford tithes, which yielded him an annuity of sixty pounds for sixty-one years, subject to a proportion of a rent-charge of twenty-seven pounds thirteen and fourpence a year, which he was to pay jointly with the other lessees ; and this, at its outside value, was not more **than** 190*l.* of our money. His income from all sources may **be** estimated at about 300*l.* a year of the present currency.

" Quiet consummation !" He wanted no recognition from princes, and **no coats of arms from Dethick—not even riches, but just enough, and** quiet. **As for courts, and gilded honour, and the strifes of the world, with its corruptions and** oppressions, and the spectacle of " captive good attending captain ill," he was tired with all these,[2] and takes leave of them in this very play.[3] He found no pleasure but in being on the spot where he had passed the innocent days of childhood, before he dreamt of such seared wisdom. So we **imagine** him pacing his garden at New Place, where he can see over the wall as he walks right into the chapel, exposed to view by its noble windows, and there he may mark the very place where he stood as a boy before Thomas Jenkins. Now it was changed, like himself : the gloom in his mind rested, **indeed, on** the whole town. Where now **were the** sheep-shearers, the morris dancers, the merry shooters at the

---

[1] This estimate includes a house and premises near the Blackfriars theatre, purchased in 1612–13. It is not known that he ever possessed any share in the theatre itself, the only evidence on this point having been pronounced a fabrication ; and no mention is made of such property in his will.

[2] **Sonnet lxvi.**          [3] ' Cymbeline,' act iii. 3.

butts? The Puritan who sang Psalms to hornpipes had driven them out. The Earl of Leicester's players would receive no welcome from the High Bailiff; for as early as 1602, it was decreed by the firm of Quiney, Sturley, and Co., who **were the present** Corporation, that "there shall **be no** plays **or** interludes played in the chamber, the guildhall, nor in any parts of the house or court," and anybody who "gave leave or licence thereunto" was to be fined ten shillings. **But** the **townsmen** of Shakespeare were stubborn on this point, **and** it **was deemed necessary to make a** more stringent decree, which raised the penalty to twelve shillings.

No sooner had Shakespeare taken up his abode at New Place, than the Puritans made a set at Stratford. His ridicule of their "bibble-babble" in 'Twelfth Night,' wounded them in the tenderest point, their gift of exorcism, and they doubtless looked upon the town as lost, if left under his influence. The task of conversion was lightened for them by the efforts already made by the Corporation, and by two fires, which providentially **almost destroyed Stratford for its** lukewarmness in the **cause —" chiefly for profaning the Lord's** day, and contemning His Word by the mouth of His faithful **minister,"**[1] and the parochial register records the fate of **one** offender after this kind :—" 1601, April 27, buried Thomas Bailey, slain at the sign of the Swan upon the Sabbath day, at the time of the sermon, being there drinking." The sign of the SWAN! the very tavern where in old time Sir Thomas Lucy, and my Lady, and Mr. Sheriff, had drunk their sack, and where Sir Thomas had consumed his burnt sugar, and which was the emblem of Shakespeare himself. But now there were to be no more such doings. **The Cor**poration had grown virtuous, and spent the **money in bribery** and sermons. Dr. Harris, of **Banbury, came in haste to**

---

[1] Beard's 'Theatre of God's Judgments.'

their aid, and as a supplement to the ordinary services, established a fortnightly lecture in the church. **Nicholas Bifield**, the Vicar, was also very active, and **Davies calls** Shakespeare a "papist," because he discountenanced their innovations. No one has instanced the refutation of **this** assertion in the explicit declaration in his will—"**I** commend my soul into the hands of God my Creator, hoping and assuredly believing through the ONLY MERITS of Jesus Christ, my Saviour, to be made partaker of life everlasting." But he never swerved from his old maxims of charity. Tradition still marks the pew in which he sat in the Guild Chapel; an entry in the Corporation accounts refers to his entertainment of one of the Puritan lecturers; and on the 5th June, 1607, he gave the hand of his eldest daughter to a Puritan leader, John Hall, a physician at Stratford.

The sermons under the new system **must have been** of prodigious length, for they were thirsty **work, and the** preacher who was the guest of Shakespeare received from the Corporation a ration of "a quart of sack, and a quart of claret wine," so that he might be said to have "drowned his tongue in sack."[1] The fee paid for the supply would say little for Shakespeare's hospitality, if the guest were **anyone** but a Puritan preacher, between whom and himself there **could** be nothing in common. Tradition, indeed, reports that he had become very religious, but we can imagine no period of his life when he was uninfluenced by such a feeling, **and even** the lapse of his youth at Bidford brought out his **reverence for Sunday.** But what religion could he see in a man who refreshed his **spiritual energies with half a** gallon of sack and claret? His own was to repeat **day by** day "prayers divine," to teach and practise forgiveness and charity, and to raise his soul by the contemplation of its

---

[1] 'Tempest,' act iii. 2.

awful destiny and the forms of things unknown.  If he had plunged into such meditations in his youth, in 'Hamlet,' how much more now, when he saw the red tide of life ebbing in his breast, and all he coveted was a quiet consummation!

Death was busy in his family, but its circle **expanded in** one direction, as it narrowed in the other; and while he lost **his** mother and two brothers,[1] his daughter, Mrs. Hall, gave **birth** to a descendant of himself, who was baptized at Strat**ford**, the 16th of February, 1607-8, under the name of Elizabeth.

His family connections in the town were in humble life, his favourite sister, Joan, being married to a hatter, named Hart; but this did not prevent the highest society in the neighbourhood from courting his acquaintance. It has always been lamented that there was no indication of his having made up his breach with the Lucys.  We have now the satisfaction of stating that this desirable result was effected, for Mrs. Lucy has found papers in the Gate-House at Charlecote, which places the point beyond doubt. Shakespeare had thought it better to **begin with the Lucys in the manner of Mrs. Malaprop, with a little aversion; but he had come to see that there** was something to forgive on both sides, and by both it was forgiven.  Indeed, the reconciliation was easy to bring about; for the Sir Thomas Lucy of his youth was dead, and Charlecote had devolved to his son, a second Sir Thomas, who was married to Constance Kingsmill; and this lady had been brought up in the family of Sir Francis Walsingham as the companion of his daughter, who was the Stella of Spenser, and THE WIFE OF SIR PHILIP SIDNEY. Sir Thomas Lucy was worthy of such associations, enjoying high repute as a scholar and the best **odour among** his neigh-

---

[1] The poet's mother, Mary Shakespeare, was buried on the 9th September, 1608.  His brother, Edmund, was buried on the 30th December, 1607, at St. Saviour's, Southwark; his brother Richard died in 1613.

bours, and we may believe that the splendid library he established at Charlecote was now thrown open to Shakespeare.

There is a Stratford tradition that the poet often resorted to a library at Radbrooke Manor House, which stands in the fields, about five miles from Stratford; but we could find no remembrance of it on the spot, nor among the oldest patriarchs of the neighbouring villages of Quinton and Adminton. It seems, however, to derive some corroboration from the proximity of Radbrooke to Wincot, which he has referred to in two of his plays, and where the old path over the fields to Radbrooke is marked by three mulberry trees said to have been planted by his hand.[1]

But Shakespeare was not left in the quiet enjoyment of either his friends or his books. In 1613 the tithe bargain imposed on him by Quiney and Co. involved him in a Chancery suit, the issue of which is unknown; but research has brought to light the draft of a bill presented by himself and two other of the lessees, against William Combe and the remaining co-sharers, to compel them to pay their proportions of the rent-charge. The next year entangled him with another of the Combes, who meditated an enclosure of the neighbouring common; and he joined the Corporation in opposing the project. A memorandum made on the occasion shows that he possessed four yards or seventy-two acres of land which there is no record of his having purchased, and this is clearly the property at Bishopton, mentioned in his will.[2] The proceedings obliged him to make a journey to London, but he succeeded in defeating the scheme, in so far

---

[1] The tradition has been handed down at the farm from father to son. Mr. Ward, the present occupant, received it from his father, who was his predecessor on the property. Nothing seems to be known of the trees elsewhere.

[2] "Mr. Shakspeare, four yard land, no common nor ground beyond Gosepl Cush, nor none in Snow Hill Field beyond Bishopton, nor none in the enclosures beyond Bishopton."

that an undertaking was give by William Replingham, one of its promoters, against any injury that should accrue from it to him or his heirs ; and eventually an interdict was put on the whole project.

The Combes were two brothers, John and William, and were the Warwickshire Shylocks, John being always spoken of as " the usurer."  Shakespeare's dealings with them, first as a buyer of land, and subsequently in these tithe and enclosure transactions, were of a nature to make him acquainted with their grasping disposition in its most unamiable light ; and it is to this period we must refer the anecdote related by Rowe, alleging that he was asked by John Combe to write his epitaph, and delivered the following impromptu strain :—

> " Ten in the hundred lies here engraved,
> 'Tis a hundred to ten his soul is not saved.
> If any man ask who lies in this tomb,
> Oh, oh ! quoth the devil, 'tis my John a Combe."

Rowe says that the usurer never forgave this rebuke ; but we have, on the contrary, ground to believe that it made a salutary impression upon him, as in his will he established an endowment of a hundred pounds for poor tradesmen of Stratford, besides bequests to the poor of the town and the poor of Warwick and Alcester ; and far from cherishing any resentment towards Shakespeare, he left him a legacy of five pounds.  The poet, on his part, evinced the same good feeling towards the Combes, as his will bequeaths his sword to Thomas Combe, the usurer's nephew.

Nothing has transpired to suggest that he resumed friendly relations with the Hathaways, nor do they appear to have come in communication with his wife.  But Shakespeare and Anne are both referred to in the will of Whittington, the shepherd of old Richard Hathaway, who mentions that they hold a small sum of money which he had placed in their care, proving that they were looked **up to by** an old follower of the family, and that they treated **him with** kindness and sympathy. Doubtless they **had many such** dependents, not all with the same claims. None of their neighbours adhered to them with more tenacity than the Quineys. They saw that Shakespeare had barns and beeves, and they saw that he had an unmarried daughter. **Judith** Shakespeare was in her thirty-second year; and **Thomas** Quiney, the brother of the Richard who borrowed the thirty pounds at the Bell, was seven-and-twenty; whether the same Mr. Quiney who forgot himself on one occasion, and is entered in the books of the Corporation as being fined for swearing, is uncertain. By trade he was a vintner, and he sued to Judith to share his fortunes. **She** might be re-**conciled to the union by his reminding** her of the happiness **enjoyed by her parents whose ages presented an even greater** disparity, and she forgot that her father, **though pleased with** his own lot, had warned others not to follow his example :—

> " Let still the woman take
> An elder than herself: so wears she to him,
> So sways she level in her husband's heart." [1]

The marriage was solemnized on the 10th February, 1615–16, but we may consider that it had not the ap-**proval** of Shakespeare, as he left Judith but a small portion **of his property and placed it beyond the control** both of **her husband and herself.**

**His will is dated** on the 25th of the **following month, and was no doubt drawn up at the time,** though it is always **said to have been commenced in January—the** words " *vicesimo quinto* **die *Martii***," having originally stood " *vice-simo quinto die Januarii*," but the day being the same, leads to the impression that he had merely made a mistake in the **month,** as men engaged in literary pursuits often find them-

<hr>

[1] 'Twelfth Night,' act ii. 4.

selves doing, and then corrected it. We may even believe that the will was made with special reference to the recent marriage of Judith, since the disposition of his property bears out such a conclusion, and it possibly took the place of a previous will, **which** being destroyed, it was unnecessary **to mention.** But his attention might be directed to the subject by the dying illness of his brother-in-law, Hart,[1] reminding him of the precarious tenure of his own life, and the possibility of his tripping on May-hill, so fatal to those suffering from consumption. Vicar Ward tells a foolish story of his being visited at this time by Drayton and Ben Jonson—"Shakespeare, Drayton, and Jonson, had a merry meeting, and it seems drank too hard, for Shakespeare died of a fever there contracted." Mr. Dyce thinks that "Drayton, a native of Warwickshire, and frequently in the neighbourhood of Stratford, may fairly be presumed to have partaken at times of Shakespeare's hospitality."[2] The fair presumption is just the contrary ; for Drayton would hardly leave **such memorable meetings without notice, when he alludes to his visits to the neighbourhood, and mentions the hospitality he received at Clifford, which is within two miles of Stratford :—**

> "—— Dear Clifford's seat, the place of health and sport,
> Which *many a time* hath been the Muse's quiet port."[3]

In fact, the negative evidence is very strong that Drayton was unacquainted with Shakespeare. Nor is it credible that Ben Jonson would omit to state that he had gone to see him just before his death, when he was constrained to prove how he "loved the man," if he had really paid such a visit. No one believes Vicar Ward's assertion **that Shake**speare obtained a thousand a year in **his** retirement by

---

[1] Hart was buried on the 17th of April, **five days** before Shakespeare.
[2] Dyce's 'Life of Shakespeare.'
[3] Drayton's 'Polyolbion.'

writing plays, yet we are willing to credit his report that he killed himself by a debauch. He had yielded, indeed, to the prevailing vice of hard drinking in his youth, but it is never connected with him afterwards, and he raised his voice against it in the most emphatic manner:—

> " —— It is a custom
> More honoured in the breach than the observance.
> This heavy-headed revel, east and west
> Makes us traduced and taxed of other nations :
> They clepe us drunkards." [1]

The only allusion in his will to his wife is a bequest of his "second-best bed," and this led to an injurious inference against her, till Mr. Knight pointed out that she was provided for by the law of the land, which secured her a proportion of his property as dower, and that the bequest of the second-best bed was a great mark of affection, the principal bed always going as an heir-loom to the heir.[2] He leaves tokens of remembrance to several friends, and settles the bulk of his property on his eldest daughter, Mrs. Hall.[3]

What would we give for a glimpse of the last scene of all, which ends this strange, eventful history! Certainly it would furnish the best of us an example, such as exists neither in tale nor chronicle—nowhere out of the Bible. He who had so often looked death in the face, more steadily than the soldier in the imminent deadly breach, scrutinizing and searching it, and following it to the grave, and beyond, must have sunk into its arms so composedly and placidly! It was the debt he was to pay to Nature! He had recognized the liability in the hey-day of youth, and kept it before him, like the Egyptian skeleton, in his wildest revels. It attends his Muse like a shadow, as well in his comedies as his tragedies, meeting us where least expected, and whispering

[1] ' Hamlet,' act i. 4.
[2] ' William Shakspere,' a Biography.
[3] Shakespeare's Will is given in the Appendix.

this text.   He saw life as a mystery, to which there was no key but God, and looked upon nothing in the world as worth possessing.   Bacon, on his deathbed, solemnly bequeathed his fame to the next generation ; Shakespeare left his works unprinted, and never mentioned them in **his will.**

So he met death like a familiar, **without** a sigh.   It was near the end of April—the anniversary of the day on which he came into the world, and the sun may have shone on the window with **the uncertain** glory of an April day.   Thus it threw its beams on the deathbed of Walter Scott, and through the open window he heard the surging of the Tweed on the unnumbered idle pebbles.   Shakespeare might think of the Avon, flowing through the osiers at the bottom of his garden, or the mulberry tree he had planted in its centre, and where his mind had often turned on this solemn moment. Only one thought seems to have disturbed his dying hour. He plainly foresaw a time when the nation would claim his remains, and desire to entomb them with her heroes and kings, in her noblest temple, and this **measure was** actually **proposed in the next generation, to which Bacon had ap-pealed in vain.**   **It was not carried out, for he had made it impracticable,** interposing an insurmountable obstacle in his **epitaph,** inscribed on the stone covering his grave as the last words of his Muse :—

> " Good frend, for Jesus sake forbeare
>   To digg the dust encloased heare:
>   Bleste be yᵉ man yᵗ spares thes stones,
>   AND CURST BE HE Yᵀ MOVES MY BONES."

He wished to rest in his native place ; and on the 25th of April, 1616, all that was mortal of the greatest of men **was** buried **in** the chancel of Stratford church—and renowned **is his grave.**

Anne Shakespeare survived her husband seven years, and by her own wish was buried by his side, where her grave is marked by a brass, doubtless placed there by her daughter, Mrs. Hall, who is supposed to have also erected the mural tablet and bust to Shakespeare. The brass bears the following inscription—

> " Here lyeth interred the body of Anne, wife of William Shakespeare, who departed this life the 6th day of Augi., 1623, being of the age of 67 yeares.

> " Ubera tu, mater, tu lac vitamque dedisti :
> Væ mihi, pro tanto munere saxa dabo.
> Quam mallem amoveat lapidem bonus angelus ore,
> Exeat Christi corpus imago tua.
> Sed nil vota valent : venias cito, Christe, resurget,
> Clausa licet tumulo, mater et astra petet."

It has been contended that Anne Shakespeare contracted a second marriage, because the registry of her burial brackets her name with another Anne, which does not occur in any similar case in the register. The entry stands thus :—

$$8 \left\{ \begin{array}{l} \text{Mrs. Shakespeare.} \\ \text{Anna, uxor Richardi James.} \end{array} \right.$$

This far-fetched surmise is sufficiently refuted by the brass on the gravestone, where there is no mention of the name of James, and we are told simply of " ANNE, WIFE OF WILLIAM SHAKESPEARE.

Judith, the second daughter of the poet, by her marriage with Thomas Quiney, became the mother of three sons, but none of them attained the age of manhood. Shakespeare Quiney, born in November, 1616, died in the May of the following year ; Richard, born in February, 1617–18, died in February, 1638 ; and Thomas, born in August, 1619, died a month before his brother Richard. Their mother lived till 1661–62.

Dr. Hall, who married Shakespeare's eldest daughter Susanna, died in 1635. His wife survived till 1649. After his death, she disposed of his manuscripts, containing notes of his medical practice, and a selection of these were published. The first edition of the work contains an introduction by the editor, Cooke, showing how they came into his possession, and giving an interesting notice of Shakespeare's daughter :—

"Being in my art an attendant to parts of some regiments to keep the pass at the bridge of Stratford-upon-Avon, there being then with me a mate, allied to the gentleman that wrote the following observations in Latin, he invited me to the house of Mrs. Hall, wife of the deceased, to see the books left by Mr. Hall. After a view of them, she told me she had some books left, by one that professed physic, with her husband, for some money. I told her if I liked them I would give her the money again ; she brought them forth, amongst which there was this, with another of the author's, both intended for the press. I being acquainted with Mr. Hall's hand, told her that one or two of them were her husband's and showed them her. She denied : I affirmed ; till I perceived she began to be offended. At last I returned her the money. After some time of trial of what had been observed, I resolved to put it to press, according to preconceived intentions, to which end I sent it to London, where, after being viewed by an able doctor, he returned answer, that it might be useful, but the Latin was so abbreviated and false, that it would require the like pains as to write a new one." Cooke also speaks of Dr. Hall, and his mode of practice : "He had been a traveller, acquainted with the French tongue, as appeared by some part of some observations, which I got help to make English. His practice was very much, and best amongst most eminent persons in the county where he lived and those adjacent." Susanna Hall was buried by the side of her husband, in the chancel of Stratford church, and the stone covering her grave bears this inscription:—

> "Here lyeth the body of Sussana, wife of John Hall, gent.; the daughter of William Shakespeare, gent.; she deceased the 11th of July, anno 1649, aged 66.

> " Witty above her sex, but that's not all,
>     Wise to salvation was good Mistress Hall:
>     Something of Shakespeare was in that; but this,
>     Wholly of him with whom she's now in bliss.
>     Then, passenger, hast ne'er a tear
>     To weep with her that wept with all?
>     That wept, yet set herself to cheer
>     Them up with comforts cordial.
>     Her love shall live, her mercy spread,
>     When thou hast ne'er a tear to shed."

Elizabeth Hall, the only child of this union, was eight years old at the time of her grandfather's death, and appears to have been a favourite with him, from the remembrance she receives in his will. She married, in 1626, Thomas Nash, a gentleman of Stratford, and bore no children. A second marriage with Sir John Bernard of Abingdon, was equally sterile. In her, therefore, the direct descendants of Shakespeare became extinct, and the only existing representatives of the family are remotely descended from his sister Joan, who married Hart, the hatter. The nearest we have been able to discover is the landlord of a publichouse at Tewkesbury, and bears the unpoetic name of William Smith.

# APPENDIX.



## TRANSFER OF THE PROPERTY RENTED BY RICHARD SHAKESPEARE AND OTHERS.

This indenture, made the 21st day of May, in the second year of the reign of our sovereign lady Elizabeth, by the grace of God Queen of England, France, and Ireland, Defender of the Faith, &c. Between Agnes Arden, of Wilmcote, in the county of Warwick, widow, on the one part, and Alexander Webb, of Bereley, in the same county, husbandman, on the other part, witnesseth that the said Agnes Arden, for divers and sundry considerations, hath demised, granted, set, and to farm let, and by these presents demiseth, granteth, setteth, and to farm letteth unto the said Alexander Webb and to his assigns all those her two messuages, with a cottage, with all and singular their appurtenances in Snitterfield, and a yard-and-a-half of arable land thereunto belonging, with all lands, meadows, pastures, commons, profits, and commodities in anywise thereunto appertaining, situate, lying, and being in the town and fields of Snitterfield aforesaid, all which now are in the occupation of Richard Shakespeare, John Henley, and John Hargreave, to have and to hold the said two messuages or tenements and cottage, with their appurtenances, a yard-and-a-half of land arable, and all other the premises, with all and singular their appurtenances, unto the said Alexander Webb, his executors and assigns, from the feast of the Annunciation of our Lady next ensuing the date hereof until the end and term of forty years next and immediately following fully to be completed and ended, if the said Agnes Arden so long do live, yielding and paying therefor yearly during the said term unto the said Agnes Arden or her assigns forty shillings of lawful money of England, to be paid at two terms in the year, that is to say, at the feast of St. Michael the Archangel, and the Annunciation of our Lady, by equal portions.   And the said Alexander Webb covenanteth by these presents to discharge, pay and save harmless the said Agnes

Arderne of all manner of chief rents, and suit of court due to the lord of the fee, and all other charges belonging to the aforesaid messuages or tenements ; and if it happen the said rent of forty shillings to be behind, unpaid in part or in all, after any of the said feasts or days of **payment at which it** ought to be paid, **as is** aforesaid, **by the space of one** month, **being** lawfully **asked and demanded, and no** sufficient distress can **or may be** found in and **upon the premises** by the space of six **weeks next after any** of the **said** feasts, **that then** it shall **be** lawful **to the said** Agnes Arden and her assigns to re-enter and have again their premises, and **every parcel** thereof, as in her first estate ; and the said Alexander **Webb, his executors and assigns** thereof, to expel and **put** out, anything herein **contained** to the contrary in anywise notwithstanding.   Also the said Agnes covenanteth and granteth, to and with the said Alexander and his assigns, that the said Alexander, his executors and assigns, shall have, enjoy, and take, during all the said term, sufficient housebote, ploughbote, cartbote, and hedgebote, with lops and shreds growing and being in and upon the premises, or any parcel thereof, for the defense and use of the same houses and closures, without doing any waste.   Also the said Alexander Webb covenanteth by these presents yearly to repair, maintain, and keep all, and all manner of necessary reparations pertaining and belonging to the aforesaid tenements, **cottages,** having sufficient timber on the aforesaid grounds, if any **be there to be had for the same.   And the said Agnes Arden and her assigns [let] the said two** messuages or tenements, **with** the said cottages, a yard-and-a-half of land, and all other the premises, with their appurtenances, unto the said Alexander Webb, his executors **and** assigns, for the said yearly rent in manner and form aforesaid, against her and her assigns, shall warrant and defend **during** the said term of forty years, if she live so long,   In witness whereof, the parties aforesaid to these present indentures interchangeably have put to their seals the day and year above written.

---

### WILL AND INVENTORY OF ROBERT ARDEN.

**In** the **name** of God, **Amen, the** 24th **day of** November, in the year of our Lord God **1556, in the third and the** fourth year of the reign of our sovereign lord and lady, **Philip** and Mary, King and Queen, &c.  I, Robert Arden, of Wilmcote, in the parish of Aston-

Cantlow, sick in body, and good and **perfect of remembrance,** make this my last will and testament in manner and form following :—

First. I bequeath my soul to Almighty God and to **our blessed** Lady **Saint** Mary, and to all the holy company of heaven, **and my** body to be buried in the churchyard of St. John the Baptist, **in** Aston aforesaid.

Also, I give **and bequeath** to my youngest daughter Mary all my land in Wilmcote, **called** Ashby, and the crop upon the ground **sown** and tilled **as it is. And** 6*l*. 13*s*. 4*d*. of money to be paid over **ere my goods be** divided. Also, I give and bequeath to my daughter **Alice the third part of all my** goods movable and unmovable in field **and** town, **after my debts and** legacies be performed, **be**sides that goods she hath of her **own** at this time. Also, I give and bequeath to Agnes, my wife, 6*l*. 13*s*. 4*d*., upon this condition, that [she] shall suffer my daughter Alice quietly to enjoy half my copyhold in Wilmcote during **the** time of her **widowhood : and if** she will not suffer my daughter Alice quietly **to occupy half with her, then I will that my wife shall have but** 3*l*. 6*s*. 8*d*. **and her jointure in Snitterfield.**

Item. I will that the residue of all my goods, **movable and unmovable, my funeral and** my **debts** discharged, **I give and bequeath to my other children,** to be equally divided amongst **them by** the discretion of Adam Palmer, Hugh Porter, of Snitterfield, and John Skerlett, whom I do ordain and make my overseers of this my last will and testament, and they to have for their painstaking in this behalf 20*s*. apiece. Also, I ordain and constitute **and make** my full executrixes, **Alice** and Mary, my daughters, of **this my last will and testament;** and they to have no more for **their** pains-taking **now as afore given them.** Also, I give and bequeath to every **house that hath no team in** the parish of Aston, to every house 4*d*.

**These being witnesses :—**

> Sir William Bouton, **curate.**
> Adam Palmer.
> John Skerlett.
> Thomas Jhenkes.
> William Pitt.
> With other mo.

Probat. fuit, &c. Wigorn, &c. 16⁹ die monsis Decembris, anno **Domini,** 1556.

*The Inventory of all the Goods movable and unmovable of Robert Arden, of Wilmcote, late deceased, made the 9th day of December, in the third and the fourth year of the reign of our Sovereign Lord and Lady Philip and Mary, King and Queen, &c. 1556.*

Imprimis. **In the hall, 2** table-boards, 3 chairs, 2 forms, **1 cup-**board, 2 **cushions, 3** benches, and one little table with **shelves,** priced at 8*s.*

Item. 2 painted **cloths in the hall and** 5 painted cloths in the chamber, 7 pairs of sheets, 2 coffers, one which priced at 19*s.*

Item. 5 board cloths, 2 towels, **and** 1 diaper towel, priced at 6*s.* 8*d.*

Item. 1 **feather-bed, 2 mattresses, 8 canvases,** 1 coverlid, **3 bol-**sters, 1 pillow, 4 painted cloths, 1 which priced at 1*l.* 6*s.* 8*d.*

**Item.** In the kitchen, **4** pans, 4 pots, **3** candlesticks, **1** bason, **1** chafing dish, 2 **catterns,** 2 skellets, 1 frying-pan, a gridiron, and pot hangings, with hooks priced at 2*l.* 11*s.* **8***d.*

Item. 1 broach, a pair of cupboards, 1 axe, a bill, **4** naggers, 2 hatchets, an adze, an mattock, a iron crow, 1 vat, 4 barrels, 4 pails, a churn, a kneading trough, a long sieve, a handsaw, priced at 1*l.* 0*s.* 2*d.*

Item. 8 oxen, 2 bullocks, 7 kine, 4 weaning calves, 24*l.*

Item. 4 horses, 3 colts, priced at 7*l.*

Item. 52 sheep, priced **at 7***l.*

Item. **The wheat in the barns and the barley, priced at 18***l.*

Item. **The hay and the peas, oats and the straw,** priced at 3*l.* 6*s.* 8*d.*

Item 9 swine, priced **at 1***l.* **6***s.* **8***d.*

**Item.** The bees and poultry, priced at 5*s.*

**Item.** Cart and cart gears, and plough and plough gears, **with** harrows, priced at 2*l.*

Item. The wood in the yard, and the batten in the roof, priced **at** 1*l.* 10*s.*

Item. The wheat in the field, priced at 6*l.* 13*s.* 4*d.*

*Summa totalis,* 77*l.* 11*s.* 10*d.*

---

## WILL OF RICHARD HATHAWAY.

In the name of God, Amen. The **1st day** of September, in the year of our Lord God 1581, and in the twenty-third **year** of the reign of our sovereign lady Elizabeth, by the grace of God Queen of England,

France, and Ireland, Defender of the Faith, &c.   I, Richard Hathaway, of Shottree, in the parish of Stratford-upon-Avon, in the
county of Warwick, husbandman, being sick in body, but of perfect
memory, I thank my Lord God, do ordain and make this my last
will and testament in manner and form following. First, I bequeath
my soul unto Almighty God, trusting to be saved by the merits
of Christ's passion, and my body to be buried in the church or churchyard of Stratford aforesaid. Item, I give and bequeath unto Thomas
my son, 6*l*. 13*s*. 4*d*., to be paid unto him at the age of twenty
years. Item, I give and bequeath unto John my son, 6*l*. 13*s*. 4*d*.,
to be paid unto him at the age of twenty years. Item, I give and bequeath unto William my son, 10*l*., to be paid unto him at the age
of twenty years. Item, I give and bequeath unto Agnes my daughter,
6*l*. 13*s*. 4*d*., to be paid unto her at the day of her marriage.   Item,
I give and bequeath unto Catherine my daughter, 6*l*. 13*s*. 4*d*., to be
paid unto her at the day of her marriage.   Item, I give and bequeath unto Margaret my daughter, 6*l*. 13*s*. 4*d*., to be paid unto
her at the age of seventeen years.   And if it fortune that any of
my said sons or daughters before named, that is to say, Thomas,
John, William, Agnes, Catherine, or Margaret, to decease before
they receive their legacies, then my will is that the legacies of he
or she so deceased to remain equally among the rest, and so unto
the longest livers of them.   Item, my will is (with consent of Joan
my wife) that my eldest son, Bartholomew, shall have the use,
commodity, and profit of one-half yard land, with all pastures and
meadowings thereto belonging, with appurtenances, to be tilled,
mucked, and sowed at the charges of Joan my wife, he only finding
seed, during the natural life or widowhood of the same Joan my
wife, to be severed from the other part of my land for his commodity and profit.   And my will is that he the same Bartholomew
shall be a guide to my said wife in her husbandry, and also a
comfort unto his brethren and sisters to his power; provided
always that if the said Joan my wife shall at any time or times
after my decease go about to disannul or to take away from my
said son Bartholomew the foresaid half yard land with the appurtenances, so that he does not enjoy the commodity and profit of
the same, according to the true meaning of this my last will and
testament, then my will is that the said Joan my wife shall give,
deliver, and pay unto my said son Bartholomew, within one year
after any such denial or discharge, the sum of 40*l*. of lawful
English money.   Item, my will is that all the ceilings in my
hall house, with two winged beds in my parlour, shall continue

and stand unremoved during the natural life or widowhood of Joan my wife, and the natural life of Bartholomew my son, and John my son, and the longest liver of them. Item, I give and bequeath unto every of my godchildren, 4*d*. apiece of them. Item, I give and bequeath unto Agnes Hathaway and Elizabeth Hathaway, daughters unto Thomas Hathaway, a sheep apiece of them. **This bequest** done, debts paid, and legacies levied, and my body **honestly** buried, then I give and bequeath all the rest of my **goods movable and** unmovable unto Joan my wife, whom I make my **sole** executrix, to **see** this my last will and testament truly performed. And I desire my trusty friend and neighbours, Stephen Burman and Fowlke Sandelles, to be my supervisors of this my last will and testament, **and** they to have for their pains therein to be taken 1*s*. apiece of them. Witnesses,—Sir William Gilman, clerk and curate in Stratford ; Richard Burman, John Richardson, and John Heming, with others. Signum Richardi Hathaway, testatoris. Debts to be paid :—Imprimis, I do owe unto my neighbour, John Pace, 2*l*. Item, I owe unto John Barber, 1*l*. 16*s*. 4*d*. Item, I owe unto Thomas Whittington, my shepherd, 4*l*. 6*s*. 8*d*. Item, I owe unto Edward Hollyock, for wood, 1*l*.

[Probatum, &c., nono die mensis Julii, 1582.]

---

## SHAKESPEARE'S ABSENCE.

**The** following **are the** Sonnets referred to in page 197 :—

### XCVII.

How like a winter hath my absence been
From thee, the pleasure of the fleeting year !
What freezings have I felt, what dark days seen !
What old December's bareness everywhere !
And yet this time remov'd was summer's time ;
The teeming autumn, big with rich increase,
Bearing the wanton burden of the prime,
Like widow'd wombs after their lords' decease :
Yet this abundant issue seem'd to me
But hope of orphans and unfather'd fruit ;
For summer and his pleasures **wait on** thee,
**And,** thou away, the very birds are **mute ;**
   Or, if they sing, 't is with so dull **a** cheer,
   That leaves look pale, dreading the winter's near.

### XCVIII.

From you have I been absent in the spring,
When proud-pied April, dress'd in all his trim,
Had put a spirit of youth in everything,
That heavy Saturn laugh'd and leap'd with him.
Yet nor the lays of birds, nor the sweet smell
Of different flowers in odour and in hue,
Could make me any summer's story tell,
Or from their proud lap pluck them where they grew:
Nor did I wonder at the lily's white,
Nor praise the deep vermilion in the rose;
They were but sweet, but figures of delight,
Drawn after you,—you pattern of all those.
    Yet seem'd it winter still, and, you away,
    As with your shadow I with these did play:

### XCIX.

The forward violet thus did I chide:—
Sweet thief, whence didst thou steal thy sweet that smells,
If not from my love's breath? The purple pride
Which on thy soft cheek for complexion dwells,
In my love's veins thou hast too grossly dy'd.
The lily I condemned for thy hand,
And buds of marjoram had stol'n thy hair:
The roses fearfully on thorns did stand,
One blushing shame, another white despair;
A third, nor red nor white, had stol'n of both,
And to his robbery had annex'd thy breath;
But, for his theft, in pride of all his growth
A vengeful canker eat him up to death.
    More flowers I noted, yet I none could see,
    But sweet or colour it had stol'n from thee.

----

## THE PROCEEDINGS AGAINST LAMBERT.

*To the Right Honourable Sir Thomas Egerton, Knight, Lord Keeper of the Great Seal of England.*

In most humble wise complaining, showeth unto your good lordship your daily orators, John Shakespeare, of Stratford-upon-Avon, in the county of Warwick, and Mary his wife, that whereas your said orators were lawfully seized in their demesne as of fee, as in the right of the said Mary, of and in one messuage and one yard land with the appurtenances, lying and being in Wilmcote, in the said county; and they being thereof so seized, for and in consideration of the sum of 40*l.* to them, by one Edmund Lambert, of Barton-on-the-Heath, in the said county, paid; your said orators were content that **he the said Edmund** Lambert should have and **enjoy the same promises, until such time as your said** orators **did repay unto him the said sum of** 40*l.*; **by** reason **whereof the said** Edmund **did enter into the** premises and **did occupy the same** for the space **of three** or four years; and the **issues and** profits thereof did **receive** and **take,** after which your **said** orators did tender **unto the** said Edmund the said sum of 40*l.*, **and desired that** they might have again the said premises according to their agreement; which money he the said Edmund **then** refused to receive, saying that he would not receive the **same, nor** suffer **your said orators to** have the **said premises** again, unless they would pay **unto him certain other money which** they did owe unto him for other matters; all which, notwithstanding, now so it is; and it may please your good lordship, that shortly after the tendering of the said 40*l.* to the said Edmund, and the desire of your said orators to have their land again from him, he the said Edmund, at Barton aforesaid, died, after whose death, one John Lambert, as son and heir of **the said** Edmund, entered into the **said premises and occupied the same;** **after which entry of the said John your said orators came to him** **and tendered the said money unto him, and likewise requested** **him that he would suffer them to have and enjoy the said** premises **according to their** right and **title therein,** and the promise of his **said father to your** said orators made, which he the said John **denied in all things, and did** withstand them for entering into the premises, and yet doth so continue **still; and** by reason that certain deeds and other evidences concerning the premises and that of right belong to your said orators, are come to the hands **and** possession **of** the said John, who wrongfully still keepeth and detaineth the possession of the said premises from your said orators, and will in no wise permit and suffer them to have and enjoy the said premises according to their right in and to the same; and he the said John Lambert hath of late **made sundry** secret estates of the premises to divers **persons to your said** orators unknown, whereby your said **orators** cannot tell against **whom to bring their actions at the common law**, **for** the recovery **of the premises. In tender consideration** whereof, and for so much **as your said orators know** not the certain dates or contents of the said writings, nor whether the same be contained in bag, box, or chest, sealed, locked, or no, and therefore have no remedy to recover the same evidences and writings by the due course of the common laws of this realm; and for that also by reason of the said secret estates so made by the said John Lambert as aforesaid, and want of your said orators having of the evidences and writings as aforesaid, your said orators cannot tell what actions or against whom, or in what manner to bring their action for the recovery of the premises at the common law; and for that also, the said John Lambert is of great wealth and ability, and well friended and allied amongst gentlemen and freeholders of the country, in the said county of Warwick, where he dwelleth, and your said orators are of small wealth and very few friends and alliance in the said county, may it therefore please your good lordship to grant unto your said orators the Queen's Majesty's most gracious writ of subpœna, to be directed to the said John Lambert, commanding him thereby, at a certain day and under a certain pain therein to be limited, personally to appear before your good lordship in her Majesty's highness Court of Chancery, then and there to answer the premises; and further, to stand to and abide such order and direction therein, as to your good lordship shall seem best to stand with right, equity, and good conscience, and your said orators shall daily pray to God for the prosperous health of your good lordship with increase of honour long to continue.

J. STOVELL.

---

## THE ANSWER OF JOHN LAMBERT, DEFENDANT, TO THE BILL OF COMPLAINT OF JOHN SHAKESPEARE AND MARY HIS WIFE, COMPLAINANTS.

THE said defendant (saving to himself both now and at all times hereafter all advantage of exception to the uncertainty and insufficiency of the said complainants' bill, and also saving to this defendant such advantage as by the order of this honourable court he shall be adjudged to have, for that the like bill, in effect containing the self-same matter, hath been heretofore exhibited into this honourable court against this defendant, whereunto this defendant hath made a full and direct answer wherein the said complainant hath not proceeded to hearing), for a second full and direct answer unto the said complainants' bill saith, that true it is (as this defendant verily thinketh) that the said complainants were, or one of them was, lawfully seized in their or one of their demesne, as of fee, of and in one messuage and one yard and four acres of land, with the appurtenances, lying and being in Wilmcote, in the parish of Aston-Cantlow, in the county of Warwick, and that they, or **one of them, so** being thereof seized, the said complainant **John** Shakespeare, by indenture bearing date upon or about the **14th** day of November, in the twentieth year of the reign of our **Sovereign Lady the** Queen's Majesty that now is, for and in con- **sideration of the sum** of 40*l.* of lawful English money unto the **said** complainant paid by Edmund Lambert, this defendant's father **in the said** bill named, did give, grant, bargain and sell the said messuage, and one yard and four acres of land with the appur- tenances, unto the said Edmund Lambert, and his heirs and assigns, to have and to hold the said messuage, one yard and four acres of land with the appurtenances, unto the said Edmund Lambert, his heirs and assigns for ever. In which indenture there is a condi- tional proviso contained, that if the said complainant did pay unto the said Edmund Lambert the sum of 40*l.* upon the feast-day of St. Michael the Archangel, which should be in the year of our Lord God 1580, at the dwelling-house of the said Edmund Lam- bert, in Barton-on-the-Heath, **in the said county of Warwick, that** then the said grant, bargain, and sale, **and all the covenants, grants, and agreements therein contained, should cease and be void, as by the said indenture, whereunto this defendant for his better certainty doth refer himself,** may appear ; **and afterwards the said com- plainant, John** Shakespeare, by his **deed-pole and livery** thereupon made, did **infeoffee the** said Edmund **Lambert of the** said pre- mises, to have and to hold unto him the said Edmund Lambert and his heirs for ever ; after all which, in the term of Easter, in the one-and-twentieth year of the Queen's Majesty's reign that **now** is, the said complainants in due **form** of law did levy a fine of the said messuage and yard land, and other the premises, before the Queen's Majesty's justices of the Common Pleas at West- minster, unto the said Edmund Lambert and his heirs, *sur conizance de droit*, as that which the said Edmund had of the gift of the said John Shakespeare, as by the said pole-deed and the chirography of the said fine, whereunto **this defendant for** his better certainty referreth **himself, it doth and may** appear : and this **defendant further saith, that the said** complainant did not tender or pay the said sum of 40*l.* unto the said Edmund Lambert, this defendant's father, upon the said feast-day, which was in the year of our Lord God 1580, according to the said proviso in the said indenture expressed. By reason whereof this defendant's said father was lawfully and absolutely seized of the said premises in his demesne as of fee, and about eleven years last past thereof, died seized : by and after whose decease the said messuage and premises with the appurtenances descended and came, as of right the same ought to descend and come, unto this defendant, as son and next heir of the said Edmund ; by virtue whereof this defendant was and yet is of the said messuage, yard land, and premises lawfully seized in his demesne as of fee, which this defendant hopeth he ought both by law and equity to enjoy, according to his lawful right and title therein : and this defendant further saith, that the said messuage, yard land, and other the said premises or the most part thereof, have ever since the purchase thereof by this defendant's father been in lease by the demise of the said complainant ; and the lease thereof being now somewhat near expired, whereby a greater value is to be yearly raised thereby, they the said complainants do now trouble and molest this defendant by unjust suits in law, thinking thereby (as it should seem) to wring from him this defendant some further recompense for the said premises than they have already received : without that, that it was agreed that the said Edmund Lambert should have and enjoy the said premises in any other manner and form (to the knowledge of this defendant), then this defendant hath in his said answer heretofore expressed, and without that, that any deeds or evidences concerning the premises that of right belong to the said complainants are come to the hands and possession of this defendant, as in the said bill is untruly supposed, and without that, that any other matter, cause, or thing, in the said complainants' bill contained, material or effectual in the law, to be answered unto, touching or concerning him this defendant, and hereinbefore not answered, unto, confessed and avoided, traversed or denied, is true, to this defendant's knowledge or remembrance, in such manner and form as in the said bill the same is set down and declared. All which matters this defendant is ready to aver and prove, as this honourable court shall award, and prayeth to be dismissed therehence with his reasonable costs and charges in this wrongful suit by him unjustly sustained.

OVERBURY.

## THE REPLICATION OF JOHN SHAKESPEARE AND MARY HIS WIFE, PLAINTIFFS, TO THE ANSWER OF JOHN LAMBERT, DEFENDANT.

THE said complainants, for replication to the answer of the said defendant, say that their bill of complaint is certain and sufficient in the law to be answered; which said bill, and matters therein contained these complainants will avow, verify, and justify to be true and sufficient in the law to be answered unto, in such sort, manner, and form as the same be set forth and declared in the said bill; and further they say that the answer of the said defendant is untrue and insufficient in law to be replied unto, for many apparent causes in the same appearing, the advantage whereof these complainants pray may be to them now and at all times saved, then and not else; for further replication to the said answer, they say that according to the condition or proviso mentioned in the said indenture of bargain and sale of the premises mentioned in the said bill of complaint, he this complainant, John Shakespeare, did come to the dwelling-house of the said Edmund Lambert, in Barton-upon-the-Heath, upon the feast-day of St. Michael the Archangel, which was in the year of our Lord God 1580, and then and there tendered to pay unto him the said Edmund Lambert the said 40*l.*, which he was to pay for the redemption of the said premises; which sum the said Edmund did refuse to receive, saying that he owed him other money, and unless that he the said John would pay him altogether, as well the said 40*l.* as the other money which he owed him over and above, he would not receive the said 40*l.*, and immediately after he the said Edmund died, and by reason thereof he the said defendant entered into the said premises, and wrongfully keepeth and detaineth the said premises from him the said complainant: without that any other matter or thing material or effectual for these complainants to reply unto, and not herein sufficiently confessed and avoided, denied and traversed, is true: all which matters and things these complainants are ready to aver and prove, as this honourable court will award, and pray as before in their said bill they have prayed.

*In dorso*, Ter. Michael. Annis. 40 et 41.          J. STOVELL.

## PURCHASE OF NEW PLACE.

TRANSLATION of the foot of the fine levied on the occasion of Shakespeare's purchase of this house. The original is now in the Public Record Office :—

This is the final agreement made in the Court of our Sovereign Lady the Queen, at Westminster, in one month from the day of St. Michael, in the forty-fourth year of the reign of Elizabeth, by the grace of God of England, France, and Ireland Queen, Defender of the Faith, &c., after the conquest; before Edmund Anderson, Thomas Walmysley, George Kingesmyll, and Peter Warburton, justices of our Lady the Queen, and others there then present; between William Shakespeare, gentleman, complainant, and Hercules Underhill, gentleman, deforciant; of one messuage, two barns, two gardens, and two orchards, with appurtenances, in Stratford-upon-Avon; whereupon a plea of covenant was summoned between them in the same court; that is to say, that the aforesaid Hercules hath acknowledged the aforesaid tenements with appurtenances to be the right of the same William, as those which he the same William hath of the gift of the aforesaid Hercules, and those he hath remised and quitclaimed from him and his heirs to the aforesaid William and his heirs for ever; and moreover, the same Hercules hath granted for him and his heirs, that they will warrant to the aforesaid William and his heirs, the aforesaid tenements with appurtenances, against him the aforesaid Hercules and his heirs, for ever; and for this acknowledgment, remise, quitclaim, warranty, fine, and agreement, the same William hath given to the aforesaid Hercules 60*l*. sterling.

---

## PURCHASE OF LAND FROM WILLIAM COMBE AND JOHN COMBE.

THE following is a translation of the foot of the fine levied on this property thirteen years after its purchase. The original is preserved in the Public Record Office :—

This is the final agreement made in the Court of our Sovereign Lord the King, at Westminster, on the morrow of the Holy Trinity, in the year of the reigns of James, by the grace of God, of England, Scotland, France, and Ireland, King, Defender of the

Faith, &c., of England, France, and Ireland the **eighth, and of** Scotland the forty-third ; before Edward Coke, Thomas Walmysley, Peter Warburton, and Thomas Foster, justices of our Lord the King, and others there then present; between William Shakespeare, gentleman, complainant, and William Combe, Esq., and John Combe, **gentleman,** deforciants, of one hundred and seven acres **of** land and twenty acres of pasture, with appurtenances in **Old Statford and** Stratford-upon-Avon , whereupon a plea of **covenant was summoned between them** in the same court, that is **to say, that the** aforesaid William Combe and John have acknowledged the aforesaid tenements with appurtenances to be the **right of** him the same William Shakespeare, as those which **the same** William hath of the gift of the aforesaid William Combe and John, and those they have remised and quitclaimed from them, the same William Combe and John and their heirs, to the aforesaid William Shakespeare and his heirs for ever ; and, moreover, the same William Combe hath granted for him and his heirs, that they will warrant to the aforesaid William Shakespeare and his heirs the aforesaid tenements, with appurtenances, against him the aforesaid William Combe and his heirs for ever ; and further, the same John hath granted for him and his heirs that they will warrant to the aforesaid William Shakespeare and his heirs, the aforesaid tenements, with appurtenances, against the aforesaid John and his heirs for **ever;** and for **this** acknowledgment, **remise,** quitclaim, warranties, fine, and agreement, **the same** William Shakespeare hath **given** to **the aforesaid William Combe and John 100***l.* sterling.

---

## SHAKESPEARE'S WILL.

[The italics denote interlineations.]

W. SHAKESPEARE,—

In the name of God, Amen. I, William Shakespeare, of Stratford-upon-Avon, in the county of Warwick, gentleman, in perfect health and memory, God be praised, do make and ordain this my last will and testament in manner and form following, that is to say :—First, I commend my soul into the hands of God my Creator, hoping, and assuredly **believing, through the** only merits of Jesus Christ my Saviour, **to be made partaker of** life everlasting, and my body to the earth whereof it **is made.** Item, I give and bequeath unto my daughter Judith, **150l. of lawful English money, to be** paid unto her in manner and form **following, that is to say :—100l.** *in discharge of her marriage portion* within **one** year **after my decease,** with consideration after the rate of 2s. in the pound **for so long** time as the same shall be unpaid unto her after my decease, **and** the 50l. residue thereof, upon her surrendering *of* or giving of such sufficient security as the overseers of this my will shall like of, to surrender or grant all her estate and right that shall descend **or** come unto her after my decease, or *that she* now hath, of, in, or **to** one copyhold tenement with the appurtenances, lying and being in Stratford-upon-Avon aforesaid, in the said county of Warwick, being parcel **or** holden of the manor of Rowington, unto my daughter **Susanna Hall, and her heirs for ever.** Item, I give and bequeath unto my said daughter Judith, 150l. more, if she, or any issue of her body, be living at the end of three years next ensuing the day of the date of this my will, during **which time my execu-** tors to pay her **consideration from my** decease according to the **rate** aforesaid ; and **if she die within the said term without** issue of her body, then my will is, and I do **give and bequeath 100l.** thereof to my niece [granddaughter] **Elizabeth Hall, and the** 50l. to **be set forth by my** executors during **the life of my sister Joan** Harte, and the use and profit there of coming shall **be paid to my** said sister Joan, and after her decease the said 50l. shall remain amongst the children of my said sister equally to be divided amongst them ; but if my said daughter Judith be living at the end of the said three years, or any issue of her body, then my will is, and so I devise and bequeath the said 150l. to be set out *by my executors* **and** *overseers* for the best benefit of her and her issue, and *the stock* not *to be* **paid unto her so** long as she shall be married and covert **barren ; but my will is, that she shall have the consideration** yearly paid unto her during her life, and after her decease the said stock and **consideration to** be **paid to her children, if she have any ;** and if not, **to her executors or assigns, she living the said term after my decease : Provided that if such husband as she shall at the end of** the said **three years be married unto, or at any [time] after, do** sufficiently **assure unto her, and the issue of her body, lands** answerable to the portion by this my will **given unto her, and to be** adjudged so by my executors and overseers, then my will is, that the said 150l. shall be paid to such husband as shall make such assurance, to his own use. Item, I give and bequeath unto my said sister Joan 20l., and all my wearing apparel, to be paid and **delivered** within one year after my decease ; and I do will and devise unto her *the house* with the appurtenances in Stratford, wherein she dwelleth, for her natural life, under the yearly rent of 1*s*.

Item, I give and bequeath unto her three sons, William Hart, [Thomas] Hart, and Michael Hart, 5*l*. apiece, to be paid within one year after my decease. Item, I give and bequeath unto *the* **said** *Elizabeth Hall* all my plate, *except my broad silver and gilt bowl*, **that I now have at the** date of this my will. Item, I give and **bequeath** unto the poor of Stratford aforesaid 10*l*. ; to Mr. Thomas Combe, my sword ; to Thomas Russell, Esq., 5*l*. ; and to Francis Collins, of the borough of Warwick, in the county of Warwick, gentleman, 13*l*. 6*s*. **8*d*., to be** paid within one year after my decease. Item, I give and bequeath to *Hamlet Sadler* 1*l*. 6*s*. 8*d*., to buy him a ring ; to *William Raynoldes, gentleman*, 1*l*. 6*s*. 8*d*., *to buy him a ring* ; to my godson William Walker, 1*l*. in gold ; to Anthony Nash, gentleman, 1*l*. 6*s*. 8*d*. ; and to Mr. John Nash, 1*l*. 6*s* 8*d*. ; *and to my fellows, John Hemings, Richard Burbage, and Henry Cundell*, 1*l*. 6*s*. 8*d*. *apiece, to buy them rings.* Item, I give, will, bequeath, and devise, unto my daughter Susanah Hall, *for better enabling of her to perform this my will, and towards the performance thereof*, all that capital, messuage, or tenement, with the appurtenances, *in Stratford aforesaid*, called the New Place, wherein I now dwell, and two messuages or tenements, with the appurtenances, situate, lying, and **being in** Henley Street, within the **borough of Stratford** aforesaid ; **and all my barns, stables, orchards,** gardens, lands, **tenements, and** hereditaments whatsoever, situate, lying, and being, or to be had, received, perceived, or taken, within **the towns, hamlets,** villages, fields, and grounds of Stratford-upon-**Avon, Old Stratford,** Bushopton, and Welcombe, or in any of them, in the said county of Warwick. And also all that messuage or tenement, with the appurtenances, wherein one John Robinson dwells, situate, lying, and being in the Blackfriars, in London, near the Wardrobe ; and all other my lands, tenements, and hereditaments whatsoever : to have and to hold all and singular the said premises, with their appurtenances, unto the said Susanna Hall, for and during the term of her natural life ; and after her decease to the first son of her body lawfully issuing, and to the heirs males of the body of the said first son lawfully issuing ; and for default of such issue, to the second son of **her body** lawfully **issuing, and to the heirs** males **of the body of the** said second son **lawfully issuing ; and for default of such** heirs, to the third son **of the body of the said Susanna** lawfully issuing, and to the heirs males of the body of the **said third son lawfully issuing ; and for** default of such issue, the same **so to be and remain to the fourth, fifth, sixth, and seventh sons of her body, lawfully issuing one after another, and** to the heirs males of the bodies of the said fourth, fifth, sixth. **and** seventh sons lawfully issuing, in such **manner as it** is before limited to be and remain to the first, second, and third sons of her body, and to their heirs males ; and for default of such issue, the said premises to be and remain to my said niece Hall, and the heirs males of her body lawfully issuing : And for default of such **issue, to** my daughter Judith and the heirs males of her body lawfully **issuing: and for default** of such **issue, to the right heirs of me the said William** Shakespeare for ever. *Item, I give unto my wife my* **second best** *bed,* **with** *the furniture.* Item, **I** give and bequeath to my said daughter Judith my broad silver-gilt bowl. All the rest of my goods, chattel, leases, plate, jewels, and household stuff whatsoever, after my debts and legacies paid, and my funeral expenses discharged, I give, devise, and bequeath to my son-in-law, John Hall, gentleman, **and my daughter Susanna** his wife, whom **I ordain and make executors of this my last will and testament.** And I do entreat and appoint *the said* Thomas Russell Esq., **and Francis Collins, gentleman, to be overseers** hereof; and **do revoke all** former **wills, and publish this to be** my last will and testament. In witness whereof I have hereunto put my *hand,* the day and year first above written.

*Witness to the publishing hereof,* Foa. Collins, Julius Shaw, John Robinson, Hamnet Sadler, Robert Whattcott.

By me, WILLIAM SHAKESPEARE.


*Probatum coram Magistro Willielmo Byrde,* **Legum Doctore** *Comiss.* *&c.,* **xxii** *die mensis Junii, anno Domini* 1616 ; **juramento** *Johannis Hall, unis executorum, &c., cui, &c.,* **de** *bene, &c., jurat. reservat., potestate, &c., Susannæ Hall, alteri executorum, &c., cum* **venerit petitur,** (**Invt. ext.**)

## THE FOLIO OF 1623, PUBLISHED BY SHAKESPEARE'S TWO FRIENDS, HEMINGE AND CONDELL.

### THE DEDICATION.

To the Most Noble and Incomparable Pair of Brethren. William Earl of Pembroke, &c., Lord Chamberlain to the King's most **excellent Majesty.** And Philip Earl of Montgomery, &c., Gentleman of His Majesty's Bed-chamber. Both Knights of **the most noble Order** of the Garter, and our singular good **Lords.**

RIGHT HONOURABLE,

Whilst we study to be thankful in our particular, for the many favours we have received from your Lordships, we are fane upon the ill-fortune to mingle two the most diverse things that can be, fear and rashness; rashness in the enterprize, and fear of the success. For, when we value the places your Honours sustain, we cannot but know their dignity greater, than to descend to the reading of these trifles; and, while we deem them trifles, we have deprived ourselves of the defence of our Dedication. But since your Lordships have been pleased to think these trifles something heretofore, **and have prosecuted both them, and** their Author living, **with so much favour, we hope that (they** out-living him, and he **not having the fate, common with some, to be executor to his own writings) you will use the like indulgence** towards **them** you have done unto their parent. **There is a great** difference whether any book choose his Patrons, **or find them.** This hath **done** both. For so **much were** your Lordships likings of the several parts, when they were acted, as before they were published, the volume asked to be yours. We have but collected them, and done an office to the dead, to procure his orphans guardians; without ambition either of self-profit, or fame: only to keep the memory of so worthy a friend and fellow alive, as was our SHAKESPEARE, by humble offer of his plays, to your most noble patronage. Wherein, as we have just observed, no man to come near your Lordships but with a kind of religious address, it hath been **the height of our** care, who are the presenters, **to make the present worthy of your Honours by the perfection. But there we must also** crave our **abilities to be considered, my Lords. We** cannot go beyond our own powers. Country hands reach forth milk, cream, fruits, or what they have ; and many nations (we have heard) that had not gums and incense, obtained their requests with **a leavened cake.** It was no fault to approach their Gods by what means **they could:** and the most, though meanest, of things are made more **precious,** when they are dedicated to temples. In that name, therefore, **we** most humbly consecrate to your Honours these remains of your servant Shakespeare ; that what delight is in them, may be ever your Lordships, the reputation his, and the faults ours, if any be committed, by a pair so careful to show their gratitude both to the living. and the dead, as is

Your Lordship's most bounden,

JOHN HEMINGE,<br>HENRY CONDELL.

## THE ADDRESS TO THE READER.

### *To the great variety of readers.*

**FROM the most able, to him that can but spell : there you are** numbered. We had **rather you were weighed.** Especially, when the fate of all books depends upon your capacities : and **not of** your heads alone, but of your purses. Well ! It is now public, and you will stand for your privileges we know : to read and censure. Do so, but buy it first. That doth best commend a book, the stationer says. Then, how odd soever your brains be, **or your wisdoms,** make your licence the same, and spare not. **Judge your** six-penny **worth,** your shilling's worth, and your five **shilling's worth** at a time, or higher, **so you raise the** just rates, **and welcome.** But, whatever **you do, buy.** Censure will not drive a trade, or make the jack **go. And** though you **be a magis-trate of wit, and sit on** the **stage at** *Blackfriars,* or **the** *cockpit* **to arrange plays daily,** know, **these plays have had their trial** already, **and stood out all appeals ; and do now come forth quitted** rather by a decree **of Court, than any purchased letters of com-**mendation.

It had been a thing, we confess, worthy **to** have been **wished,** that the author **himself had** lived to have set forth, and overseen **his own** writings ; but since it hath been ordained otherwise, and **he by death** departed from that right, we pray you do not envy his friends, the office of their care, and pain, to have collected and published them ; and so to have published them, as where (before) you were abused with diverse stolen, and surreptitious copies, maimed, and deformed by the frauds and stealths of injurious impostors, that exposed them: even those, are now offered **to** your **view cured, and** perfect of their limbs ; and all the rest, absolute **in** their numbers, as he conceived the. Who, as he was **a happy imitator of** nature, was a most gentle expressor of it. **His mind and** hand went together: and what he thought, he **uttered with that easiness,** that we have scarce received from **him a blot** in his papers. **But it is not our province, who only** gather his works, and give **them you, to praise him. And there** we hope, to your divers capacities, you **will** find enough, both to draw and hold you : for his wit can **no more** lie hid, then it could be **lost.** Read him, therefore ; and **again,** and again ; and if then you do not like him, surely you are **in** some manifest danger, not to understand him. And so we leave you to other of his friends, whom if you need, can be your guides : if you need them not, you can lead yourselves and others. And such readers we wish him.

JOHN HEMINGE,
HENRY CONDELL.

## THE WORKS OF WILLIAM SHAKESPEARE,

**Containing all his** Comedies, Histories, and Tragedies: Truly set forth, **according to** their first ORIGINAL.

*The Names of the Principal Actors in all these Plays.*

| | |
|---|---|
| William Shakespeare. | Samuel Gilburne. |
| Richard Burbadge. | Robert Armin. |
| John Hemmings. | William Ostler. |
| Augustine Phillips. | Nathan Field. |
| William Kempt. | John Underwood. |
| Thomas Poope. | Nicholas Tooley. |
| George Bryan. | William Ecclestone. |
| Henry Condell. | Joseph Taylor. |
| William Slye. | Robert **Benfield.** |
| Richard Cowley. | Robert **Goughe.** |
| John Lowine. | **Richard** Robinson. |
| **Samuel Crosse.** | John Shancke. |
| **Alexander Cooke.** | John Rice. |

*A Catalogue of the several Comedies, Histories, and Tragedies contained in this Volume.*

## COMEDIES.

The Tempest.
The Two Gentlemen of Verona.
The Merry Wives of Windsor.
Measure for Measure.
The Comedy of Errors.
Much Ado about Nothing.
Love's Labour's Lost.
Midsummer Night's Dream.
The Merchant of Venice.
As You Like It.
The Taming of the Shrew.
All is Well that Ends Well.
Twelfth Night, or What You Will.
The Winter's Tale.

## HISTORIES.

The Life and Death of King John.
The Life and Death of Richard the Second.
The First Part of King Henry the Fourth.
The Second Part of King Henry the Fourth.
The Life of King Henry the Fifth.
The First Part of King Henry the Sixth.
The Second Part of King Henry the Sixth.
The Third Part of King Henry the Sixth.
The Life and Death of Richard the Third.
The Life of King Henry the Eighth.

## TRAGEDIES.

The Tragedy of Coriolanus.
Titus Andronicus.
Romeo and Juliet.
Timon of Athens.
The Life and Death of Julius Cæsar.
The Tragedy of Macbeth.

The Tragedy of Hamlet.
King Lear.
Othello, the Moor of Venice.
Anthony and **Cleopatra.**
**Cymbeline, King of Britain.**

[This **list** omits '**Troilus and** Cressidus,' doubtless by accident, **as it is**
included in the collection.]

---

## COMMENDATORY VERSES

### PREFIXED TO THE FOLIO OF 1623.

*To the* Reader. (*Fronting the Portrait of Shakespeare.*)

THIS Figure that thou here seest put,
It was for gentle Shakespeare cut ;
Wherein the Graver had a strife
With Nature, to outdo the life :
Oh, could he but have drawn his wit
As well in brass as he hath hit
His face; the print would **then surpass**
**All** that was ever writ in brass ;
But, since he cannot, reader, look
Not on his picture, but his book.—B. J.

---

To THE MEMORY *of the deceased Author*, MR. W. SHAKESPEARE.

SHAKESPEARE, at length thy pious fellows give
The world thy Works : thy Works, by which outlive
Thy tomb, thy name must : when that stone is rent,
And time dissolves thy Stratford monument,
Here we alive shall view thee still. This book,
When brass and marble fade, shall make thee look
Fresh to all ages; when posterity
Shall loathe what's new, think all is **prodigy**
**That is** not Shakespeare's ; **every line, each verse,**
**Here** shall revive, redeem **thee** from **thy** hearse.
**Nor fire,** nor cankering age, **as** Naso said,

Of his, thy wit-fraught book shall once invade.
Nor shall I e'er believe, or think thee dead
(Though miss'd) until our bankrupt stage be sped
(Impossible) with some new strain t'outdo
Passions of Juliet and her Romeo;
Or till I hear a scene more nobly take,
Than when thy half-sword parlying Romans spake,
Till these, till any of thy volumes rest,
Shall with more fire, more feeling be express'd,
Be sure, our Shakespeare, thou canst never die,
But crowned with laurel, live eternally.

L. DIGGES.

---

### *To the Memory of* MR. W. SHAKESPEARE.

WE wondered (Shakespeare) that thou wentst so soon
From the world's stage to the grave's tiring room.
We thought thee dead, but this thy printed worth,
Tells thy spectators, that thou wentst but forth
To enter with applause. An actor's art
Can die, and live to act a second part.
That's but an exit of mortality;
This, a re-entrance to a plaudit.—I. M.

---

### *To the Memory of my beloved, the* AUTHOR, MR. WILLIAM SHAKE- SPEARE, *and what he hath left us.*

To draw no envy (Shakespeare) on thy name,
Am I thus ample to thy book and Fame;
While I confess thy writings to be such,
As neither man nor Muse can praise too much.
'Tis true, and all men's suffrage. But these ways
Were not the paths I meant unto thy praise;
For seeliest ignorance on these may light,
Which, when it sounds at best, but echo's right;
Or blind affection, which doth ne'er advance
The truth, but gropes, and urgeth all by chance;

Or crafty malice might pretend this praise,
And think to ruin where it seem'd to raise.
These are, as some infamous bawd or whore,
Should praise a matron:—what could hurt her more?
But thou art proof against them, and, indeed,
Above th' ill fortune of them, or the need.
I, therefore, will begin.  Soul of the age!
The applause! delight! the wonder of our stage!
My Shakespeare, rise!  I will not lodge thee by[1]
Chaucer or Spenser, or bid Beaumont lie
A little further, to make thee a room:
Thou art a monument, without a tomb,
And art alive still, while thy book doth live,
And we have wits to read, and praise to give.
That I not mix thee so, my brain excuses,—
I mean with great, but disproportion'd Muses;
For if I thought my judgment were of years,
I should commit thee surely with thy peers,
And tell, how far thou did'st our Lily outshine,
Or sporting Kid, or Marlowe's mighty line.
And though thou hadst small Latin and less Greek,
From thence to honour thee, I would not seek
For names; but call forth thund'ring Æschilus,
Euripides, and Sophocles to us,
Paccuvius, Accius, him of Cordova dead,
To life again, to hear thy buskin tread,

[1] An allusion to the following lines by Bassen:—

> " Renownèd Spenser, lie a thought more nigh
> To learned Chaucer; and, rare Beaumont, lie
> A little nearer Spenser; to make room
> For Shakespeare in your threefold, fourfold tomb:
> To lodge all four in one bed make a shift
> Until doomsday; for hardly will a fifth,
> Betwixt this day and that, by fate be slain,
> For whom your curtains may be drawn again.
> But if precedency in death doth bar
> A fourth place in your sacred sepulchre,
> Under this carved marble of thine own,
> Sleep, rare tragedian, Shakespeare, sleep alone:
> Thy unmolested peace, unsharèd cave,
> Possess as lord, not tenant, of thy grave;
> That unto us and others it may be
> Honour hereafter to be laid by thee."

And shake a stage : Or, when thy socks were on,
Leave thee alone for the comparison
Of all that insolent Greece or haughty Rome
Sent forth, or since did from their ashes come.
Triumph, my Britain! thou hast one to show,
To whom all scenes of Europe homage owe.
He was not of an age, but for all time!
And all the Muses still were in their prime,
When, like Apollo, he came forth to warm
Our ears, or like a Mercury to charm!
Nature herself was proud of his designs,
And joy'd to wear the dressing of his lines!
Which were so richly spun, and woven so fit,
As, since, she will vouchsafe no other wit.
The merry Greek, tart Aristophanes,
Neat Terence, witty Plautus, now not please ;
But antiquated and deserted lie,
As they were not of nature's family.
Yet must I not give nature all ; thy art,
My gentle Shakespeare, must enjoy a part :
For though the poet's matter nature be,
His art doth give the fashion.  And, that he,
Who casts to write a living line, must sweat
(Such as thine are) and strike the second heat
Upon the Muses' anvil : turn the same,
(And himself with it) that he thinks to frame ;
Or, for the laurel, he may gain a scorn.—
For a good poet's made, as well as born.
And such wert thou.  Look how the father's face
Lives in his issue, even so the race
Of Shakespeare's mind and manners brightly shines
In his well-turned and true-filed lines :
In each of which he seems to shake a lance,
As brandish'd at the eyes of ignorance.
Sweet Swan of Avon! what a sight it were
To see thee in our waters yet appear,
And make those flights upon the banks of Thames,
That so did take Eliza and our James!
But stay, I see thee in the hemisphere
Advanc'd, and made a constellation there!

Shine forth, thou star of poets, and with rage
Or influence, chide or cheer the drooping stage;
Which, since thy flight from hence, hath mourn'd like night,
And despairs day, but for thy volumes' light.

BEN JONSON.

---

*Upon the Lines and Life of the Famous Scenic Poet, Master*
WILLIAM SHAKESPEARE.

THOSE hands which you so clapt, go now and wring,
**You Britons brave**; for done are Shakespeare's days:
**His days** are done, that made the dainty plays
**Which** make the globe **of** heav'n and earth to ring.
**Dry'd is that** vein, dry'd is the Thespian spring,
**Turn'd all to** tears, and Phœbus clouds his rays:
**That** corpse, that coffin, now bestick those bays,
Which crown'd him poet first, then poet's king.
If tragedies might any prologue have,
All those he made, would scarce make one to this:
Where fame, now that he is gone to the grave,
(Earth's public tiring house) the Nuncius is.
  **For,** though his line of life went soon about,
  **The life yet of his lines shall never out.**

HUGH HOLLAND.

---

## ADDITIONAL COMMENDATORY POEMS,

### PREFIXED TO THE FOLIO EDITION OF 1623.

*Upon the Effigies of my worthy Friend, the* **Author,** *Master William*
*Shakespeare, and his Works.*

SPECTATOR, this life's shadow is; to see
The truer image and a livelier he,
Turn, reader. But, observe his comic vein,
Laugh, and proceed next to a tragic strain,
Then weep, so when thou find'st **two contraries,**
Two different passions from thy **rapt soul rise;**
**Say (who alone effect such wonders could),**
**Rare Shakespeare to the life thou** dost behold.

*An Epitaph on the admirable Dramatic Poet, William Shakespeare.*

BY JOHN MILTON.

WHAT need my Shakespeare for his honour'd bones,
The labour of an age in piled stones;
Or that his hallow'd relics should be hid
Under a star-pointing pyramid?
Dear son of Memory, great heir of Fame,
What need'st thou such dull witness of thy name?
Thou in our wonder and astonishment
**Hast built** thyself a lasting monument:
**For whilst,** to the shame of slow-endeavouring art,
**Thy** easy numbers flow; and that each heart
**Hath** from the leaves of thy unvalued book
**Those** Delphic lines with deep impression took;
**Then** thou, our fancy of herself bereaving,
**Dost** make us marvel, **with too** much conceiving;
And, so sepulchred, in such pomp dost lie,
That kings for such a tomb would wish to die.

---

*On worthy Master Shakespeare and his Poems.*

[Anonymous, but attributed, with equal probability, to Milton,
Jasper Mayne, and Richard James.]

A MIND reflecting ages past, whose clear
And equal surface can make things appear
**Distant a thousand years,** and represent
Them in their lively colours, just extent.
**To outrun** hasty Time, retrieve the fates,
**Roll back** the heavens, blow ope the iron gates
**Of Death** and Lethe, where (confused) lie
**Great heaps of ruinous mortality.**
**In that deep, dusky dungeon to discern**
A royal ghost from **Churles; by art to learn**
The physiognomy of **shades, and give**
Them sudden birth, wondering how oft they live.
What story coldly tells, what poets fain
**At** second hand, and pictures without brain,
**Senseless** and soulless shows. To give a stage

(Ample and true with life) voice, action, age,
As Plato's year and new scene of the world
Them unto us, or us to them had hurl'd:
To raise our ancient sovereigns from their hearse
Make **kings his subjects ; by** exchanging verse
Enlive **their pale trunks, that** the present age
**Joys in their** joy, **and trembles at their rage:**
Yet so to temper **passion, that our ears**
**Take pleasure in their pain : and** eyes in tears
**Both weep and smile : fearful** at plots **so sad,**
**Then, laughing at our** fear ; abus'd and glad
**To** be abus'd ; affected with that truth
**Which** we perceive is false ; pleas'd in that ruth
**At** which we start ; and by elaborate play
Tortur'd and tickled ; by a crab-like way
Time past made pastime, and in ugly sort
Disgorging up his ravine for our sport——
—— While the plebeian imp, from lofty throne,
Creates and rules a world, and works upon
Mankind by secret engines ; now to move
A chilling pity, then a rigorous love :
To strike up and stroke down, both joy **and ire ;**
To **steer** th' **affections; and by** heavenly **fire**
**Mould us anew.   Stol'n from ourselves——**
    **This, and much more which cannot be express'd**
**But by himself,** his tongue, and his own breast,
**Was** Shakespeare's freehold ; which his cunning brain
**Improv'd by favour of the ninefold train,**
**The** buskin'd **Muse, the comic Queen, the** grand
**And louder tone of Clio ; nimble hand,**
**And nimbler foot of the** melodious pair,
**The silver-voiced Lady ; the most** fair
Calliope, **whose** speaking silence daunts,
And she whose praise the heavenly body chants.
These jointly woo'd him, envying one another
(Obey'd by all as spouse, but lov'd as brother),
And wrought a curious robe of sable **grave,**
**Fresh** green, and **pleasant yellow, red most brave,**
**And constant blue, rich** purple, guiltless white,
**The lowly russet, and** the scarlet bright ;

Branch'd and embroider'd like the painted spring,
Each leaf match'd with a flower, and each string
Of golden wire, each line of silk; there run
Italian works whose thread the Sisters spun;
And there did sing, or seem to sing, the choice
Birds of a foreign note and various voice.
Here hangs a mossy rock; there plays a fair
But chiding fountain, purled: not the air,
Nor clouds, nor thunder, but were living drawn,
Not out of common tiffany or lawn,
But fine materials, which the Muses know,
And only know the countries where they grow.
  Now, when they could no longer him enjoy,
In mortal garments pent, "death may destroy,"
They say, "his body, but his verse shall live,
And more than nature takes, our hands shall give.
In a less volume, but more strongly bound,
Shakespeare shall breathe and speak, with laurel crown'd,
Which never fades. Fed with Ambrosian meat,
In a well-lined vesture, rich and neat."
  So with this robe they clothe him, bid him wear it,
For time shall never stain, nor envy tear it.

The friendly admirer of his endowments,

I. M. S.

---

## DOCUMENTS REFERRING TO THE PROPERTY OF SHAKE-SPEARE, DISCOVERED IN THE ROLLS CHAPEL.

Mr. STAUNTON, in the Appendix to his valuable edition of the poet's works, gives the following account of these documents:—

" Shakespeare by his will, dated 25th March, 1616, bequeathed, as we have seen, to his daughter Susanna Hall [wife of John Hall] the capital messuage in Stratford-upon-Avon, called the New Place, wherein he then dwelt, and two messuages in Henley Street within the said borough, and all his other lands and tenements in Stratford-upon-Avon, Old Stratford, Bishopton, and Welcombe, in the county of Warwick; also all that messuage wherein John Robinson

2 A

dwells, in the Blackfriars, in London, near the Wardrobe ; to hold for the term of her life, and after her decease, to the heirs male of her body ; and in default of heirs male of her body, the said premises to remain to his *niece* [grand-daughter], Elizabeth Hall, and the **heirs male of her** body ; for default of such **issue to** his daughter **Judith** [**wife of** Thomas Quiney], and the heirs male **of her body, and for** default of such **issue to** his right heirs.

"**This lady,** Elizabeth Hall, **it** has been shown, at eighteen years of age became the wife of Thomas Nash, and as the three sons **of Judith Quiney all died** without children, the last of them in January, **1639, the poet's** elder daughter, Susanna Hall, her daughter, Elizabeth Nash, and her husband, Thomas Nash, suffered **a fine and recovery in** the fifteenth of Charles I., **A.D.** 1639-40, **by which all the** estates in question **were** confirmed **to** Mrs. Hall **for her life, with remainder to Mr. and** Mrs. Nash and her issue ; and **in default of** such issue, then upon Mr. Nash.

" Mr. Nash died without issue 4th April, 1647, having by his **will** dated 25th August, 1642, bequeathed all the said estate to his wife Elizabeth, for her life, and the reversionary interest thereof to his cousin Edward Nash.

" Mrs. Nash advised that her husband had no right to make such a will, as the fine and recovery settled the estates upon her **and** her issue, and **considering** that she might marry again and **have** children (being then only thirty-nine years old), refused, it seems, to carry out her husband's will. Whereupon the said Edward Nash filed his bill in Chancery against her and others, setting out the will in question, and calling upon the **Court to compel Mrs.** Nash to produce and execute the same, &c.

" These circumstances, **and the** consequent fact that by another fine and recovery Shakespeare's estate was again limited to his descendants, were first made public by the late Mr. Wheeler, of **Stratford.** Neither he, however, nor Malone, who was indefatigable in his inquiries concerning the poet's grand-daughter and the ultimate disposition of the property, was fortunate enough to find the legal papers in the suit in Chancery between Mrs. Nash and Edward Nash. The instruments in question appear to have remained untouched in their original depository, the Rolls Chapel, for above two hundred years until a few month since, when, during some alterations in the chapel, they were brought to light, together with the **original will of** Thomas Nash. By the liberality of **Sir John** Romilly, the Right Honourable the Master of the **Rolls, I am** enabled to print the whole of these documents, as well as some others relating **to the poet's property which have never,** to my knowledge, been published."

----

We annex the several documents, as given by Mr. Staunton.

## CHANCERY PROCEEDINGS.

### N. N. 17. No. 65.

The several Answers of ELIZABETH NASH, Widow, one of the Defendants to the Bill of Complaint of EDWARD NASH, Complainant.

ALL advange of exception to the uncertainties and insufficiencies of the said Bill of Complaint, **now and at all times hereafter saved and reserved** unto the defendant, **for** answer saith : **That the complainant** is cousin to the defendant's late husband, **Thomas** Nash, Esq., **deceased, but** not heir to the said Thomas **Nash ; for that the said Thomas Nash hath a sister living who is one of the defendants to the said Bill of Complaint, besides other kindred, who are nearer in blood to the said Thomas Nash,** deceased, **than** the said complainant as the defendant takes it. And the defendant saith, that the said Thomas Nash, in his lifetime, was seized of divers messuages, lands, tenements, and hereditaments, and possessed of **a** personal estate ; and that he, being so seized and possessed, made his last will and testament in writing, in or about the 25th day of August, 1642, and thereby devised unto this defendant and the other defendant, his sister and the complainant **and other persons, the lands and legacies, in such sort and to such purpose, word for word,** as the complainant hath set forth in **his said Bill of Complaint, which** the complainant might well do, **for that the defendant gave** unto the said complainant a true copy **of the said last will and testament of the said Thomas Nash and of the codicil to the said will annexed, which codicil the said Thomas Nash** made, or caused to be made, **in his sickness, in or** about the **3rd day of April, anno Domini, 1647, and published the** same for as part **of his said last will and testament, and to be added** to the same ; and that shortly after, **that is to say, in** or about the **4th** day of the same month, the said Thomas Nash died, having in **or by** his said last will appointed and made this defendant his sole **executrix,** who proved the said will, with the said codicil thereunto annexed in due form of law in the Prerogative Court of

Canterbury, where the said last will and codicil are entered, and remain upon record amongst the records there, to which the defendant for more certainty referreth herself, for and concerning all and every the matters contained in the said will and codicil, and complained **of, in, or by** the said Bill of Complaint ; and the defendant **saith, that the said** messuage, **called the New Place, in Stratford, with the** appurtenances, and **four yards** of land in the common **fields** of Old Stratford, and the messuage in London, **near the Wardrope, there** supposed to be **devised to the** complainant and **his heirs by the** said Thomas Nash, **could** not be devised, **given, or disposed** of by the said Thomas Nash, for that the said **messuage, four** yards of land, and house in London, were the Inheritance of William Shakespeare, the Defendant's Grandfather, **who was seized thereof in fee** simple long **before the defendant's** marriage with the said Thomas Nash, and being so seized by his last will and testament in writing, bearing date on or **about** the 25th day of March, in the fourteenth year of the reign of our late sovereign Lord King James, devised the same to Susan Hall, the daughter and co-heir of the said William, and mother to the defendant, for and during her life, and after her death to this defendant and the heirs of her body, as in and by the said will ready to be produced, **to** which due reference being had, **may** more fully **appear ;** and **the defendant** saith, that **the said** Susan, the defendant's, **mother, to whom the said messuage, four yards of land, and the house aforesaid, was** devised by the said William Shakespeare, is yet living, and enjoyeth the same ; and that the said Susan and the defendant, since the death of the said Thomas Nash, have acknowledged and levied one or more fines, and suffered a recovery of the said messuage called the New Place, and the said four yards of land, and the house in London, to the use of the said Susan, the defendant's mother, for her life, and after her decease to this defendant and her heirs for ever, as was lawful for them so to do, which are all the conveyances and estates that the defendant, since the death of the said Thomas Nash, hath made, granted, or suffered of any the lands mentioned in the said Bill of Complaint ; and the defendant denies that she hath a mind to suppress the said last will of the said Thomas Nash, or that the same can be suppressed to the knowledge of the defendant, or that the said Thomas Nash made no codicil to his said last will, or that the said Thomas Nash died without making any alteration of the said will set forth by the said complainant, other than is expressed in or by the said codicil of the said Thomas Nash ; and the defendant denies that she the defendant or any other to her knowledge, give out that the said Thomas Nash died intestate, and that he made no will; or that he the said Thomas revoked the said will, and made a new will, to the knowledge of the defendant. But true it is she the defendant hath given forth that the said Thomas Nash made the said codicil as part of his said last will, which the defendants proved as aforesaid; and that he the said Thomas Nash had no power to give and devise the said messuage, called the New Place, the four yards of land, and the house in London, being the defendant's inheritance as aforesaid. But that the defendant, with her said mother, may dispose thereof as they please; and the defendant denies that she doth refuse to prove the will, or to assent to such legacies as are given to the said complainant, saving the right and inheritance in the said messuage, four yards of land, and house in London. *And saith that she this defendant hath in her hands or custody many deeds, evidences, writings, charters, escripts, and muniments, which concern the lands and premises which the defendant claimeth as her inheritance, and other the lands which are the defendant's jointure*, and are devised to her by the said Thomas Nash in or by his said last will, which writings concerning the defendant's jointure she may keep for her life, as she is informed; but the defendant is ready to produce the same by copies or otherwise to make known the same to the complainant, in such manner as the honourable Court shall appoint; and the defendant denies that she doth suppress or conceal the said writings, or hath cancelled the same, or doth refuse to set forth the same; or that this defendant doth know that the said writings do concern the complainant during the defendant's life; or that she this defendant hath made, or consented to the making, any estate of the premises to any person or persons whatsoever, other than as aforesaid, without that any other matter or thing material or effectual in the law to be answered unto by this defendant, and not herein and hereby well and sufficiently answered unto, confessed, traversed, or denied, is true: all which matters and things this defendant is and will be ready to aver, maintain, and prove, as this honourable Court shall award; and humbly prayeth to be hence dismissed with her reasonable costs and charges, &c., &c.

Predict. Def. Jur. 17 die  
Aprilis, anno r. R. Carol.     Thos. Dighton,  
24 apud     John Eston.  
Avon, in Com Warr.coram

Veneris 11 Februarii Termino Hillarii Anno Dni. 1648.

Inter EDRU. NASH. . . . . Quer.

and

ELIZA NASH . . . Deftem.

**Forasmuch as** this Court was this present day informed by **Mr. Catlin, being of** the plaintiff's counsel, that the plaintiff having **exhibited his bill into** this Court to be relieved touching certain **lands devised to the defendant** for her life, the remainder to the **plaintiff and his heirs, the** defendant by her answer hath confessed **the having of the original** will and the plaintiff's estate, which **being an estate of an** inheritance, and the defendant's but an estate **for life, and witnesses** being examined in the cause, it was prayed **that the defendant** might bring the said original will confessed in **her answer** into **this** Court, there to remain indifferently for both parties, which is ordered accordingly, unless the defendant having notice thereof, shall within a week after such notice show unto this Court good cause to the contrary.

F. BODWELL, *Clerk.*

B 1648 folio 343 C.

---

Lune 15 May Termino Pas Anno Regni **Caroli Regis 24** 1648.

Inter EDWARDU NASH . . . Quer.

ELIZABETH NASH (executrix), ⎤  
THOMAS NASH, . . ⎬ Deftes.  
THOMAS WITHERS, . . ⎦ -

Upon motion **this day** made unto this Court by Mr. Catlin, being of the plaintiff's counsel, it is ordered that process of duces tecum be awarded against the defendants, to bring into this Court the will, evidences, and writings confessed by their answer to be in their custody, or at the return thereof to show unto this Court good cause to the contrary.

F. BODWELL, *Clerk.*

B 1647 folio 573 C.

Sabbi 10 Junii Term Trin A Rs Car 24 1648.

Inter Edru. Nash . . . Quer.

Eliza Nash (executrix),
Thos. Nash, and . . } Deftes.
Thomas Withers . .

Whereas, by an order of the 15th of May last, process of duces tecum was awarded against the defendants to bring into this Court the will, evidences, and writings confessed by their answer to be in their custody, or at the return thereof to show unto this Court good cause to the contrary, upon opening of the matter this present day unto this Court by Mr. Dighton, being of the defendant's counsel, in the presence of Mr. Chute, being of the plaintiff's counsel, and upon reading of the said order, it was alleged that the defendant Elizabeth hath an estate for life in the lands in question, and being executrix of the said Thomas Nash, hath proved the will, and justifies the detaining of the said evidences in her hands, for the maintenance of her title, but the plaintiff's counsel, alleging that the inheritance of the lands being in the plaintiff, the said evidences do properly belong to the plaintiff. Whereupon, and upon hearing what was alleged on either side, it is ordered that the will be brought into this Court, to the end the plaintiff may examine witnesses thereupon, and then to be delivered back to the defendant, and that the defendant shall also bring the said evidences and writings into Court, upon oath, the first day of the next term, there to remain for the equal benefit of both parties, and shall, within ten days after notice, deliver unto the plaintiff a true schedule thereof.

F. Bodwell, *Clerk.*

B 1647 folio 742 C.

---

### THE WILL OF THOMAS NASH.

By this will, dated August 25, 1642, which appears to have been kept in the Chapel of the Rolls from the period when Mrs. Nash was ordered to produce it in Court, Thomas Nash makes the following disposition of that portion of his property in which alone we are interested,—the inheritance of the poet's grand-daughter :—

"That is to say :—First, I give, dispose, and bequeath unto

Elizabeth, my well beloved wife, and her assigns, for and during the term of her natural life, in lieu of her jointure and thirds, all that messuage or tenement, with the appurtenances, situate, lying, and being in Stratford-upon-Avon, in the said county of **Warwick,** in a street there called or known by the **name of the Chapel Street,** and now **in the tenure, use, and occupation, of one Johan Nor-man, widow ;** and also one meadow, with the appurtenances, lying and **being within the** parish of Old Stratford, in the said county of **Warwick, and** called or known by **the name of the** Square **Meadow, and lying near** unto the great **stone bridge of** Strat-**ford aforesaid, and now in** the tenure, use, and occupation of one **William** Abbotts, innholder ; and also one other meadow, **with the** appurtenances, lying and being within the parish of Old Stratford **aforesaid, in** the said county of Warwick, and called **or known by the name of the Wash** Meadow, and lying near unto **the** said great stone bridge of Stratford. . . . . . . Item, I give, dispose, and bequeath unto my loving kinsman, Edward Nash, gentleman's son and heir of my uncle, George Nash, of London, gentleman, and to his heirs and assigns for ever after the death and decease of Elizabeth my said wife, all that the said messuage or tenement, with the appurtenances, situate, lying, and being in Stratford-upon-Avon aforesaid, in the said county of Warwick, in the said **street there** called the **Chapel Street, and** now in the tenure, **use, and occupation of the said Johan Norman,** and also the said meadow, with the appurtenances, **lying and being** within the parish of Old **Stratford aforesaid, in the said county of Warwick, called or known by the** name of the Square Meadow, **and lying near unto the said great stone** bridge of Stratford afore-**said, and now in the tenure, use, and occupation** of one William **Abbots, innholder. . . . . . Item, 1 give, dispose, and bequeath** unto my **said** kinsman, Edward Nash, and **to his heirs and assigns for ever, one messuage or tenement, with** the appurtenances, com-**monly called or known** by **the name of** the New Place, situate, lying, **and** being in Stratford-upon-Avon aforesaid, in the said county of Warwick, in a street there called or known by the name of the Chapel Street, together also with all and singular houses, outhouses, barns, stables, orchards, gardens, easements, profits, and commodities to the same belonging, or in anywise appertaining or **reputed,** taken, **esteemed,** or enjoyed **as thereunto** belonging, **and now in the tenure, use, and occupation of me the said** Thomas Nash. And **also four yard land of** arable land, meadow and pasture, with the **appurtenances,** lying and being in the common fields of Old Stratford, in the said county of **Warwick, together** with all easements, profits, commons, commodities, **and hereditaments** to the same four yard lands, or any **of them belonging, or** in anywise appertaining . . . . ; and also one other **messuage** or tenement, with the appurtenances, situate, lying, and **being in** the parish of in London, **and** called or known by the name of the Wardrop, and now in the tenure, use, and occupation of one Dicks . . . . ; and also the said messuage **or tenement, with the appurtenances, situate,** lying, and being in Stratford-upon-Avon aforesaid, in the said county of Warwick, in the said street, there called the Henley Street, and now in **the** tenure, use, and occupation of the said John Hornby, blacksmith ; **and also one** other messuage or tenement, with the appurtenances situate, lying, and being in Stratford-upon-Avon **aforesaid, in the** said county of Warwick, in a certain street, there called **the Chapel** Street, and now in the **tenure, use, and occupation of the said** Nicholas Ingram. . . . . . . **All the rest and other of** my goods, chattels, **cattles, leases, jewels, plate, household** stuff, and implements of **household, movable and unmovable, my** debts **and legacies being paid, and my funeral expenses being discharged,** **I** give and **bequeath unto Elizabeth my wife, whom I make full** and whole executrix **of this my** last **will and testament ; and I** revoke and renounce all former and other will and wills by **me** made ; and I appoint and entreat my loving friends, Edmund Rawlins, gentleman, William Smith, and John Easton, to be the overseers of this my last will and testament, desiring them to see this my last will to be performed so far as in them lieth ; and for **their** pains therein, I give them and every of them 40*s.* apiece. **In witness to** this my will I have put my hand and seal, the day **and year above** written.

Thos. Nash.

**Witnesses to** the sealing and publishing hereof :—
    John Soch.
    Michael Johnson.
    Samuel Rawlins.

---

The following are translations of two Recoveries, hitherto unpublished, by which Mrs. Nash, after disputing the will in question, **succeeded** in limiting a portion of the poet's estates to his descendants. **The first** refers to the land purchased by him in 1602, of William and John Combe: the other, to the house in Blackfriars, bought in 1612-13. It will be observed that the parties concerned with Mrs. Nash in this confirmation of the property are two of the Hathaways, or Hathways, an additional proof, to that afforded by her will, of her friendly intercourse with the members of her grandmother's **family.**

RECOVERY ROLL, 23 CHARLES I. MICHAELMAS. ROLL 103
*(on the back).*

> Pleas of Land enrolled at Westminster before PETER PHESANT and JOHN GODBOLD, Justices of the Lord the King of the Common Pleas, of Michaelmas Term, in the twenty-third year of the reign of Lord CHARLES, by the grace of God, of England, Scotland, France, and Ireland, King, Defender of the Faith, &c.

Warwick Ss.—William Hathway and Thomas Hathway, in their proper persons, demand against Richard Lane, gentleman, and William Smyth, gentleman, three messuages, three gardens, 107 acres of land and 20 acres of pasture, with appurtenances in Stratford-upon-Avon, Old Stratford, Bishopton, and Welcombe, as their right and inheritance; and into which the same Richard and William Smyth have not entry, but after the decision which Hugh Hunt thereof unjustly and without judgment hath made to **the aforesaid** William Hathway **and Thomas** within thirty years, &c.; **and** whereupon they say that they were seized of the tenements aforesaid, with appurtenances, in their demesne as of fee and **right in time** of peace, in the time of our Lord the King that now **is, by taking** the profits thereof to the value, &c.; and into which, **&c.;** and thereof they bring suit, &c.

And the aforesaid Richard and William Smyth, in their proper **persons,** come and defend their right, when, &c.; and thereupon **vouch to** warrant Elizabeth Nash, widow, who is present here in **Court in** her **proper** person; and freely warrants the tenements aforesaid, with appurtenances, to them, &c.; and hereupon the aforesaid William Hathway and Thomas demand against the same Elizabeth, tenant, by her own warranty, the tenements aforesaid, with appurtenances in form aforesaid, &c.; and whereupon they say that they were seized of the tenements aforesaid, with appurtenances in their demesne as of fee and right in time of peace in the time of our Lord the King that now is, by taking the profits thereof to the value, &c.; and into which, &c.; and thereof they bring suit, &c.

And the aforesaid Elizabeth, tenant by her own warranty, defends her right, when, &c. And thereupon further voucheth to warrant **Robert Lee**, who is **also present here in Court, in his** proper person, and freely warrants the tenements aforesaid **with** appurtenances to her, &c. And hereupon the aforesaid William Hathaway and Thomas demand against the same Robert, tenant by his own warranty, the tenements aforesaid, with appurtenances in form aforesaid, &c. And whereupon they say that they were seized of the tenements aforesaid, with appurtenances in their demesne, as of fee and right in time of peace, in the time of our Lord the King that now is, by taking the profits thereof, **to the** value, &c. And into which, &c. And thereof they bring suit, &c.

And the **aforesaid** Robert, **tenant by** his own warranty, de**fends his** right, when, &c. **And saith that the aforesaid Hugh** did not disseize the aforesaid William Hathaway and Thomas of the tenements aforesaid, with appurtenances, as the same William Hathaway and Thomas, by their writ and declaration aforesaid above, do suppose, and of this he putteth himself upon the **country, &c.** And the aforesaid **William Hathaway and** Thomas thereupon crave **license to imparl, and they have it, &c. And** afterwards, the same William Hathaway and Thomas come **again** here into Court in this same Term, in their proper persons ; **and** the aforesaid Robert, although solemnly called, cometh not again, but departed in contempt of the Court, and maketh default. Therefore it is considered that the aforesaid William Hathaway and Thomas recover their seisin against the aforesaid Richard and William Smyth, of the tenements aforesaid, with appurtenances, and that the same Richard and William Smyth have **of** the land of the aforesaid Elizabeth, to the value, &c. And that **the same** Elizabeth further have of the land of the aforesaid Robert, to the value, &c. And the same Robert in mercy, **&c. And hereupon** the aforesaid William Hathaway and Thomas pray a writ of our Lord the King, to be directed to the sheriff of the **county aforesaid, to** cause full seisin of the tenements aforesaid, **with appurtenances to be delivered to** them, and **it is** granted to them returnable here **without delay, &c. Afterwards, that is to** say, on the 29th day **of November, in this same Term, come** here into Court, **the** aforesaid William Hathaway and Thomas, in their proper persons, and the sheriff, namely, Richard Lucy, Esq., now returns that he, by virtue of the said **writ** to him, directed on the 26th **day of** November last past, did cause full seisin of the tenements **aforesaid,** with appurtenances, to be **delivered** to the aforesaid William Hathaway and Thomas, as by the said writ he was commanded, &c.

RECOVERY ROLL, 23 CHARLES **I.** MICHAELMAS. ROLL 103
*(on the back).*

> **Pleas** of Land enrolled **at** Westminster before PETER PHESANT and JOHN GODBOLD, Justices of the Lord the King of the Common Pleas, of Michaelmas Term, in the twenty-third year of the reign of Lord CHARLES, by the grace of God, of England, Scotland, France, and Ireland King, Defender **of** the Faith, &c.

London Ss.—William Hathway and Thomas Hathway, in their proper persons, demand against Richard Lane, gentleman, and William Smyth gentleman, one messuage, with appurtenances, in the parish of St. Anne, Blackfriars, as their right and inheritance; and into which the same Richard and William Smyth have not entry but after the decision which Hugh Hunt thereof, unjustly and without judgment hath made to the aforesaid William Hathway and Thomas within thirty years, &c.; and whereupon they say that they were seized of the messuage aforesaid, with appurtenances, in their demesne as of fee and right in time of peace, in the time of our Lord the King, that now is, by taking the profits thereof, to the value, &c.; and into which, &c.; and thereof they bring suit, &c.

And the aforesaid Richard and William Smyth, in their proper persons, come and defend their right, when, &c.; and thereupon vouch to warrant Elizabeth Nash, widow, who is present here in court, in her proper person; and freely warrants the messuage aforesaid, with appurtenances, to them, &c.; and hereupon, the aforesaid William Hathway and Thomas, demand against the same Elizabeth, tenant by her own warranty, the messuage aforesaid, with appurtenances in form aforesaid, &c.; and whereupon, they say that they were seized of the messuage aforesaid, with appurtenances, in their demesne, as of fee and right in time of peace, in the time of the Lord the King, that now is by taking the profits thereof, to the value, &c.; and into which, &c.; and thereof they bring suit, &c.

And the aforesaid Elizabeth Tenant by her own warranty defends her right when, &c. And thereupon further voucheth to warrant Robert Lee, who is also present here in court in his proper person ; and freely warrants the messuage aforesaid, with appurtenances to her, &c. ; and hereupon the aforesaid William Hathaway and Thomas demand against the said Robert Tenant, by his own warranty, the messuage aforesaid with appurtenances in form aforesaid, &c. And whereupon, they say that they were seised of the messuage aforesaid, with appurtenances, in their demense as of fee and right in time of peace in the time of the Lord the King that now is, by taking the profits thereof to the value, &c. ; and into which, &c. ; and thereof they bring suit, &c. ; and the aforesaid Robert Tenant, by his own warranty, defends his right when, &c. ; and saith, that the aforesaid Hugh did not diseise the aforesaid William Hathaway and Thomas of the messuage aforesaid, with appurtenances, as the same William Hathaway and Thomas by their writ and declaration aforesaid above do suppose ; and of this he putteth himself upon the country, &c.

And the aforesaid William Hathaway and Thomas thereupon crave leave to imparl ; and they have it, &c. And afterwards the same William Hathaway and Thomas come again here into court in this same term in their proper persons ; and the aforesaid Robert, although solemnly called, cometh not again but departed, in contempt of the court, and maketh default.

Therefore it is considered, that the aforesaid William Hathaway and Thomas recover their seisin against the afore said Richard and William Smith of the messuage aforesaid, with appurtenances ; and that the same Richard and William Smyth have of the land of the aforesaid Elizabeth to the value, &c. ; and that the same Elizabeth have lastly of the land of the aforesaid Robert to the value, &c. ; and the same Robert, in mercy, &c. ; and hereupon the aforesaid William Hathaway and Thomas pray a writ of our Lord the King to be directed to the sheriffs of London aforesaid, to cause full seisin of the messuage aforesaid, with appurtenances, to be delivered to them ; and it is granted to them, returnable here without delay, &c. Afterwards, that is to say, on the 29th day of November in this same term, come here into court the aforesaid William Hathaway and Thomas in their proper person ; and the sheriffs, namely, Samuel Avery and John Bide now return that they, by virtue of the said writ to them directed, on the 2 th day of November last past did cause full seisin of the messuage aforesaid, with appurtenances, to be delivered to the aforesaid William Hathaway and Thomas, as by the said writ they were prayed, &c.

## DISPUTED SHAKESPEARE DOCUMENTS, DISCOVERED BY MR. COLLIER.

### In Bridgewater House.

**1.** Memorial of the players, James Burbidge, Richard Burbidge, John Laneham, &c. &c., November, 1589.

**2. List of** claims made by R. Burbidge; Laz. Fletcher; W. Shakespeare, &c. *No date*, which Mr. Collier describes as "a **paper, which shows,** with great exactness and particularity, the amount of interest then claimed by each sharer, those sharers being Richard Burbage, Laurence Fletcher, William Shakespeare, John Heming, Henry Condell, Joseph Taylor, and Lowen, with four other persons not named, each the owner of half a share."— *Collier's 'Life of Shakespeare,'* p. 189.

*" For avoiding of the playhouse in the Blackfriars :—*

|  | £. | s. | d. |
|---|---|---|---|
| *Impr.* Richard Burbidge oweth the fee, and is also a sharer therein. His interest he rateth at the gross sum of 1000*l.* for the fee, and for his four shares the sum of 933*l.* 7*s.* 8*d.* . . | 1933 | 6 | 8 |
| *Item.* Laz. Fletcher oweth three shares, which he rateth at 700*l.*, that is at seven years' purchase for each share, or 33*l.* 6*s.* 8*d.*, one year with another . . . . . . . . . | 700 | 0 | 0 |
| *Item.* W. Shakespeare asketh for the wardrobe and properties of the same playhouse 500*l.*, and for his four shares, the same as his fellows, Burbidge and Fletcher, viz., 933*l.* **6s. 8d.** . | 1433 | 6 | 8 |
| *Item.* Hemings and Condell, each two shares . . . | 933 | 6 | 8 |
| *Item.* Joseph Taylor, **one** share and an half . . . | 350 | 0 | 0 |
| *Item.* Lowing, one share and an half . . . . . | 350 | 0 | 0 |
| *Item.* Four more players, with one half share unto each of them . . . . . . . . . . . . | 466 | 13 | 4 |
| Sum total . . . . . £6166 | | 13 | 4 |

" Moreover, the hired men of the company demand some recompense for their great loss, and the widows and orphans of players, who are paid by the sharers at divers rates and proportions, so as in **the whole it will cost the** Lord Mayor and citizens, at the least, 7000*l.*"

## DANIEL'S LETTER.

*To the Right Honorable Sir* **Thomas** *Egerton,* **Knight,** *Lord Keeper of the* **Great** *Seal of England.*

I WILL not endeavour, right honourable, to thank **you in words** for this new, great, and unlooked-for favour shown unto me ; whereby **I** am bound to you for **ever, and hope** one day, with true heart and simple skill, to prove that I am not unmindful.

Most earnestly do I wish I could praise as your honour is **known to deserve,** for then should I, like my master Spenser, whose memory your honour cherisheth, leave behind me some worthy work, **to be** treasured by posterity ; what my poor muse could perform **in haste** is here set down, and though it be far below what other poets and better pens have written, it cometh from a grateful heart, and therefore may be accepted. **I** shall now be able **to** live free from those cares and troubles that hitherto have been my continual and wearisome companions. **But a little time is** past since I 'was called upon to thank **your honour for my brother's advancement, and now I** thank **you for my own, which double kindness will always receive double gratefulness at both our hands.**

I cannot but know that I am less deserving **than some that** sued by other of the nobility unto her Majesty for this room, **if** M. Drayton, my good friend, had been chosen I should not have murmured, for sure I am he would have filled it most excellently ; but it seemeth to my humble judgment, that one which is the author **of** plays now daily presented on the public stages of London, and the possessor of no small gains, and, moreover, himself an actor in the king's company of comedians, could not with reason pretend to be member of the Queen's Majesty's revelers, for as much as he would sometimes be asked to approve and allow of his own writing. Therefore he and more of like quality cannot justly be disappointed **because, through** your honour's gracious interposition, **the chance was haply mine. I** owe this and all else to your honour, **and if ever I have time** and ability to finish any noble undertaking, **as God grant one day I shall, the work** will rather be your honour's **than mine. God makes the poet, but his** creation would be in vain if patrons did not **make** him to live. Your honour hath ever shown yourself the friend of desert, and pity it were if this should be the first exception to the rule. It shall not be while my poor wit and strength do remain to me, though the verses which I now send be indeed no proof of mine

ability ; I only entreat your honour to accept the same the rather
as an earnest of my good will than as an example of my good deed.
In all things I am your honour's

Most bounden in duty and observance,

S. DANIELL.

## SUPPOSED LETTER FROM LORD SOUTHAMPTON.

MY VERY HONOURED LORD, — The many good offices I have received at your Lordship's hands, which ought to make me backward in asking further favours, only emboldeneth me to require
more in the same kind.   Your Lordship will be warned how hereafter you grant any suit, seeing it draweth on more and greater
demands : this which now presseth is to request your Lordship, in
all you can, to be good to the poor players of the Blackfriars, who
call themselves by authority the servants of his Majesty, and ask
for the protection of their most gracious master and sovereign in
this the time of their trouble.   They are threatened by the Lord
Mayor and Aldermen of London, never friendly to their calling,
with the destruction of their means of livelihood by the pulling
down of their playhouse, which is a private theatre, and hath
never given occasion of anger by any disorders.   These bearers
are two of the chief of the company, one of them by name Richard
Burbidge, who humbly sueth for your lordship's kind help, for that
he is a man famous as our English Roscius, one who fitteth the
action to the word, and the word to the action, most admirably.
By the exercise of his quality, industry, and good behaviour, he
hath become possessed of the Blackfriars playhouse, which hath
been employed for plays since it was built by his father, now near
fifty years ago.   The other is a man no wit less deserving favour,
and my especial friend, till of late an actor of good account in the
company, now a sharer in the same, and writer of some of our
best English plays, which, as your lordship knoweth, were most
singularly liked of Queen Elizabeth when the company was called
upon to perform before her Majesty at court at Christmas and
Shrovetide.   His Most Gracious Majesty King James also, since
his coming to the crown, hath extended his royal favour to the
company in divers ways, and at sundry times.   This other hath to
name William Shakespeare, and they are both of one county, and,
indeed, almost of one town ; both are right famous in their qualities, though it longeth not of your lordship's gravity and wisdom

to resort unto the places where they are wont to delight the public ear. Their trust and suit now is not to be molested in their way of life, whereby they maintain themselves and their wives and families (being both married and of good reputation), as well as the widows and orphans of some of their dead fellows. Your lordship most bounden at command.

*Copia vera.* H. S.

---

Draft of warrant naming Robert Daborne, William Shakespeare, and others, instructors of the children of the Queen's revels.—*Collier's ' Life of Shakespeare,'* pp. 197–8 :—

Right trusty and well beloved &c. James, &c. To all mayors sheriffs, justices of the peace, &c. Whereas the Queen, our dearest wife, hath for her pleasure and recreation appointed her servants Robert Daborne, &c., to provide and bring up a convenient number of children, who shall be called the children of her Majesty's revels. Know ye that we have appointed and authorized, and by these presents do appoint and authorize, the said Robert Daborne, William Shakespeare, Nathaniel Field, and Edward Kirkham, from time to time to provide and bring up a convenient number of children, and them to instruct and exercise in the quality of playing tragedies, comedies, &c., by the name of the children of the revels to the Queen, within the Blackfriars, in our city of London, and elsewhere within our realm of England. Wherefore, we will and command you, and every of you, to permit her said servants to keep a convenient number of children, by the name of the children of the revels to the Queen, and them to exercise in the quality of playing according to our royal pleasure. Provided always, that no plays, &c., shall be by them presented but such plays, &c., as have received the approbation and allowance of our Master of the Rolls for the time being. And these our lines shall be your sufficient warrant in this behalf. In witness whereof, &c. 4th day of January, 1609.

| Bl. Fr. & Globe, | Curten & Fortune, | } All in & near |
| Wh. Fr. & Parish Garden, | Hope & Swan. | } London. |

| | |
|---|---|
| Proud Poverty | English Tragedy. |
| Widow's Mite. | False Friends. |
| Antonio Kinsmen. | Hate and Love. |
| Triumph of Truth. | Taming of S. |
| Touchstone. | King Edward II. |
| Mirror of Life. | |
| Grissel. | Stayed. |

2 B

IN DULWICH COLLEGE.

Mr. Collier found a notice of a wager, which he thus describes :—

"But there **is another paper of a very** similar kind, apparently referring **to the preceding, or to some** other like contest, but **containing several remarkable allusions,** which Malone did not notice. **Perhaps it never met his eye, or** perhaps **he** reserved it for his **Life of Shakespeare, and was** unwilling to forestall that production by inserting **it elsewhere. It** seems to be of a later date, and it mentions not **only** Tarlton, Knell, and Bentley, but Kempe, Phillips, and Pope, while Alleyn's rival, Burbage, is sneered at as ' Roscius Richard,' and Shakespeare introduced under the name of Will, by which we have Thomas Heywood's authority (in his ' Hierarchy of the Blessed Angels,' 1635, p. 206) for saying **he** was known among his companions. The paper is in verse, and runs precisely as follows :—

> "'Sweet Ned, now win another wager
> For thine old friend and fellow-stager;
> Tarlton himself thou dost excel,
> And Bentley beat, and conquer Knell,
> **And now shall** Kempe **o'ercome as well.**
> **The money's down, the place the Hope,**
> **Phillips shall hide his head, and Pope,**
> Fear not, the victory is thine;
> Thou still as matchless Ned shall shine.
> If Roscius Richard foams and fumes,
> The Globe shall have but empty rooms,
> If thou dost act ; and Will's new play
> Shall be rehearsed some other day.
> Consent, then, Ned ; do us this grace :
> Thou **cannot fail in any case ;**
> For in the trial, come what **may,**
> All sides shall brave Ned Alleyn say.'"

*Memoirs of Alleyn*, p. 13, ed. J. P. Collier, 1841.

2. The following list of players is appended to a memorandum ; **and of this** Mr. Collier says :—

" Malone also appears to have reserved another circumstance, of very considerable importance in relation to Shakespeare, for his life of the poet. To the last-quoted document, but in a different hand and in different ink, is appended a list of the king's players. The name of Shakespeare there occurs second, and as it could not be written at the bottom of the letter of the Council to the Lord Mayor, &c., prior to the date of that letter, it proves that up to 9th April, 1604, our great dramatist continued to be numbered among the *actors* of the company. Hitherto the last trace we have had of Shakespeare as actually on the stage, has been as one of the performers in Ben Jonson's 'Sejanus,' which was produced in 1603. We will insert the list as it stands at the foot of the Council's letter to the Lord Mayor, &c.

" ' K's. Comp.

| | |
|---|---|
| Burbidge. | Armyn. |
| Shakespeare. | Slye. |
| Fletcher. | Cowley. |
| Phillips. | Hostler. |
| Condle. | Day.' " |
| Hemmings. | |

Collier's Memoirs of Alleyn, p. 68.

3. A letter from John Marston to Henslow, thus described :—

" The following undated note from Marston to Henslowe may not be unfitly introduced here : it refers to a play by Marston on the subject of Columbus, of which we hear on no other authority. It is one of the scraps of correspondence between Henslow and the poets in his employ, existing at Dulwich College, of the major part of which Malone has given copies, but omitting the subsequent, which is certainly one of the most interesting of the whole collection.

" ' Mr. Henslow, at the Rose on the Bankside.

" ' If you like my play of Columbus it is very well, and you shall give me no more than 20*l.* for it, but if not, let me have it by this bearer again, as I know the King's men will freely give me as much for it, and the profits of the third day moreover.

" ' So I rest, yours,

" ' JOHN MARSTON.' "

Collier's Memoirs of Alleyn, p. 154.

4. A list of the inhabitants of Southwark who made a complaint in 1596.

5. " A brief note taken out of the poor's book, containing the names of all the inhabitants of this liberty, which are rated and assessed to a weekly payment towards the relief of the poor, as it stands now increased, this 6th day of April, 1609," &c.

THE END.

LONDON: PRINTED BY W. CLOWES AND SONS, 14, CHARING CROSS.